The Collected Supernatural and Weird Fiction of Robert W. Chambers Volume 1

The Collected Supernatural and Weird Fiction of Robert W. Chambers Volume 1

Including One Novel 'The Slayer of Souls',
One Novelette 'The Man at the Next Table',
and Fourteen Short Stories
of the Strange and Unusual

Robert W. Chambers

LEONAUR

The Collected
Supernatural and Weird
Fiction of
Robert W. Chambers
Volume 1
Including One Novel 'The Slayer of Souls',
One Novelette 'The Man at the Next Table',
and Fourteen Short Stories
of the Strange and Unusual
by Robert W. Chambers

FIRST EDITION

Leonaur is an imprint
of Oakpast Ltd

ISBN: 978-0-85706-192-8 (hardcover)
ISBN: 978-0-85706-191-1 (softcover)

http://www.leonaur.com

Contents

The Slayer of Souls

CHAPTER 1

THE YEZIDEE

Only when the *Nan-yang Maru* sailed from Yuen-San did her terrible sense of foreboding begin to subside.

For four years, waking or sleeping, the awful sub-consciousness of supreme evil had never left her.

But now, as the Korean shore, receding into darkness, grew dimmer and dimmer, fear subsided and grew vague as the half-forgotten memory of horror in a dream.

She stood near the steamer's stern apart from other passengers, a slender, lonely figure in her silver-fox furs, her ulster and smart little hat, watching the lights of Yuen-San grow paler and smaller along the horizon until they looked like a level row of stars.

Under her haunted eyes Asia was slowly dissolving to a streak of vapour in the misty lustre of the moon.

Suddenly the ancient continent disappeared, washed out by a wave against the sky; and with it vanished the last shreds of that accursed nightmare which had possessed her for four endless years. But whether during those unreal years her soul had only been held in bondage, or whether, as she had been taught, it had been irrevocably destroyed, she still remained uncertain, knowing nothing about the death of souls or how it was accomplished.

As she stood there, her sad eyes fixed on the misty East, a passenger passing—an Englishwoman—paused to say something

7

kind to the young American; and added, "if there is anything my husband and I can do it would give us much pleasure." The girl had turned her head as though not comprehending. The other woman hesitated.

"This is Doctor Norne's daughter, is it not?" she inquired in a pleasant voice.

"Yes, I am Tressa Norne. . . . I ask your pardon. . . . Thank you, madam:—I am—I seem to be—a trifle dazed—"

"What wonder, you poor child! Come to us if you feel need of companionship."

"You are very kind. . . . I seem to wish to be alone, some-how."

"I understand. . . . Goodnight, my dear."

Late the next morning Tressa Norne awoke, conscious for the first time in four years that it was at last her own familiar self stretched out there on the pillows where sunshine streamed through the port-hole. All that day she lay in her bamboo steam-er chair on deck. Sun and wind conspired to dry every tear that wet her closed lashes. Her dark, glossy hair blew about her face; scarlet tinted her full lips again; the tense hands relaxed. Peace came at sundown.

That evening she took her Yu-kin from her cabin and found a chair on the deserted hurricane deck.

And here, in the brilliant moonlight of the China Sea, she curled up cross-legged on the deck, all alone, and sounded the four futile strings of her moon-lute, and hummed to herself, in a still voice, old songs she had sung in Yian before the tragedy. She sang the tent-song called "Tchinguiz". She sang "Camel Bells" and "The Blue Bazaar,"—children's songs of the Yiort. She sang the ancient Khiounnou song called "The Saghalien":

1

In the month of Saffar
Among the river-reeds
I saw two horsemen
Sitting on their steeds.
Tulugum!

Heitulum!
By the river-reeds

2

In the month of Saffar
A demon guards the ford.
Tokhta, my Lover!
Draw your shining sword!
Tulugum!
Heitulum!
Slay him with your sword!

3

In the month of Saffar
Among the water-weeds
I saw two horsemen
Fighting on their steeds.
Tulugum!
Heitulum!
How my lover bleeds!

4

In the month of Saffar,
The Year I should have wed—
The Year of The Panther—
My lover lay dead,—
Tulugum!
Heitulum!
Dead without a head.

And songs like these—the one called "Keuke Mongol," and
an ancient air of the Tchortchas called "The Thirty Thousand
Calamities," and some Chinese boatmen's songs which she had
heard in Yian before the tragedy; these she hummed to herself there in the moonlight playing on her round-faced, short-
necked lute of four strings.

Terror indeed seemed ended for her, and in her heart a great
overwhelming joy was welling up which seemed to overflow
across the entire moonlit world. She had no longer any fear;

no premonition of further evil. Among the few Americans and English aboard, something of her story was already known.

People were kind; and they were also considerate enough to subdue their sympathetic curiosity when they discovered that this young American girl shrank from any mention of what had happened to her during the last four years of the Great World War.

It was evident, also, that she preferred to remain aloof; and this inclination, when finally understood, was respected by her fellow passengers. The clever, efficient and polite Japanese officers and crew of the *Nan-yang Maru* were invariably considerate and courteous to her, and they remained nicely reticent, although they also knew the main outline of her story and very much desired to know more. And so, surrounded now by the friendly security of civilised humanity, Tressa Norne, reborn to light out of hell's own shadows, awoke from four years of nightmare which, after all, perhaps, never had seemed entirely actual.

And now God's real sun warmed her by day; His real moon bathed her in creamy coolness by night; sky and wind and wave thrilled her with their blessed assurance that this was once more the real world which stretched illimitably on every side from horizon to horizon; and the fair faces and pleasant voices of her own countrymen made the past seem only a ghastly dream that never again could enmesh her soul with its web of sorcery.

And now the days at sea fled very swiftly; and when at last the Golden Gate was not far away she had finally managed to persuade herself that nothing really can harm the human soul; that the monstrous devil-years were ended, never again to return; that in this vast, clean Western Continent there could be no occult threat to dread, no gigantic menace to destroy her body, no secret power that could consign her soul to the dreadful abysm of spiritual annihilation.

Very early that morning she came on deck. The November day was delightfully warm, the air clear save for a belt of mist low on the water to the southward.

She had been told that land would not be sighted for twenty-four hours, but she went forward and stood beside the starboard rail, searching the horizon with the enchanted eyes of hope.

As she stood there a Japanese ship's officer crossing the deck, forward, halted abruptly and stood staring at something to the southward.

At the same moment, above the belt of mist on the water, and perfectly clear against the blue sky above, the girl saw a fountain of gold fire rise from the fog, drift upward in the daylight, slowly assume the incandescent outline of a serpentine creature which leisurely uncoiled and hung there floating, its lizard-tail undulating, its feet with their five stumpy claws closing, relaxing, like those of a living reptile. For a full minute this amazing shape of fire floated there in the sky, brilliant in the morning light, then the reptilian form faded, died out, and the last spark vanished in the sunshine.

When the Japanese officer at last turned to resume his promenade, he noticed a white-faced girl gripping a stanchion behind him as though she were on the point of swooning. He crossed the deck quickly. Tressa Norne's eyes opened.

"Are you ill, Miss Norne?" he asked.

"The—the Dragon," she whispered.

The officer laughed. "Why, that was nothing but Chinese day-fireworks," he explained. "The crew of some fishing boat yonder in the fog is amusing Itself." He looked at her narrowly, then with a nice little bow and smile he offered his arm: "If you are indisposed, perhaps you might wish to go below to your stateroom, Miss Norne?"

She thanked him, managed to pull herself together and force a ghost of a smile.

He lingered a moment, said something cheerful about being nearly home, then made her a punctilious salute and went his way.

Tressa Norne leaned back against the stanchion and closed her eyes. Her pallor became deathly. She bent over and laid her white face in her folded arms.

After a while she lifted her head, and, turning very slowly,

11

stared at the fog-belt out of frightened eyes.

And saw, rising out of the fog, a pearl-tinted sphere which gradually mounted into the clear daylight above like the full moon's phantom in the sky.

Higher, higher rose the spectral moon until at last it swam in the very zenith. Then it slowly evaporated in the blue vault above.

A great wave of despair swept her; she clung to the stanchion, staring with half-blinded eyes at the flat fog-bank in the south.

But no more "Chinese day-fireworks" rose out of it. And at length she summoned sufficient strength to go below to her cabin and lie there, half senseless, huddled on her bed.

When land was sighted, the following morning, Tressa Norne had lived a century in twenty-four hours. And in that space of time her agonised soul had touched all depths.

But now as the Golden Gate loomed up in the morning light, rage, terror, despair had burned themselves out. From their ashes within her mind arose the cool wrath of desperation armed for anything, wary, alert, passionately determined to survive at whatever cost, recklessly ready to fight for bodily existence.

That was her sole instinct now, to go on living, to survive, no matter at what price. And if it were indeed true that her soul had been slain, she defied its murderers to slay her body also.

That night, at her hotel in San Francisco, she double-locked her door and lay down without undressing, leaving all lights burning and an automatic pistol underneath her pillow.

Toward morning she fell asleep, slept for an hour, started up in awful fear. And saw the double-locked door opposite the foot of her bed slowly opening of its own accord.

Into the brightly illuminated room stepped a graceful young man in full evening dress carrying over his left arm an overcoat, and in his other hand a top hat and silver tipped walking-stick.

With one bound the girl swung herself from the bed to the carpet and clutched at the pistol under her pillow.

"Sanang!" she cried in a terrible voice.

"Keuke Mongol!" he said, smilingly.

For a moment they confronted each other in the brightly lighted bedroom, then, partly turning, he cast a calm glance at the open door behind him; and, as though moved by a wind, the door slowly closed. And she heard the key turn of itself in the lock, and saw the bolt slide smoothly into place again.

Her power of speech came back to her presently—only a broken whisper at first: "Do you think I am afraid of your accursed magic?" she managed to gasp. "Do you think I am afraid of you, Sanang?"

"You are afraid," he said serenely.

"You lie!"

"No, I do not lie. To one another the Yezidees never lie."

"You lie again, assassin! I am no Yezidee!"

He smiled gently. His features were pleasing, smooth, and regular; his cheek-bones high, his skin fine and of a pale and delicate ivory colour. Once his black, beautifully shaped eyes wandered to the levelled pistol which she now held clutched desperately close to her right hip, and a slightly ironical expression veiled his gaze for an instant.

"Bullets?" he murmured. "But you and I are of the Hassanis."

"The third lie, Sanang!" Her voice had regained its strength. Tense, alert, blue eyes ablaze, every faculty concentrated on the terrible business before her, the girl now seemed like some supple leopardess poised on the swift verge of murder.

"*Tókhta!*"[1] She spat the word. "Any movement toward a hidden weapon, any gesture suggesting recourse to magic and I kill you, Sanang, exactly where you stand!"

"With a pistol?" He laughed. Then his smooth features altered subtly. He said: "Keuke Mongol, who call yourself Tressa Norne,—Keuke—heavenly azure-blue,—named so in the temple because of the colour of your eyes—listen attentively, for this is the Yarlig which I bring to you by word of mouth from Yian, as from Yezidee to Yezidee:

"Here, in this land called the United States of America, the

---

1. "Look out!" Nomad-Mongol dialect.

Temple girl, Keuke Mongol, who has witnessed the mysteries of Erlik and who understands the magic of the Sheiks-el-Djebel, and who has seen Mount Alamout and the eight castles and the fifty thousand Hassanis in white turbans and in robes of white;—*you*—Azure-blue eyes—heed the Yarlig!—or may thirty thousand calamities overtake you!"

There was a dead silence; then he went on seriously: "It is decreed: You shall cease to remember that you are a Yezidee, that you are of the Hassanis, that you ever have laid eyes on Yian the Beautiful, that you ever set naked foot upon Mount Alamout. It is decreed that you remember nothing of what you have seen and heard, of what has been told and taught during the last four years reckoned as the Christians reckon from our Year of the Bull. Otherwise—my Master sends you this for your *convenience*."

Leisurely, from under his folded overcoat, the young man produced a roll of white cloth and dropped it at her feet and the girl shrank aside, shuddering, knowing that the roll of white cloth was meant for her winding-sheet.

Then the colour came back to lip and cheek; and, glancing up from the soft white shroud, she smiled at the young man: "Have you ended your Oriental mummery?" she asked calmly. "Listen very seriously in your turn, Sanang, Sheik-el-Djebel, Prince of the Hassanis who, God knows when and how, have come out into the sunshine of this clean and decent country, out of a filthy darkness where devils and sorcerers make earth a hell.

"If you, or yours, threaten me, annoy me, interfere with me, I shall go to our civilised police and tell all I know concerning the Yezidees. I mean to live. Do you understand? You know what you have done to me and mine. I come back to my own country alone, without any living kin, poor, homeless, friendless,—and, perhaps, damned. I intend, nevertheless, to survive. I shall not relax my clutch on bodily existence whatever the Yezidees may pretend to have done to my soul. I am determined to live in the body, anyway."

He nodded gravely.

She said: "Out at sea, over the fog, I saw the sign of Yu-lao in fire floating in the day-sky. I saw his spectral moon rise and vanish in mid-heaven. I understood. But—" And here she suddenly showed an edge of teeth under the full scarlet upper lip: "Keep your signs and your shrouds to yourself, dog of a Yezidee!— toad!—tortoise-egg!—he-goat with three legs! Keep your threats and your messages to yourself! Keep your accursed magic to yourself! Do you think to frighten me with your sorcery by showing me the Moons of Yu-lao?—by opening a bolted door? I know more of such magic than do you, Sanang—Death Adder of Alamout!"

Suddenly she laughed aloud at him—laughed insultingly in his expressionless face:

"I saw you and Gutchlug Khan and your cowardly Tchortchas in red-lacquered jackets slink out of the Temple of Erlik where the bronze gong thundered and a cloud settled down raining little yellow snakes all over the marble steps—all over you, Prince Sanang! You were *afraid*, my *Tougtchi*! you and Gutchlug and your red Tchortchas with their halberds all dripping with human entrails! And I saw you mount and gallop off into the woods while in the depths of the magic cloud which rained little yellow snakes all around you, we temple girls laughed and mocked at you—at you and your cowardly Tchortcha horsemen."

A slight tinge of pink came into the young man's pale face. Tressa Norne stepped nearer, her levelled pistol resting on her hip.

"Why did you not complain of us to your Master, the Old Man of the Mountain?" she asked jeeringly. "And where, also, was your Yezidee magic when it rained little snakes?—What frightened you away—who had boldly come to seize a temple girl—you who had screwed up your courage sufficiently to defy Erlik in his very shrine and snatch from his temple a young thing whose naked body wrapped in gold was worth the chance of death to you?"

The young man's top-hat dropped to the floor. He bent over

15

to pick it up. His face was quite expressionless, quite colourless, now.

"I went on no such errand," he said with an effort. "I went with a thousand prayers on scarlet paper made in—"

"A lie, Yezidee! You came to seize *me*!"

He turned still paler. "By Abu, Omar, Otman, and Ali, it is not true!"

"You lie!—by the Lion of God, Hassini !"

She stepped closer. "And I'll tell you another thing you fear-you Yezidee of Alamout—you robber of Yian—you sorcerer of Sabbah Khan, and chief of his sect of Assassins! You fear this native land of mine, America; and its laws and customs, and its clear, clean sunshine; and its cities and people; and its police! Take that message back. We Americans fear nobody save the true God!—nobody—neither Yezidee nor Hassani nor Russ nor German nor that sexless monster born of hell and called the Bolshevik!"

"*Tokhta!*" he cried sharply.

"Damn you!" retorted the girl; "get out of my room! Get out of my sight! Get out of my path! Get out of my life! Take that to your Master of Mount Alamout! I do what I please; I go where I please; I live as I please. And if I please, *I turn against him!*"

"In that event," he said hoarsely, "there lies your winding-sheet on the floor at your feet! Take up your shroud; and make Erlik seize you!"

"Sanang," she said very seriously.

"I hear you, Keuke-Mongol."

"Listen attentively. I wish to live. I have had enough of death in life. I desire to remain a living, breathing thing—even if it be true—as you Yezidees tell me, that you have caught my soul in a net and that your sorcerers really control its destiny.

"But damned or not, I passionately desire to live. And I am coward enough to hold my peace for the sake of living. So—I remain silent. I have no stomach to defy the Yezidees; because, if I do, sooner or later I shall be killed. I know it. I have no desire to die for others—to perish for the sake of the common good. I am young. I have suffered too much; I am determined to live-

16

and let my soul take its chances between God and Erlik."

She came close to him, looked curiously into his pale face.

"I laughed at you out of the temple cloud," she said. "I know how to open bolted doors as well as you do. And I know *other things*. And if you ever again come to me in this life I shall first torture you, then slay you. Then I shall tell all! . . . and unroll my shroud."

"I keep your word of promise until you break it," he interrupted hastily. "Yarlig! It is decreed!" And then he slowly turned as though to glance over his shoulder at the locked and bolted door.

"Permit me to open it for you, Prince Sanang," said the girl scornfully. And she gazed steadily at the door.

Presently, all by itself, the key turned in the lock, the bolt slid back, the door gently opened.

Toward it, white as a corpse, his overcoat on his left arm, his stick and top-hat in the other hand, crept the young man in his faultless evening garb.

Then, as he reached the threshold, he suddenly sprang aside. A small yellow snake lay coiled there on the door sill. For a full throbbing minute the young man stared at the yellow reptile in unfeigned horror. Then, very cautiously, he moved his fascinated eyes sideways and gazed in silence at Tressa Norne.

The girl laughed.

"Sorceress!" he burst out hoarsely. "Take that accursed thing from my path!"

"What thing, Sanang?" At that his dark, frightened eyes stole toward the threshold again, seeking the little snake. But there was no snake there. And when he was certain of this he went, twitching and trembling all over.

Behind him the door closed softly, locking and bolting itself.

And behind the bolted door in the brightly lighted bedroom Tressa Norne fell on both knees, her pistol still clutched in her right hand, calling passionately upon Christ to forgive her for the dreadful ability she had dared to use, and begging Him to save her body from death and her soul from the snare of the Yezidee.

17

CHAPTER 2
THE YELLOW SNAKE

When the young man named Sanang left the bedchamber of Tressa Norne he turned to the right in the carpeted corridor outside and hurried toward the hotel elevator. But he did not ring for the lift; instead he took the spiral iron stairway which circled it, and mounted hastily to the floor above.

Here was his own apartment and he entered it with a key bearing the hotel tag. A dusky-skinned powerful old man wearing a grizzled beard and a greasy broadcloth coat of old-fashioned cut known to provincials as a "Prince Albert" looked up from where he was seated cross-legged upon the sofa, sharpening a curved knife on a whetstone.

"Gutchlug," stammered Sanang, "I am afraid of her! What happened two years ago at the temple happened again a moment since, there in her very bedroom! She made a yellow death-adder out of nothing and placed it upon the threshold, and mocked me with laughter. May Thirty Thousand Calamities overtake her! May Erlik seize her! May her eyes rot out and her limbs fester! May the seven score and three principal devils—"

"You chatter like a temple ape," said Gutchlug tranquilly. "Does Keuke Mongol die or live? That alone interests me."

"Gutchlug," faltered the young man, "thou knowest that m-my heart is inclined to mercy toward this young Yezidee—"

"I know that it is inclined to lust," said the other bluntly.

Sanang's pale face flamed.

"Listen," he said. "If I had not loved her better than life had I dared go that day to the temple to take her for my own?"

"You loved life better," said Gutchlug. "You fled when it rained snakes on the temple steps—you and your Tchortcha horsemen! *Kai!* I also ran. But I gave every soldier thirty blows with a stick before I slept that night. And you should have had your thirty, also, conforming to the Yarlig, my *Tougtchi.*"

Sanang, still holding his hat and cane and carrying his overcoat over his left arm, looked down at the heavy, brutal features of Gutchlug Khan—at the cruel mouth with its crooked smile

18

under the grizzled beard; at the huge hands—the powerful hands of a murderer—now deftly honing to a razor-edge the Kalmuck knife held so firmly yet lightly in his great blunt fingers.

"Listen attentively, Prince Sanang," growled Gutchlug, pausing in his monotonous task to test the blade's edge on his thumb—"Does the Yezidee Keuke Mongol live? Yes or no?"

Sanang hesitated, moistened his pallid lips. "She dares not betray us."

"By what pledge?"

"Fear."

"That is no pledge. You also were afraid, yet you went to the temple!"

"She has listened to the Yarlig. She has looked upon her shroud. She has admitted that she desires to live. Therein lies her pledge to us."

"And she placed a yellow snake at your feet!" sneered Gutchlug. "Prince Sanang, tell me, what man or what devil in all the chronicles of the past has ever tamed a Snow-Leopard?" And he continued to hone his *yataghan*.

"Gutchlug—"

"No, she dies," said the other tranquilly.

"Not yet!"

"When, then?"

"Gutchlug, thou knowest me. Hear my pledge! At her first gesture toward treachery—her first thought of betrayal—I myself will end it all."

"You promise to slay this young snow-leopardess?"

"By the four companions, I swear to kill her with my own hands !"

Gutchlug sneered. "Kill her—yes—with the kiss that has burned thy lips to ashes for all these months. I know thee, Sanang. Leave her to me. Dead she will no longer trouble thee."

"Gutchlug!"

"I hear, Prince Sanang."

"Strike when I nod. Not until then."

"I hear, *Tougtchi*. I understand thee, my *Banneret*. I whet my

19

knife. *Kai!*"

Sanang looked at him, put on his top-hat and overcoat, pulled on a pair of white evening gloves.

"I go forth," he said more pleasantly.

"I remain here to talk to my seven ancestors and sharpen my knife," remarked Gutchlug.

"When the white world and the yellow world and the brown world and the black world finally fall before the Hassanis," said Sanang with a quick smile, "I shall bring thee to her. Gutchlug—once—before she is veiled, thou shalt behold what is lovelier than Eve."

The other stolidly whetted his knife.

Sanang pulled out a gold cigarette case, lighted a cigarette with an air.

"I go among Germans," he volunteered amiably. "The *huns* swam across two oceans, but, like the unclean swine, it is their own throats they cut when they swim! Well, there is only one God. And not very many angels. Erlik is greater. And there are many million devils to do his bidding. *Adieu.* There is rice and there is *koumiss* in the frozen closet. When I return you shall have been asleep for hours."

When Sanang left the hotel one of two young men seated in the hotel lobby got up and strolled out after him.

A few minutes later the other man went to the elevator, ascended to the fourth floor, and entered an apartment next to the one occupied by Sanang.

There was another man there, lying on the lounge and smoking a cigar. Without a word, they both went leisurely about the matter of disrobing for the night.

When the shorter man who had been in the apartment when the other entered, and who was dark and curly-headed, had attired himself in pyjamas, he sat down on one of the twin beds to enjoy his cigar to the bitter end.

"Has Sanang gone out?" he inquired in a low voice.

"Yes. Benton went after him."

The other man nodded. "Cleves," he said, "I guess it looks as though this Norne girl is in it, too."

"What happened?"

"As soon as she arrived, Sanang made straight for her apartment. He remained inside for half an hour. Then he came out in a hurry and went to his own rooms, where that surly servant of his squats all day, shining up his arsenal, and drinking *koumiss*."

"Did you get their conversation?"

"I've got a record of the gibberish. It requires, an interpreter, of course."

"I suppose so. I'll take the records east with me tomorrow, and by the same token I'd better notify New York that I'm leaving."

He went, half-undressed, to the telephone, got the telegraph office, and sent the following message:

> Recklow, New York:
> Leaving tomorrow for N.Y. with samples. Retain expert in Oriental fabrics.
>
> Victor Cleves.

"Report for me, too," said the dark young man, who was still enjoying his cigar on his pillows.

So Cleves sent another telegram, directed also to

> Recklow, New York:
> Benton and I are watching the market. Chinese importations fluctuate. Recent consignment per *Nan-yang Maru* will be carefully inspected and details forwarded.
>
> Alek Selden.

In the next room Gutchlug could hear the voice of Cleves at the telephone, but he merely shrugged his heavy shoulders in contempt. For he had other things to do beside eavesdropping.

Also, for the last hour in fact, ever since Sanang's departure-something had been happening to him—something that happens to a Hassani only once in a lifetime. And now this unique thing had happened to him—to him, Gutchlug Khan—to him before whose Khiounnou ancestors eighty-one thousand nations had bowed the knee.

It had come to him at last, this dread thing, unheralded, totally unexpected, a few minutes after Sanang had departed.

And he suddenly knew he was going to die.

And, when, presently, he comprehended it, he bent his grizzled head and listened seriously. And, after a little silence, he heard his soul bidding him farewell.

So the chatter of white men at a telephone in the next apartment had no longer any significance for him. Whether or not they had been spying on him; whether they were plotting, made no difference to him now.

He tested his knife's edge with his thumb and listened gravely to his soul bidding him farewell.

But, for a Yezidee, there was still a little detail to attend to before his soul departed;—two matters to regulate. One was to select his shroud. The other was to cut the white throat of this young snow-leopardess called Keuke Mongol, the Yezidee temple girl.

And he could steal down to her bedroom and finish that matter in five minutes.

But first he must choose his shroud, as is the custom of the Yezidee.

That office, however, was quickly accomplished in a country where fine white sheets of linen are to be found on every hotel bed.

So, on his way to the door, his naked knife in his right hand, he paused to fumble under the bedcovers and draw out a white linen sheet.

Something hurt his hand like a needle. He moved it, felt the thing squirm under his fingers and pierce his palm again and again. With a shriek, he tore the bedclothes from the bed.

A little yellow snake lay coiled there.

He got as far as the telephone, but could not use it. And there he fell heavily, shaking the room and dragging the instrument down with him.

There was some excitement. Cleves and Selden in their bathrobes went in to look at the body. The hotel physician diagnosed it as heart-trouble. Or, possibly, poison. Some gazed significantly at the naked knife still clutched in the dead man's hands.

Around the wrist of the other hand was twisted a pliable gold bracelet representing a little snake. It had real emeralds for eyes.

It had not been there when Gutchlug died.

But nobody except Sanang could know that. And later when Sanang came back and found Gutchlug very dead on the bed and a policeman sitting outside, he offered no information concerning the new bracelet shaped like a snake with real emeralds for eyes, which adorned the dead man's left wrist.

Toward evening, however, after an autopsy had confirmed the house physician's diagnosis that heart-disease had finished Gutchlug, Sanang mustered enough courage to go to the desk in the lobby and send up his card to Miss Norne.

It appeared, however, that Miss Norne had left for Chicago about noon.

CHAPTER 3
GREY MAGIC

To Victor Cleves came the following telegram in code:

Washington,
April 14th.1919.

Investigation ordered by the State Department as the result of frequent mention in despatches of Chinese troops operating with the Russian Bolsheviki forces has disclosed that the Bolsheviki are actually raising a Chinese division of 30,000 men recruited in Central Asia. This division has been guilty of the greatest cruelties. A strange rumour prevails among the Allied forces at Archangel that this Chinese division is led by Yezidee and Hassani officers belonging to the sect of devil-worshipers and that they employ black arts and magic in battle.

From information so far gathered by the several branches of the United States Secret Service operating throughout the world, it appears possible that the various revolutionary forces of disorder, in Europe and Asia, which now are violently threatening the peace and security, of all established civilisation on earth, may have had a common origin. This origin, it is now suspected, may date back to a very remote epoch; the wide-spread forces of violence and merciless destruction may have had their beginning among some ancient and predatory race whose existence was maintained solely by robbery and murder.

Anarchists, terrorists, Bolshevists, Reds of all shades and degrees, are now believed to represent in modern times what perhaps once was a tribe of Assassins—a sect whose religion was founded upon a common predilection for crimes of violence.

On this theory then, for the present, the United States Government will proceed with this investigation of Bolshevism; and the Secret Service will continue to pay particular attention to all Orientals in the United States and other countries. You personally are formally instructed to keep in touch with XLY-371 (Alek Selden) and ZB-303 (James Benton), and to employ every possible means to become friendly with the girl Tressa Norne, win her confidence, and, if possible, enlist her actively in the Government Service as your particular aid and comrade.

It is equally important that the movements of the Oriental, called Sanang, be carefully observed in order to discover the identity and whereabouts of his companions. However, until further instructions he is not to be taken into custody.   M. H. 2479.

(Signed)

(John Recklow.)

The long despatch from John Recklow made Cleves's duty plain enough.

For months, now, Selden and Benton had been watching Tressa Norne. And they had learned practically nothing about her.

And now the girl had come within Cleves's sphere of operation. She had been in New York for two weeks. Telegrams from Benton in Chicago, and from Selden in Buffalo, had prepared him for her arrival.

He had his men watching her boarding-house on West Twenty-eighth Street, men to follow her, men to keep their eyes on her at the theatre, where every evening, at 10:45, her *entr'acte* was staged. He knew where to get her. But he, himself, had been on the watch for the man Sanang; and had failed to find the slightest trace of him in New York, although warned that he had arrived.

So, for that evening, he left the hunt for Sanang to others, put on his evening clothes, and dined with fashionable friends at the Patroons' Club, who never for an instant suspected that young Victor Cleves was in the Service of the United States Government. About half-past nine he strolled around to the theatre, desiring to miss as much as possible of the popular show without being too late to see the curious little *entr'acte* in which this girl, Tressa Norne, appeared alone.

He had secured an aisle seat near the stage at an outrageous price; the main show was still thundering and fizzing and glittering as he entered the theatre; so he stood in the rear behind the orchestra until the descending curtain extinguished the outrageous glare and din.

Then he went down the aisle, and as he seated himself Tressa Norne stepped from the wings and stood before the lowered curtain facing an expectant but oddly undemonstrative audience.

The girl worked rapidly, seriously, and in silence. She seemed a mere child there behind the footlights, not more than sixteen anyway—her winsome eyes and wistful lips unspoiled by the world's wisdom.

Yet once or twice the mouth drooped for a second and the winning eyes darkened to a remoter blue—the brooding iris hue of far horizons.

She wore the characteristic *tabard* of stiff golden tissue and the gold *pagoda*-shaped headpiece of a Yezidee temple girl. Her flat, slipper-shaped footgear was of stiff gold, too, and curled upward at the toes.

All this accentuated her apparent youth. For in face and throat no firmer contours had as yet modified the soft fullness of immaturity; her limbs were boyish and frail, and her bosom more undecided still, so that the embroidered breadth of gold fell flat and straight from her chest to a few inches above the ankles.

She seemed to have no stock of paraphernalia with which to aid the performance; no assistant, no orchestral diversion, nor did she serve herself with any magician's patter. She did her work close to the footlights.

Behind her loomed a black curtain; the strip of stage in front was bare even of carpet; the orchestra remained mute.

But when she needed anything—a little table, for example-well, it was suddenly there where she required it—a tripod, for instance, evidently fitted to hold the big iridescent bubble of glass in which swarmed little tropical fishes—and which arrived neatly from nowhere. She merely placed her hands before her as though ready to support something weighty which she expected—and suddenly, the huge crystal bubble was visible, resting between her hands. And when she tired of holding it, she set it upon the empty air and let go of it; and instead of crashing to the stage with its finny rainbow swarm of swimmers, out of thin air appeared a tripod to support it.

Applause followed, not very enthusiastic, for the sort of audience which sustains the shows of which her performance was merely an *entr'acte* is an audience responsive only to the obvious.

Nobody ever before had seen that sort of magic in America. People scarcely knew whether or not they quite liked it. The lightning of innovation stupefies the dull; ignorance is always suspicious of innovation—always afraid to put itself on record until its mind is made up by somebody else.

So in this typical New York audience approbation was cautious, but every fascinated eye remained focused on this young girl who continued to do incredible things, which seemed to resemble "putting something over" on them; a thing which no uneducated American conglomeration ever quite forgives.

The girl's silence, too, perplexed them; they were accustomed to gabble, to noise, to jazz, vocal and instrumental, to that incessant metropolitan clamour which fills every second with sound in a city whose only distinction is its din. Stage, press, art, letters, social existence unless noisy mean nothing in Gotham; reticence, leisure, repose are the three lost arts. The megaphone is the city's symbol; its chiefest crime, silence.

The girl having finished with the big glass bubble full of tiny fish, picked it up and tossed it aside. For a moment it apparently floated there in space like a soap-bubble. Changing rainbow tints waxed and waned on the surface, growing deeper and more gorgeous until the floating globe glowed scarlet, then suddenly burst into flame and vanished. And only a strange, sweet perfume lingered in the air.

But she gave her perplexed audience no time to wonder; she had seated herself on the stage and was already swiftly busy unfolding a white veil with which she presently covered herself, draping it over her like a tent.

The veil seemed to be translucent; she was apparently visible seated beneath it. But the veil turned into smoke, rising into the air in a thin white cloud; and there, where she had been seated, was a statue of white stone the image of herself!—in all the frail springtide of early adolescence—a white statue, cold, opaque, exquisite in its sculptured immobility.

There came, the next moment, a sound of distant thunder; flashes lighted the blank curtain; and suddenly a vein of lightning and a sharper peal shattered the statue to fragments.

There they lay, broken bits of her own sculptured body, glistening in a heap behind the footlights. Then each fragment began to shimmer with a rosy internal light of its own, until the pile of broken marble glowed like living coals under thickening and reddening vapours. And, presently, dimly perceptible, there she was in the flesh again, seated in the fiery centre of the conflagration, stretching her arms luxuriously, yawning, seemingly awakening from refreshing slumber, her eyes unclosing to rest with a sort of confused apology upon her astounded audience.

As she rose to her feet nothing except herself remained on the stage—no debris, not a shred of smoke, not a spark.

She came down, then, across an inclined plank into the orchestra among the audience.

In the aisle seat nearest her sat Victor Cleves. His business was to be there that evening. But she didn't know that, knew nothing about him—had never before set eyes on him.

At her gesture of invitation he made a cup of both his hands. Into these she poured a double handful of unset diamonds—or what appeared to be diamonds—pressed her own hands above his for a second—and the diamonds in his palms had become pearls.

These were passed around to people in the vicinity, and finally returned to Mr. Cleves, who, at her request, covered the heap of pearls with both his hands, hiding them entirely from view.

At her nod he uncovered them. The pearls had become emeralds. Again, while he held them, and without even touching him, she changed them into rubies. Then she turned away from him, apparently forgetting that he still held the gems, and he sat very still, one cupped hand over the other, while she poured silver coins into a woman's gloved hands, turned them into gold coins, then flung each coin into the air, where it changed to a living, fragrant rose and fell among the audience.

Presently she seemed to remember Cleves, came back down the aisle, and under his close and intent gaze drew from his cupped hands, one by one, a score of brilliant little living birds, which continually flew about her and finally perched, twittering, on her golden headdress—a rainbow-crest of living jewels.

As she drew the last warm, breathing little feathered miracle from Cleves's hands and released it, he said rapidly under his breath: "I want a word with you later. Where?"

She let her clear eyes rest on him for a moment, then with a shrug so slight that it was perceptible, perhaps, only to him, she moved on along the inclined way, stepped daintily over the footlights, caught fire, apparently, nodded to a badly rattled audience, and sauntered off, burning from head to foot.

What applause there was became merged in a dissonant instrumental outburst from the orchestra; the great god Jazz resumed direction, the mindless audience breathed freely again as the curtain rose upon a familiar, yelling turbulence, including all that Gotham really understands and cares for—legs and noise.

Victor Cleves glanced up at the stage, then continued to study the name of the girl on the programme. It was featured in rather pathetic solitude under "*Entr'acte.*" And he read further:

During the *entr'acte* Miss Tressa Norne will entertain you with several phases of Black Magic. This strange knowledge was acquired by Miss Norne from the Yezidees, among which almost unknown people still remain descendants of that notorious and formidable historic personage known in the twelfth century as The Old Man of the Mountain—or The Old Man of Mount Alamout.

The pleasant profession of this historic individual was assassination; and some historians now believe that genuine occult power played a part in his dreadful record—a record which terminated only when the infantry of Genghis Khan took Mount Alamout by storm and hanged the Old Man of the Mountain and burned his body under a boulder of You-Stone.

For Miss Norne's performance there appears to be no plausible, practical or scientific explanation.

During her performance the curtain will remain lowered for fifteen minutes and will then rise on the last act of *You Betcha Life.*

The noisy show continued while Cleves, paying it scant attention, brooded over the programme. And ever his keen, grey eyes reverted to her name, Tressa Norne.

Then, for a little while, he settled back and let his absent gaze wander over the galloping battalions of painted girls and the slapstick principals whose perpetual motion evoked screams of

29

approbation from the audience amid the din of the great god Jazz.

He had an aisle seat; he disturbed nobody when he went out and around to the stage door.

The aged man on duty took his card, called a boy and sent it off. The boy returned with the card, saying that Miss Norne had already dressed and departed.

Cleves tipped him and then tipped the doorman heavily.

"Where does she live?" he asked.

"Say," said the old man, "I dunno, and that's straight. But them ladies mostly goes up to the roof for a look in at the *Moonlight Masque* and a dance afterward. Was you ever up there?"

"Yes."

"Seen the new show?"

"No."

"Well, g'wan up while you can get a table. And I bet the little girl will be somewheres around."

"The little girl" *was* "somewheres around." He secured a table, turned and looked about at the vast cabaret into which only a few people had yet filtered, and saw her at a distance in the carpeted corridor buying violets from one of the flower-girls.

A waiter placed a reserve card on his table; he continued on around the outer edge of the auditorium.

Miss Norne had already seated herself at a small table in the rear, and a waiter was serving her with iced orange juice and little French cakes.

When the waiter returned Cleves went up and took off his hat.

"May I talk with you for a moment, Miss Norne?" he said.

The girl looked up, the wheat-straw still between her scarlet lips. Then, apparently recognising in him the young man in the audience who had spoken to her, she resumed her business of imbibing orange juice.

The girl seemed even frailer and younger in her hat and street gown. A silver-fox stole hung from her shoulders; a gold bag lay on the table under the bunch of violets.

30

She paid no attention whatever to him. Presently her wheat-straw buckled, and she selected a better one.

He said: "There's something rather serious I'd like to speak to you about if you'll let me. I'm not the sort you evidently suppose. I'm not trying to annoy you."

At that she looked around and upward once more.

Very, very young, but already spoiled, he thought, for the dark-blue eyes were coolly appraising him, and the droop of the mouth had become almost sullen. Besides, traces of paint still remained to incarnadine lip and cheek and there was a hint of hardness in the youthful plumpness of the features.

"Are you a professional?" she asked without curiosity.

"A theatrical man? No."

"Then if you haven't anything to offer me, what is it you wish?"

"I have a job to offer if you care for it and if you are up to it," he said.

Her eyes became slightly hostile:

"What kind of job do you mean?"

"I want to learn something about you first. Will you come over to my table and talk it over?"

"No."

"What sort do you suppose me to be?" he inquired, amused.

"The usual sort, I suppose."

"You mean a Johnny?"

"Yes—of sorts."

She let her insolent eyes sweep him once more, from head to foot.

He was a well-built young man and in his evening dress he had that something about him which placed him very definitely where he really belonged.

"Would you mind looking at my card?" he asked.

He drew it out and laid it beside her, and without stirring she scanned it sideways.

"That's my name and address," he continued. "I'm not contemplating mischief. I've enough excitement in life without seeking adventure. Besides, I'm not the sort who goes about annoying women."

She glanced up at him again:

"You are annoying me !"

"I'm sorry. I was quite honest. Goodnight."

He took his *congé* with unhurried amiability; had already turned away when she said:

"Please . . . what do you desire to say to me?" He came back to her table:

"I couldn't tell you until I know a little more about you."

"What—do you wish to know?"

"Several things. I could scarcely ask you—go over such matters with you—standing here."

There was a pause; the girl juggled with the straw on the table for a few moments, then, partly turning, she summoned a waiter, paid him, adjusted her stole, picked up her gold bag and her violets and stood up. Then she turned to Cleves and gave him a direct look, which had in it the impersonal and searching gaze of a child.

When they were seated at the table reserved for him the place already was filling rapidly—backwash from the theatres slopped through every aisle—people not yet surfeited with noise, not yet sufficiently sodden by their worship of the great god Jazz.

"Jazz," said Cleves, glancing across his dinner-card at Tressa Norne—"what's the meaning of the word? Do you happen to know?"

"Doesn't it come from the French '*jaser*'?"

He smiled. "Possibly. I'm rather hungry. Are you?"

"Yes."

"Will you indicate your preferences?"

She studied her card, and presently he gave the order.

"I'd like some champagne," she said, "unless you think it's too expensive."

He smiled at that, too, and gave the order.

"I didn't suggest any wine because you seem so young," he said.

"How old do I seem?"

"Sixteen perhaps."

"I am twenty-one."

"Then you've had no troubles."

"I don't know what you call trouble," she remarked, indifferently, watching the arriving throngs.

The orchestra, too, had taken its place.

"Well," she said, "now that you've picked me up, what do you really want of me?" There was no mitigating smile to soften what she said. She dropped her elbows on the table, rested her chin between her palms and looked at him with the same searching, undisturbed expression that is so disconcerting in children. As he made no reply: "May I have a cocktail?" she inquired.

He gave the order. And his mind registered pessimism. "There is nothing doing with this girl," he thought. "She's already on the toboggan." But he said aloud: "That was beautiful work you did down in the theatre, Miss Norne."

"Did you think so?"

"Of course. It was astounding work."

"Thank you. But managers and audiences differ with you."

"Then they are very stupid," he said.

"Possibly. But that does not help me pay my board."

"Do you mean you have trouble in securing theatrical engagements?"

"Yes, I am through here tonight, and there's nothing else in view, so far."

"That's incredible I" he exclaimed.

She lifted her glass, slowly drained it.

For a few moments she caressed the stem of the empty glass, her gaze remote.

"Yes, it's that way," she said. "From the beginning I felt that my audiences were not in sympathy with me. Sometimes it even amounts to hostility. Americans do not like what I do, even if it holds their attention. I don't quite understand why they don't like it, but I'm always conscious they don't. And of course that settles it—tonight has settled the whole thing, once and for all."

"What are you going to do?"

"What others do, I presume."

"What do others do?" he inquired, watching the lovely sullen eyes.

"Oh, they do what I'm doing now, don't they?—let some man pick them up and feed them." She lifted her indifferent eyes. "I'm not criticising you. I meant to do it someday—when I had courage. That's why I just asked you if I might have some champagne—finding myself a little scared at my first step. . . . But you *did* say you might have a job for me. Didn't you?"

"Suppose I haven't. What are you going to do?"

The curtain was rising. She nodded toward the bespangled chorus. "Probably that sort of thing. They've asked me."

Supper was served. They both were hungry and thirsty; the music made conversation difficult, so they supped in silence and watched the imbecile show conceived by vulgarians, produced by vulgarians and served up to mental degenerates of the same species—the average metropolitan audience.

For ten minutes a pair of comedians fell up and down a flight of steps, and the audience shrieked approval.

"Miss Norne?"

The girl who had been watching the show turned in her chair and looked back at him.

"Your magic is by far the most wonderful I have ever seen or heard of. Even in India such things are not done."

"No, not in India," she said, indifferently.

"Where then?"

"In China."

"You learned to do such things there?"

"Yes."

"Where, in China, did you learn such amazing magic?"

"In Yian."

"I never heard of it. Is it a province?"

"A city."

"And you lived there?"

34

"Fourteen years."

"When?"

"From 1904 to 1918."

"During the great war," he remarked, "you were in China?"

"Yes."

"Then you arrived here very recently."

"In November, from the Coast."

"I see. You played the theatres from the Coast eastward."

"And went to pieces in New York," she added calmly, finishing her glass of champagne.

"Have you any family?" he asked.

"No."

"Do you care to say anything further?" he inquired, pleasantly.

"About my family? Yes, if you wish. My father was in the spice trade in Yian. The Yezidees took Yian in 1910, threw him into a well in his own compound and filled it up with dead imperial troops. I was thirteen years old. . . The Hassani did that. They held Yian nearly eight years, and I lived with my mother, in a garden *pagoda*, until 1914. In January of that year Germans got through from Kiaou-Chou. They had been six months on the way. I think they were Hassanis. Anyway, they persuaded the Hassanis to massacre every English-speaking prisoner. And so—my mother died in the garden *pagoda* of Yian. . . . I was not told for four years."

"Why did they spare you?" he asked, astonished at her story so quietly told, so utterly destitute of emotion.

"I was seventeen. A certain person had placed me among the temple girls in the temple of Erlik. It pleased this person to make of me a Mongol temple girl as a mockery at Christ. They gave me the name Keuke Mongol. I asked to serve the shrine of Kwann-an—she being like to our Madonna. But this person gave me the choice between the halberds of the Tchortchas and the sorcery of Erlik."

She lifted her sombre eyes. "So I learned how to do the things you saw. But—what I did there on the stage is not—

35

respectable."

An odd shiver passed over him. For a second he took her literally, suddenly convinced that her magic was not white but black as the demon at whose shrine she had learned it. Then he smiled and asked her pleasantly, whether indeed she employed hypnosis in her miraculous exhibitions.

But her eyes became more sombre still, and, "I don't care to talk about it," she said. "I have already said too much."

"I'm sorry. I didn't mean to pry into professional secrets—"

"I can't talk about it," she repeated. ". . . Please—my glass is quite empty."

When he had refilled it:

"How did you get away from Yian?" he asked.

"The Japanese."

"What luck!"

"Yes. One battle was fought at Buldak. The Hassanis and Blue Flags were terribly cut up. Then, outside the walls of Yian, Prince Sanang's Tchortcha infantry made a stand. He was there with his Yezidee horsemen, all in leather and silk armour with *casques* and corselets of black Indian steel.

"I could see them from the temple—saw the Japanese gunners open fire. The Tchortchas were blown to shreds in the blast of the Japanese guns. . . . Sanang got away with some of his Yezidee horsemen."

"Where was that battle?"

"I told you, outside the walls of Yian."

"The newspapers never mentioned any such trouble in China," he said, suspiciously.

"Nobody knows about it except the Germans and the Japanese."

"Who is this Sanang?" he demanded.

"A Yezidee-Mongol. He is one of the Sheiks-el-Djebel—a servant of The Old Man of Mount Alamout."

"What is *he*?"

"A sorcerer—assassin."

"What!" exclaimed Cleves incredulously.

"Why, yes," she said, calmly. "Have you never heard of The Old Man of Mount Alamout?"

"Well, yes —"

"The succession has been unbroken since 1090 b.c. A Hassan Sabbah is still the present Old Man of the Mountain. His Yezidees worship Erlik. They are sorcerers. But you would not believe that."

Cleves said with a smile, "Who is Erlik?"

"The Mongols' Satan."

"Oh! So these Yezidees are devil-worshipers!"

"They are more. They *are* actually devils."

"You don't really believe that even in unexplored China there exists such a creature as a real sorcerer, do you?" he inquired, smilingly.

"I don't wish to talk of it."

To his surprise her face had flushed, and he thought her sensitive mouth quivered a little.

He watched her in silence for a moment; then, leaning a little way across the table:

"Where are you going when the show here closes?"

"To my boarding-house."

"And then?"

"To bed," she said, sullenly.

"And tomorrow what do you mean to do?"

"Go out to the agencies and ask for work."

"And if there is none?"

"The chorus," she said, indifferently.

"What salary have you been getting?"

She told him.

"Will you take three times that amount and work with me?"

CHAPTER 4
BODY AND SOUL

The girl's direct gaze met his with that merciless searching intentness he already knew. "What do you wish me to do?"

"Enter the service of the United States."

"Wh-what?"

"Work for the Government."

She was too taken aback to answer.

"Where were you born?" he demanded abruptly.

"In Albany, New York," she replied in a dazed way.

"You are loyal to your country?"

"Yes—certainly."

"You would not betray her?"

"No."

"I don't mean for money; I mean from fear."

After a moment, and, avoiding his gaze: "I am afraid of death," she said very simply.

He waited.

"I—I don't know what I might do—being afraid," she added in a troubled voice. "I desire to—live."

He still waited.

She lifted her eyes: "I'd try not to betray my country," she murmured.

"Try to face death for your country's honour?"

"Yes."

"And for your own?"

"Yes; and for my own."

He leaned nearer: "Yet you're taking a chance on your own honour tonight."

She blushed brightly: "I didn't think I was taking a very great chance with you."

He said: "You have found life too hard. And when you faced failure in New York you began to let go of life—real life, I mean. And you came up here tonight wondering whether you had courage to let yourself go. When I spoke to you it scared you. You found you hadn't the courage. But perhaps tomorrow you might find it—or next week—if sufficiently scared by hunger—you might venture to take the first step along the path that you say others usually take sooner or later."

The girl flushed scarlet, sat looking at him out of eyes grown dark with anger.

He said: "You told me an untruth. You *have* been tempted to betray your country. You have resisted. You *have* been threatened with death. You *have* had courage to defy threats and temptations where your country's honour was concerned !"

"How do you know?" she demanded.

He continued, ignoring the question: "From the time you landed in San Francisco you have been threatened. You tried to earn a living by your magician's tricks, but in city after city, as you came East, your uneasiness grew into fear, and your fear into terror, because every day more terribly confirmed your belief that people were following you determined either to use you to their own purposes or to murder you—"

The girl turned quite white and half rose in her chair, then sank back, staring at him out of dilated eyes. Then Cleves smiled: "So you've got the nerve to do Government work," he said, "and you've got the intelligence, and the knowledge, and something else—I don't know exactly what to call it—Skill? Dexterity? Sorcery?" he smiled—"I mean your professional ability. That's what I want—that bewildering dexterity of yours, to help your own country in the fight of its life. Will you enlist for service?"

"W-what fight?" she asked faintly.

"The fight with the Red Spectre."

"Anarchy?"

"Yes . . . Are you ready to leave this place? I want to talk to you."

"Where?"

"In my own rooms."

After a moment she rose.

"I'll go to your rooms with you," she said. She added very calmly that she was glad it was to be his rooms and not some other man's.

Out of countenance, he demanded what she meant, and she said quite candidly that she'd made up her mind to live at any cost, and that if she couldn't make an honest living she'd make a living anyway.

He offered no reply to this until they had reached the street and he had called a taxi.

On their way to his apartment he reopened the subject rather bluntly, remarking that life was not worth living at the price she had mentioned.

"That is the accepted Christian theory," she replied coolly, "but circumstances alter things."

"Not such things."

"Oh, yes, they do. If one is already damned, what difference does anything else make?"

He asked, sarcastically, whether she considered herself already damned.

She did not reply for a few moments, then she said, in a quick, breathless way, that souls have been entrapped through ignorance of evil. And asked him if he did not believe it.

"No," he said, "I don't."

She shook her head. "You couldn't understand," she said. "But I've made up my mind to one thing; even if my soul has perished, my body shall not die for a long, long time. I mean to live," she added. "I shall not let my body be slain! They shall not steal life from me, whatever they have done to my soul—"

"What in heaven's name are you talking about?" he exclaimed. "Do you actually believe in soul-snatchers and life-stealers?"

She seemed sullen, her profile turned to him, her eyes on the brilliantly lighted avenue up which they were speeding. After a while: "I'd rather live decently and respectably if I can," she said. "That is the natural desire of any girl, I suppose. But if I can't, nevertheless I shall beat off death at any cost. And whatever the price of life is, I shall pay it. Because I am absolutely determined to go on living. And if I can't provide the means I'll have to let some man do it, I suppose."

"It's a good thing it was I who found you when you were out of a job," he remarked coldly.

"I hope so," she said. "Even in the beginning I didn't really believe you meant to be impertinent" a tragic smile touched her lips "and I was almost sorry—"

"Are you quite crazy?" he demanded.

"No, my mind is untouched. It's my soul that's gone. . . . Do you know I was very hungry when you spoke to me? The management wouldn't advance anything, and my last money went for my room. . . . Last Monday I had three dollars to face the future and no job. I spent the last of it tonight on violets, orange juice and cakes. My furs and my gold bag remain. I can go two months more on them. Then it's a job or—" She shrugged and buried her nose in her violets.

"Suppose I advance you a month's salary?" he said.

"What am I to do for it?"

The taxi stopped at a florist's on the corner of Madison Avenue and 58th Street. Overhead were apartments. There was no elevator—merely the street door to unlock and four dim nights of stairs rising steeply to the top.

He lived on the top floor. As they paused before his door in the dim corridor:

"Are you afraid?" he asked.

She came nearer, laid a hand on his arm:

"Are *you* afraid?"

He stood silent, the latch-key in his hand.

"I'm not afraid of myself—if that is what you mean," he said.

"That is partly what I mean . . . you'll have to mount guard over your soul."

"I'll look out for my soul," he retorted dryly.

"Do so. I lost mine. I—I would not wish any harm to yours through our companionship."

"Don't you worry about my soul," he remarked, fitting the key to the lock. But again her hand fell on his wrist:

"Wait. I can't—can't help warning you. Neither your soul nor your body are safe if—if you ever do make of me a companion. I've *got* to tell you this!"

"What are you talking about?" he demanded bluntly.

"Because you have been courteous—considerate—and you *don't* know—oh, you don't realise what spiritual peril is!—What

41

your soul and body have to fear if you—if you win me over—if you ever manage to make of me a friend!"

He said: "People follow and threaten you. We know that. I understand also that association with you involves me, and that I shall no doubt be menaced with bodily harm."

He laid his hand on hers where it still rested on his sleeves:

"But that's my business, Miss Norne," he added with a smile. "So, otherwise, it being merely a plain business affair between you and me, I think I may also venture my immortal soul alone with you in my room."

The girl flushed darkly.

"You have misunderstood," she said.

He looked at her coolly, intently; and arrived at no conclusion. Young, very lovely, confessedly without moral principle, he still could not believe her actually depraved. "What did you mean?" he said bluntly.

"In companionship with the lost, one might lose one's way-unawares. . . . Do you know that there is an Evil loose in the world which is bent upon conquest by *obtaining control of men's minds*?"

"No," he replied, amused.

"And that, through the capture of men's minds and souls the destruction of civilisation is being planned?"

"Is that what you learned in your captivity, Miss Norne?"

"You do not believe me."

"I believe your terrible experiences in China have shaken you to your tragic little soul Horror and grief and loneliness have left scars on tender, impressionable youth. They would have slain maturity broken it, crushed it. But youth is flexible, pliable, and bends—gives way under pressure. Scars become slowly effaced. It shall be so with you. You will learn to understand that nothing really can harm the soul."

For a few moments' silence they stood facing each other on the dim landing outside his locked door.

"Nothing can slay our souls," he repeated in a grave voice. "I do not believe you really ever have done anything to wound

42

even your self-respect. I do not believe you are capable of it, or ever have been, or ever will be. But somebody has deeply wounded you, spiritually, and has wounded your mind to persuade you that your soul is no longer in God's keeping. For that is a lie!"

He saw her features working with poignant emotions as though struggling to believe him.

"Souls are never lost," he said. "Ungoverned passions of every sort merely cripple them for a space. God always heals them in the end."

He laid his hand on the door-knob once more and lifted the latch-key.

"Don't!" she whispered, catching his hand again, "if there should be somebody in there waiting for us!"

"There is not a soul in my rooms. My servant sleeps out."

"There is somebody there !" she said, trembling.

"Nobody, Miss Norne. Will you come in with me?"

"I don't dare —."

"Why?"

"You and I alone together—no! oh, please—please! I am afraid!"

"Of what?"

"Of—giving you my c-confidence and trust—and—and f-friendship."

"I want you to."

"I must not! It would destroy us both, soul and body!"

"I tell you," he said, impatiently, "that there is no destruction of the soul—and it's a clean comradeship anyway—a fighting friendship I ask of you—*all* I ask; all I offer! Wherein, then, lies this peril in being alone together?"

"Because I am finding it in my heart "to believe in you, trust you, hold fast to your strength and protection. And if I give way—yield—and if I make you a promise—*and if there is any-body in that room to see us and hear us—then we shall be destroyed,* both of us, soul and body—"

He took her hands, held them until their trembling ceased.

"I'll answer for our bodies. Let God look after the rest. Will you trust Him?"

She nodded.

"And me?"

"Yes."

But her face blanched as he turned the latch-key, switched on the electric light, and preceded her into the room beyond.

The place was one of those accentless, typical bachelor apartments made comfortable for anything masculine, but quite unliveable otherwise.

Live coals still glowed in the hob grate; he placed a lump of cannel coal on the embers, used a bellows vigorously and the flame caught with a greasy crackle.

The girl stood motionless until he pulled up an easy chair for her, then he found another for himself. She let slip her furs, folded her hands around the bunch of violets and waited.

"Now," he said, "I'll come to the point. In 1916 I was at Plattsburg, expecting a commission. The Department of Justice sent for me. I went to Washington where I was made to understand that I had been selected to serve my country in what is vaguely known as the Secret Service—and which includes government agents attached to several departments.

"The great war is over; but I am still retained in the service. Because something more sinister than a *hun* victory over civilisation threatens this Republic. And threatens the civilised world."

"Anarchy," she said.

"Bolshevism."

She did not stir in her chair.

She had become very white. She said nothing. He looked at her with his quiet, reassuring smile.

"That's what I want of you," he repeated.

"I want your help," he went on, "I want your valuable knowledge of the Orient. I want whatever secret information you possess. I want your rather amazing gifts, your unprecedented experience almost unknown people, your familiarity with occult

44

things, your astounding powers—whatever they are—hypnotic, psychic, material.

"Because, today, civilisation is engaged in a secret battle for existence against gathering powers of violence, the force and limit of which are still unguessed.

"It is a battle between righteousness and evil, between sanity and insanity, light and darkness, God and Satan! And if civilisation does not win, then the world perishes."

She raised her still eyes to his, but made no other movement.

"Miss Norne," he said, "we in the International Service know enough about you to desire to know more.

"We already knew the story you have told to me. Agents in the International Secret Service kept in touch with you from the time that the Japanese escorted you out of China.

"From the day you landed, and all across the Continent to New York, you have been kept in view by agents of this government.

"Here, in New York, my men have kept in touch with you. And now, tonight, the moment has come for a personal understanding between you and me."

The girl's pale lips moved—became stiffly articulate: "I—I wish to live," she stammered, "I fear death."

"I know it. I know what I ask when I ask your help."

She said in the ghost of a voice: "If I turn against *them*—they will kill me."

"They'll try," he said quietly.

"They will not fail, Mr. Cleves."

"That is in God's hands."

She became deathly white at that.

"No," she burst out in an agonised voice, "it is not in God's hands! If it were, I should not be afraid! It is in the hands of those who stole my soul!"

She covered her face with both arms, fairly writhing on her chair.

"If the Yezidees have actually made you believe any such

45

nonsense"—he began; but she dropped her arms and stared at him out of terrible blue eyes:

"I don't want to die, I tell you! I am afraid!—*afraid*! If I reveal to you what I know they'll kill me. If I turn against them and aid you, they'll slay my body, and send it after my soul!"

She was trembling so violently that he sprang up and went to her. After a moment he passed one arm around her shoulders and held her firmly, close to him.

"Come," he said, "do your duty. Those who enlist under the banner of Christ have nothing to dread in this world or the next."

"If—if I could believe I were safe there."

"I tell you that you are. So is every human soul! What mad nonsense have the Yezidees made you believe? Is there any surer salvation for the soul than to die in Christ's service?"

He slipped his arm from her quivering shoulders and grasped both her hands, crushing them as though to steady every fibre in her tortured body.

"I want you to live. I want to live, too. But I tell you it's in God's hands, and we soldiers of civilisation have nothing to fear except failure to do our duty. Now, then, are we comrades under the United States Government?"

"O God—I—dare not!"

"*Are* we?"

Perhaps she felt the physical pain of his crushing grip for she turned and looked him in the eyes.

"I don't want to die," she whispered. "Don't make me!"

"Will you help your country?"

The terrible directness of her child's gaze became almost unendurable to him.

"Will you offer your country your soul and body?" he insisted in a low, tense voice.

Her stiff lips formed a word.

"Yes!" he exclaimed.

"Yes."

For a moment she rested against his shoulder, deathly white, then in a flash she had straightened, was on her feet in one bound and so swiftly that he scarcely followed her movement—was unaware that she had risen until he saw her standing there with a pistol glittering in her hand, her eyes fixed on the *portieres* that hung across the corridor leading to his bedroom.

"What on earth," he began, but she interrupted him, keeping her gaze focused on the curtains, and the pistol resting level on her hip.

"I'll answer you if I die for it!" she cried. "I'll tell you everything I know! You wish to learn what is this monstrous evil that threatens the world with destruction—what you call anarchy and Bolshevism? It is an Evil that was born before Christ came! It is an Evil which not only destroys cities and empires and men but which is more terrible still for it obtains control of the human mind, and uses it at will; and it obtains sovereignty over the soul, and makes it prisoner. Its aim is to dominate first, then to destroy. It was conceived in the beginning by Erlik and by Sorcerers and devils. . . . Always, from the first, there have been sorcerers and living devils.

"And when human history began to be remembered and chronicled, devils were living who worshiped Erlik and practised sorcery.

"They have been called by many names. A thousand years before Christ Hassan Sabbah founded his sect called Hassanis or Assassins. The Yezidees are of them. Their Chief is still called Sabbah; their creed is the annihilation of civilisation!"

Cleves had risen. The girl spoke in a clear, accentless monotone, not looking at him, her eyes and pistol centred on the motionless curtains.

"Look out!" she cried sharply.

"What is the matter?" he demanded. "Do you suppose anybody is hidden behind that curtain in the passageway?"

"If there is," she replied in her excited but distinct voice, "here is a tale to entertain him:

"The Hassanis are a sect of assassins which has spread out of Asia all over the world, and they are determined upon the an-

47

nihilation of everything and everybody in it except themselves!

"In Germany is a branch of the sect. The *hun* is the lineal descendant of the ancient Yezidee; the gods of the *hun* are the old demons under other names; the desire and object of the *hun* is the same desire—to rule the minds and bodies and souls of men and use them to their own purposes!"

She lifted her pistol a little, came a pace forward:

"Anarchist, Yezidee, Hassani, Boche, Bolshevik—all are the same—all are secretly swarming in the hidden places for the same purpose!"

The girl's blue eyes were aflame, now, and the pistol was lifting slowly in her hand to a deadly level.

"Sanang!" she cried in a terrible voice.

"Sanang!" she cried again in her terrifying young voice—"Toad! Tortoise egg! Spittle of Erlik! May the Thirty Thousand Calamities overtake you! Sheik-el-Djebel!—cowardly Khan whom I laughed at from the temple when it rained yellow snakes on the marble steps when all the gongs in Yian sounded in your frightened ears!"

She waited.

"What! You won't step out? *Tokhta!*" she exclaimed in a ringing tone, and made a swift motion with her left hand. Apparently out of her empty open palm, like a missile hurled, a thin, blinding beam of light struck the curtains, making them suddenly transparent.

A man stood there.

He came out, moving very slowly as though partly stupefied. He wore evening dress under his overcoat, and had a long knife in his right hand.

Nobody spoke.

"So—I really was to die then, if I came here," said the girl in a wondering way.

Sanang's stealthy gaze rested on her, stole toward Cleves. He moistened his lips with his tongue. "You deliver me to this government agent?" he asked hoarsely.

"I deliver nobody by treachery. You may go, Sanang."

He hesitated, a graceful, faultless, metropolitan figure in top-hat and evening attire. Then, as he started to move, Cleves covered him with his weapon.

"I can't let that man go free!" cried Cleves angrily.

"Very well!" she retorted in a passionate voice "then take him if you are able! *Tokhta!* Look out for yourself!"

Something swift as lightning struck the pistol from his grasp,- blinded him, half stunned him, set him reeling in a drenching blaze of light that blotted out all else,

He heard the door slam; he stumbled, caught at the back of a chair while his senses and sight were clearing.

"By heavens!" he whispered with ashen lips, "you—you *are* a sorceress—or something. What—what are you doing to me?"

There was no answer. And when his vision cleared a little more he saw her crouched on the floor, her head against the locked door, listening, perhaps—or sobbing—he scarcely understood which until the quiver of her shoulders made it plainer.

When at last Cleves went to her and bent over and touched her she looked up at him out of wet eyes, and her grief-drawn mouth quivered.

"I—I don't know," she sobbed, "if he truly stole away my soul—there—there in the temple dusk of Yian. But he—he stole my heart—for all his wickedness—Sanang, Prince of the Yezidees—and I have been fighting him for it all these years—all these long years—fighting for what he stole in the temple dusk! . . . And now—now I have it back—my heart—all broken to pieces—here on the floor behind your—your bolted door."

CHAPTER 5
THE ASSASSINS

On the wall hung a map of Mongolia, that indefinite region a million and a half square miles in area, vast sections of which have never been explored.

Turkestan and China border it on the south, and Tibet almost touches it, not quite.

Even in the twelfth century, when the wild Mongols broke

49

loose and nearly overran the world, the Tibet infantry under Genghis, the Tchortcha horsemen drafted out of Black China, and a great cloud of Mongol cavalry under the Prince of the Vanguard commanding half a hundred Hezars, never penetrated that grisly and unknown waste. The "Eight Towers of the Assassins" guarded it—still guard it, possibly.

The vice-regent of Erlik, Prince of Darkness, dwelt within this unknown land. And dwells there still, perhaps.

In front of this wall-map stood Tressa Norne.

Behind her, facing the map, four men were seated—three of them under thirty.

These three were volunteers in the service of the United States Government—men of independent means, of position, who had volunteered for military duty at the outbreak of the great war. However, they had been assigned by the Government to a very different sort of duty no less exciting than service on the fighting line, but far less conspicuous, for they had been drafted into the United States Department of Justice.

The names of these three were Victor Cleves, a professor of ornithology at Harvard University before the war; Alexander Selden, junior partner in the banking firm of Milwyn, Selden, and Co., and James Benton, a New York architect.

The fourth man's name was John Recklow. He might have been over fifty, or under. He was well-built, in a square, athletic way, clear-skinned and ruddy, grey-eyed, quiet in voice and manner. His hair and moustache had turned silvery. He had been employed by the Government for many years. He seemed to be enormously interested in what Miss Norne was saying.

Also he was the only man who interrupted her narrative to ask questions. And his questions revealed a knowledge which was making the girl more sensitive and uneasy every moment.

Finally, when she spoke of the Scarlet Desert, he asked if the Scarlet Lake were there and if the Xin was still supposed to inhabit its vermilion depths. And at that she turned and looked at him, her forefinger still resting on the map.

"Where have you ever heard of the Scarlet Lake and the

Xin?" she asked as though frightened.

Recklow said quietly that as a boy he had served under Gordon and Sir Robert.

"If, as a boy, you served under Chinese Gordon, you already know much of what I have told you, Mr. Recklow. Is it not true?" she demanded nervously.

"That makes no difference," he replied with a smile. "It is all very new to these three young gentlemen. And as for myself, I am checking up what you say and comparing it with what I heard many, many years ago when my comrade Barres and I were in Yian."

"Did you really know Sir Robert Hart?"

"Yes."

"Then why do you not explain to these gentlemen?"

"Dear child," he interrupted gently, "what did Chinese Gordon or Sir Robert Hart, or even my comrade Barres, or I myself know about occult Asia in comparison to what you know?—a girl who has actually served the mysteries of Erlik for four amazing years!"

She paled a trifle, came slowly across the room to where Recklow was seated, laid a timid hand on his sleeve.

"Do you believe there are sorcerers in Asia?" she asked with that child-like directness which her wonderful blue eyes corroborated.

Recklow remained silent.

"Because," she went on, "if, in your heart, you do not believe this to be an accursed fact, then what I have to say will mean nothing to any of you."

Recklow touched his short, silvery moustache, hesitating. Then:

"The worship of Erlik is devil worship," he said. "Also I am entirely prepared to believe that there are, among the Yezidees, adepts who employ scientific weapons against civilisation—who have probably obtained a rather terrifying knowledge of psychic laws which they use scientifically, and which to ordinary, God-fearing folk appear to be the black magic of sorcerers."

Cleves said: "The employment by the *huns* of poison gases and long-range cannon is a parallel case. Before the war we could not believe in the possibility of a cannon that threw shells a distance of seventy miles."

The girl still addressed herself to Recklow: "Then you do not believe there are real sorcerers in Asia, Mr. Recklow?"

"Not sorcerers with supernatural powers for evil. Only degenerate human beings who, somehow, have managed to tap invisible psychic currents, and have learned how to use terrific forces about which, so far, we know practically nothing."

She spoke again in the same uneasy voice: "Then you do not believe that either God or Satan is involved?"

"No," he replied smilingly, "and you must not so believe."

"Nor the—the destruction of human souls," she persisted; "you do not believe it is being accomplished today?"

"Not in the slightest, dear young lady," he said cheerfully.

"Do you not believe that to have been instructed in such unlawful knowledge is damning? Do you not believe that ability to employ unknown forces is forbidden of God, and that to disobey His law means death to the soul?"

"No!"

"That it is the price one pays to Satan for occult power over people's minds?" she insisted.

"Hypnotic suggestion is not one of the cardinal sins," explained Recklow, still smiling—"unless wickedly employed. The Yezidee priesthood is a band of so-called sorcerers only because of their wicked employment of whatever hypnotic and psychic knowledge they may have obtained.

"There was nothing intrinsically wicked in the *huns'* discovery of phosgene. But the use they made of it made devils out of them. My ability to manufacture phosgene gas is no crime. But if I manufacture it and use it to poison innocent human beings, then, in that sense, I am, perhaps, a sort of modern sorcerer."

Tressa Norne turned paler:

"I had better tell you that I *have* used—forbidden knowledge—which the Yezidees taught me in the temple of Erlik."

"Used it how?" demanded Cleves.

"To—to earn a living. . . . And once or twice to defend myself."

There was the slightest scepticism in Recklow's bland smile. "You did quite right, Miss Norne."

She had become very white now. She stood beside Recklow, her back toward the suspended map, and looked in a scared sort of way from one to the other of the men seated before her, turning finally to Cleves, and coming toward him.

"I—I once killed a man," she said with a catch in her breath.

Cleves reddened with astonishment. "Why did you do that?" he asked.

"He was already on his way to kill me in bed."

"You were perfectly right," remarked Recklow coolly.

"I don't know . . . I was in bed. . . . And then, on the edge of sleep, I felt his mind groping to get hold of mine—feeling about in the darkness to get hold of my brain and seize it and paralyse it."

All colour had left her face. Cleves gripped the arm of his chair and watched her intently.

"I—I had only a moment's mental freedom," she went on in a ghost of a voice. "I was just able to rouse myself, fight off those murderous brain-fingers—let loose a clear mental ray. . . . And then, O God! I saw him in his room with his Kalmuck knife—saw him already on his way to murder me—Gutchlug Khan, the Yezidee—looking about in his bedroom for a shroud. . . . And when—when he reached for the bed to draw forth a fine, white sheet for the shroud without which no Yezidee dares journey deathward—then—then I became frightened. . . . And I killed him—I slew him there in his hotel bedroom on the floor above mine!"

Selden moistened his lips: "That Oriental, Gutchlug, died from heart-failure in a San Francisco hotel," he said. "I was there at the time."

"He died by the fangs of a little yellow snake," whispered the girl.

"There was no snake in his room," retorted Cleves.

"And no wound on his body," added Selden. "I attended the autopsy."

She said, faintly: "There was no snake, and no wound, as you say. . . . Yet Gutchlug died of both there in his bedroom. . . . And before he died he heard his soul bidding him farewell; and he saw the death-adder coiled in the sheet he clutched saw the thing strike him again and again saw and felt the tiny wounds on his left hand; felt the fangs pricking deep, deep into the veins; died of it there within the minute—died of the swiftest poison known. And yet—"

She turned her dead-white face to Cleves—"And *yet there was no snake there*! . . . And never had been. . . . And so I—I ask you, gentlemen, if souls do not die when minds learn to fight death with death and deal it so swiftly, so silently, while one's body lies, unstirring on a bed—in a locked room on the floor—"

She swayed a little, put out one hand rather blindly.

Recklow rose and passed a muscular arm around her; Cleves, beside her, held her left hand, crushing it, without intention, until she opened her eyes with a cry of pain.

"Are you all right?" asked Recklow bluntly.

"Yes." She turned and looked at Cleves and he caressed her bruised hand as though dazed.

"Tell me," she said to Cleves—"you who know—know more about my mind than anybody living—" a painful colour surged into her face but she went on steadily, forcing herself to meet his gaze: "tell me, Mr. Cleves—do you still believe that nothing can really destroy my soul? And that it shall yet win through to safety?"

He said: "Your soul is in God's keeping, and always shall be. . . And if the Yezidees have made you believe otherwise, they lie."

Recklow added in a slow, perplexed way: "I have no personal knowledge of psychic power. I am not psychic, not susceptible. But if you actually possess such ability, Miss Norne, and if you have employed such knowledge to defend your life, then you have done absolutely right."

"No guilt touches you," added Selden with an involuntary shiver, "if by hypnosis or psychic ability you really did put an end to that would-be murderer, Gutchlug."

Selden said: "If Gutchlug died by the fangs of a yellow death-adder which existed only in his own mind, and if you actually had anything to do with it you acted purely in self-defence."

"You did your full duty," added Benton—"but—good God!—it seems incredible to me, that such power can actually be available in the world!"

Recklow spoke again in his pleasant, undisturbed voice: "Go back to the map, Miss Norne, and tell us a little more about this rather terrifying thing which you believe menaces the civilised world with destruction."

Tressa Norne laid a slim finger on the map. Her voice had become steady. She said:

"The devil-worship, of which one of the modern develop-ments is Bolshevism, and another the terrorism of the *hun*, be-gan in Asia long before Christ's advent: At least so it was taught us in the temple of Erlik.

"It has always existed, its aim always has been the annihila-tion of good and the elevation of evil; the subjection of right by might, and the worldwide triumph of wrong.

"Perhaps it is as old as the first battle between God and Sa-tan. I have wondered about it, sometimes. There in the dusk of the temple when the Eight Assassins came—the eight Sheiks-el-Djebel, all in white—chanting the Yakase of Sabbah—always that dirge when they came and spread their eight white shrouds on the temple steps—"

Her voice caught; she waited to recover her composure. Then went on:

"The ambition of Genghis was to conquer the world by force of arms. It was merely of physical subjection that he dreamed. But the Slayer of Souls—"

"Who?" asked Recklow sharply.

"The Slayer of Souls—Erlik's vice-regent on earth—Hassan

Sabbah. The Old Man of the Mountain. It is of him I am speaking," exclaimed Tressa Norne—with quiet resolution. "Genghis sought only physical conquest of man; the Yezidee's ambition is more awful, *for he is attempting to surprise and seize the very minds of men!*"

There was a dead silence. Tressa looked palely upon the four.

"The Yezidees—who you tell me are not sorcerers—are using power—which you tell me is not magic accursed by God—to waylay, capture, enslave, and destroy *the minds and souls of mankind*.

"It may be that what they employ is hypnotic ability and psychic power and can be, some day, explained on a scientific basis when we learn more about the occult laws which govern these phenomena.

"But could anything render the threat less awful? For there have existed for centuries—perhaps always—a sect of Satanists determined upon the destruction of everything that is pure and holy and good on earth; and they are resolved to substitute for righteousness the dreadful reign of hell.

"In the beginning there were comparatively few of these human demons. Gradually, through the eras, they have increased. In the twelfth century there were fifty thousand of the Sect of Assassins.

"Beside the castle of the Slayer of Souls on Mount Alamout—" she laid her finger on the map—"eight other towers were erected for the Eight Chief Assassins, called Sheiks-el-Djebel.

"In the temple we were taught where these eight towers stood." She picked up a pencil, and on eight blank spaces of unexplored and unmapped Mongolia she made eight crosses. Then she turned to the men behind her.

"It was taught to us in the temple that from these eight *foci* of infection the disease of evil has been spreading throughout the world; from these eight towers have gone forth every year the emissaries of evil—perverted missionaries—to spread the poisonous propaganda, to teach it, to tamper stealthily with the minds of men, dominate them, pervert them, instruct them in the creed of the Assassin of Souls.

"All over the world are people, already contaminated, whose minds are already enslaved and poisoned, and who are infecting the still healthy brains of others—stealthily possessing themselves of the minds of mankind—teaching them evil, inviting them to mock the precepts of Christ.

"Of such lost minds are the degraded brains of the Germans—the pastors and philosophers who teach that might is right.

"Of such crippled minds are the Bolsheviki, poisoned long, long ago by close contact with Asia which, before that, had infected and enslaved the minds of the ruling classes with ferocious philosophy.

"Of such minds are all anarchists of every shade and stripe—all terrorists, all disciples of violence,—the murderously envious, the slothful slinking brotherhood which prowls through the world taking every opportunity to set it afire; those mentally dulled by reason of excesses; those weak intellects become unsound through futile gabble,—parlour socialists, amateur revolutionists, theoretical incapables excited by discussion fit only for healthy minds."

She left the map and came over to where the four men were seated terribly intent upon her every word.

"In the temple of Erlik, where my girlhood was passed after the murder of my parents, I learned what I am repeating to you," she said.

"I learned this, also, that the Eight Towers still exist—still stand today,—at least theoretically—and that from the Eight Towers pours forth across the world a stream of poison.

"I was told that, to every country, eight Yezidees were allotted—eight sorcerers—or adepts in scientific psychology if you prefer it—whose mission is to teach the gospel of hell and gradually but surely to win the minds of men to the service of the Slayer of Souls.

"That is what was taught us in the temple. We were educated in the development of occult powers—for it seems all human beings possess this psychic power latent within them—only few, even when instructed, acquire any ability to control and use this force. . . .

"I—I learned—rapidly, I even thought, sometimes, that the Yezidees were beginning to be a little afraid of me,—even the Hassani priests. . . . And the Sheiks-el-Djebel, spreading their shrouds on the temple steps, looked at me with unquiet eyes, where I stood like a corpse amid the incense clouds—"

She passed, her fingers over her eyelids, then framed her face between both hands for a moment's thought lost in tragic retrospection.

"*Kai!*" she whispered dreamily as though to herself—"what Erlik awoke within my body that was asleep, God knows, but it was as though a twin comrade arose within me and looked out through my eyes upon a world which never before had been visible."

Utter silence reigned in the room: Cleves's breathing seemed almost painful to him so intently was he listening and watching this girl; Benton's hands whitened with his grip on the chair-arms; Selden, tense, absorbed, kept his keen gaze of a business man fastened on her face. Recklow slowly caressed the cold bowl of his pipe with both thumbs.

Tressa Norne's strange and remote eyes subtly altered, and she lifted her head and looked calmly at the men before her.

"I think that there is nothing more for me to add," she said. "The Red Spectre of Anarchy, called Bolshevism at present, threatens our country. Our Government is now awake to this menace and the Secret Service is moving everywhere.

"Great damage already has been done to the minds of many people in this Republic; poison has spread; is spreading. The Eight Towers still stand. The Eight Assassins are in America.

"But these eight Assassins know me to be their enemy. . . . They will surely attempt to kill me. . . . I don't believe I can avoid—death—very long. . . . But I want to serve my country and—and mankind."

"They'll have to get me first," said Cleves, bluntly. "I shall not permit you out of my sight."

Recklow said in a musing voice: "And these eight gentlemen, who are very likely to hurt us, also, are the first people we ought to hunt."

"To get them," added Selden, "we ought to choke the stream at its source."

"To find out who they are is what is going to worry us," added Benton. Cleves had stood holding a chair for Tressa Norne. Finally she noticed it and seated herself as though tired.

"Is Sanang one of these eight?" he asked her. The girl turned and looked up at him, and he saw the flush mounting in her face.

"Sometimes," she said steadily, "I have almost believed he was Erlik's own vice-regent on earth—the Slayer of Souls himself."

Benton and Selden had gone. Recklow left a little later. Cleves accompanied him out to the landing.

"Are you going to keep Miss Norne here with you for the present?" inquired the older man.

"Yes. I dare not let her out of my sight, Recklow. What else can I do?"

"I don't know. Is she prepared for the consequences?"

"Gossip? Slander?"

"Of course."

"I can get a housekeeper."

"That only makes it look worse."

Cleves reddened. "Well, do you want to find her in some hotel or apartment with her throat cut?"

"No," replied Recklow, gently, "I do not."

"Then what else is there to do but keep her here in my own apartment and never let her out of my sight until we can find and lock up the eight gentlemen who are undoubtedly bent on murdering her?"

"Isn't there some woman in the Service who could help out? I could mention several."

"I tell you I can't trust Tressa Norne to anybody except myself," insisted Cleves. "I got her into this; I am responsible if she

59

is murdered; I dare not entrust her safety to anybody else. And, Recklow, it's a ghastly responsibility for a man to induce a young girl to face death, even in the service of her country."

"If she remains here alone with you she'll face social destruction," remarked Recklow.

Cleves was silent for a moment, then he burst out: "Well, what am I to do? What is there left for me to do except to watch over her and see her through this devilish business? What other way have I to protect her, Recklow?"

"You could offer her the protection of your name," suggested the other, carelessly.

"What? You mean—marry her?"

"Well, nobody else would be inclined to, Cleves, if it ever becomes known she has lived here quite alone with you."

Cleves stared at the elder man.

"This is nonsense," he said in a harsh voice. "That young girl doesn't want to marry anybody. Neither do I. She doesn't wish to have her throat cut, that's all. And I'm determined she shan't."

"There are stealthier assassins, Cleves,—the slayers of reputations. It goes badly with their victim. It does indeed."

"Well, hang it, what do you think I ought to do?"

"I think you ought to marry her if you're going to keep her here."

"Suppose she doesn't mind the unconventionality of it?"

"All women mind. No woman, at heart, is unconventional, Cleves."

"She—she seems to agree with me that she ought to stay here. . . . Besides, she has no money, no relatives, no friends in America—"

"All the more tragic. If you really believe it to be your duty to keep her here where you can look after her bodily safety, then the other obligation is still heavier. And there may come a day when Miss Norne will wish that you had been less conscientious concerning the safety of her pretty throat. . . . For the knife of the Yezidee is swifter and less cruel than the tongue that slays with a smile. . . . And this young girl has many years to live, after this business of Bolshevism is dead and forgotten in our Republic."

"Recklow!"

"Yes?"

"You think I might dare try to find a room somewhere else for her and let her take her chances? *Do* you?"

"It's your affair."

"I know hang it! I know it's my affair. I've unintentionally made it so. But can't you tell me what I ought to do?"

"I can't."

"What would *you* do?"

"Don't ask me," returned Recklow, sharply. "If you're not man enough to come to a decision you may turn her over to me."

Cleves flushed brightly. "Do you think *you* are old enough to take my job and avoid scandal?"

Recklow's cold eyes rested on him: "If you like," he said, "I'll assume your various kinds of personal responsibility toward Miss Norne."

Cleve's visage burned. "I'll shoulder my own burdens," he retorted.

"Sure. I knew you would." And Recklow smiled and held out his hand. Cleves took it without cordiality. Standing so, Recklow, still smiling, said: "What a rotten deal that child has had—is having. Her father and mother were fine people. Did you ever hear of Dr. Norne?"

"She mentioned him once."

"They were up-State people of most excellent antecedents and no money.

"Dr. Norne was our Vice-Consul at Yarkand in the province of Sin Kiang. All he had was his salary, and he lost that and his post when the administration changed. Then he went into the spice trade.

"Some Jew syndicate here sent him up the Yarkand River to see what could be done about jade and gold concessions. He was on that business when the tragedy happened. The Kalmuks and Khirghiz were responsible, under Yezidee instigation. And there you are:—and here is his child, Cleves—back, by some miracle, from that flowering hell called Yian, believing in her heart that she really lost her soul there in the temple. And now, here in her own native land, she is exposed to actual and hourly danger of assassination. . . . Poor kid! . . . Did you ever hear of a rottener deal, Cleves?"

Their hands had remained clasped while Recklow was speaking. He spoke again, clearly, amiably:

"To lay down one's life for a friend is fine. I'm not sure that it's finer to offer one's honour in behalf of a girl whose honour is at stake."

After a moment Cleves's grip tightened

"All right," he said.

Recklow went downstairs.

Chapter 6
In Battle

Cleves went back into the apartment; he noticed that Miss Norne's door was ajar.

To get to his own room he had to pass that way; and he saw her, seated before the mirror, partly undressed, her dark, lustrous hair being combed out and twisted up for the night.

Whether this carelessness was born of innocence or of indifference mattered little; he suddenly realised that these conditions wouldn't do. And his first feeling was of anger.

"If you'll put on your robe and slippers," he said in an unpleasant voice, "I'd like to talk to you for a few moments."

She turned her head on its charming neck and looked around and up at him over one naked shoulder.

"Shall I come into your room?" she inquired.

"No! . . . when you've got some clothes on, call me."

"I'm quite ready now," she said calmly, and drew the Chinese slippers over her bare feet and passed a silken loop over the silver bell buttons on her right shoulder. Then, undisturbed, she continued to twist up her hair, following his movements in the mirror with unconcerned blue eyes.

He entered and seated himself, the impatient expression still creasing his forehead and altering his rather agreeable features,

"Miss Norne," he said, "you're absolutely convinced that these people mean to do you harm. Isn't that true?"

"Of course," she said simply.

"Then, until we get them, you're running a serious risk. In fact, you live in hourly peril. That is your belief, isn't it?"

She put the last peg into her thick, curly hair, lowered her arms, turned, dropped one knee over the other, and let her candid gaze rest on him in silence.

"What I mean to explain," he said coldly, "is that as long as I induced you to go into this affair I'm responsible for you. If I let you out of my sight here in New York and if anything happens to you, I'll be as guilty as the dirty beast who takes your life. What is your opinion? It's up to me to stand by you now, isn't it?"

"I had rather be near you—for a while," she said timidly.

"Certainly. But, Miss Norne, our living here together, in my apartment—or living together anywhere else—is never going to be understood by other people. You know that, don't you?"

After a silence, still looking at him out of clear, unembarrassed eyes:

"I know. . . . But . . . I don't want to die."

"I told you," he said sharply, "they'll have to kill me first. So that's all right. But how about what I am doing to your reputation?"

"I understand."

"I suppose you do. You're very young. Once out of this blooming mess, you will have all your life before you. But if I kill your reputation for you while saving your body from death, you'll find no happiness in living. Do you realise that?"

"Yes."

"Well, then? Have you any solution for this problem that confronts you?"

"No."

"Haven't you any idea to suggest?"

"I don't—don't want to die," she repeated in an unsteady voice.

He bit his lip; and after a moment's scowling silence under the merciless scrutiny of her eyes: "Then you had better marry me," he said.

It was some time before she spoke. For a second or two he sustained the searching quality of her gaze, but it became unendurable.

Presently she said: "I don't ask it of you. I can shoulder my own burdens." And he remembered what he had just said to Recklow.

"You've shouldered more than your share," he blurted out. "You are deliberately risking death to serve your country. I enlisted you. The least I can do is to say my affections are not engaged; so naturally the idea of—of marrying anybody never entered my head."

"Then you do not care for anybody else?"

Her candour amazed and disconcerted him.

"No." He looked at her, curiously. "Do you care for anybody in that way?"

A light blush tinted her face. She said gravely: "If we really are going to marry each other I had better tell you that I did care for Prince Sanang."

"What!" he cried, astounded.

"It seems incredible, doesn't it? Yet it is quite true. I fought him; I fought myself; I stood guard over my mind and senses there in the temple; I knew what he was and I detested him and I mocked him there in the temple. . . . And I loved him."

"Sanang!" he repeated, not only amazed but also oddly incensed at the naive confession.

"Yes, Sanang. . . . If we are to marry, I thought I ought to tell you. Don't you think so?"

"Certainly," he replied in an absent-minded way, his mind still grasping at the thing. Then, looking up: "Do you still care for this fellow?"

She shook her head.

"Are you perfectly sure, Miss Norne?"

"As sure as that I am alive when I awake from a nightmare. My hatred for Sanang is very bitter," she added frankly, "and yet somehow it is not my wish to see him harmed."

"You still care for him a little?"

"Oh, no. But—can't you understand that it is not in me to wish him harm? . . . No girl feels that way—once having cared. To become indifferent to a familiar thing is perhaps natural; but to desire to harm it is not in my character."

"You have plenty of character," he said, staring at her.

"You don't think so. Do you?"

"Why not?"

"Because of what I said to you on the roof-garden that night. It was shameful, wasn't it?"

"You behaved like many a thoroughbred," he returned bluntly; "you were scared, bewildered, ready to bolt to any shelter offered."

"It's quite true I didn't know what to do to keep alive. And that was all that interested me—to keep on living—having lost my soul and being afraid to die and find myself in hell with Erlik."

He said: "Isn't that absurd notion out of your head yet?"

"I don't know. . . . I can't suddenly believe myself safe after all those years. It is not easy to root out what was planted in childhood and what grew to be part of one during the tender and formative period. . . . You can't understand, Mr. Cleves—you can't ever feel or visualise what became my daily life in a region which was half paradise and half hell—"

She bent her head and took her face between her fingers, and sat so, brooding.

After a little while: "Well," he said, "there's only one way to manage this affair—if you are willing, Miss Norne."

She merely lifted her eyes.

"I think," he said, "there's only that one way out of it. But you

65

understand"—he turned pink—"it will be quite all right—your liberty—privacy—I shan't bother you—annoy—"

She merely looked at him.

"After this Bolshevistic flurry is settled—in a year or two—or three—then you can very easily get your freedom; and you'll have all life before you" . . . he rose:—"and a jolly good friend in me—a good comrade, Miss Norne. And that means you can count on me when you go into business—or whatever you decide to do."

She also had risen, standing slim and calm in her exquisite Chinese robe, the sleeves of which covered her finger tips.

"Are you going to marry me?" she asked.

"If you'll let me."

"Yes—I will . . . it's so generous and considerate of you. I—I don't ask it; I really don't—"

"But *I* do."

"—And I never dreamed of such a thing."

He forced a smile. "Nor I. It's rather a crazy thing to do. But I know of no saner alternative. . . . So we had better get our license tomorrow. . . . And that settles it."

He turned to go; and, on her threshold, his feet caught in something on the floor and he stumbled, trying to free his feet from a roll of soft white cloth lying there on the carpet. And when he picked it up, it unrolled, and a knife fell out of the folds of cloth and struck his foot.

Still perplexed, not comprehending, he stooped to recover the knife. Then, straightening up, he found himself looking into the colourless face of Tressa Norne.

"What's all this?" he asked—"this sheet and knife here on the floor outside your door?"

She answered with difficulty: "They have sent you your shroud, I think."

"Are not those things yours? Were they not already here in your baggage?" he demanded incredulously. Then, realising that they had not been there on the door-sill when he entered her room a few moments since, a rough chill passed over him—the

66

icy caress of fear.

"Where did that thing come from?" he said hoarsely. "How could it get here when my door is locked and bolted? Unless there's somebody hidden here!"

Hot anger suddenly flooded him; he drew his pistol and sprang into the passageway.

"What the devil is all this!" he repeated furiously, flinging open his bedroom door and switching on the light.

He searched his room in a rage, went on and searched the dining-room, smoking-room, and kitchen, and every clothes-press and closet, always aware of Tressa's presence close behind him. And when there remained no tiniest nook or cranny in the place unsearched, he stood in the centre of the carpet glaring at the locked and bolted door.

He heard her say under her breath: "This is going to be a sleepless night. And a dangerous one." And, turning to stare at her, saw no fear in her face, only excitement.

He still held clutched in his left hand the sheet and the knife. Now he thrust these toward her.

"What's this damned foolery, anyway?" he demanded harshly. She took the knife with a slight shudder. "There is something engraved on the silver hilt," she said.

He bent over her shoulder.

"Eighur," she added calmly, "not Arabic. The Mongols had no written characters of their own."

She bent closer, studying the inscription. After a moment, still studying the Eighur characters, she rested her left hand on his shoulder—an impulsive, unstudied movement that might have meant either confidence or protection.

"Look," she said, "it is not addressed to you after all, but to a symbol—a series of numbers, 53-6-26."

"That is my designation in the Federal Service," he said, sharply.

"Oh!" she nodded slowly. "Then this is what is written in the Mongol-Yezidee dialect, traced out in Eighur characters: 'To 53-6-26! By one of the Eight Assassins the Slayer of Souls sends this shroud and this knife from Mount Alamout. Such a blade shall divide your heart. This sheet is for your corpse."'

After a grim silence he flung the soft white cloth on the floor.

"There's no use my pretending I'm not surprised and worried," he said; "I don't know how that cloth got here. Do you?"

"It was sent."

"How?"

She shook her head and gave him a grave, confused look.

"There are ways. You could not understand. . . . This is going to be a sleepless night for us."

"You can go to bed, Tressa. I'll sit up and read and keep an eye on that door."

"I can't let you remain alone here. I'm afraid to do that."

He gave a laugh, not quite pleasant, as he suddenly comprehended that the girl now considered their *rôles* to be reversed.

"Are *you* planning to sit up in order to protect *me*?" he asked, grimly amused.

"Do you mind?"

"Why, you blessed little thing, I can take care of myself. How funny of you, when I am trying to plan how best to look out for *you*!"

But her face remained pale and concerned, and she rested her left hand more firmly on his shoulder.

"I wish to remain awake with you," she said. "Because I myself don't fully understand this"—she looked at the knife in her palm, then down at the shroud. "It is going to be a strange night for us," she sighed. "Let us sit together here on the lounge where I can face *that bolted door*. And if you are willing, I am going to turn out the lights—" She suddenly bent forward and switched them off—"because I must keep my mind on guard."

"Why do you do that?" he asked, "you can't see the door, now."

"Let me help you in my own way," she whispered. "I—I am very deeply disturbed, and very, very angry. I do not understand this new menace. Yezidee that I am, I do not understand what kind of danger threatens you through your loyalty to me."

She drew him forward, and he opened his mouth to remonstrate, to laugh; but as he turned, his foot touched the shroud, and an uncontrollable shiver passed over him.

They went close together, across the dim room to the lounge, and seated themselves. Enough light from Madison Avenue made objects in the room barely discernible.

Sounds from the street below became rarer as the hours wore away. The iron jar of trams, the rattle of vehicles, the harsh warning of taxicabs broke the stillness at longer and longer intervals, until, save only for that immense and ceaseless vibration of the monstrous iron city under the foggy stars, scarcely a sound stirred the silence.

The half-hour had struck long ago on the bell of the little clock. Now the clear bell sounded three times.

Cleves stirred on the lounge beside Tressa. Again and again he had thought that she was asleep for her head had fallen back against the cushions, and she lay very still. But always, when he leaned nearer to peer down at her, he saw her eyes open, and fixed intently upon the bolted door.

His pistol, which still rested on his knee, was pointed across the room, toward the door. Once he reminded her in a whisper that she was unarmed and that it might be as well for her to go and get her pistol. But she murmured that she was sufficiently equipped; and, in spite of himself, he shivered as he glanced down at her frail and empty hands.

It was sometime between three and half-past, he judged, when a sudden movement of the girl brought him upright on his seat, quivering with excitement.

"Mr. Cleves!"

"Yes?"

"The Sorcerers!"

"Where? Outside the door ?"

"Oh, my God," she murmured, "*they are after my mind again!* Their fingers are groping to seize my brain and get possession of it!"

"What!" he stammered, horrified.

"Here—in the dark," she whispered—"and I feel their fingers caressing me—searching—moving stealthily to surprise and grasp my thoughts. . . . I know what they are doing . . . I am resisting . . . I am fighting—fighting!"

She sat bolt upright with clenched hands at her breast, her face palely aglow in the dimness as though illumined by some vivid inward light—or, as he thought—from the azure blaze in her wide-open eyes.

"Is—is this what you call—what you believe to be magic?" he asked unsteadily. "Is there some hostile psychic influence threatening you?"

"Yes. I'm resisting. I'm fighting—fighting. They shall not trap me. They shall not harm you! . . . I know how to defend myself and you! . . . And *you*!"

Suddenly she flung her left arm around his neck and the delicate clenched hand brushed his cheek.

"They shall not have you," she breathed. "I am fighting. I am holding my own. There are eight of them—eight Assassins! My mind is in battle with theirs—fiercely in battle. . . . I hold my own! I am armed and waiting!"

With a convulsive movement she drew his head closer to her shoulder. "Eight of them!" she whispered,—"trying to entrap and seize my brain. But my thoughts are free! My mind is defending you—you, here in my arms!"

After a breathless silence: "Look out!" she whispered with terrible energy; "they are after *your* mind at last. Fix your thoughts on me! Keep your mind clear of their net! Don't let their ghostly fingers touch it. Look at me!" She drew him closer. "Look at *me*! Believe in *me*! I can resist. I can defend you. Does your head feel confused?"

"Yes—numb."

"*Don't sleep*! Don't close your eyes! Keep them open and look at me!"

"I can scarcely see you—"

"You *must* see me!"

"My eyes are heavy," he said drowsily. "I can't see you, Tres-sa—"

"Wake! Look at me! Keep your mind clear. Oh, I beg you—I beg you! They're after our minds and souls, I tell you! Oh, believe in me," she beseeched him in an agonised whisper—"Can't you believe in me for a moment,—as if you loved me!"

His heavy lids lifted and he tried to look at her.

"Can you see me? *Can* you?"

He muttered something in a confused voice.

"Victor!"

At the sound of his own name, he opened his eyes again and tried to straighten up, but his pistol fell to the carpet.

"Victor!" she gasped, "clear your mind in the name of God!"

"I cannot—"

"I tell you hell is opening beyond that door!—outside your bolted door, there I Can't you believe me! Can't you hear me! Oh, what will hold you if the love of God cannot!" she burst out. "I'd crucify myself for you if you'd look at me—if you'd only fight hard enough to believe in me—as though you loved me!"

His eyes unclosed but he sank back against her shoulder.

"Victor!" she cried in a terrible voice.

There was no answer.

"If the love of God could only hold you for a moment more!"—she stammered with her mouth against his ear, "just for a moment, Victor! Can't you hear me?"

"Yes—very far away."

"Fight for me! Try to care for me! Don't let Sanang have me!"

He shuddered in her arms, reached out and resting heavily on her shoulder, staggered to his feet and stood swaying like a drunken man.

"No, by God," he said thickly, "Sanang shall not touch you."

The girl was on her feet now, holding him upright with an arm around his shoulders.

"They can't—can't harm us together," she stammered. "Hark! Listen! Can you hear? Oh, can you hear?"

"Give me my pistol," he tried to say, but his tongue seemed twisted. "No—by God—Sanang shall not touch you."

She stooped lithely and recovered the weapon. "Hush," she said close to his burning face. "Listen. Our minds are safe! I can hear somebody's soul bidding its body farewell!"

White-lipped she burst out laughing, kicked the shroud out of the way, thrust the pistol into his right hand, went forward, forcing him along beside her, and drew the bolts from the door.

Suddenly he spoke distinctly:

"Is there anything outside that door on the landing?"

"Yes . . . I don't know what. Are you ready?" She laid her hand on lock and knob.

He nodded. At the same instant she jerked open the door; and a hunchback who had been picking at the lock fell headlong into the room, his pistol exploding on the carpet in a streak of fire.

It was a horrible struggle to secure the powerful misshapen creature, for he clawed and squealed and bounced about on the floor, striking blindly with ape-like arms. But at last Cleves held him down, throttled and twitching, and Tressa ripped strips from the shroud to truss up the writing thing.

Then Cleves switched on the light.

"Why—why—you rat!" he exclaimed in hysterical relief at seeing a living man whom he recognised there at his feet. "What are you doing here?"

The hunchback's red eyes blazed up at him from the floor.

"Who—who is he?" faltered the girl.

"He's a German tailor named Albert Feke—one of the Chicago Bolsheviki—the most dangerous sort we harbour one of their vile leaders who preaches that might is right and tells his disciples to go ahead and take what they want."

He looked down at the malignant cripple.

"You're wanted for the I. W. W. bomb murder, Albert. Did you know it?"

The hunchback licked his bloody lips. Then he kicked himself to a sitting position, squatted there like a toad and looked steadily at Tressa Norne out of small red-rimmed eyes. Blood dripped on his beard; his huge hairy fists, tied and crossed behind his back, made odd, spasmodic movements.

Cleves went to the telephone. Presently Tressa heard his voice, calm and distinct as usual:

"We've caught Albert Feke. He's here at my rooms. I'd like to have you come over, Recklow. . . . Oh, yes, he kicked and scuffled and scratched like a cat. . . . What? . . . No, I hadn't heard that he'd been in China. . . . Who? . . . Albert Feke? You say he was one of the Germans who escaped from Shantung four years ago? . . . You think he's a Yezidee! You mean one of the Eight Assassins?"

The hunchback, staring at Tressa out of red-rimmed eyes, suddenly snarled and lurched his misshapen body at her.

"*Teufelstuck!*" he screamed, "ain't I tell efferybody in Yian already it iss safer if we cut your throat! Devil-slut of Erlik—snow-leopardess!—cat of the Yezidees who has made of Sanang a fool!—it iss I who haf said always, always, that you know too damn much! . . . *Kai!* . . . I hear my soul bidding me farewell. Gif me my shroud!"

Cleves came back from the telephone. With the toe of his left foot he lifted the shroud and kicked it across the hunchback's knees.

"So you were one of the *huns* who instigated the massacre in Yian," he said, curiously. At that Tressa turned very white and a cry escaped her.

But the hunchback's features were all twisted into ferocious laughter, and he beat on the carpet with the heels of his great splay feet.

"*Ja! Ja!*" he shrieked, "in Yian it vas a goot hunting! English and Yankee men und vimmens ve haff dropped into dose deep wells down. Py *Gott in Himmel*, how dey schream up out of dose deep wells in Yian!" He began to cackle and shriek in his frenzy. "*Ach Gott ja!* It iss not you either—you there, Keuke Mongol, who shall escape from the Sheiks-el-Djebel! It iss dot Old Man of the Mountain who shall tell your soul it iss time to say farewell! *Ja! Ja! Ach Gott!*—it iss my only regret that I shall not see the world when it is all afire! *Ja! Ja!*—all on fire like hell! But you shall see it, slut-leopard of the snows! You shall see it und you shall burn! *Kai! Kai!* My soul it iss bidding my body farewell. *Kai!* May Erlik curse you, Keuke Mongol—Heavenly Azure-Sorceress of the temple!—"

He spat at her and rolled over in his shroud.

The girl looking down on him closed her eyes for a moment, and Cleves saw her bloodless lips move, and bent nearer, listening. And he heard her whispering to herself:

"Preserve us all, O God, from the wrath of Satan who was stoned."

CHAPTER 7
THE BRIDAL

Over the United States stretched an unseen network of secret intrigue woven tirelessly night and day by the busy enemies of civilisation—Reds, parlour-socialists, enemy-aliens, terrorists, Bolsheviki, pseudo-intellectuals, I.W.W.'s, social faddists, and amateur meddlers of every nuance—all the various varieties of the vicious, witless, and mentally unhinged—brought together through the "cohesive power of plunder" and the degeneration of cranial tissue.

All over the United States the various departmental divisions of the Secret Service were busily following up these threads of intrigue leading everywhere through the obscurity of this vast and secret maze.

To meet the constantly increasing danger of physical violence and to uncover secret plots threatening sabotage and revolution, there were capable agents in every branch of the Secret Service, both Federal and State.

But in the first months of 1919 something more terrifying than physical violence suddenly threatened civilised America,—a wild, grotesque, incredible threat of a *war on human minds*!

And, little by little, the United States Government became convinced that this ghastly menace was no dream of a disordered imagination, but that it was real: that among the enemies of civilisation there actually existed a few powerful but perverted minds capable of wielding psychic forces as terrific weapons: that by the sinister use of psychic knowledge controlling these mighty forces the very minds of mankind could be stealthily approached, seized, controlled and turned upon civilisation to aid in the world's destruction.

In terrible alarm the Government turned to England for advice. But Sir William Crookes was dead.

However, in England, Sir Conan Doyle immediately took up the matter, and in America Professor Hyslop was called into consultation.

And then, when the Government was beginning to realise what this awful menace meant, and that there were actually in the United States possibly half a dozen people who already had begun to carry on a diabolical warfare by means of psychic power, for the purpose of enslaving and controlling the very minds of men,—then, in the terrible moment of discovery, a young girl landed in America after fourteen years' absence in Asia.

And this was the amazing girl that Victor Cleves had just married, at Recklow's suggestion, and in the line of professional duty,—and moral duty, perhaps.

It had been a brief, matter-of-fact ceremony. John Recklow, of the Secret Service, was there; also Benton and Selden of the same service.

The bride's lips were unresponsive; cold as the touch of the groom's unsteady hand.

She looked down at her new ring in a blank sort of way, gave her hand listlessly to Recklow and to the others in turn, whispered a timidly comprehensive "Thank you," and walked away beside Cleves as though dazed.

There was a taxicab waiting. Tressa entered. Recklow came out and spoke to Cleves in a low voice.

"Don't worry," replied Cleves dryly. "That's why I married

her."

"Where are you going now?" inquired Recklow.

"Back to my apartment."

"Why don't you take her away for a month?"

Cleves flushed with annoyance: "This is no occasion for a wedding trip. You understand that, Recklow."

"I understand. But we ought to give her a breathing space. She's had nothing but trouble. She's worn out."

Cleves hesitated: "I can guard her better in the apartment. Isn't it safer to go back there, where your people are always watching the street and house day and night?"

"In a way it might be safer, perhaps. But that girl is nearly exhausted. And her value to us is unlimited. She may be the vital factor in this fight with anarchy. Her weapon is. her mind. And it's got to have a chance to rest."

Cleves, with one hand on the cab door, looked around impatiently.

"Do you, also, conclude that the psychic factor is actually part of this damned problem of Bolshevism?"

Recklow's cool eyes measured him: "Do *you*?"

"My God, Recklow, I don't know—after what my own eyes have seen."

"I don't know either," said the other calmly, "but I am taking no chances. I don't attempt to explain certain things that have occurred. But if it be true that a misuse of psychic ability by foreigners—Asiatics—among the anarchists is responsible for some of the devilish things being done in the United States, then your wife's unparalleled knowledge of the occult East is absolutely vital to us. And so I say, better take her away somewhere and give her mind a chance to recover from the incessant strain of these tragic years."

The two men stood silent for a moment, then Recklow went to the window of the taxicab.

"I have been suggesting a trip into the country, Mrs. Cleves," he said pleasantly,—"into the real country, somewhere,—a month's quiet in the woods, perhaps. Wouldn't it appeal to you?"

Cleves turned to catch her low-voiced answer.

"I should like it very much," she said in that odd, hushed way of speaking, which seemed to have altered her own voice and manner since the ceremony a little while before.

Driving back to his apartment beside her, he strove to realise that this girl was his wife.

One of her gloves lay across her lap, and on it rested a slender hand. And on one finger was his ring.

But Victor Cleves could not bring himself to believe that this brand-new ring really signified anything to him,—that it had altered his own life in any way. But always his incredulous eyes returned to that slim finger resting there, unstirring, banded with a narrow circlet of virgin gold.

In the apartment they did not seem to know exactly what to do or say—what attitude to assume—what effort to make.

Tressa went into her own room, removed her hat and furs, and came slowly back into the living-room, where Cleves still stood gazing absently out of the window.

A fine rain was falling.

They seated themselves. There seemed nothing better to do.

He said, politely: "In regard to going away for a rest, you wouldn't care for the North Woods, I fancy, unless you like winter sports. Do you?"

"I like sunlight and green leaves," she said in that odd, still voice.

"Then, if it would please you to go South for a few weeks' rest—"

"Would it inconvenience you?"

Her manner touched him.

"My dear Miss Norne," he began, and checked himself, flushing painfully. The girl blushed, too; then, when he began to laugh, her lovely, bashful smile glimmered for the first time.

"I really can't bring myself to realise that you and I are married," he explained, still embarrassed, though smiling.

Her smile became an endeavour. "I can't believe it either, Mr. Cleves," she said. "I feel rather stunned."

"Hadn't you better call me Victor—under the circumstances?" he suggested, striving to speak lightly.

"Yes. . . . It will not be very easy to say it—not for some time, I think."

"Tressa?"

"Yes."

"Yes—*what?*"

"Yes—Victor."

"That's the idea," he insisted with forced gaiety.

"The thing to do is to face this rather funny situation and take it amiably and with good humour. You'll have your freedom some day, you know."

"Yes—I—know."

"And we're already on very good terms. We find each other interesting, don't we?"

"Yes."

"It even seems to me," he ventured, "it certainly seems to me, at times, as though we are approaching a common basis of—of mutual—er—esteem."

"Yes. I—I do esteem you, Mr. Cleves."

"In point of fact," he concluded, surprised, "we *are* friends-in a way. Wouldn't you call it—friendship?"

"I think so, I think I'd call it that," she admitted.

"I think so, too. And that is lucky for us. That makes this crazy situation more comfortable—less—well, perhaps less ponderous."

The girl assented with a vague smile, but her eyes remained lowered.

"You see," he went on, "when two people are as oddly situated as we are, they're likely to be afraid of being in each other's way. But they ought to get on without being unhappy as long as they are quite confident of each other's friendly consideration. Don't you think so, Tressa?"

Her lowered eyes rested steadily on her ring-finger. "Yes," she said. "And I am not—unhappy, or—afraid."

She lifted her blue gaze to his; and, somehow, he thought of her barbaric name, Keuke,—and its Yezidee significance, "heavenly—azure."

"Are we really going away together?" she asked timidly.

"Certainly, if you wish."

"If you, also, wish it, Mr. Cleves."

He found himself saying with emphasis that he always wished to do what she desired. And he added, more gently:

"You *are* tired, Tressa—tired and lonely and unhappy."

"Tired, but not the—others."

"Not unhappy?"

"No."

"Aren't you lonely?"

"Not with you."

The answer came so naturally, so calmly, that the slight sensation of pleasure it gave him arrived only as an agreeable afterglow.

"We'll go South," he said. . . . "I'm so glad that you don't feel lonely with me."

"Will it be warmer where we are going, Mr. Cleves?"

"Yes—you poor child! You need warmth and sunshine, don't you? Was it warm in Yian, where you lived so many years?"

"It was always June in Yian," she said under her breath.

She seemed to have fallen into a reverie; he watched the sensitive face. Almost imperceptibly it changed; became altered, younger, strangely lovely.

Presently she looked up—and it seemed to him that it was not Tressa Norne at all he saw, but little Keuke—Heavenly Azure—of the Yezidee temple, as she dropped one slim knee over the other and crossed her hands above it.

"It was very beautiful in Yian," she said, "—Yian of the thousand bridges and scented gardens so full of lilies. Even after they took me to the temple, and I thought the world was ending, God's skies still remained soft overhead, and His weather fair and golden. . . . And when, in the month of the Snake, the Eight Sheiks-el-Djebel came to the temple to spread their shrouds on the rose-marble steps, then, after they had departed, chanting the

Prayers for the Dead, each to his Tower of Silence, we temple girls were free for a week....And once I went with Tchagane—a girl—and with Yulun—another girl—and we took our *keutch*, which is our luggage, and we went to the *yaïlak*, or summer pavilion on the Lake of the Ghost. Oh, wonderful,—a silvery world of pale-gilt suns and of moons so frail that the cloud-fleece at high-noon has more substance!"

Her voice died out; she sat gazing down at her spread fingers, on one of which gleamed her wedding-ring.

After a little, she went on dreamily:

"On that week, each three months, we were free. . . . If a young man should please us. . . ."

"Free?" he repeated.

"To love," she explained coolly.

"Oh." He nodded, but his face became rather grim.

"There came to me at the *yaïlak*," she went on carelessly, "one Khassar Noïane—Noïane means Prince—all in a *surcoat* of gold tissue with green vines embroidered, and wearing a green cap trimmed with dormouse, and green boots inlaid with stiff gold.

"He was so young ... a boy. I laughed. I said: 'Is this a *Yaçaoul*? An Urdu-envoy of Prince Erlik?'—mocking him as young and thoughtless girls mock—not in unfriendly manner—though I would not endure the touch of any man at all.

"And when I laughed at him, this Eighur boy flew into such a rage! *Kai*! I was amazed.

"'*Sou-sou*! Squirrel!' he cried angrily at me. 'Learn the *Yacaz*, little chatterer! Little mocker of men, it is ten blows with a stick you require, not kisses!'

"At that I whistled my two dogs, Bars and Alaga, for I did not think what he said was funny.

"I said to him: 'You had better go home, Khassar Noïane, for if no man has ever pleased me where I am at liberty to please myself, here on the Lake of the Ghost, then be very certain that no boy can please Keuke-Mongol here or anywhere!'

"And at that—*kai*! What did he say—that monkey?" She looked at her husband, her splendid eyes ablaze with wrathful laughter, and made a gesture full of angry grace:

"'Squirrel!' he cries—'little malignant sorceress of Yian! May everything high about you become a sandstorm, and everything long a serpent, and everything broad a toad, and everything—'

"But I had had enough, Victor," she added excitedly, "and I made a wild bee bite him on the lip! *What* do you think of such a courtship?" she cried, laughing. But Cleves's face was a study in emotions.

And then, suddenly, the laughing mask seemed to slip from the bewitching features of Keuke Mongol; and there was Tressa Norne—Tressa Cleves—disconcerted, paling a little as the memory of her impulsive confidence in this man beside her began to dawn on her more clearly.

"I—I'm sorry—" she faltered. . . . "You'll think me silly think evil of me, perhaps—"

She looked into his troubled eyes, then suddenly she took her face into both hands and covered it, sitting very still.

"We'll go South together," he said in an uncertain voice. "I hope you will try to think of me as a friend. . . . I'm just troubled because I am so anxious to understand you. That is all. . . . I'm—I'm troubled, too, because I am anxious that you should think well of me. Will you try, always?"

She nodded.

"I want to be your friend, always," he said.

"Thank you, Mr. Cleves."

It was a strange spot he chose for Tressa—strange but lovely in its own unreal and rather spectral fashion—where a pearl-tinted mist veiled the St. Johns, and made exquisite ghosts of the palmettos, and softened the sun to a silver-gilt wafer pasted on a nacre sky.

It was a still country, where giant water-oaks towered, fantastic under their misty camouflage of moss, and swarming with small birds.

Among the trees the wood-ibis stole; without on the placid glass of the stream the eared grebe floated. There was no wind, no stirring of leaves, no sound save the muffled splash of silver mullet, the breathless whirr of a humming-bird, or the hushed rustle of lizards in the woods.

For Tressa this was the blessed balm that heals,—the balm of silence. And, for the first week, she slept most of the time, or lay in her hammock watching the swarms of small birds creeping and flitting amid the moss-draped labyrinths of the live-oaks at her very door.

It had been a little club house before the war, this bungalow on the St. Johns at Orchid Hammock. Its members had been few and wealthy; but some were dead in France and Flanders, and some still remained overseas, and others continued busy in the North.

And these two young people were quite alone there, save for a negro cook and a maid, and an aged negro kennel-master who wore a scarlet waistcoat and cords too large for his shrunken body, and who pottered, pottered through the fields all day, with his whip clasped behind his bent back and the pointers ranging wide, or plodding in at heel with red tongues lolling.

Twice Cleves went a little way for quail, using Benton's dogs; but even here in this remote spot he dared not move out of view of the little house where Tressa lay asleep.

So he picked up only a few brace of birds, and confined his sport to impaling too-familiar scorpions on the blade of his knife.

And all the while life remained unreal for him; his marriage seemed utterly unbelievable; he could not realise it, could not reconcile himself to conditions so incomprehensible.

Also, ever latent in his mind, was knowledge that made him restless—the knowledge that the young girl he had married had been in love with another man: Sanang.

And there were other thoughts—thoughts which had scarcely even taken the shape of questions.

One morning he came from his room and found Tressa on the veranda in her hammock. She had her moon-lute in her lap.

"You feel better—much better!" he said gaily, saluting her

extended hand.

"Yes. Isn't this heavenly? I begin to believe it is life to me, this pearl-tinted world, and the scent of orange bloom and the stillness of paradise itself."

She gazed out over the ghostly river. Not a wing stirred its glassy surface.

"Is this dull for you?" she asked in a low voice.

"Not if you are contented, Tressa."

"You're so nice about it. Don't you think you might venture a day's real shooting?"

"No, I think I won't," he replied.

"On my account?"

"Well—yes."

"I'm so sorry."

"It's all right as long as you're getting rested. What is that instrument?"

"My moon-lute."

"Oh, is that what it's called?"

She nodded, touched the strings. He watched her exquisite hands.

"Shall I?" she inquired a little shyly.

"Go ahead. I'd like to hear it!"

"I haven't touched it in months—not since I was on the steamer." She sat up in her hammock and began to swing there; and played and sang while swinging in the flecked shadow of the orange bloom:

Little Isle of Cispangou,
Isle of iris, isle of cherry,
Tell your tiny maidens merry
Clouds are looming over you!
La-e-la!
La-e-la!
All your ocean's but a ferry;
Ships are bringing death to you!
La-e-lou!
La-e-lou!

Little Isle of Cispangou,
Half a thousand ships are sailing;
Captain Death commands each crew;
Lo! the ruddy moon is paling!
La-e-la!
La-e-la!
Clouds the dying moon are veiling,
Every cloud a shroud for you!
La-e-lou!
La-e-lou!"

"Cispangou," she explained, "is the very, very ancient name, among the Mongols, for Japan."

"It's not exactly a gay song," he said. "What's it about?"

"Oh, it's a very ancient song about the Mongol invasion of Japan. I know scores and scores of such songs."

She sang some other songs. Afterward she descended from the hammock and came and sat down beside him on the veranda steps.

"I wish I could amuse you," she said wistfully.

"Why do you think I'm bored, Tressa? I'm not at all."

But she only sighed, lightly, and gathered her knees in both arms.

"I don't know how young men in the Western world are entertained," she remarked presently.

"You don't have to entertain me," he said, smiling.

"I should be happy to, if I knew how."

"How are young men entertained in the Orient?"

"Oh, they like songs and stories. But I don't think you do."

He laughed in spite of himself.

"Do you really wish to entertain me?"

"I do," she said seriously.

"Then please perform some of those tricks of magic which you can do so amazingly well."

Her dawning smile faded a trifle. "I don't—I haven't—" She hesitated.

"You haven't your professional paraphernalia with you," he

suggested.

"Oh—as for that—"

"Don't you need it?"

"For some things—some kinds of things. . . . I *could* do-other things—"

He waited. She seemed disconcerted. "Don't do anything you don't wish to do, Tressa," he said.

"I was only—only afraid—that if I should do some little things to amuse you, I might stir—stir up—interfere—encounter some sinister current—and betray myself—betray my whereabouts—"

"Well, for heaven's sake don't venture then!" he said with emphasis. "Don't do anything to stir up any other wireless—any Yezidee—"

"I am wondering," she reflected, "just what I dare venture to do to amuse you."

"Don't bother about me. I wouldn't have you try any psychic stunt down here, and run the chance of stirring up some Asiatic devil somewhere !"

She nodded absently, occupied with her own thoughts, sitting there, chin on hand, her musing eyes intensely blue.

"I think I can amuse you," she concluded, "without bringing any harm to myself."

"Don't try it, Tressa!—"

"I'll be very careful. Now, sit quite still—closer to me, please."

He edged closer; and became conscious of an indefinable freshness in the air that enveloped him, like the scent of something young and growing. But it was no magic odour,—merely the virginal scent of her hair and skin that even clung to her summer gown.

He heard her singing under her breath to herself:

La-e-la!
La-e-la!

and murmuring caressingly in an unknown tongue.

85

Then, suddenly in the pale sunshine, scores of little birds came hovering around them, alighting all over them. And he saw them swarming out of the mossy festoons of the water-oaks—scores and scores of tiny birds—Parula warblers, mostly—all flitting fearlessly down to alight upon his shoulders and knees, all keeping up their sweet, dreamy little twittering sound.

"This is wonderful," he whispered.

The girl laughed, took several birds on her forefinger.

"This is nothing," she said. "If I only dared—wait a moment!—" And, to the Parula warblers: "Go home, little friends of God!"

The air was filled with the musical whisper of wings. She passed her right arm around her husband's neck.

"Look at the river," she said.

"Good God!" he blurted out. And sat dumb.

For, over the St. John's misty surface, there was the span of a bridge—a strange, marble bridge humped up high in the centre.

And over it were passing thousands of people—he could make them out vaguely—see them passing in two never-ending streams—tinted shapes on the marble bridge.

And now, on the farther shore of the river, he was aware of a city—a vast one, with spectral *pagoda* shapes against the sky—

Her arm tightened around his neck.

He saw boats on the river—like the grotesque shapes that decorate ancient *lacquer*.

She rested her face lightly against his cheek.

In his ears was a far confusion of voices—the stir and movement of multitudes—noises on ships, boatmen's cries, the creak of oars.

Then, far and sonorous, quavering across the water from the city, the din of a temple gong.

There were bells, too—very sweet and silvery—camel bells, bells from the Buddhist temples.

He strained his eyes, and thought, amid the *pagodas*, that there were minarets, also.

Suddenly, clear and ringing came the distant *muezzin's* cry: "There is no other god but God! . . . It is noon. Mussulmans, pray!"

The girl's arm slipped from his neck and she shuddered and pushed him from her.

There was nothing, now, on the river or beyond it but the curtain of hanging mist; no sound except the cry of a gull, sharp and querulous in the vapours overhead.

"Have—have you been amused?" she asked.

"What did you do to me!" he demanded harshly.

She smiled and drew a light breath like a sigh.

"God knows what we living do to one another,—or to ourselves," she said. "I only tried to amuse you—after taking counsel with the birds."

"What was that bridge I saw!"

"The Bridge of Ten Thousand Felicities."

"And the city?"

"Yian."

"You lived there?"

"Yes."

He moistened his dry lips and stole another glance at this very commonplace Florida river. Sky and water were blank and still, and the ghostly trees stood tall, reflected palely in the translucent tide.

"You merely made me visualise what you were thinking about," he concluded in a voice which still remained unsteady.

"Did you *hear* nothing?"

He was silent, remembering the bells and the enormous murmur of a living multitude.

"And—there were the birds, too." She added, with an uncertain smile: "I do not mean to worry you. . . . And you did ask me to amuse you."

"I don't know how you did it," he said harshly. "And the details—those thousands and thousands of people on the bridge! . . . And there was one, quite near this end of the bridge, who looked back. . . . A young girl who turned and laughed at us—"

"That was Yulun."

"Who?"

"Yulun. I taught her English."

"A temple girl?"

"Yes. From Black China."

"How could you make *me* see *her*!" he demanded.

"Why do you ask such things? I do not know how to tell you how I do it."

"It's a dangerous, uncanny knowledge!" he blurted out; and suddenly checked himself, for the girl's face went white.

"I don't mean uncanny," he hastened to add. "Because it seems to me that what you did by juggling with invisible currents to which, when attuned, our five senses respond, is on the same lines as the wireless telegraph and telephone."

She said nothing, but her colour slowly returned.

"You mustn't be so sensitive," he added. "I've no doubt that it's all quite normal—quite explicable on a perfectly scientific basis. Probably it's no more mysterious than a man in an airplane over mid-ocean conversing with people ashore on two continents."

For the remainder of the day and evening Tressa seemed subdued—not restless, not nervous, but so quiet that, sometimes, glancing at her askance, Cleves involuntarily was reminded of some lithe young creature of the wilds, intensely alert and still, immersed in fixed and dangerous meditation.

About five in the afternoon they took their golf sticks, went down to the river, and embarked in the canoe.

The water was glassy and still. There was not a ripple ahead, save when a sleeping gull awoke and leisurely steered out of their way.

Tressa's arms and throat were bare and she wore no hat. She sat forward, wielding the bow paddle and singing to herself in a low voice.

"You feel all right, don't you?" he asked.

"Oh, I am so well, physically, now! It's really wonderful, Victor—like being a child again," she replied happily.

"You're not much more," he muttered.

She heard him: "Not very much more—in years," she said. "Does Scripture tell us how old Our Lord was when He descended into Hell?"

"I don't know," he replied, startled.

After a little while Tressa tranquilly resumed her paddling and singing:

> —And eight tall towers
> Guard the route
> Of human life,
> Where at all hours
> Death looks out,
> Holding a knife
> Rolled in a shroud.
>
> For every man,
> Humble or proud,
> Mighty or bowed,
> Death has a shroud;—for every man,—
> Even for Tchingniz Khan!
> Behold them pass!—lancer,
> Baroulass,
> Temple dancer
> In tissue gold,
> Khiounnou,
> Karlik bold,
>
> Christian, Jew,—
> Nations swarm to the great Urdu.
> Yaçaoul, with your kettledrum,
> Warn your Khan that his hour is come!
> Shroud and knife at his spurred feet throw,
> And bid him stretch his neck for the blow!—

"You know," remarked Cleves, "that some of those songs you sing are devilish creepy."

Tressa looked around at him over her shoulder, saw he was smiling, smiled faintly in return.

They were off Orchid Cove now. The hotel and cottages loomed dimly in the silver mist. Voices came distinctly across the water. There were people on the golf course paralleling the river; laughter sounded from the clubhouse veranda.

They went ashore.

CHAPTER 8
THE MAN IN WHITE

It was at the sixth hole that they passed the man ahead who was playing all alone—a courteous young fellow in white flannels, who smiled and bowed them "through" in silence.

They thanked him, drove from the tee, and left the polite and reticent young man still apparently hunting for a lost ball.

Like other things which depended upon dexterity and precision, Tressa had taken most naturally to golf. Her supple muscles helped.

At the ninth hole they looked back but did not see the young man in white flannels.

Hammock, set with pine and *palmetto*, and intervals of evil-looking swamp, flanked the course. Rank wire-grass, bayberry and scrub *palmetto* bounded the fairgreen.

On every blossoming bush hung butterflies—Palomedes swallowtails—drugged with sparkle-berry honey, their gold and black velvet wings conspicuous in the sunny mist.

"Like the ceremonial vestments of a Yezidee executioner," murmured the girl. "The Tchortchas wear red when they robe to do a man to death."

"I wish you could forget those things," said Cleves.

"I am trying. . . . I wonder where that young man in white went."

Cleves searched the links. "I don't see him. Perhaps he had to go back for another ball."

"I wonder who he was," she mused.

"I don't remember seeing him before," said Cleves. . . . "Shall we start back?"

They walked slowly across the course toward the tenth hole.

Tressa teed up, drove low and straight. Cleves sliced, and they walked together into the scrub and towards the woods, where his ball had bounded into a bunch of palm trees.

Far in among the trees something white moved and vanished.

"Probably a white egret," he remarked, knocking about in the scrub with his midiron.

"It was that young man in white flannels," said Tressa in a low voice.

"What would he be doing in there?" he asked incredulously. "That's merely a jungle, Tressa—swamp and cypress, thorn and creeper,—and no man would go into that mess if he could. There is no bottom to those swamps."

"But I saw him in there," she said in a troubled voice.

"But when I tell you that only a wild animal or a snake or a bird could move in that jungle! The bog is one vast black quicksand. There's death in those depths."

"Victor."

"Yes?" He looked around at her. She was pale. He came up and took her hand inquiringly.

"I don't feel well," she murmured. "I'm not ill, you understand—"

"What's the matter, Tressa?"

She shook her head drearily: "I don't know. . . . I wonder whether I should have tried to amuse you this morning—"

"You don't think you've stirred up any of those Yezidee beasts, do you?" he asked sharply.

And as she did not answer, he asked again whether she was afraid that what she had done that morning might have had any occult consequences. And he reminded her that she had hesitated to venture anything on that account.

His voice, in spite of him, betrayed great nervousness now, and he saw apprehension in her eyes, also.

"Why should that man in white have followed us, keeping out of sight in the woods?" he went on. "Did you notice about him anything to disturb you, Tressa?"

"Not at the time. But—it's odd—I can't put him out of my mind. Since we passed him and left him apparently hunting a lost ball, I have not been able to put him out of my mind."

"He seemed civil and well bred. He was perfectly good-humoured—all courtesy and smiles."

"I think—perhaps—it was the way he smiled at us," murmured the girl. "Everybody in the East smiles when they draw a knife. . . ."

He placed his arm through hers. "Aren't you a trifle morbid?" he said pleasantly.

She stooped for her golf ball, retaining a hold on his arm. He picked up his ball, too, put away her clubs and his, and they started back together in silence, evidently with no desire to make it eighteen holes.

"It's a confounded shame," he muttered, "just as you were becoming so rested and so delightfully well, to have anything—any unpleasant flash of memory cut in to upset you—"

"I brought it on myself. I should not have risked stirring up the sinister minds that were asleep."

"Hang it all!—and I asked you to amuse me."

"It was not wise in me," she said under her breath. "It is easy to disturb the unknown currents which enmesh the globe. I ought not to have shown you Yian. I ought not to have shown you Yulun. It was my fault for doing that. I was a little lonely, and I wanted to see Yulun."

They came down the river back to the canoe, threw in their golf bags, and embarked on the glassy stream.

Over the calm flood, stained deep with crimson, the canoe glided in the sanguine evening light. But Tressa sang no more and her head was bent sideways as though listening—always listening—to something inaudible to Cleves—something very, very far away which she seemed to hear through the still drip of the paddles.

They were not yet in sight of their landing when she spoke to him, partly turning:

"I think some of your men have arrived."

"Where?" he asked, astonished.

"At the house."

"Why do you think so?"

"I think so."

They paddled a little faster. In a few minutes their dock came into view.

"It's funny," he said, "that you should think some of our men have arrived from the North. I don't see anybody on the dock."

"It's Mr. Recklow," she said in a low voice. "He is seated on our veranda."

As it was impossible to see the house, let alone the veranda, Cleves made no reply. He beached the canoe; Tressa stepped out; he followed, carrying the golf bags.

A mousy light lingered in the shrubbery; bats were flying against a salmon-tinted sky as they took the path homeward.

With an impulse quite involuntary, Cleves encircled his young wife's shoulders with his left arm.

"Girl-comrade," he said lightly, "I'd kill any man who even looked as though he'd harm you."

He smiled, but she had not missed the ugly undertone in his words.

They walked slowly, his arm around her shoulders. Suddenly he felt her start. They halted.

"What was it?" he whispered.

"I thought there was something white in the woods."

"Where, dear?" he asked coolly.

"Over there beyond the lawn."

What she called the "lawn" was only a vast sheet of pink and white phlox, now all misty with the whirring wings of sphinx-moths and *Noctuidae*.

The oak grove beyond was dusky. Cleves could see nothing among the trees.

After a moment they went forward. His arm had fallen away from her shoulders.

There were no lights except in the kitchen when they came

in sight of the house. At first nobody was visible on the screened veranda under the orange trees. But when he opened the swing door for her a shadowy figure arose from a chair.

It was John Recklow. He came forward, bent his strong white head, and kissed Tressa's hand.

"Is all well with you, Mrs. Cleves?"

"Yes. I am glad you came."

Cleves clasped the elder man's firm hand.

"I'm glad too, Recklow. You'll stop with us, of course."

"Do you really want me?"

"Of course," said Cleves.

"All right. I've a coon and a surrey behind your house."

So Cleves went around in the dusk and sent the outfit back to the hotel, and he himself carried in Recklow's suitcase.

Then Tressa went away to give instructions, and the two men were left together on the dusky veranda.

"Well?" said Recklow quietly.

Cleves went to him and rested both hands on his shoulders:

"I'm playing absolutely square. She's a perfectly fine girl and she'll have her chance some day, God willing."

"Her chance?" repeated Recklow.

"To marry whatever man she will some day care for."

"I see," said Recklow drily.

There was a silence, then:

"She's simply a splendid specimen of womanhood," said Cleves earnestly. "And intensely interesting to me. Why, Recklow, I haven't known a dull moment—though I fear she has known many—"

"Why?"

"Why? Well, being married to a—a sort of temporary figurehead—shut up here all day alone with a man of no particular interest to her—"

"Don't you interest her?"

"Well, how could I? She didn't choose me because she liked me particularly."

"Didn't she?" asked Recklow, still more drily. "Well, that does make it a trifle dull for you both."

"Not for me," said the younger man naively. "She is one of the most interesting women I ever met. And good heavens!-what psychic knowledge that child possesses! She did a thing today—merely to amuse me—" He checked himself and looked at Recklow out of sombre eyes.

"What did she do?" inquired the older man.

"I think I'll let her tell you—if she wishes. . . . And that reminds me. Why did you come down here, Recklow?"

"I want to show you something, Cleves. May we step into the house?"

They went into a little lamplit living-room. Recklow handed a newspaper clipping to Cleves: the latter read it, standing:

Had Deadliest Gas Ready For Germans, 'Lewisite' Might Have Killed Millions

Washington, April 24.—Guarded night and day and far out of human reach on a pedestal at the Interior Department Exposition here is a tiny vial. It contains a specimen of the deadliest poison ever known, 'Lewisite,' the product of an American scientist.

Germany escaped this poison by signing the armistice before all the resources of the United States were turned upon her.

Ten airplanes carrying 'Lewisite' would have wiped out, it is said, every vestige of life—animal and vegetable—in Berlin. A single day's output would snuff out the millions of lives on Manhattan Island. A drop poured in the palm of the hand would penetrate to the blood, reach the heart and kill the victim in agony.

What was coming to Germany may be imagined by the fact that when the armistice was signed 'Lewisite' was being manufactured at the rate of ten tons a day. Three thousand tons of this most terrible instrument ever conceived for killing would have been ready for business on the American front in France on November 1.

'Lewisite' is another of the big secrets of the war just leaking out. It was developed in the Bureau of Mines by Professor W. Lee Lewis, of Northwestern University, Evanston, Ill., who took a commission as a captain in the army.

The poison was manufactured in a specially built plant near Cleveland, called the 'Mouse Trap,' because every workman who entered the stockade went under an agreement not to leave the eleven-acre space until the war was won. The object of this, of course, was to protect the secret.

Work on the plant was started eighteen days after the Bureau of Mines had completed its experiments.

Experts are certain that no one will want to steal the sample. Everybody at the Exposition, which shows what Secretary Lane's department is doing, keeps as far away from it as possible.

When Cleves had finished reading, he raised his eyes in silence.

"That vial was stolen a week ago," said Recklow gravely, "by a young man who killed one guard and fatally wounded the other."

"Was there any ante-mortem statement?"

"Yes. I've followed the man. I lost all trace of him at Palm Beach, but I picked it up again at Ormond. *And now I'm here*, Cleves."

"You don't mean you've traced him here!" exclaimed Cleves under his breath.

"He's here on the St. Johns River, somewhere. He came up in a motor-boat, but left it east of Orchard Cove. Benton knows this country. He's covering the motor-boat. And I—came here to see how you are getting on."

"And to warn us," added Cleves quietly.

"Well—yes. He's got that stuff. It's deadlier than the newspaper suspects. And I guess—I guess, Cleves, he's one of those damned Yezidee witchdoctors—or sorcerers, as they call them;—one of that sect of Assassins sent over here to work havoc on feeble minds and do murder on the side."

"Why do you think so?"

"Because the dirty beast lugs his shroud around with him—a bed-sheet stolen from the New Willard in Washington.

"We were so close to him in Jacksonville that we got it, and his luggage. But we didn't get him, the rat! God knows how he knew we were waiting for him in his room. He never came back to get his luggage.

"But he stole a bed-sheet from his hotel in St. Augustine, and that is how we picked him up again. Then, at Palm Beach, we lost the beggar, but somehow or other I felt it in my bones that he was after you—you and your wife. So I sent Benton to Ormond and I went to Palatka. Benton picked up his trail. It led toward you—toward the St. Johns. And the reptile has been here forty-eight hours, trying to nose you out, I suppose—"

Tressa came into the room. Both men looked at her.

Cleves said in a guarded voice:

"Today, on the golf links at Orchard Cove, there was a young man in white flannels—very polite and courteous to us—but—Tressa thought she saw him slinking through the woods as though following and watching us."

"My man, probably," said Recklow. He turned quietly to Tressa and sketched for her the substance of what he had just told Cleves.

"The man in white flannels on the golf links," said Cleves, "was well built and rather handsome, and not more than twenty-five. I thought he was a Jew."

"I thought so too," said Tressa, calmly, "until I saw him in "the woods. And then and then suddenly it came to me that his smile was the smile of a treacherous Shaman sorcerer.

"...And the idea haunts me—the memory of those smooth-faced, smiling men in white—men who smile only when they slay—when they slay body and soul under the iris skies of Yian!—O God, merciful, long suffering," she whispered, staring into the East, "deliver our souls from Satan who was stoned, and our bodies from the snare of the Yezideel"

CHAPTER 9
THE WEST WIND

The night grew sweet with the scent of orange bloom, and all the perfumed darkness was vibrant with the feathery whirr of hawkmoths' wings.

Tressa had taken her moon-lute to the hammock, but her fingers rested motionless on the strings.

Cleves and Recklow, shoulder to shoulder, paced the moonlit path along the hedges of oleander and hibiscus which divided garden from jungle.

And they moved cautiously on the white-shell road, not too near the shadow line. For in the cypress swamp the bloated grey death was awake and watching under the moon; and in the scrub *palmetto* the diamond-dotted death moved lithely.

And somewhere within the dark evil of the jungle a man in white might be watching.

So Recklow's pistol swung lightly in his right hand and Cleves' weapon lay in his side-pocket, and they strolled leisurely around the drive and up and down the white-shell walks, passing Tressa at regular intervals, where she sat in her hammock with the moon-lute across her knees.

Once Cleves paused to place two pink hibiscus blossoms in her hair above her ears; and the girl smiled gravely at him in the light.

Again, pausing beside her hammock on one of their tours of the garden, Recklow said in a low voice: "If the beast would only show himself, Mrs. Cleves, we'd not miss him. Have you caught a glimpse of anything white in the woods?"

"Only the night mist rising from the branch and a white ibis stealing through it."

Cleves came nearer: "Do you think the Yezidee is in the woods watching us, Tressa?"

"Yes, he is there," she said calmly.

"You *know* it?"

"Yes."

Recklow stared at the woods. "We can't go in to hunt for

him," he said. "That fellow would get us with his Lewisite gas before we could discover and destroy him."

"Suppose he waits for a west wind and squirts his gas in this direction?" whispered Cleves.

"There is no wind," said Tressa tranquilly. "He has been waiting for it, I think. The Yezidee is very patient. And he is a Shaman sorcerer."

"My God!" breathed Recklow. "What sort of hellish things has the Old World been dumping into America for the last fifty years? An ordinary anarchist is bad enough, but this new breed of devil—these Yezidees—this sect of Assassins—"

"Hush!" whispered Tressa.

All three listened to the great cat-owl howling from the jungle. But Tressa had heard another sound—the vague stir of leaves in the live-oaks. Was it a passing breeze? Was a night wind rising? She listened. But heard no brittle clatter from the palm-fronds.

"Victor," she said.

"Yes, Tressa."

"If a wind comes, we must hunt him. That will be necessary."

"Either we hunt him and get him, or he kills us here with his gas," said Recklow quietly.

"If the night wind comes," said Tressa, "we must hunt the darkness for the Yezidee." She spoke coolly.

"If he'd only show himself," muttered Recklow, staring into the darkness.

The girl picked up her lute, caught Cleves' worried eyes fixed on her, suddenly comprehended that his anxiety was on her account, and blushed brightly in the moonlight. And he saw her teeth catch at her underlip; saw her look up again at him, confused.

"If I dared leave you," he said, "I'd go into the hammock and start that reptile. This won't do—this standing pat while he comes to some deadly decision in the woods there."

"What else is there to do?" growled Recklow.

"Watch," said the girl. "Out-watch the Yezidee. If there is no night-wind he may tire of waiting. Then you must shoot fast-very, very fast and straight. But if the night-wind comes, then we must hunt him in darkness."

Recklow, pistol in hand, stood straight and sturdy in the moonlight, gazing fixedly at the forest. Cleves sat down at his wife's feet.

She touched her moon-lute tranquilly and sang in her childish voice:

Ring, ring, Buddha bells,
Gilded gods are listening.
Swing, swing, lily bells,
In my garden glistening.
Now I hear the Shaman drum;
Now the scarlet horsemen come;
Ding-dong!
Ding-dong!
Through the chanting of the throng
Thunders now the temple gong.
Boom-boom!
Ding-dong!

Let the gold gods listen!
In my garden; what care I
Where my lily bells hang mute!
Snowy-sweet they glisten
Where I'm singing to my lute.
In my garden; what care I
Who is dead and who shall die?
Let the gold gods save or slay
Scented lilies bloom in May.
Boom, boom, temple gong!
Ding-dong!
Ding-dong!

"What are you singing?" whispered Cleves.
"'The Bells of Yian.'"
"Is it old?"

"Of the 13th century. There were few Buddhist bells in Yian then. It is Lamaism that has destroyed the Mongols and that has permitted the creed of the Assassins to spread—the devil worship of Erlik."

He looked at her, not understanding. And she, pale, slim prophetess, in the moonlight, gazed at him out of lost eyes-eyes which saw, perhaps, the bloody age of men when mankind took the devil by the throat and all Mount Alamout went up in smoking ruin; and the Eight Towers were dark as death and as silent before the blast of the silver clarions of Ghenghis Khan.

"Something is stirring in the forest," whispered Tressa, her fingers on her lips.

"Damnation," muttered Recklow, "it's the wind!"

They listened. Far in the forest they heard the clatter of palm-fronds. They waited. The ominous warning grew faint, then rose again,—a long, low rattle of palm-fronds which became a steady monotone.

"We hunt," said Recklow bluntly. "Come on!"

But the girl sprang from the hammock and caught her husband's arm and drew Recklow back from the hibiscus hedge.

"Use me," she said. "You could never find the Yezidee. Let me do the hunting; and then shoot very, very fast."

"We've got to take her," said Recklow. "We dare not leave her."

"I can't let her lead the way into those black woods," muttered Cleves.

"The wind is blowing in my face," insisted Recklow. "We'd better hurry."

Tressa laid one hand on her husband's arm.

"I can find the Yezidee, I think. You never could find him before he finds you! Victor, let me use my own *knowledge*! Let me find the way. Please let me lead! Please, Victor. Because, if you don't, I'm afraid we'll all die here in the garden where we stand."

Cleves cast a haggard glance at Recklow, then looked at his wife.

"All right," he said.

The girl opened the hedge gate. Both men followed with pistols lifted.

The moon silvered the forest. There was no mist, but a night-wind blew mournfully through palm and cypress, carrying with it the strange, disturbing pungency of the jungle—wild, unfamiliar perfumes,—the acrid aroma of swamp and rotting mould.

"What about snakes?" muttered Recklow, knee deep in wild phlox.

But there was a deadlier snake to find and destroy, somewhere in the blotched shadows of the forest.

The first sentinel trees were very near, now; and Tressa was running across a ghostly tangle, where once had been an orange grove, and where aged and dying citrus stumps rose stark amid the riot of encroaching jungle.

"She's circling to get the wind at our backs," breathed Recklow, running forward beside Cleves. "That's our only chance to kill the dirty rat catch him with the wind at our backs!"

Once, traversing a dry hammock where streaks of moon-light alternated with velvet-black shadow a rattlesnake sprang his goblin alarm.

They could not locate the reptile. They shrank together and moved warily, chilled with fear.

Once, too, clear in the moonlight, the Grey Death reared up from bloated folds and stood swaying rhythmically in a horrible shadow dance before them. And Cleves threw one arm around his wife and crept past, giving death a wide berth there in the checkered moonlight.

Now, under foot, the dry hammock lay everywhere and the night wind blew on their backs.

Then Tressa turned and halted the two men with a gesture. And went to her husband where he stood in the palm forest, and laid her hands on his shoulders, looking him very wistfully in the eyes.

Under her searching gaze he seemed oddly to comprehend her appeal.

"You are going to use—to use your *knowledge*," he said mechanically. "You are going to find the man in white."

"Yes."

"You are going to find him in a way we don't understand," he continued, dully.

"Yes. . . . You will not hold me in—in horror—will you?"

Recklow came up, making no sound on the spongy palm litter underfoot.

"Can you find this devil?" he whispered.

"I—think so."

"Does your super-instinct—finer sense—knowledge—whatever it is—give you any inkling as to his whereabouts, Mrs. Cleves?"

"I think he is here in this hammock. Only—" she turned again, with swift impulse, to her husband, "—only if you—if *you* do not hold me in—in horror—because of what I do—"

There was a silence; then:

"What are you about to do?" he asked hoarsely.

"Slay this man."

"We'll do that," said Cleves with a shudder. "Only show him to us and we'll shoot the dirty reptile to slivers—"

"Suppose we hit the jar of gas," said Recklow.

After a silence, Tressa said:

"I have got to give him back to Satan. There is no other way. I understood that from the first. He cannot die by your pistols, though you shoot very fast and straight. No!"

After another silence, Recklow said:

"You had better find him before the wind changes. We hunt down wind or—we die here together."

She looked at her husband.

"Show him to us in your own way," he said, "and deal with him as he must be dealt with."

A gleam passed across her pale face and she tried to smile at her husband.

Then, turning down the hammock to the east, she walked noiselessly forward over the fibrous litter, the men on either side of her, their pistols poised.

103

They had halted on the edge of an open glade, ringed with young pines in fullest plumage.

Tressa was standing very straight and still in a strange, supple, agonised attitude, her left forearm across her eyes, her right hand clenched, her slender body slightly twisted to the left.

The men gazed pallidly at her with tense, set faces, knowing that the girl was in terrible mental conflict against another mind a powerful, sinister mind which was seeking to grasp her thoughts and control them.

Minute after minute sped: the girl never moved, locked in her psychic duel with this other brutal mind,—beating back its terrible thought-waves which were attacking her, fighting for mental supremacy, struggling in silence with an unseen adversary whose mental dominance meant death.

Suddenly her cry rang out sharply in the moonlight, and then, all at once, a man in white stood there in the lustre of the moon—a young, graceful man dressed in white flannels and carrying on his right arm what seemed to be a long white cloak.

Instantly the girl was transformed from a living statue into a lithe, supple, lightly moving thing that passed swiftly to the west of the glade, keeping the young man in white facing the wind, which was blowing and tossing the plumy young pines.

"So it is *you*, young man, with whom I have been wrestling here under the moon of the only God!" she said in a strange little voice, all vibrant and metallic with menacing laughter.

"It is I, Keuke Mongol," replied the young man in white, tranquilly; yet his words came as though he were tired and out of breath, and the hand he raised to touch his small black moustache trembled as if from physical exhaustion.

"Yarghouz!" she exclaimed. "Why did I not know you there on the golf links, Assassin of the Seventh Tower? And why do you come here with your shroud over your arm and hidden under it, in your right hand, a flask full of death?"

He said, smiling:

"I come because you are to die, Heavenly-Azure Eyes. I bring you your shroud." And he moved warily westward around the open circle of young pines.

Instantly the girl flung her right arm straight upward.

"Yarghouz!"

"I hear thee, Heavenly Azure."

"Another step to the west and I shatter thy flask of gas."

"With what?" he demanded; but stood discreetly motionless.

"With what I grasp in an empty palm. Thou knowest, Yarghouz."

"I have heard," he said with smiling uncertainty, "but to hear of force that can be hurled out of an empty palm is one thing, and to see it and feel it is another. I think you lie, Heavenly Azure."

"So thought Gutchlug. And died of a yellow snake."

The young man seemed to reflect. Then he looked up at her in his frank, smiling way.

"Wilt thou listen, Heavenly Eyes?"

"I hear thee, Yarghouz."

"Listen then, Keuke Mongol. Take life from us as we offer it. Life is sweet. Erlik, like a spider, waits in darkness for lost souls that flutter to his net."

"You think my soul was lost there in the temple, Yarghouz?"

"Unutterably lost, little temple girl of Yian. Therefore, live. Take life as a gift!"

"Whose gift?"

"Sanang's."

"It is written," she said gravely, "that we belong to God and we return to him. Now then, Yezidee, do your duty as I do mine! *Kai* !"

At the sound of the formula always uttered by the sect of Assassins when about to do murder, the young man started and shrank back. The west wind blew fresh in his startled eyes.

"Sorceress," he said less firmly, "you leave your Yiort to come all alone into this forest and seek me. Why then have you come, if not to submit!—if not to take the gift of life—if not to turn away from your seducers who are hunting me, and who have

105

corrupted you?"

"Yarghouz, I come to slay you," she said quietly.

Suddenly the man snarled at her, flung the shroud at her feet, and crept deliberately to the left.

"Be careful!" she cried sharply; "look what you're about! Stand still, son of a dog! May your mother bewail your death!"

Yarghouz edged toward the west, clasping in his right hand the flask of gas.

"Sorceress," he laughed, "a witch of Thibet prophesied with a drum that the three purities, the nine perfections, and the nine times nine felicities shall be lodged in him who slays the treacherous temple girl, Keuke Mongol! There is more magic in this bottle which I grasp than in thy mind and body. Heavenly Eyes! I pray God to be merciful to this soul I send to Erlik!"

All the time he was advancing, edging cautiously around the circle of little plumy pines; and already the wind struck his left cheek.

"Yarghouz Khan!" cried the girl in her clear voice. "Take up your shroud and repeat the *fatha*!"

"Backward!" laughed the young man, "—as do you, Keuke Mongol!"

"Heretic!" she retorted. "Do you also refuse to name the ten Imaums in your prayers? Dog! Toad! Spittle of Erlik! May all your cattle die and all your horses take the glanders and all your dogs the mange!"

"Silence, sorceress!" he shouted, pale with fear and fury. "Witch! Mud worm! May Erlik seize you! May your skin be covered with putrefying sores! May all the demons torment you! May God remember you in hell!"

"Yarghouz! Stand still!"

"Is your word then the Rampart of Gog and Magog, you young witch of Yian, that a Khan of the Seventh Tower need fear you!" he sneered, stealing stealthily westward through the feathery pines.

"I give thee thy last chance, Yarghouz Khan," she said in an excited voice that trembled. "Recite thy prayer naming the ten, because with their holy names upon thy lips thou mayest escape damnation. For I am here to slay thee, Yarghouz! Take up thy shroud and pray!"

The young man felt the west wind at the back of his left ear. Then he began to laugh.

"Heavenly Eyes," he said, "thy end is come—together with the two police who hide in the pines yonder behind thee! Behold the bottle magic of Yarghouz Khan!"

And he lifted the glass flask in the moonlight as though he were about to smash it at her feet.

Then a terrible thing occurred. The entire flask glowed red hot in his grasp; and the man screamed and strove convulsively to fling the bottle; but it stuck to his hand, melted into the smoking flesh.

Then he screamed again—or tried to—but his entire lower jaw came off and he stood there with the awful orifice gaping in the moonlight—stood, reeled a moment—and then—and *then*—his whole face slid off, leaving nothing but a bony mask out of which burst shriek after shriek—

Keuke Mongol had fainted dead away. Cleves took her into his arms.

Recklow, trembling and deathly white, went over to the thing that lay among the young pines and forced himself to bend over it.

The glass flask still stuck to one charred hand, but it was no longer hot. And Recklow rolled the unspeakable thing into the white shroud and pushed it into the swamp.

An evil ooze took it, slowly sucked it under and engulfed it. A few stinking bubbles broke.

Recklow went back to the little glade among the pines.

A young girl lay sobbing convulsively in her husband's arms, asking God's pardon and his for the justice she had done upon an enemy of all mankind.

CHAPTER 10
AT THE RITZ

Then Victor Cleves telegraphed from St. Augustine to Washington that he and his wife were on their way North, and that they desired to see John Recklow as soon as they arrived, John Recklow remarked that he knew of no place as private as a public one. And he came on to New York and established himself at the Ritz, rather regally.

To dine with him that evening were two volunteer agents of the United States Secret Service, ZB-303, otherwise James Benton, a fashionable architect; and XYL-371, Alexander Selden, sometime junior partner in the house of Milwin, Selden & Co.

A single lamp was burning in the white-and-rose rococo room. Under its veiled glow these three men sat conversing in guarded voices over coffee and cigars, awaiting the advent of 53-6-26, otherwise Victor Cleves, recently Professor of Ornithology at Cambridge; and his young wife, Tressa, known officially as V-69.

"Did the trip South do Mrs. Cleves any good?" inquired Benton.

"Some," said Recklow. "When Selden and I saw her she was getting better."

"I suppose that affair of Yarghouz upset her pretty thoroughly."

"Yes." Recklow tossed his cigar into the fireplace and produced a pipe. "Victor Cleves upsets her more," he remarked.

"Why?" asked Benton, astonished.

"She's beginning to fall in love with him and doesn't know what's the matter with her," replied the elder man drily. "Selden noticed it, too."

Benton looked immensely surprised. "I supposed," he said, "that she and Cleves considered the marriage to be merely a temporary necessity. I didn't imagine that they cared for each other."

"I don't suppose they did at first," said Selden. "But I think she's interested in Victor. And I don't see how he can help falling in love with her, because she's a very beautiful thing to gaze on, and a most engaging one to talk to."

"She's about the prettiest girl I ever saw," admitted Benton, "and about the cleverest. All the same—"

"All the same—*what*?"

"Well, Mrs. Cleves has her drawbacks, you know—as a real wife, I mean."

Recklow said: "There is a fixed idea in Cleves's head that Tressa Norne married him as a last resort, which is true. But he'll never believe she's changed her ideas in regard to him unless she herself enlightens him. And the girl is too shy to do that. Besides, she believes the same thing of him. There's a mess for you!"

Recklow filled his pipe carefully.

"In addition," he went on, "Mrs. Cleves has another and very terrible fixed idea in her charming head, and that is that she really did lose her soul among those damned Yezidees. She believes that Cleves, though kind to her, considers her merely as something uncanny—something to endure until this Yezidee campaign is ended and she is safe from assassination."

Benton said: "After all, and in spite of all her loveliness, I myself should not feel entirely comfortable with such a girl for a real wife."

"Why?" demanded Recklow.

"Well—good heavens, John!—those uncanny things she does—her rather terrifying psychic knowledge and ability-make a man more or less uneasy." He laughed without mirth.

"For example," he added, "I never was nervous in any physical crisis; but since I've met Tressa Norne—to be frank—I'm not any too comfortable in my mind when I remember Gutchlug and Sanang and Albert Feke and that dirty reptile Yarghouz-and when I recollect *how that girl dealt with them!* Good God, John, I'm not a coward, I hope, but that sort of thing worries me!"

Recklow lighted his pipe. He said: "In the Government's campaign against these eight foreigners who have begun a psychic campaign against the unsuspicious people of this decent Republic, with the purpose of surprising, overpowering and enslaving the minds of mankind by a misuse of psychic power, we agents of the Secret Service are slowly gaining the upper hand.

"In this battle of minds we are gaining a victory. But we are winning solely and alone through the psychic ability and the loyalty and courage of a young girl who, through tragedy of circumstances, spent the years of her girlhood in the infamous Yezidee temple at Yian, and who learned from the devil-worshipers themselves not only this so-called magic of the Mongol sorcerers, but also how to meet its psychic menace and defeat it."

He looked at Benton, shrugged:

"If you and if Cleves really feel the slightest repugnance toward the strange psychic ability of this brave and generous girl, I for one do not share it."

Benton reddened: "It isn't exactly repugnance—" But Recklow interrupted sharply:

"Do you realise, Benton, what she's already accomplished for us in our secret battle against Bolshevism?—against the very powers of hell itself, led by these Mongol sorcerers?

"Of the Eight Assassins—or Sheiks-el-Djebel—who came to the United States to wield the dreadful weapon of psychic power against the minds of our people, and to pervert them and destroy all civilisation,—of the Eight Chief Assassins of the Eight Towers, this girl already has discovered and identified four,—Sanang, Gutchlug, Albert Feke, and Yarghouz; and she has destroyed the last three."

He sat calmly enjoying his pipe for a few moments' silence, then:

"Five of this sect of Assassins remain—five sly, murderous, psychic adepts who call themselves sorcerers. Except for Prince Sanang, I do not know who these other four men may be. I haven't a notion. Nor have you. Nor do I believe that with all the resources of the United States Secret Service we ever should be able to discover these four Sheiks-el-Djebel except for the astounding spiritual courage and psychic experience of the young wife of Victor Cleves."

After a moment Selden nodded. "That is quite true," he said simply. "We are utterly helpless against unknown psychic forces. And I, for one, feel no repugnance toward what Mrs. Cleves has done for all mankind and in the name of God."

"She's a brave girl," muttered Benton, "but it's terrible to possess such knowledge and horrible to use it."

Recklow said: "The horror of it nearly killed the girl herself. Have you any idea how she must suffer by being forced to employ such terrific knowledge? by being driven to use it to combat this menace of hell? Can you imagine what this charming, sensitive, tragic young creature must feel when, with powers natural to her but unfamiliar to us, she destroys with her own mind and will-power demons in human shape who are about to destroy her?

"Talk of nerve! Talk of abnegation! Talk of perfect loyalty and courage! There is more than these in Tressa Cleves. There is that dauntless bravery which faces worse than physical death. Because the child still believes that her soul is damned for whatever happened to her in the Yezidee temple; and that when these Yezidees succeed in killing her body, Erlik will surely seize the soul that leaves it." There was a knocking at the door. Benton got up and opened it. Victor Cleves came in with his young wife.

Tressa Cleves seemed to have grown since she had been away. Taller, a trifle paler, yet without even the subtlest hint of that charming maturity which the young and happily married woman invariably wears, her virginal allure now verged vaguely on the delicate edges of austerity.

Cleves, sunburnt and vigorous, looked older, somehow- far less boyish—and he seemed more silent than when, nearly seven months before, he had been assigned to the case of Tressa Norne.

Recklow, Selden and Benton greeted them warmly; to each in turn Tressa gave her narrow, sun-tanned hand. Recklow led her to a seat. A servant came with iced fruit juice and little cakes and cigarettes.

111

Conversation, aimless and general, fulfilling formalities, gradually ceased.

A full June moon stared through the open windows—searching for the traditional bride, perhaps—and its light silvered a pale and lovely figure that might possibly have passed for the pretty ghost of a bride, but not for any girl who had married because she was loved.

Recklow broke the momentary silence, bluntly:

"Have you anything to report, Cleves?"

The young fellow hesitated:

"My wife has, I believe."

The others turned to her. She seemed, for a moment, to shrink back in her chair, and, as her eyes involuntarily sought her husband, there was in them a vague and troubled appeal.

Cleves said in a sombre voice: "I need scarcely remind you how deeply distasteful this entire and accursed business is to my wife. But she is going to see it through, whatever the cost. And we four men understand something of what it has cost her—is costing her—in violence to her every instinct."

"We honour her the more," said Recklow quietly.

"We couldn't honour her too much," said Cleves.

A slight colour came into Tressa's face; she bent her head, but Recklow saw her eyes steal sideways toward her husband.

Still bowed a little in her chair, she seemed to reflect for a while concerning what she had to say; then, looking up at John Recklow:

"I saw Sanang."

"Good heavens! Where?" he demanded.

"I—don't—know."

Cleves, flushing with embarrassment, explained: "She saw him clairvoyantly. She was lying in the hammock. You remember I had a trained nurse for her after—what happened in Orchid Lodge."

Tressa looked miserably at Recklow,—dumbly, for a moment. Then her lips unclosed.

"I saw Prince Sanang," she repeated. "He was near the sea.

There were rocks—cottages on cliffs—and very brilliant flowers in tiny, pocket-like gardens.

"Sanang was walking on the cliffs with another man. There were forests, inland."

"Do you know who the other man was?" asked Recklow gently.

"Yes. He was one of the Eight. I recognised him. When I was a girl he came once to the Temple of Yian, all alone, and spread his shroud on the pink marble steps. And we temple girls mocked him and threw stemless roses on the shroud, telling him they were human heads with which to grease his *toug*."

She became excited and sat up straighter in her chair, and her strange little laughter rippled like a rill among pebbles.

"I threw a big rose without a stem upon the shroud," she exclaimed, "and I cried out, '*Niaz!*' which means, 'Courage,' and I mocked him, saying, 'Djamouk Khagan,' when he was only a Khan, of course; and I laughed and rubbed one finger against the other, crying out, '*Toug ia glachakho!*' which means, 'The *toug* is anointed.' And which was very impudent of me, because Djamouk was a Sheik-el-Djebel and Khan of the Fifth Tower, and entitled to a *toug* and to eight men and a Toughtchi. And it is a grave offence to mock at the anointing of a *toug*."

She paused, breathless, her splendid azure eyes sparkling with the memory of that girlish mischief.

Then their brilliancy faded; she bit her lip and stole an un-certain glance at her husband.

And after a pause she explained in a very subdued voice that the "*Iagla michi*," or action of "greasing the *toug*," or standard, was done when a severed human head taken in battle was cast at the foot of the lance shaft stuck upright in the ground.

"You see," she said sadly, "we temple girls, being already damned, cared little what we said, even to such a terrible man as Djamouk Khan. And even had the ghost of old Tchinguiz Khagan himself come to the temple and looked at us out of his tawny eyes, I think we might have done something saucy."

Tressa's pretty face was spiritless, now; she leaned back in her

113

armchair and they heard an unconscious sigh escape her.

"*Ai-ya! Ai-ya!*" she murmured to herself, "what crazy things we did on the rose-marble steps, Yulun and I, so long—so long ago."

Cleves got up and went over to stand beside his wife's chair.

"What happened is this," he said heavily. "During my wife's convalescence after that Yarghouz affair, she found herself, at a certain moment, clairvoyant. And she thought she saw—she *did* see—Sanang, and an Asiatic she recognised as being one of the chiefs of the Assassins sect, whose name is Djamouk.

"But, except that it was somewhere near the sea—some summer colony probably on the Atlantic coast—she does not know where this pair of jailbirds roost. And this is what we have come here to report."

Benton, politely appalled, tried not to look incredulous. But it was evident that Selden and Recklow had no doubts.

"Of course," said Recklow calmly, "the thing to do is for you and your wife to try to find this place she saw."

"Make a tour of all such ocean-side resorts until Mrs. Cleves recognises the place she saw," added Selden. And to Recklow he added: "I believe there are several perfectly genuine cases on record where clairvoyants have aided the police."

"Several authentic cases," said Recklow quietly. But Benton's face was a study.

Tressa looked up at her husband. He dropped his hand reassuringly on her shoulder and nodded with a slight smile.

"There—there was something else," she said with considerable hesitation—"something not quite in line of duty—perhaps—"

"It seems to concern Benton," added Cleves, smiling.

"What is it?" inquired Selden, smiling also as Benton's features froze to a mask.

"Let me tell you, first," interrupted Cleves, "that my wife's psychic ability and skill can make me visualise and actually see scenes and people which, God knows, I never before laid eyes upon, but which she has both seen and known.

"And one morning, in Florida, I asked her to do something strange—something of that sort to amuse me—and we were sitting on the steps of our cottage—you know, the old club-house at Orchid!—and the first I knew I saw, in the mist on the St. Johns, a Chinese bridge humped up over that very commonplace stream, and thousands of people passing over it,—and a city beyond—the town of Yian, Tressa tells me,—and I heard the Buddhist bells and the big temple gong and the noises in streets and on the water—"

He was becoming considerably excited at the memory, and his lean face reddened and he gesticulated as he spoke:

"It was astounding, Recklow! There was that bridge, and all those people moving over it; and the city beyond, and the boats and shipping, and the vast murmur of multitudes. . . . And then, there on the bridge crossing toward Yian, I saw a young girl, who turned and looked back at my wife and laughed."

"And I told him it was Yulun," said Tressa, simply.

"A playfellow of my wife's in Yian," explained Cleves. "But if she were really Chinese she didn't look like what are my own notions of a Chinese girl."

"Yulun came from Black China," said Mrs. Cleves. "I taught her English. I loved her dearly. I was her most intimate friend in Yian."

There ensued a silence, broken presently by Benton; and:

"Where do I appear in this?" he asked stiffly.

Tressa's smile was odd; she looked at Selden and said:

"When I was convalescent I was lonely. . . . I made *the effort* one evening. And I found Yulun. And again she was on a bridge. But she was dressed as I am. And the bridge was one of those great, horrible steel monsters that sprawl across the East River. And I was astonished, and I said, 'Yulun, darling, are you really here in America and in New York, or has a demon tangled the threads of thought to mock my mind in illness?'

"Then Yulun looked very sorrowfully at me and wrote in Arabic characters, in the air, the name of our enemy who once came to the Lake of Ghosts for love of her Yaddin-ed-Din,

Tougtchi to Djamouk the Fox. . . . And who went his way again amid our scornful laughter. . . . He is a demon. And he was tangling my thread of thought!"

Tressa became exceedingly animated once more. She rose and came swiftly to where Benton was standing.

"And what do you think!" she said eagerly. "I said to her, 'Yulun! Yulun! Will you *make the effort* and come to me if I *make the effort*? Will you come to me, beloved?' And Yulun made 'Yes,' with her lips."

After a silence: "But—where do I come in?" inquired Benton, stiffly fearful of such matters.

"You *came* in."

"I don't understand."

"You came in the door while Yulun and I were talking."

"When?"

"When you came to see me after I was better, and you and Mr. Selden were going North with Mr. Recklow. Don't you remember; I was lying in the hammock in the moonlight, and Victor told you I was asleep?"

"Yes, of course—"

"I was not asleep. I had *made the effort* and I was with Yulun. . . . I did not know you were standing beside my hammock in the moonlight until Yulun told me. . . . And *that* is what I am to tell you; Yulun saw you. . . . And Yulun has written it in Chinese, in Eighur characters and in Arabic, tracing them with her forefinger in the air—that Yulun, loveliest in Yian, flame-slender and very white, has seen her heart, like a pink pearl afire, burning between your august hands."

"My hands!" exclaimed Benton, very red.

There fell an odd silence. Nobody laughed.

Tressa came nearer to Benton, wistful, uncertain, shy.

"Would you care to see Yulun?" she asked.

"Well—no," he said, startled. "I—I shall not deny that such things worry me a lot, Mrs. Cleves. I'm a—an Episcopalian."

The tension released, Selden was the first to laugh.

"There's no use blinking the truth," he said; "we're up against something absolutely new. Of course, it isn't magic. It can, of course, be explained by natural laws about which we happen to know nothing at present."

Recklow nodded. "What do we know about the human mind? It has been proven that no thought can originate within that mass of convoluted physical matter called the brain. It has been proven that *something outside* the brain originates thought and uses the brain as a vehicle to incubate it. What do we know about thought?"

Selden, much interested, sat cogitating and looking at Mrs. Cleves. But Benton, still flushed and evidently nervous, sat staring out of the window at the full moon, and twisting an unlighted cigarette to shreds.

"Why didn't you tell Benton when the thing occurred down there at Orchid Lodge, the night we called to say goodbye?" asked Selden, curiously.

Tressa gave him a distressed smile: "I was afraid he wouldn't believe me. And I was afraid that you and Mr. Recklow, even if you believed it, might not like—like me any the better for—for being clairvoyant."

Recklow came over, bent his handsome grey head, and kissed her hand.

"I never liked any woman better, nor respected any woman as deeply," he said. And, lifting his head, he saw tears sparkling in her eyes.

"My dear," he said in a low voice, and his firm hand closed over the slim fingers he had kissed.

Benton got up from his chair, went to the window, turned shortly and came over to Tressa.

"You're braver than I ever could learn to be," he said shortly., "I ask your pardon if I seem sceptical. I'm more worried than incredulous. There's something born in me—part of me—that shrinks from anything that upsets my orthodox belief in the future life. But—if you wish me to see this—this girl—Yulun—it's quite all right."

She said softly, and with gentle wonder: "I know of nothing

117

that could upset your belief, Mr. Benton. There is only one God. And if Mahomet be His prophet, or if he be Lord Buddha, or if your Lord Christ be vice-regent to the Most High, I do not know. All I know is that God is God, and that He prevailed over Satan who was stoned. And that in Paradise is eternal life, and in hell demons hide where dwells Erlik, Prince of Darkness."

Benton, silent and secretly aghast at her theology, said nothing. Recklow pleasantly but seriously denied that Satan and his demons were actual and concrete creatures.

Again Cleves's hand fell lightly on his wife's shoulder, in a careless gesture of reassurance. And, to Benton, "No soul is ever lost," he said, calmly. "I don't exactly know how that agrees with your orthodoxy, Benton. But it is surely so."

"I don't know myself," said Benton. "I hope it's so." He looked at Tressa a moment and then blurted out: "Anyway, if ever there was a soul in God's keeping and guarded by His angels, it's your wife's!"

"That also is true," said Cleves quietly.

"By the way," remarked Recklow carelessly, "I've arranged to have you stop at the Ritz while you're in town, Mrs. Cleves. You and your husband are to occupy the apartment adjoining this. Where is your luggage, Victor?"

"In our apartment."

"That won't do," said Recklow decisively. "Telephone for it."

Cleves went to the telephone, but Recklow took the instrument out of his hand and called the number. The voice of one of his own agents answered.

Cleves was standing alone by the open window when Recklow hung up the telephone. Tressa, on the sofa, had been whispering with Benton. Selden, looking over the evening paper by the rose-shaded lamp, glanced up as Recklow went over to Cleves.

"Victor," he said, "your man has been murdered. His throat was cut; his head was severed completely. Your luggage has been ransacked and so has your apartment. Three of my men are in possession, and the local police seem to comprehend the necessity of keeping the matter out of the newspapers. What was in your baggage?"

"Nothing," said Cleves, ghastly pale.

"All right. We'll have your effects packed up again and brought over here. Are you going to tell your wife?"

Cleves, still deathly pale, cast a swift glance toward her. She sat on the sofa in animated conversation with Benton. She laughed once, and Benton smiled at what she was saying.

"Is there any need to tell her, Recklow?"

"Not for a while, anyway."

"All right. I suppose the Yezidees are responsible for this horrible business."

"Certainly. Your poor servant's head lay at the foot of a curtain-pole which had been placed upright between two chairs. On the pole were tied three tufts of hair from the dead man's head. The pole had been rubbed with blood."

"That's Mongol custom," muttered Cleves. "They made a *toug* and 'greased' it!—the murderous devils !"

"They did more. They left at the foot of your bed and at the foot of your wife's bed two white sheets. And a knife lay in the centre of each sheet. That, of course, is the symbol of the Sect of Assas- sins."

Cleves nodded. His body, as he leaned there on the window sill in the moonlight, trembled. But his face had grown dark with rage.

"If I could—could only get my hands on one of them," he whispered hoarsely.

"Be careful. Don't wear a face like that. Your wife is looking at us," murmured Recklow.

With an effort Cleves raised his head and smiled across the room at his wife.

"Our luggage will be sent over shortly," he said. "If you're tired, we'll say goodnight."

So she rose and the three men came to make their *adieux* and pay their compliments and devoirs. Then, with a smile that

119

seemed almost happy, she went into her own apartment on her husband's arm.

Cleves and his wife had connecting bedrooms and a sitting-room between. Here they paused for a moment before the always formal ceremony of leave-taking at night. There were roses on the centre table. Tressa dropped one hand on the table and bent over the flowers.

"They seem so friendly," she said under her breath.

He thought she meant that she found even in flowers a refuge from the solitude of a loveless marriage.

He said quietly: "I think you will find the world very friendly, if you wish." But she shook her head, looking at the roses.

Finally he said goodnight and she extended her hand, and he took it formally.

Then their hands fell away. Tressa turned and went toward her bedroom. At the door she stopped, turned slowly.

"What shall I do about Yulun?" she asked.

"What is there to do? Yulun is in China."

"Yes, her body is."

"Do you mean that the rest of her—whatever it is—could come here?"

"Why, of course."

"So that Benton could see her?"

"Yes."

"Could he see her just as she is? Her face and figure—clothes and everything?"

"Yes."

"Would she seem real or like a ghost—spirit—whatever you choose to call such things?"

Tressa smiled. "She'd be exactly as real as you or I, Victor. She'd seem like anybody else."

"That's astonishing," he muttered. "Could Benton hear her speak?"

"Certainly."

"Talk to her?"

Tressa laughed: "Of course. If Yulun should *make the effort* she could leave her body as easily as she undresses herself. It is no more difficult to divest one's self of one's body than it is to put off one garment and put on another. . . . And, somehow, I think Yulun will do it tonight."

"Come *here*?"

"It would be like her." Tressa laughed. "Isn't it odd that she should have become so enamoured of Mr. Benton—just seeing him there in the moonlight that night at Orchid Lodge?"

For a moment the smile curved her lips, then the shadow fell again across her eyes, veiling them in that strange and lovely way which Cleves knew so well; and he looked into her impenetrable eyes in troubled silence.

"Victor," she said in a low voice, "were you afraid to tell me that your man had been murdered?"

After a moment: "You always know everything," he said unsteadily. "When did you learn it?"

"Just before Mr. Recklow told you."

"How did you learn it, Tressa?"

"I looked into our apartment."

"When?"

"While you were telephoning."

"You mean you looked into our rooms from *here*?'

"Yes, clairvoyantly."

"What did you see?"

"The *Iaglamichi*!" she said with a shudder. "*Kai*! The *Toug* of Djamouk is anointed at last!"

"Is that the beast of a Mongol who did this murder ?"

"Djamouk and Prince Sanang planned it," she said, trembling a little. "But that butchery was Yaddin's work, I think. *Kai*! The work of Yaddined-Din, Tougtchi to Djamouk the Fox!"

They stood confronting each other, the length of the sitting-room between them. And after the silence had lasted a full minute Cleves reddened and said: "I am going to sleep on the couch at the foot of your bed, Tressa."

His young wife reddened too.

He said: "This affair has thoroughly scared me. I can't let you sleep out of my sight."

"I am quite safe. And you would have an uncomfortable night," she murmured.

"Do you mind if I sleep on the couch, Tressa?"

"No."

"Will you call me when you are ready?"

"Yes."

She went into her bedroom and closed the door.

When he was ready he slipped a pistol into the pocket of his dressing-gown, belted it over his pyjamas, and walked into the sitting-room. His wife called him presently, and he went in. Her night-lamp was burning and she extended her hand to extinguish it.

"Could you sleep if it burns?" he asked bluntly.

"Yes."

"Then let it burn. This business has got on my nerves," he muttered.

They looked at each other in an expressionless way. Both really understood how useless was this symbol of protection—this man the girl called husband;—how utterly useless his physical strength, and the pistol sagging in the pocket of his dressing-gown. Both understood that the only real projection to be looked for must come from her—from the gifted and guardian mind of this young girl who lay there looking at him from the pillows.

"Goodnight," he said, flushing; "I'll do my best. But only one of God's envoys, like you, knows how to do battle with things that come out of hell."

After a moment's silence she said in a colourless voice: "I wish you'd lie down on the bed."

"Had you rather I did?"

"Yes."

So he went slowly to the bed, placed his pistol under the pillow, drew his dressing-gown around him, and lay down.

After he had lain unstirring for half an hour: "Try to sleep, Tressa," he said, without turning his head.

"Can't you seem to sleep, Victor?" she asked. And he heard her turn her head.

"No."

"Shall I help you?"

"Do you mean use hypnosis—the power of suggestion on me?"

"No. I can help you to sleep very gently. I can make you very drowsy. . . . You are drowsy now. . . . You are very close to the edge of sleep. . . . Sleep, dear. . . . Sleep, easily, naturally, confidently as a tired boy. . . . You are sleeping, . . . deeply . . . sweetly . . . my dear . . . my dear, dear husband."

CHAPTER 11
YULUN THE BELOVED

Cleves opened his eyes. He was lying on his left side. In the pink glow of the night-lamp he saw his wife in her night-dress, seated sideways on the farther edge of the bed, talking to a young girl.

The strange girl wore what appeared to be a chamber-robe of frail gold tissue that clung to her body and glittered as she moved. He had never before seen such a dress; but he had seen the girl; he recognised her instantly as the girl he had seen turn to look back at Tressa as she crossed the phantom bridge over that misty Florida river. And Clever Comprehended that he was looking at Yulun.

But this charming young thing was no ghost, no astral projection. This girl was warm, living, breathing flesh. The delicate scent of her strange garments and of her hair, her very breath, was in the air of the room. Her half-hushed but laughing voice was deliciously human; her delicate little hands, caressing Tressa's, were too eagerly real to doubt.

Both talked at the same time, their animated voices mingling in the breathless delight of the reunion. Their exclamations, enchanting laughter, bubbling chatter, filled his ears. But not one word of what they were saying to each other could he understand.

Suddenly Tressa looked over her shoulder and met his astonished eyes.

"*Tokhta!*" she exclaimed. "Yulun! My lord is awake!"

Yulun swung around swiftly on the edge of the bed and looked laughingly at Cleves. But when her red lips unclosed she spoke to Tressa: and, "Darling," she said in English, "I think your dear lord remembers that he saw me on the Bridge of Dreams. And heard the bells of Yian across the mist."

Tressa said, laughing at her husband: "This is Yulun, flame-slender, very white, loveliest in Yian. On the rose-marble steps of the Yezidee Temple she flung a stemless rose upon Djamouk's shroud, where he had spread it like a patch of snow in the sun.

"And at the Lake of the Ghosts, where there is freedom to love, for those who desire love, came Yaddin, Tougtchi to Djamouk the Fox, in search of love—and Yulun, flame-slim, and flower-white. . . . Tell my dear lord, Yulun!"

Yulun laughed at Cleves out of her dark eyes that slanted charmingly at the corners.

"*Kai!*" she cried softly, clapping her palms. "I took his roses and tore them with my hands till their petals rained on him and their golden hearts were a powdery cloud floating across the water.

"I said: 'Even the damned do not mate with demons, my Tougtchi! So go to the devil, my *Banneret*, and may Erlik seize you!' "

Cleves, his ears ringing with the sweet confusion of their girlish laughter, rose from his pillow, supporting himself on one arm.

"You are Yulun. You are alive and real—"

He looked at Tressa: "She is real, isn't she?" And, to Yulun: "Where do you come from?"

The girl replied seriously: "I come from Yian." She turned to Tressa with a dazzling smile: "Thou knowest, my heart's gold, how it was I came. Tell thy dear lord in thine own way, so that it shall be simple for his understanding. . . . And now—because my visit is ending—I think thy dear lord should sleep. Bid him

124

sleep, my heart's gold!"

At that calm suggestion Cleves sat upright on the bed,—or attempted to. But sank back gently on his pillow and met there a dark, delicious rush of drowsiness.

He made an effort—or tried to: the smooth, sweet tide of sleep swept over him to the eyelids, leaving him still and breathing evenly on his pillow.

The two girls leaned over and looked down at him.

"Thy dear lord," murmured Yulun. "Does he love thee, rosebud of Yian?"

"No," said Tressa, under her breath.

"Does he know thou art damned, heart of gold?"

"He says no soul is ever really harmed," whispered Tressa.

"*Kai*! Has he never heard of the Slayer of Souls?" exclaimed Yulun incredulously.

"My lord maintains that neither the Assassin of Khorassan nor the Sheiks-el-Djebel of the Eight Towers, nor their dark prince Erlik, can have power over God to slay the human soul."

"*Tokhta*, Rose of Yian! Our souls were slain there in the Yezfdee temple."

Tressa looked down at Cleves:

"My dear lord says no," she said under her breath.

"And—Sanang?"

Tressa paled: "His mind and mine did battle. I tore my heart from his grasp. I have laid it, bleeding, at my dear lord's feet. Let God judge between us, Yulun."

"There was a day," whispered Yulun, "when Prince Sanang went to the Lake of the Ghosts."

Tressa, very pallid, looked down at her sleeping husband. She said:

"Prince Sanang came to the Lake of the Ghosts. The snow of the cherry-trees covered the young world.

"The water was clear as sunlight; and the lake was afire with scarlet carp . . . Yulun—beloved—the nightingale sang all night long—all night long . . . Then I saw Sanang shining, all gold, in the moonlight . . . May God remember him in hell!"

125

"May God remember him."

"Sanang Noïane. May he be accursed in the Namaz Ga!"

"May he be tormented in Jehaunum!—Sanang, Slayer of Souls."

Tressa leaned forward on the bed, stretched herself out, and laid her face gently across her husband's feet, touching them with her lips.

Then she straightened herself and sat up, supported by one hand, and looking silently down at the sleeping man.

"No soul shall die," she said. "*Niaz!*"

"Is it written?" asked Yulun, surprised.

"My lord has said it."

"*Allahou Ekber,*" murmured Yulun; "thy lord is only a man."

Tressa said: "Neither the Tekbir nor the *fatha*, nor the warning of Khidr, nor the Yacaz of the Khagan, nor even the prayers of the Ten Imaums are of any value to me unless my dear lord confirms the truth of them with his own lips."

"And Erlik? Is he nothing, then?"

"Erlik!" repeated Tressa insolently. "Who is Erlik but the servant of Satan who was stoned?"

Her beautiful, angry lips were suddenly distorted; her blue eyes blazed. Then she spat, her mouth still tremulous with hatred. She said in a voice shaking with rage:

"Yulun, beloved! Listen attentively. I have slain two of the Slayers of the Eight Towers. With God's help I shall slay them all—all!—Djamouk, Yaddin, Arrak Sou-Sou—all! every one!-Tiyang Khan, Togrul,—all shall I slay, even to the last one among them!"

"*Sanang, also?*"

"I leave him to God. It is a fearful thing to fall into the hands of the living God!"

Yulun calmly paraphrased the cant phrase of the Assassins: "For it is written that we belong to God and we return to Him. Heart of gold, I shall execute my duty!"

Then Yulun slipped from the edge of the bed to the floor, and stood there looking oddly at Tressa, her eyes rain-bright as though choking back tears—or laughter.

"Heart of a rose," she said in a suppressed voice, "my time is nearly ended. ... So. ... I go to the chamber of this strange young man who holds my soul like a pearl afire between his hands. ... I think it is written that I shall love him."

Tressa rose also and placed her lips close to Yulun's ear: "His name, beloved, is Benton. His room is on this floor. Shall we *make the effort* together?"

"Yes," said Yulun. "Lay your body down upon the bed beside your lord who sleeps so deeply. ... And now stretch out. ... And fold both hands. ... And now put off thy body like a silken garment. ... So! And leave it there beside thy lord, asleep."

They stood together for a moment, shining like dewy shapes of tall flowers, whispering and laughing together in the soft glow of the night lamp.

Cleves slept on, unstirring. There was the white and sleeping figure of his wife lying on the bed beside him.

But Tressa and Yulun were already melting away between the wall and the confused rosy radiance of the lamp.

Benton, in night attire and chamber-robe belted in, fresh from his bath and still drying his curly hair on a rough towel, wandered back into his bedroom.

When his short, bright hair was dry, he lighted a cigarette, took the automatic from his dresser, examined the clip, and shoved it under his pillow.

Then he picked up the little leather-bound Testament, seated himself, and opened it. And read tranquilly while his cigarette burned.

When he was ready he turned out the ceiling light, leaving only the night lamp lighted. Then he knelt beside his bed,—a custom surviving the nursery period,—and rested his forehead against his folded hands.

Then, as he prayed, something snapped the thread of prayer as though somebody had spoken aloud in the still room; and, like one who has been suddenly interrupted, he opened his eyes and looked around and upward.

The silent shock of her presence passed presently. He got up from his knees, looking at her all the while.

"You are Yulun," he said very calmly.

The girl flushed brightly and rested one hand on the foot of the bed.

"Do you remember in the moonlight where you walked along the hedge of white hibiscus and oleander—that night you said goodbye to Tressa in the South?"

"Yes."

"Twice," she said, laughing, "you stopped to peer at the blossoms in the moonlight."

"I thought I saw a face among them."

"You were not sure whether it was flowers or a girl's face looking at you from the blossoming hedge of white hibiscus," said Yulun.

"I know now," he said in an odd, still voice, unlike his own.

"Yes, it was I," she murmured. And of a sudden the girl dropped to her knees without a sound and laid her head on the velvet carpet at his feet.

So swiftly, noiselessly was it done that he had not comprehended—had not moved—when she sat upright, resting on her knees, and grasped the collar of her tunic with both gemmed hands.

"Have pity on me, lord of my lost soul !" she cried softly.

Benton stooped in a dazed way to lift the girl; but found himself knee deep in a snowy drift of white hibiscus blossoms-touched nothing but silken petals—waded in them as he stepped forward. And saw her standing before him still grasping the collar of her golden tunic.

A great white drift of bloom lay almost waist deep between them; the fragrance of oleander, too, was heavy in the room.

"There are years of life before the flaming gates of Jehaunum open. And I am very young," said Yulun wistfully.

Somebody else laughed in the room. Turning his head, he saw Tressa standing by the empty fireplace.

"What you see and hear need not disturb you," she said, looking at Benton out of brilliant eyes. "There is no god but God; and His prophet has been called by many names." And to Yulun: "Have I not told you that nothing can harm our souls?"

Yulun's expression altered and she turned to Benton: "Say it to me!" she pleaded.

As in a dream he heard his own words: "Nothing can ever really harm the soul."

Yulun's hands fell from her tunic collar. Very slowly she lifted her head, looking at him out of lovely, proud young eyes.

She said, evenly, her still gaze on him: "I am Yulun of the Temple. My heart is like a blazing pearl which you hold between your hands. May the four Blessed Companions witness the truth of what I say."

Then a delicate veil of colour wrapped her white skin from throat to temple; she looked at Benton with sudden and exquisite distress, frightened and ashamed at his silence.

In the intense stillness Benton moved toward her. Into his outstretched hands her two hands fell; but, bending above them, his lips touched only two white hibiscus flowers that lay fresh and dewy in his palms.

Bewildered, be straightened up; and saw the girl standing by the mantel beside Tressa, who had caught her by the left hand.

"*Tokhta*! Look out!" she said distinctly.

Suddenly he saw two men in the room, close to him—their broad faces, slanting eyes, and sparse beards thrust almost against his shoulder.

"Djamouk! Yaddin-ed-Din!" cried Tressa in a terrible voice. But quick as a flash Yulun tore a white sheet from the bed, flung it on the floor, and, whipping a tiny, jewelled knife from her sleeve, threw it glittering upon the sheet at the feet of the two men.

"One shroud for two souls!" she said breathlessly. "—and a knife like that to sever them from their bodies!"

The two men sprang backward as the sheet touched their feet, and now they stood there as though confounded.

"Djamouk, Kahn of the Fifth Tower!" cried Tressa in a clear

voice, "you have put off your body like a threadbare cloak, and your form that stands there Is only your mind! And it is only the evil will of Yaddin in the shape of his body that confronts us in this room of a man you have doomed!"

Yulun, intent as a young leopardess on her prey, moved soundlessly toward Yaddin.

"Tougtchi!" she said coldly, "you did murder this day, my *Banneret*, and the *Toug* of Djamouk has been greased. Now look out for yourself!"

"Don't stir!" came Tressa's warning voice, as Benton snatched his pistol from the pillow. "Don't fire! Those men have no real substance! For God's sake don't fire! I tell you they have no bodies!"

Suddenly something—some force—flung Benton on the bed. The two men did not seem to touch him at all, but he lay there struggling, crushed, held by something that was strangling him.

Through his swimming eyes he saw Yaddin trying to drive a long nail into his skull with a hammer,—felt the piercing agony of the first crashing blow,—struggled upright, drenched in blood, his ears ringing with the screaming of Yaddin.

Then, there in the little *rococo* bedroom of the Ritz-Carlton, began a strange and horrible struggle—the more dreadful because the struggle was not physical and the combatants never touched each other—scarcely moved at all.

Yaddin, still screaming, confronted Yulun. The girl's eyes were ablaze, her lips parted with the violence of her breathing. And Yaddin writhed and screamed under the terrible concentration of her gaze, his inferior but ferocious mind locked with her mind in deadly battle.

The girl said slowly, showing a glimmer of white teeth: "Your will to do evil to my young lord is breaking, Yaddin-ed-Din. . . . . I am breaking it. The nail and hammer were but symbols. It was your brain that brooded murder—that willed he should die as though shattered by lightning when that blood-vessel burst in his brain!"

"Sorceress!" shrieked Yaddin, "what are you doing to my heart, where my body lies asleep in a berth on the Montreal Express!"

"Your heart is weak, Yaddin. Soon the valves shall fail. A negro porter shall discover you dead in your berth, my *Banneret!*"

The man's swarthy face became livid with the terrific mental battle.

"Let me go back to my body !" he panted. "What are you doing to me that I cannot go back? I will go back! I wish it!—I—"

"Let us go back and rejoin our bodies!" cried Djamouk in an agonised voice. "There are teeth in my throat, deep in my throat, biting and tearing out the cords."

"Cancer," said Tressa calmly. "Your body shall die of it while your soul stumbles on through darkness."

"My Tougtchi!" shouted Djamouk, "I hear my soul bidding my body farewell! I must go before my mind expires in the terrible gaze of this young sorceress!"

He turned, drifted like something misty to the solid wall.

"My soul be ransom for yours!" cried Yulun to Tressa. "Bar that man's path to life !"

Tressa flung out her right hand and, with her forefinger, drew a barrier through space, bar above bar.

And Benton, half swooning on his bed, saw a cage of terrible and living light penning in Djamouk, who beat upon the incandescent bars and grasped them and clawed his way about, squealing like a tortured rat in a red-hot cage.

Through the deafening tumult Yulun's voice cut like a sword:

"Their bodies are dying, Heart of a Rose! . . . Listen! I hear their souls bidding their minds farewell!"

And, after a dreadful silence: "The train speeding north carries two dead men! God is God. *Niaz!*"

The bars of living fire faded. Two cinder-like and shapeless shadows floated and eddied like whitened ashes stirred by a wind on the hearth; then drifted through the lamplight, fading, dissolving, lost gradually in thin air.

Tressa, leaning back against the mantel, covered her face with both hands.

Yulun crept to the bed where Benton lay, breathing evenly in deepest sleep.

With the sheer sleeve of her tunic she wiped the blood from his face. And, at her touch, the wound in the temple closed and the short, bright hair dried and curled over a forehead as clean and fresh as a boy's.

Then Yulun laid her lips against his, rested so a moment.

"Seek me, dear lord," she whispered. "Or send me a sign and I shall come."

And, after a pause, she said, her lips scarcely stirring: "Love me. My heart is a flaming pearl burning between your hands."

Then she lifted her head.

But Tressa had rejoined her body, where it lay asleep beside her deeply sleeping husband.

So Yulun stood a moment, her eyes remote. Then, after a while, the little *rococo* bedroom in the Ritz-Carlton was empty save for a young man asleep on the bed, holding in his clenched hand a white hibiscus blossom.

Chapter 12
His Excellency

His Excellency President Tintinto, Chief Executive of one of the newer and cruder republics, visiting New York *incognito* with his Secretaries of War and of the Navy, had sent for John Recklow. And now the reception was in full operation.

Recklow was explaining. "In the beginning," he said, "the Bolsheviks' aim was to destroy everything and everybody except themselves, and then to reorganise for their own benefit what was left of a wrecked world. That was their programme—"

"Quite a programme," interrupted the Secretary of War, with something that almost resembled a giggle. But his prominent eyes continued to stare at Recklow untouched by the mirth which stretched his large, silly mouth.

The face of the Secretary of the Navy resembled the countenance of a benevolent manatee. The visage of the President was a study in tinted chalks.

Recklow said: "To combat that sort of Bolshevism was a business that we of the United States Secret Service understood—or supposed we understood.

"Then, suddenly, out of unknown Mongolia and into the civilised world stepped eight men."

"Yezidees," said the President mechanically. "Your Government has sent me a very full report."

"Yezidees of the Sect of the Assassins," continued Recklow; "—the most ancient sect in the world surviving from ancient times—the Sorcerers of Asia. And, as it was in ancient times, so it is now: the Yezidees are devil worshipers; their god is Satan; *his* prophet is Erlik, Prince of Darkness; *his* regent on earth is the old man of Mount Alamout; and to this ancient and sinister title a Yezi- dee sorcerer called Prince Sanang, or Sanang Noïane, has succeeded.

"His murderous deputies were the Eight Khans of the Eight Towers. Four of these assassins are dead—Gutchlug, Yarghouz, Djamouk the Fox, and Yaddin-ed-Din. One is in prison charged with murder,—Albert Feke.

"Four of the sorcerers remain alive: Tiyang Khan, Togrul, Arrak, Sou-Sou, called The Squirrel, and the Old Man of the Mountain himself, Saï-Sanang, Prince of the Yezidees."

Recklow paused; the pop-eyes of the War Secretary were upon him; the benevolent manatee gazed mildly at him; the countenance of the President seemed more like a Rocky Mountain goat than ever—chiselled out of a block of tinted chalk.

Recklow said: "To the menace of Bolshevism, which endangers this Republic and yours, has been added a more terrible threat—the threat of powerful and evil minds made formidable by psychic knowledge.

"For these Yezidee Sorcerers are determined to conquer, seize, and subdue the minds of mankind. They are here for that frightful purpose. Powerfully, terrifically equipped to surprise and capture the unarmed minds of our people, enslave their very thoughts and use them to their own purposes, these Sorcerers of the Yezidees assumed control of the Bolsheviki, who were merely envious and ferocious bandits, but whose crippled minds are now utterly enslaved by these Assassins from Asia.

"And this is what the United States Secret Service has to combat. And its weapons are not warrants, not pistols. For in this awful battle between decency and evil, it is mind against mind in an occult death grapple. And our only weapon against these minds made powerful by psychic knowledge and made terrible by an esoteric ability akin to what is called black magic,—our only weapon is the mind of a young girl."

"I understand," said the President, "that she became an adept in occult practices while imprisoned in the Yezidee Temple of Erlik at Yian."

Recklow looked into the President's face, which had grown very pale.

"Yes, sir," he said. "God alone knows what this child learned in the Yezidee Temple. All I know is that with this knowledge she has met the Yezidees in a battle of minds, has halted them, confounded them, fought them with their own occult knowledge, and has slain four of them."

The intense silence was broken by the frivolous titter of the Secretary of War:

"Of course I don't believe any of this supernatural stuff," he said with the split grin which did not modify his protruding stare. "This girl is merely a clever detective, that is the gist of the matter. And I don't believe anything else."

"Perhaps, sir, you will believe this, then," said John Recklow quietly. "I cut it from the *Times* this morning." And he handed the clipping to the Secretary of War.

New Plot In East
Moslem and Hindu Conspirators
Have Formed Secret
Organisation
Have World Revolution in View

Think to Rouse Asia, America, and Africa
to Outbreaks by Their
Propaganda.

July 1.—A significant event has recently taken place. Under the name of the Oriental League has recently been established a central organisation uniting all the various secret societies of Moslem and Hindu nationalists. The aim of the new association is to prepare for joint revolutionary action in Asia, America, and Africa.

The effects of this vast conspiracy may already be traced in recent events in Egypt, India, and Afghanistan. For the first time, through the creation of this league, the racial and religious differences which have divided Eastern conspirators have been overcome. The Ottoman League, founded by Mahmud Muktar Pasha, Munir Pasha, and Ahmed Rechid Bey, has adhered to the new organisation. So have the extreme Egyptian nationalists and the Hindu revolutionary group, "Pro India," emissaries of which were recently sentenced for bringing bombs into Switzerland during the war at the instigation of the German General Staff.

At a "Constituent Assembly" of the league, which took place in Yian, there were present, besides Young Turks, Egyptians and Hindus, delegates representing Persia, Afghanistan, Algeria, Morocco, and Mongolia.

The league is of Mongolian origin. Its leading spirit is a certain Prince Sanang, of whom little is known.

Associated with this mischievous and rather mysterious Mongolian personage are three better known criminals, now fugitives from justice—Talaat, Enver, and Djemal. It is to Enver Pasha's talent for intrigue that the union between Moslems and Hindus, the most striking and dangerous feature of the movement, is chiefly due.

Considerable funds are at the disposal of the league. These are partly supplied from Germany. Besides enjoying the support of the Germans, the league is also in close touch with Lenine, who very soon after his advent to power organised an Oriental Department in Moscow.

The alliance between the league and the Russian Bolsheviki was brought about by the notorious German Socialist agent, "Parvus," who is now in Switzerland. Many weeks ago he conferred with the Soviet rulers in Moscow, whence he went to Afghanistan, hoping to reorganise the new *Amir's* army and establish lines of communication for propaganda in India.

Evidence exists that the recent insurrection in Egypt, the sudden attack of the Afghans, and the rising in India, remarkable for co-operation between Moslems and Hindus, were connected with the activities of the league.

The Secretary looked up after he finished the reading.

"I don't see anything about Black Magic in this?" he remarked flippantly.

Recklow's features became very grave.

"I think," he said, "that everybody—myself included—and, with all respect, even yourself, sir,—and your honourable colleague,—and perhaps even his Excellency your President,—should be on perpetual guard over their minds, and the thoughts that range there, lest, surreptitiously, stealthily, some taint of Yezidee infection lodge there and take root—and spread—perhaps—throughout your new Republic."

The Secretary of War grinned. "They say I'm something of a socialist already," he chuckled. "Do you think your magic Yezidees are responsible ?"

The President, troubled and pallid, gazed steadily at Recklow.

"Mine is a single-track mind," he remarked as though to himself.

Recklow said nothing. It is one kind of mind, after all. However, single-track roads are now obsolete.

"A single-track mind," repeated the President. "And—I should not like anything to happen to the switch. It would mean ditching—or a rusty siding at best. . . . Please do all that is possible to get those four Yezidees, Mr. Recklow."

Recklow said calmly: "Our only hope is in this young girl, Tressa Norne, who is now Mrs. Cleves."

"My conscience!" piped the Secretary of the Navy. "What would happen to us if these Yezidees should murder her?"

"God knows," replied John Recklow, unsmiling.

"Why not put her aboard our new dreadnought?" suggested the Secretary, "and keep her cruising until you United States Secret Service fellows get the rest of these infernal Yezidees and clap 'em into jail?"

"We can do nothing without her," said Recklow sombrely.

There was a painful silence. The President joined his finger tips and stared palely into space.

"May I not say," he suggested, "that I think it a vital necessity that these Yezidees be caught and destroyed before they do any damage to the minds of myself and my cabinet?"

"God grant it, sir," said Recklow grimly.

"Mine," murmured the President, "is a single-track mind. I should be very much annoyed if anybody tampered with the rails—very much annoyed indeed, Mr. Recklow."

"They mustn't murder that girl," said the Secretary of the Navy. "Do you need any Marines, Mr. Recklow? Why not ask your Government for a few?"

Recklow rose: "Mr. President," he said, "I shall not deny that my Government is very deeply disturbed by this situation. In the beginning, these eight Assassins, and Sanang, came here for the purpose of attacking, overpowering, and enslaving the minds of the people of the United States and of the South American Republics.

"But now, after four of their infamous colleagues have been destroyed, the ferocious survivors, thoroughly alarmed, have turned their every energy toward accomplishing the death of Mrs. Cleves! Why, sir, scarcely a day passes but that some attempt upon her life is made by these Yezidees.

"Scarcely a day passes that this young girl is not suddenly

summoned to defend her mind as well as her body against the occult attacks of these Mongol Sorcerers. Yes, sir, Sorcerers!" repeated Recklow, his calm voice deep with controlled passion, "—whatever your honourable Secretary of War may think about it!"

His cold, grey eyes measured the President as he stood there.

"Mr. President, I am at my wits' end to protect her from assassination! Her husband is always with her—Victor Cleves, sir, of our Secret Service. But wherever he takes her these devils follow and send their emissaries to watch her, to follow, to attempt her mental destruction or her physical death.

"There is no end to their stealthy cunning, to their devilish devices, to their hellish ingenuity!

"And all we can do is to guard her person from the approach of strangers, and stand ready, physically, to aid her.

"She is our only barrier—*your* only defence—between civilisation and horrors worse than Bolshevism.

"I believe, Mr. President, that civilisation in North and South America—in your own Republic as well as in ours—depends, literally, upon the safety of Tressa Cleves. For, if the Yezidees kill her, then I do not see what is to save civilisation from utter disintegration and total destruction."

There was a silence. Recklow was not certain, that the President had been listening.

His Excellency sat with finger tips joined, gazing pallidly into space; and Recklow heard him murmuring under his breath and all to himself, as though to fix the deathless thought forever in his brain:

"May I not say that mine is a single-track mind? May I not say it? May I not,—may I not,—not, not, not—"

CHAPTER 13
SA-N'SA

June sunshine poured through the window of his bedroom in the Ritz; and Cleves had just finished dressing when he heard his wife's voice in the adjoining sitting-room.

He had not supposed that Tressa was awake. He hastened to tie his tie and pull on a smoking jacket, listening all the while to his wife's modulated but gay young voice.

Then he opened the sitting-room door and went in. And found his wife entirely alone.

She looked up at him, her lips still parted as though checked in what she had been saying, the smile still visible in her blue eyes.

"Who on earth are you talking to?" he asked, his bewildered glance sweeping the sunny room again.

She did not reply; her smile faded as a spot of sunlight wanes, veiled by a cloud—yet a glimmer of it remained in her gaze as he came over to her.

"I thought they'd brought our breakfast," he said, "—hearing your voice. . . . Did you sleep well?"

"Yes, Victor."

He seated himself, and his perplexed scrutiny included her frail morning robe of China silk, her lovely bare arms, and her splendid hair twisted up and pegged down with a jade dagger. Around her bare throat and shoulders, too, was a magnificent necklace of imperial jade which he had never before seen; and on one slim, white finger a superb jade ring.

"By Jove!" he said, "you're very exotic this morning, Tressa. I never before saw that negligee effect."

The girl laughed, glanced at her ring, lifted a frail silken fold and examined the amazing embroidery.

"I wore it at the Lake of the Ghosts," she said.

The name of that place always chilled him. He had begun to hate it, perhaps because of all that he did not know about it—about his wife's strange girlhood—about Yian and the devil's Temple there—and about Sanang.

He said coldly but politely that the robe was unusual and the jade very wonderful.

The alteration in his voice and expression did not escape her. It meant merely masculine jealousy, but Tressa never dreamed he cared in that way.

139

Breakfast was brought, served; and presently these two young people were busy with their melons, coffee, and toast in the sunny room high above the softened racket of traffic echoing through avenue and street below.

"Recklow telephoned me this morning," he remarked.

She looked up, her face serious.

"Recklow says that Yezidee mischief is taking visible shape. The Socialist Party is going to be split into bits and a new party, impudently and publicly announcing itself as the Communist Party of America, is being organised. Did you ever hear of anything as shameless—as outrageous—in this Republic?"

She said very quietly: "Sanang has taken prisoner the minds of these wretched people. He and his remaining Yezidees are giving battle to the unarmed minds of our American people."

"Gutchlug is dead," said Cleves, "—and Yarghouz and Djamouk, and Yaddin."

"But Tiyang Khan is alive, and Togrul, and that cunning demon Arrak Sou-Sou, called The Squirrel," she said. She bent her head, considering the jade ring on her finger. "—And Prince Sanang," she added in a low voice.

"Why didn't you let me shoot him when I had the chance?" said Cleves harshly.

So abrupt was his question, so rough his sudden manner, that the girl looked up in dismayed surprise. Then a deep colour stained her face.

"Once," she said, "Prince Sanang held my heart prisoner—as Erlik held my soul. . . . I told you that."

"Is that the reason you gave the fellow a chance?"

"Yes."

"Oh. . . . And possibly you gave Sanang a chance because he still holds your—affections !"

She said, crimson with the pain of the accusation: "I tore my heart out of his keeping. . . . I told you that. . . . And, —trying to believe what you say to me, I have tried to tear my soul out of the claws of Erlik. . . . Why are you angry?"

"I don't know. . . . I'm not angry. . . . The whole horrible situation is breaking my nerve, I guess. . . . With whom were you talking before I came in?"

After a silence the girl's smile glimmered.

"I'm afraid you won't like it if I tell you."

"Why not?"

"You—such things perplex and worry you. . . . I am afraid you won't like me any the better if I tell you who it was I had been talking with."

His intent gaze never left her. "I want you to tell me," he repeated.

"I—I was talking with Sa-n'sa," she faltered.

"With whom?"

"With Sa-n'sa. . . . We called her Sansa."

"Who the dickens is Sansa?"

"We were three comrades at the Temple," she said timidly, "—Yulun, Sansa, and myself. We loved each other. We always went to the Lake of the Ghosts together—for protection—"

"Go on!"

"Sansa was a girl of the Aroulads, born at Buldak—as was Temujin. The night she was born three moon-rainbows made circles around her Yaïlak. The Baroulass horsemen saw this and prayed loudly in their saddles. Then they galloped to Yian and came crawling on their bellies to Sanang Noïane with the news of the miracle. And Sanang came with a thousand riders in leather armour. And, 'What is this child's name?' he shouted, riding into the Yaïlak with his black banners flapping around him like devil's wings.

"A poor Manggoud came out of the tent of skins, carrying the new born infant, and touched his head to Sanang's stirrup. 'This babe is called Tchagane,' he said, trembling all over. 'No!' cries Sanang, 'she is called Sansa. Give her to me and may Erlik seize you!'

"And he took the baby on his saddle in front of him and struck his spurs deep; and so came Sansa to Yian under a roaring rustle of black silk banners. . . . It is so written in the *Book of Iron*. . . . *Allahou Ekber*."

Cleves had leaned his elbow on the table, his forehead rested in his palm.

Perhaps he was striving in a bewildered way to reconcile such occult and amazing things with the year 1920—with the commonplace and noisy city of New York with this pretty, modern, sunlit sitting-room in the Ritz-Carlton on Madison Avenuewith this girl in her morning negligee opposite, her coffee and melon fragrant at her elbow, her wonderful blue eyes resting on him.

"Sansa," he repeated slowly, as though striving to grasp even a single word from the confusion of names and phrases that were sounding still in his ears like the vibration of distant and unfamiliar seas.

"Is this the girl you were talking with just now? In—in *this* room?" he added, striving to understand.

"Yes."

"She wasn't here, of course."

"Her body was not."

"Oh!"

Tressa said in her sweet, humorous way: "You must try to accustom yourself to such things, Victor. You know that Yulun talks to me. . . . I wanted to talk to Sansa. The longing awakened me. So—*I made the effort.*"

"And she came—I mean the part of her which is not her body."

"Yes, she came. We talked very happily while I was bathing and dressing. Then we came in here. She is such a darling!"

"Where is she?"

"In Yian, feeding her silk-worms and making a garden. You see, Sansa is quite wealthy now, because when the Japanese came she filled a bullock cart with great lumps of spongy gold from the Temple and filled another cart with Yu-stone, and took the Hezar of Baroulass horsemen on guard at the Lake of the Ghosts. And with this Keutch, riding a Soubz horse, and dressed like an Urieng lancer, my pretty little comrade Tchagane, who is called Sansa, marched north preceded by two kettle-drums and a *toug* with two tails—"

142

Tressa's clear laughter checked her; she clapped her hands, breathless with mirth at the picture she evoked.

"*Kai!*" she laughed; "what adorable impudence has Sansa! Neither Tchortcha nor Khiounnou dared ask her who were her seven ancestors! No! And when her caravan came to the lovely Yliang River, my darling Sansa rode out and grasped the lance from her Tougtchi and drove the point deep into the fertile soil, crying in a clear voice: 'A place for Tchagane and her people! Make room for the *toug!*'

"Then her Manggoud, who carried the spare steel tip for her lance, got out of his saddle and, gathering a handful of mulberry leaves, rubbed the shaft of the lance till it was all pale green.

"'*Toug iaglachakho!*' cries my adorable Sansa! 'Build me here my *Urdu!*[1]—my *Mocalla!*[2] And upon it pitch my tent of skins!'"

Again Tressa's laughter checked her, and she strove to control it with the jade ring pressed to her lips.

"Oh, Victor," she added in a stifled voice, looking at him out of eyes full of mischief, "you don't realise how funny it was- Sansa and her *toug* and her *Urdu*—Oh, Allah!—the bones of Tchinguiz must have rattled in his tomb!"

Her infectious laughter evoked a responsive but perplexed smile from Cleves; but it was the smile of a bewildered man who has comprehended very little of an involved jest; and he looked around at the modern room as though to find his bearings.

Suddenly Tressa leaned forward swiftly and laid one hand on his.

"You don't think all this is very funny. You don't like it," she said in soft concern.

"It isn't that, Tressa. But this is New York City in the year 1920. And I can't—I absolutely cannot get into touch—hook up, mentally, with such things—with the unreal Oriental life that is so familiar to you."

She nodded sympathetically: "I know. You feel like a Mergued Pagan from Lake Baikal when all the lamps are lighted in

---

1. *Urdu* = An imperial encampment.
2. *Mocalla* = A platform used as a Moslem pulpit.

the Mosque;—like a camel driver with his jade and gold when he enters Yarkand at sunrise."

"Probably I feel like that," said Cleves, laughing outright. "I take your word, dear, anyway."

But he took more; he picked up her soft hand where it still rested on his, pressed it, and instantly reddened because he had done it. And Tressa's bright flush responded so quickly that neither of them understood, and both misunderstood.

The girl rose with heightened colour, not knowing why she stood up or what she meant to do. And Cleves, misinterpreting her emotion as a silent rebuke to the invasion of that convention tacitly accepted between them, stood up, too, and began to speak carelessly of commonplace things.

She made the effort to reply, scarcely knowing what she was saying, so violently had his caress disturbed her heart,—and she was still speaking when their telephone rang.

Cleves went; listened, then, still listening, summoned Tressa to his side with a gesture.

"It's Selden," he said in a low voice. "He says he has the Yezidee Arrak Sou-Sou under observation, and that he needs you desperately. Will you help us?"

"I'll go, of course," she replied, turning quite pale.

Cleves nodded, still listening. After a while: "All right. We'll be there. Goodbye," he said sharply; and hung up.

Then he turned and looked at his wife.

"I wish to God," he muttered, "that this business were ended. I—I can't bear to have you go."

"I am not afraid. . . . Where is it?"

"I never heard of the place before. We're to meet Selden at 'Fool's Acre.'"

"Where is it, Victor?"

"I don't know. Selden says there are no roads,—not even a spotted trail. It's a wilderness left practically blank by the Geological Survey. Only the contours are marked, and Selden tells me that the altitudes are erroneous and the unnamed lakes and water courses are all wrong. He says it is his absolute conviction that the Geological Survey never penetrated this wilderness at all, but merely skirted it and guessed at what lay inside, because the map he has from Washington is utterly misleading, and the entire region is left blank except for a few vague blue lines and spots indicating water, and a few heights marked '1800.'"

He turned and began to pace the sitting-room, frowning, perplexed, undecided.

"Selden tells me," he said, "that the Yezidee, Arrak Sou-Sou, is in there and very busy doing something or other. He says that he can do nothing without you, and will explain why when we meet him."

"Yes, Victor."

Cleves turned on his heel and came over to where his wife stood beside the sunny window.

"I hate to ask you to go. I know that was the understanding. But this incessant danger—your constant peril—"

"That does not count when I think of my country's peril," she said in a quiet voice. "When are we to start? And what shall I pack in my trunk?"

"Dear child," he said with a brusque laugh, "it's a wilderness and we carry what we need on our backs. Selden meets us at a place called Glenwild, on the edge of this wilderness, and we follow him in on our two legs."

He glanced across at the mantel clock.

"If you'll dress," he said nervously, "we'll go to some shop that outfits sportsmen for the North. Because, if we can, we ought to leave on the one o'clock train."

She smiled; came up to him. "Don't worry about me," she said. "Because I also am nervous and tired; and I mean to make an end of every Yezidee remaining in America."

"Sanang, too?"

They both flushed deeply.

She said in a steady voice: "Between God and Erlik there is a black gulf where a million million stars hang, lighting a million million other worlds.

"Prince Sanang's star glimmers there. It is a sun, called Yramid. And it lights the planet, Yu-tsung. Let him reign there between God and Erlik."

"You will slay this man?"

"God forbid!" she said, shuddering. "But I shall send him to his own star. Let my soul be ransom for his! And may Allah judge between us—between this man and me."

Then, in the still, sunny room, the girl turned to face the East. And her husband saw her lips move as though speaking, but heard no sound.

"What on earth are you saying there, all to yourself?" he demanded at last.

She turned her head and looked at him across her left shoulder.

"I asked Sansa to help me. . . . And she says she will."

Cleves nodded in a dazed way. Then he opened a window and leaned there in the sunshine, looking down into Madison Avenue. And the roar of traffic seemed to soothe his nerves.

But "Good heavens!" he thought; "do such things really go on in New York in 1920! Is the entire world becoming a little crazy? Am I really in my right mind when I believe that the girl I married is talking, without wireless, to another girl in China!"

He leaned there heavily, gazing down into the street with sombre eyes.

"What a ghastly thing these Yezidees are trying to do to the world—these Assassins of men's minds!" he thought, turning away toward the door of his bedroom.

As he crossed the threshold he stumbled, and looking down saw that he had tripped over a white sheet lying there. For a moment he thought it was a sheet from his own bed, and he started to pick it up. Then he saw the naked blade of a knife at his feet.

With an uncontrollable shudder he stepped out of the shroud and stood staring at the knife as though it were a snake. It had a curved blade and a bone hilt coarsely inlaid with Arabic characters in brass.

The shroud was a threadbare affair perhaps a bed-sheet from some cheap lodging house. But its significance was so repulsive that he hesitated to touch it.

However, he was ashamed to have it discovered in his room. He picked up the brutal-looking knife and kicked the shroud out into the corridor, where they could guess if they liked how such a rag got into the Ritz-Carlton.

Then he searched his bedroom, and, of course, discovered nobody hiding. But chills crawled on his spine while he was about it, and he shivered still as he stood in the centre of the room examining the knife and testing edge and point.

Then, close to his ear, a low voice whispered:

"Be careful, my lord; the Yezidee knife is poisoned. But it is written that a poisoned heart is more dangerous still."

He had turned like a flash; and he saw, between him and the sitting-room door, a very young girl with slightly slanting eyes, and rose and ivory features as perfect as though moulded out of tinted bisque.

She wore a loose blue linen robe, belted in, short at the elbows and skirt, showing two creamy-skinned arms and two bare feet in straw sandals. In one hand she had a spray of purple mulberries, and she looked coolly at Cleves and ate a berry or two.

"Give me the knife," she said calmly.

He handed it to her; she wiped it with a mulberry leaf and slipped it through her girdle.

"I am Sansa," she said with a friendly glance at him, busy with her fruit.

Cleves strove to speak naturally, but his voice trembled.

"Is it you—I mean your real self—your own body?"

"It's my real self. Yes. But my body is asleep in my mulberry grove."

"In—in China?"

"Yes," she said calmly, detaching another mulberry and eating it. A few fresh leaves fell on the centre table.

Sansa chose another berry. "You know," she said, "that I came to Tressa this morning,—to my little Heart of Fire I came when she called me. And I was quite sleepy, too. But I heard her, though there was a night wind in the mulberry trees, and the river made

147

a silvery roaring noise in the dark. . . . And now I must go. But I shall come again very soon."

She smiled shyly and held out her lovely little hand, "—As Tressa tells me is your custom in America," she said, "I offer you a goodbye."

He took her hand and found it a warm, smooth thing of life and pulse.

"Why," he stammered in his astonishment, "you *are* real! You are not a ghost!"

"Yes, I am real," she answered, surprised, "but I'm not in my body,—if you mean that." Then she laughed and withdrew her hand, and, going, made him a friendly gesture.

"Cherish, my lord, my darling Heart of Fire. Serpents twist and twine. So do rose vines. May their petals make your path of velvet and sweet scented. May everything that is round be a pomegranate for you two to share; may everything that sways be lilies bordering a path wide enough for two. In the name of the Most Merciful God, may the only cry you hear be the first sweet wail of your firstborn. And when the tenth shall be born, may you and Heart of Fire bewail your fate because both of you desire more children!"

She was laughing when she disappeared. Cleves thought she was still there, so radiant the sunshine, so sweet the scent in the room.

But the golden shadow by the door was empty of her. If she had slipped through the doorway he had not noticed her departure. Yet she was no longer there. And, when he understood, he turned back into the empty room, quivering all over. Suddenly a terrible need of Tressa assailed him—an imperative necessity to speak to her hear her voice.

"Tressa!" he called, and rested his hand on the centre table, feeling weak and shaken to the knees. Then he looked down and saw the mulberry leaves lying scattered there, tender and green and still dewy with the dew of China.

"Oh, my God!" he whispered, "such things *are*! It isn't my mind that has gone wrong. There *are* such things!"

The conviction swept him like a tide till his senses swam. As though peering through a mist of gold he saw his wife enter and come to him;—felt her arm about him, sustaining him where he swayed slightly with one hand on the table among the mulberry leaves.

"Ah," murmured Tressa, noticing the green leaves, "she oughtn't to have done that. That was thoughtless of her, to show herself to you."

Cleves looked at her in a dazed way. "The body is nothing," he muttered. "The rest only is real. That is the truth, isn't it?"

"Yes."

"I seem to be beginning to believe it. . . . Sansa said things—I shall try to tell you—someday—dear. . . . I'm so glad to hear your voice."

"Are you?" she murmured.

"And so glad to feel your touch. . . . I found a shroud on my threshold. And a knife."

"The Yezidees are becoming mountebanks. . . . Where is the knife?" she asked scornfully.

"Sansa said it was poisoned. She took it. She—she said that a poisoned heart is more dangerous still."

Then Tressa threw up her head and called softly into space: "Sansa! Little Silk-Moth! What are these mischievous things you have told to my lord?"

She stood silent, listening. And, in the answer which he could not hear, there seemed to be something that set his young wife's cheeks aflame.

"Sansa! Little devil!" she cried, exasperated. "May Erlik send his imps to pinch you if you have said to my lord these shameful things. It was impudent! It was mischievous! You cover me with shame and confusion, and I am humbled in the dust of my lord's feet!"

Cleves looked at her, but she could not sustain his gaze.

"Did Sansa say to you what she said to me?" he demanded unsteadily.

"Yes. ... I ask your pardon. . . . And I had already *told* her you did not—did not—*were* not in—in love—with me. . . . I ask your pardon."

"Ask more. . . . Ask your heart whether it would care to hear that I am in love. And with whom. Ask your heart if it could ever care to listen to what my heart could say to it."

"Y-yes—I'll ask—my heart," she faltered. . . . "I think I had better finish dressing—" She lifted her eyes, gave him a breathless smile as he caught her hand and kissed it.

"It—it would be very wonderful," she stammered, "—if our necessity should be-become our choice."

But that speech seemed to scare her and she fled, leaving her husband standing tense and upright in the middle of the room.

Their train on the New York Central Railroad left the Grand Central Terminal at one in the afternoon.

Cleves had made his arrangements by wire. They travelled lightly, carrying, except for the clothing they wore, only camping equipment for two.

It was raining in the Hudson valley; they rushed through the outlying towns and Po'keepsie in a summer downpour.

At Hudson the rain slackened. A golden mist enveloped Albany, through which the beautiful tower and facades along the river loomed, masking the huge and clumsy Capitol and the spires beyond.

At Schenectady, rifts overhead revealed glimpses of blue. At Amsterdam, where they descended from the train, the flag on the arsenal across the Mohawk flickered brilliantly in the sunny wind.

By telegraphic arrangement, behind the station waited a touring car driven by a trooper of State Constabulary, who, with his comrade, saluted smartly as Cleves and Tressa came up.

There was a brief, low-voiced conversation. Their camping outfit was stowed aboard, Tressa sprang into the *tonneau* followed by Cleves, and the car started swiftly up the inclined roadway, turned to the right across the railroad bridge, across the trolley tracks, and straight on up the steep hill paved with blocks of granite.

On the level road which traversed the ridge at last they speeded up, whizzed past the great hedged farm where racing horses are bred, rushing through the afternoon sunshine through the old-time Scotch settlements which once were outposts of the old New York frontier.

Nine miles out the macadam road ended. They veered to the left over a dirt road, through two hamlets; then turned to the right.

The landscape became rougher. To their left lay the long, low Maxon hills; behind them the Mayfield range stretched northward into the open jaws of the Adirondacks.

All around them were woods, now. Once a Gate House appeared ahead; and beyond it they crossed four bridges over a foaming, tumbling creek where Cleves caught glimpses of shadowy forms in amber-tinted pools—big yellow trout that sank unhurriedly out of sight among huge submerged boulders wet with spray.

The State trooper beside the chauffeur turned to Cleves, his purple tie whipping in the wind.

"Yonder is Glenwild, sir," he said.

It was a single house on the flank of a heavily forested hill. Deep below to the left the creek leaped two cataracts and went flashing out through a belt of cleared territory ablaze with late sunshine.

The car swung into the farmyard, past the barn on the right, and continued on up a very rough trail.

"This is the road to the Ireland Vlaie," said the trooper. "It is possible for cars for another mile only."

Splendid spruce, pine, oak, maple, and hemlock fringed the swampy, uneven trail which was no more than a wide, rough *vista* cut through the forest.

And, as the trooper had said, a little more than a mile farther the trail became a tangle of bushes and swale; the car slowed down and stopped; and a man rose from where he was seated on a mossy log and came forward, his rifle balanced across the hollow of his left arm.

The man was Alek Selden.

It was long after dark and they were still travelling through pathless woods by the aid of their electric torches.

There was little underbrush; the forest of spruce and hemlock was first growth.

Cleves shined the trees but could discover no blazing, no trodden path.

In explanation, Selden said briefly that he had hunted the territory for years.

"But I don't begin to know it," he added. "There are vast and ugly regions of bog and swale where a sea of alders stretches to the horizon. There are desolate wastes of cat-briers and witch-hopple under leprous tangles of grey birches, where stealthy little brooks darkle deep under matted debris. Only wild things can travel such country.

"Then there are strange, slow-flowing creeks in the perpetual shadows of tamarack woods, where many a man has gone in never to come out."

"Why?" asked Tressa.

"Under the tender carpet of green cresses are shining black bogs set with tussock; and under the bog stretches quicksand,-and death."

"Do you know these places?" asked Cleves.

"No."

Cleves stepped forward to Tressa's side.

"Keep flashing the ground," he said harshly. "I don't want you to step into some hell-hole. I'm sorry I brought you, anyway."

"But I had to come," she said in a low voice.

Like the two men, she wore a grey flannel shirt, knickers, and spiral *puttees*.

They, however, carried rifles as well as packs; and the girl's pack was lighter.

They had halted by a swift, icy rivulet to eat, with- out building a fire. After that they crossed the Ireland Vlaie and the main creek, where remains of a shanty stood on the bluff above the right bank—the last sign of man.

Beyond lay the uncharted land, skimped and shirked entirely in certain regions by map-makers;—an unknown wilderness on the edges of which Selden had often camped when deer shooting.

It was along this edge he was leading them, now, to a lean-to which he had erected, and from which he had travelled in to Glenwild to use the superintendent's telephone to New York.

There seemed to be no animal life stirring in this forest; their torches illuminated no fiery orbs of dazed wild things surprised at gaze in the wilderness; no leaping furry form crossed their flashlights' fan-shaped radiance.

There were no nocturnal birds to be seen or heard, either: no bittern squawked from hidden sloughs; no herons howled; not an owl-note, not a whispering cry of a whippoorwill, not the sudden uncanny twitter of those little birds that become abruptly vocal after dark, interrupted the dense stillness of the forest.

And it was not until his electric torch glimmered repeatedly upon reaches of dusk-hidden bog that Cleves understood how Selden took his bearings—for the night was thick and there were no stars.

"Yes," said Selden tersely, "I'm trying to skirt the bog until I shine a peeled stick."

An hour later the peeled alder-stem glittered in the beam of the torches. In ten minutes something white caught the electric rays.

It was Selden's spare undershirt drying on a bush behind the lean-to.

"Can we have a fire?" asked Cleves, relieving his wife of her pack and striding into the open-faced camp.

"Yes, I'll fix it," replied Selden. "Are you all right, Mrs. Cleves?"

Tressa said: "Delightfully tired, thank you." And smiled faintly at her husband as he let go his own pack, knelt, and spread a blanket for his wife.

He remained there, kneeling, as she seated herself.

"Are you quite fit?" he asked bluntly. Yet, through his brusqueness her ear caught a vague undertone of something else—anxiety perhaps—perhaps tenderness. And her heart stirred deliciously in her breast.

He inflated a pillow for her; the firelight glimmered, brightened, spread glowing across her feet. She lay back with a slight sigh, relaxed.

Then, suddenly, the thrill of her husband's touch flooded her face with colour; but she lay motionless, one arm flung across her eyes, while he unrolled her *puttees* and unlaced her muddy shoes.

A heavenly warmth from the fire dried her stockinged feet. Later, on the edge of sleep, she opened her eyes and found herself propped upright on her husband's shoulder.

Drowsily, obediently she swallowed spoonfuls of the hot broth which he administered.

"Are you really quite comfortable, dear?" he whispered.

"Wonderfully. . . . And so very happy. . . . Thank you—dear."

She lay back, suffering him to bathe her face and hands with warm water.

When the fire was only a heap of dying coals, she turned over on her right side and extended her hand a little way into the darkness. Searching, half asleep, she touched her husband, and her hand relaxed in his nervous clasp. And she fell into the most perfect sleep which she had known in years.

She dreamed that somebody whispered to her, "Darling, darling, wake up. It is morning, beloved."

Suddenly she opened her eyes; and saw her husband set a tray, freshly plaited out of Indian willow, beside her blanket.

"Here's your breakfast, pretty lady," he said, smilingly. "And over there is an exceedingly frigid pool of water. You're to have the camp to yourself for the next hour or two."

"You dear fellow," she murmured, still confused by sleep, and reached out to touch his hand. He caught hers and kissed it, back and palm, and got up hastily as though scared.

"Selden and I will stand sentry," he muttered. "There is no hurry, you know."

She heard him and his comrade walking away over dried leaves; their steps receded; a dry stick cracked distantly; then silence stealthily invaded the place like a cautious living thing, creeping unseen through the golden twilight of the woods.

Seated in her blanket, she drank the coffee; ate a little; then lay down again in the early sun, feeling the warmth of the heap of whitening coals at her feet, also.

For an hour she dozed awake, drowsily opening her eyes now and then to look across the glade at the pool over which a single dragon-fly glittered on guard.

Finally she rose resolutely, grasped a bit of soap, and went down to the edge of the pool.

Tressa was in flannel shirt and knickers when her husband and Selden hailed the camp and presently appeared walking slowly toward the dead fire.

Their grave faces checked her smile of greeting; her husband came up and laid one hand on her arm, looking at her out of thoughtful, preoccupied eyes.

"What is the *Tchordagh?*" he said in a low voice.

The girl's quiet face went white.

"The—the *Tchordagh!*" she stammered.

"Yes, dear. What is it?"

"I don't—don't know where you heard that term," she whispered. "The *Tchordagh* is the—the power of Erlik. It is a term. . . . In it is comprehended all the evil, all the cunning, all the perverted spiritual intelligence of Evil,—its sinister might,—its menace. It is an Alouäd-Yezidee term, and it is written in brass in Eighur characters on the Eight Towers, and on the Rampart of Gog and Magog;—nowhere else in the world!"

"It is written on a pine tree a few paces from this camp," said Cleves absently.

Selden said: "It has not been there more than an hour or two, Mrs. Cleves. A square of bark was cut out and on the white surface of the wood this word is written in English."

"Can you tell us what it signifies?" asked Cleves, quietly.

Tressa's studied effort at self-control was apparent to both men.

She said: "When that word is written, then it is a death struggle between all the powers of Darkness and those who have read the written letters of that word. . . . For it is written in *The Iron Book* that no one but the Assassin of Khorassan—excepting the Eight Sheiks—shall read that written word and live to boast of having read it."

"Let us sit here and talk it over," said Selden soberly.

And when Tressa was seated on a fallen log, and Cleves settled down cross-legged at her feet, Selden spoke again, very soberly:

"On the edges of these woods, to the northwest, lies a sea of briers, close growing, interwoven and matted, strong and murderous as barbed wire.

"Miles out in this almost impenetrable region lies a patch of trees called Fool's Acre.

"At Wells I heard that the only man who had ever managed to reach Fool's Acre was a trapper, and that he was still living.

"I found him at Rainbow Lake—a very old man, who had a fairly clear recollection of Fool's Acre and his exhausting journey there.

"And he told me that man had been there before he had. For there was a roofless stone house there, and the remains of a walled garden. And a skull deep in the wild grasses."

Selden paused and looked down at the recently healed scars on his wrists and hands.

"It was a rotten trip," he said bluntly. "It took me three days to cut a tunnel through that accursed tangle of matted brier and grey birch. . . . Fool's Acre is a grove of giant trees—first growth pine, oak, and maple. Great outcrops of limestone ledges bound it on the east. A brook runs through the woods.

"There is a house there, *no longer roofless*, and built of slabs of fossil-pitted limestone. The glass in the windows is so old that it is iridescent.

"A seven-foot wall encloses the house, built also of slabs blasted out of the rock outcrop, and all pitted with fossil shells.

"Inside is a garden—not the *remains* of one—a beautiful gar-

156

den full of unfamiliar flowers. And in this garden I saw the Yezidee on his knees *making living things out of lumps of dead earth!*"

"The *Tchordagh!*" whispered the girl.

"What was the Yezidee doing?" demanded Cleves nervously.

Involuntarily all three drew nearer each other there in the sunshine.

"It was difficult for me to see," said Selden in his quiet, serious voice. "It was nearly twilight: I lay flat on top of the wall under the curving branches of a huge syringa bush in full bloom. The Yezidees—"

"Were there two!" exclaimed Clever

"Two. They were squatting on the old stone path, bordering one of the flower-beds." He turned to Tressa: "They both wore white cloths twisted around their heads, and long soft garments of white. Under these their bare, brown legs showed, but they wore things on their naked feet which were shaped like what we call Turkish slippers—only different."

"Black and green," nodded Tressa with the vague horror growing in her face.

"Yes. The soles of their shoes were bright green."

"Green is the colour sacred to Islam," said Tressa. "The priests of Satan defile it by staining with green the soles of their footwear."

After an interval: "Go on," said Cleves nervously.

Selden drew closer, and they bent their heads to listen:

"I don't, even now, know what the Yezidees were actually doing. In the twilight it was hard to see clearly. But I'll tell you what it looked like to me. One of these squatting creatures would scoop out a handful of soil from the flower-bed, and mould it for a few moments between his lean, sinewy fingers, and then he'd open his hands and—and something *alive*—something small like a rat or a toad, or God knows what, would escape from between his palms and run out into the grass—"

Selden's voice failed and he looked at Cleves with sickened eyes.

"I can't—can't make you understand how repulsive to me it

157

was to see a wriggling live thing creep out between their fingers and—and go running or scrambling away little loathsome things with humpy backs that hopped or scurried through the grass—"

"What on earth *were* these Yezidees doing, Tressa?" asked Cleves almost roughly.

The girl's white face was marred by the imprints of deepening horror.

"It is the Tchor-Dagh," she said mechanically. "They are using every resource of hell to destroy me—testing the gigantic power of Evil—as though it were some vast engine charged with thunderous destruction!—and they were testing it to discover its terrific capacity to annihilate—"

Her voice died in her dry throat; she dropped her bloodless visage into both hands and remained seated so.

Both men looked at her in silence, not daring to interfere. Finally the girl lifted her pallid face from her hands.

"That is what they were doing," she said in a dull voice. "Out of inanimate earth they were making things animate—living creatures—to—to test the hellish power which they are storing—concentrating—for my destruction."

"What is their purpose?" asked Cleves harshly. "What do these Mongol Sorcerers expect to gain by making little live things out of lumps of garden dirt?"

"They are testing their power," whispered the girl.

"Like tuning up a huge machine?" muttered Selden.

"Yes."

"For what purpose?"

"To make larger living creatures out of—of clay."

"They can't—they can't *create*!" exclaimed Cleves. "I don't know how—by what filthy tricks—they make rats out of dirt. But they can't make a—anything—like a—like a man!"

Tressa's body trembled slightly.

"Once," she said, "in the temple, Prince Sanang took dust which was brought in sacks of goat-skin, and fashioned the heap of dirt with his hands, so that it resembled the body of a man lying there on the marble floor under the shrine of Erlik. . . . And—and then, there in the shadows where only the Dark Star burned—that black lamp which is called the Dark Star—the long heap of dust lying there on the marble pavement began to—to *breathe*!—"

She pressed both hands over her breast as though to control her trembling body: "I saw it; I saw the long shape of dust begin to breathe, to stir, move, and slowly lift itself—"

"A Yezidee trick!" gasped Cleves; but he also was trembling now.

"God!" whispered the girl. "*Allah* alone knows—the Merciful, the Long Suffering—He knows what it was that we temple girls saw there—that Yulun saw—that Sa-n'sa and I beheld there rising up like a man from the marble floor—and standing erect in the shadowy twilight of the Dark Star. . . ."

Her hands gripped at her breast; her face was deathly.

"Then," she said, "I saw Prince Sanang draw his sabre of Indian steel, and he struck . . . once only. . . . And a dead man fell down where the *thing* had stood. And all the marble was flooded with scarlet blood."

"A trick," repeated Cleves, in the ghost of his own voice. But his gaze grew vacant.

Presently Selden spoke in tones that sounded weakly querulous from emotional reaction:

"There is a path—a tunnel under the matted briers. It took me more than a week to cut it out. It is possible to reach Fool's Acre. We can try—with our rifles if—you say so, Mrs. Cleves."

The girl looked up. A little colour came into her cheeks. She shook her head.

"Their bodies may not be there in the garden," she said absently. "What you saw may not have been that part of them—the material which dies by knife or bullet. . . . And it is necessary that these Yezidees should die."

"Can you do anything?" asked Cleves, hoarsely.

She looked at her husband; tried to smile:

"I must try. . . . I think we had better not lose any time—if Mr.

Selden will lead us."

"Now?"

"Yes, we had better go, I think," said the girl. Her smile still remained stamped on her lips, but her eyes seemed preoccupied as though following the movements of something remote that was passing across the far horizon.

CHAPTER 14
A DEATH TRAIL

The way to Fool's Acre was under a tangled canopy of thorns, under rotting windfalls of grey mirch, through tunnel after tunnel of fallen debris woven solidly by millions of strands of tough cat-briers which cut the flesh like barbed wire.

There was blood on Tressa, where her flannel shirt had been pierced in a score of places. Cleves and Selden had been painfully slashed.

Silent, thread-like streams flowed darkling under the tangled mass that roofed them. Sometimes they could move upright; more often they were bent double; and there were long stretches where they had to creep forward on hands and knees through sparse wild grasses, soft, rotten soil, or paths of sphagnum which cooled their feverish skin in velvety, icy depths.

At noon they rested and ate, lying prone under the matted roof of their tunnel.

Cleves and Selden had their rifles. Tressa lay like a slender boy, her brier-torn hands empty.

And, as she lay there, her husband made a sponge of a handful of sphagnum moss, and bathed her face and her arms, cleansing the dried blood from the skin, while the girl looked up at him out of grave, inscrutable eyes.

The sun hung low over the wilderness when they came to the woods of Fool's Acre. They crept cautiously out of the briers, among ferns and open spots carpeted with pine needles and dead leaves which were beginning to burn ruddy gold under the level rays of the sun.

Lying flat behind an enormous oak, they remained listening

for a while. Selden pointed through the woods, eastward, whispering that the house stood there not far away.

"Don't you think we might risk the chance and use our rifles?" asked Cleves in a low voice.

"No. It is the Tchor-Dagh that confronts us. I wish to talk to Sansa," she murmured.

A moment later Selden touched her arm.

"My God," he breathed, "who is that!"

"It is Sansa," said Tressa calmly, and sat up among the ferns. And the next instant Sansa stepped daintily out of the red sunlight and seated herself among them without a sound.

Nobody spoke. The newcomer glanced at Selden, smiled slightly, blushed, then caught a glimpse of Cleves where he lay in the brake, and a mischievous glimmer came into her slanting eyes.

"Did I not tell my lord truths?" she inquired in a demure whisper. "As surely as the sun is a dragon, and the flaming pearl burns between his claws, so surely burns the soul of Heart of Flame between thy guarding hands. There are as many words as there are demons, my lord, but it is written that *Niaz* is the greatest of all words save only the name of God."

She laughed without any sound, sweetly malicious where she sat among the ferns.

"Heart of Flame," she said to Tressa, "you called me and I *made the effort*."

"Darling," said Tressa in her thrilling voice, "the Yezidees are making living things out of dust,—as Sanang Noïane made that thing in the Temple. . . . And slew it before our eyes."

"The Tchor-Dagh," said Sansa calmly.

"The Tchor-Dagh," whispered Tressa.

Sansa's smooth little hands crept up to the collar of her odd, blue tunic; grasped it.

"In the name of God the Merciful," she said without a tremor, "listen to me, Heart of Flame, and may my soul be ransom for yours!"

"I hear you, Sansa."

Sansa said, her fingers still grasping the em- broidered collar of her tunic:

"Yonder, behind walls, two Tower Chiefs meddle with the Tchor-Dagh, making living things out of the senseless dust they scrape from the garden."

Selden moistened his dry lips. Sansa said:

"The Yezidees who have come into this wilderness are Arrak Sou-Sou, the Squirrel; and Tiyang Khan. . . . May God remember them in Hell!"

"May God remember them," said Tressa mechanically.

"And these two Yezidee Sorcerers," continued Sansa coolly, "have advanced thus far in the Tchor-Dagh; for they now roam these woods, digging like demons for the roots of Ginseng; and thou knowest,

Heart of Flame, what that indicates."

"Does Ginseng grow in these woods!" exclaimed Tressa with a new terror in her widening eyes.

"Ginseng grows here, little Rose-Heart, and the roots are as perfect as human bodies. And Tiyang Khan squats in the walled garden moulding the Ginseng roots in his unclean hands, while Sou-Sou the Squirrel scratches among the dead leaves of the woods for roots as perfect as a naked human body.

"All day long the Sou-Sou rummages among the trees; all day long Tiyang pats and rubs and moulds the Ginseng roots in his skinny fingers. It is the Tchor-Dagh, Heart of Flame. And these Sorcerers must be destroyed."

"Are their bodies here?"

"Arrak is in the body. And thus it shall be accomplished: listen attentively, Rose Heart Afire!—I shall remain here with—" she looked at Selden and flushed a trifle, "—with you, my lord. And when the Squirrel comes a-digging, so shall my lord slay him with a bullet. . . . And when I hear his soul bidding his body farewell, then I shall make prisoner his soul. . . . And send it to the Dark Star. . . . And the rest shall be in the hands of Allah."

She turned to Tressa and caught her hands in both of her own:

"It is written on the Iron Pages," she whispered, "that we belong to Erlik and we return to him. But in the *Book of Gold* it is written otherwise: '*God preserve us from Satan who was stoned!*' . . . Therefore, in the name of *Allah!* Now then, Heart of Flame, do your duty!"

A burning flush leaped over Tressa's features.

"Is my soul, then, my own!"

"It belongs to God," said Sansa gravely.

"And—Sanang?"

"God is greatest."

"But—was God there—at the Lake of the Ghosts?"

"God is everywhere. It is so written in the *Book of Gold*," replied Sansa, pressing her hands tenderly.

"Recite the *Fatha*, Heart of Flame. Thy lips shall not stiffen; God listens."

Tressa rose in the sunset glory and stood as though dazed, and all crimsoned in the last fiery bars of the declining sun.

Cleves also rose.

Sansa laughed noiselessly: "My lord would go whither thou goest, Heart of Fire I" she whispered. "And thy ways shall be his ways!"

Tressa's cheeks flamed and she turned and looked at Cleves.

Then Sansa rose and laid a hand on Tressa's arm and on her husband's:

"Listen attentively. Tiyang Khan must be destroyed. The signal sounds when my lord's rifleshot makes a loud noise here among these trees."

"Can I prevail against the Tchor-Dagh?" asked Tressa, steadily.

"Is not that event already in God's hands, darling?" said Sansa softly. She smiled and resumed her seat beside Selden, amid the drooping fern fronds.

"Bid thy dear lord leave his rifle here," she added quietly.

Cleves laid down his weapon. Selden pointed eastward in silence.

So they went together into the darkening woods.

In the dusk of heavy foliage overhanging the garden, Tressa lay flat as a lizard on the top of the wall. Beside her lay her husband.

In the garden below them flowers bloomed in scented thickets, bordered by walks of flat stone slabs split from boulders. A little lawn, very green, centred the garden.

And on this lawn, in the clear twilight still tinged with the sombre fires of sundown, squatted a man dressed in a loose white garment.

Save for a twisted breadth of white cloth, his shaven head was bare. His sinewy feet were naked, too, the lean, brown toes buried in the grass.

Tressa's lips touched her husband's ear.

"Tiyang Khan," she breathed. "Watch what he does!"

Shoulder to shoulder they lay there, scarcely daring to breathe. Their eyes were fastened on the Mongol Sorcerer, who, squatted below on his haunches, grave and deliberate as a great grey ape, continued busy with the obscure business which so intently preoccupied him.

In a short semi-circle on the grass in front of him he had placed a dozen wild Ginseng roots. The roots were enormous, astoundingly shaped like the human body, almost repulsive in their weird symmetry.

The Yezidee had taken one of these roots into his hands. Squatting there in the semi-dusk, he began to massage it between his long, muscular fingers, rubbing, moulding, pressing the root with caressing deliberation.

His unhurried manipulation, for a few moments, seemed to produce no result. But presently the Ginseng root became lighter in colour and more supple, yielding to his fingers, growing ivory pale, sinuously limber in a newer and more delicate symmetry.

"Look!" gasped Cleves, grasping his wife's arm. '*What* is that man doing!"

'The Tchor-Dagh!" whispered Tressa. "Do you see what lies twisting there in his hands !"

164

The Ginseng root had become the tiny naked body of a woman—a little ivory-white creature, struggling to escape between the hands that had created it—dark, powerful, masterly hands, opening leisurely now, and releasing the living being they had fashioned.

The thing scrambled between the fingers of the Sorcerer, leaped into the grass, ran a little way and hid, crouched down, panting, almost hidden by the long grass. The shocked watchers on the wall could still see the creature. Tressa felt Cleves' body trembling beside her. She rested a cool, steady hand on his.

"It is the Tchor-Dagh," she breathed close to his face. "The Mongol Sorcerer is becoming formidable."

"Oh, God!" murmured Cleves, "that thing he made is *alive*! I saw it. I can see it hiding there in the grass. It's frightened— breathing! It's alive!"

His pistol, clutched in his right hand, quivered. His wife laid her hand on it and cautiously shook her head.

"No," she said, "that is of no use."

"But what that Yezidee is doing is—is blasphemous—"

"Watch him! His mind is stealthily feeling its way among the laws and secrets of the Tchor-Dagh. He has found a thread. He is following it through the maze into hell's own labyrinth! He has created a tiny thing in the image of the Creator. He will try to create a larger being now. Watch him with his Ginseng roots!"

Tiyang, looming ape-like on his haunches in the deepening dusk, moulded and massaged the Ginseng roots, one after another. And one after another, tiny naked creatures wriggled out of his palms between his fingers and scuttled away into the herbage.

Already the dim lawn was alive with them, crawling, scurrying through the grass, creeping in among the flower-beds, little, ghostly-white things that glimmered from shade into shadow like moonbeams.

Tressa's mouth touched her husband's ear:

"It is for the secret of Destruction that the Yezidee seeks. But first he must learn the secret of creation. He is learning. . . . And

165

he must learn no more than he has already learned."

"That Yezidee is a living man. Shall I fire?"

"No."

"I can kill him with the first shot."

"Hark!" she whispered excitedly, her hand closing convulsively on her husband's arm.

The whip-crack of a rifleshot still crackled in their ears.

Tiyang had leaped to his feet in the dusk, a Ginseng root, half-alive, hanging from one hand and beginning to squirm.

Suddenly the first moonbeam fell across the wall. And in its lustre Tressa rose to her knees and flung up her right hand.

Then it was as though her palm caught and reflected the moon's ray, and hurled it in one blinding shaft straight into the dark visage of Tiyang-Khan.

The Yezidee fell as though he had been pierced by a shaft of steel, and lay sprawling there on the grass in the ghastly glare.

And where his features had been there gaped only a hole into the head.

Then a dreadful thing occurred; for everywhere the grass swarmed with the little naked creatures he had made, running, scrambling, scuttling, darting into the black hole which had been the face of Tiyang-Khan.

They poured into the awful orifice, crowding, jostling one another so violently that the head jerked from side to side on the grass, a wabbling, inert, soggy mass in the moonlight.

And presently the body of Tiyang-Khan, Warden of the Rampart of Gog and Magog, and Lord of the Seventh Tower, began to burn with white fire—a low, glimmering combustion that seemed to clothe the limbs like an incandescent mist.

On the wall knelt Tressa, the glare from her lifted hand streaming over the burning form below.

Cleves stood tall and shadowy beside his wife, the useless pistol hanging in his grasp.

Then, in the silence of the woods, and very near, they heard Sansa laughing. And Selden's anxious voice:

"Arrak is dead. The Sou-Sou hangs across a rock, head down,

166

like a shot squirrel. Is all well with you?"

"Tiyang is on his way to his star," said Tressa calmly. "Somewhere in the world his body has bid its mind farewell. . . . And so his body may live for a little, blind, in mental darkness, fed by others, and locked in all day, all night, until the end."

Sansa, at the base of the wall, turned to Selden.

"Shall I bring my body with me, one day, my lord?" she asked demurely.

"Oh, Sansa—" he whispered, but she placed a fragrant hand across his lips and laughed at him in the moonlight.

CHAPTER 15
IN THE FIRELIGHT

In 1920 the whole spiritual world was trembling under the thundering shock of the Red Surf pounding the frontiers of civilisation from pole to pole.

Up out of the hell-pit of Asia had boiled the molten flood, submerging Russia, dashing in giant waves over Germany and Austria, drenching Italy, France, England with its bloody spindrift.

And now the Red Rain was sprinkling the United States from coast to coast, and the mindless administration, scared out of its stupidity at last, began a frantic attempt to drain the country of the filthy flood and throw up barriers against the threatened deluge.

In every state and city Federal agents made wholesale arrests—too late!

A million minds had already been perverted and dominated by the terrible Sect of the Assassins. A million more were sickening under the awful psychic power of the Yezidee.

Thousands of the disciples of the Yezidee devil-worshipers had already been arrested and held for deportation,—poor, wretched creatures whose minds were no longer their own, but had been stealthily surprised, seized and mastered by Mongol adepts and filled with ferocious hatred against their fellow men.

Yet, of the Eight Yezidee Assassins only two now remained

alive in America,—Togrul, and Sanang, the Slayer of Souls.

Yarghouz was dead; Djamouk the Fox, Kahn of the Fifth Tower was dead; Yaddin-ed-Din, Arrak the Sou-Sou, Gutchlug, Tiyang Khan, all were dead. Six Towers had become dark and silent. From them the last evil thought, the last evil shape had sped; the last wicked prayer had been said to Erlik, Khagan of all Darkness.

But his emissary on earth, Prince Sanang, still lived. And at Sanang' s heels stole Togrul, Tougtchi to Sanang Noïane, the Slayer of Souls.

In the United States there had been a cessation of the active campaign of violence toward those in authority. Such unhappy dupes of the Yezidees as the I. W. W. and other radicals were, for the time, physically quiescent. Crude terrorism with its more brutal outrages against life and law ceased. But two million sullen eyes, in which all independent human thought had been extinguished, watched unblinking the wholesale arrests by the government—watched panic-stricken officials rushing hither and thither to execute the mandate of a miserable administration—watched and waited in dreadful silence.

In that period of ominous quiet which possessed the land, the little group of Secret Service men that surrounded the young girl who alone stood between a trembling civilisation and the threat of hell's own chaos, became convinced that Sanang was preparing a final and terrible effort to utterly overwhelm the last vestige of civilisation in the United States.

What shape that plan would develop they could not guess.

John Recklow sent Benton to Chicago to watch that centre of infection for the appearance there of the Yezidee Togrul.

Selden went to Boston where a half-witted group of parlour-socialists at Cambridge were talking too loudly and loosely to please even the most tolerant at Harvard.

But neither Togrul nor Sanang had, so far, materialised in either city; and John Recklow prowled the purlieus of New York, haunting strange byways and obscure quarters where the dull embers of revolution always smouldered, watching for the

Yezidee who was the deep-bedded, vital root of this psychic evil which menaced the minds of all mankind,—Sanang, the Slayer of Souls.

Recklow's lodgings were tucked away in Westover Court-three bedrooms, a parlour and a kitchenette. Tressa Cleves occupied one bedroom; her husband another; Recklow the third.

And in this tiny apartment, hidden away among a group of old buildings, the very existence of which was unknown to the millions who swarmed the streets of the greatest city in the world,—here in Westover Court, a dozen paces from the roar of Broadway, was now living a young girl upon whose psychic power the only hope of the world now rested.

The afternoon had turned grey and bitter; ragged flakes still fell; a pallid twilight possessed the snowy city, through which lighted trains and taxis moved in the foggy gloom.

By three o'clock in the afternoon all shops were illuminated; the south windows of the Hotel Astor across the street spread a sickly light over the old buildings of Westover Court as John Recklow entered the tiled hallway, took the stairs to the left, and went directly to his apartment.

He unlocked the door and let himself in and stood a moment in the entry shaking the snow from his hat and overcoat.

The sitting-room lamp was unlighted but he could see a fire in the grate, and Tressa Cleves seated near, her eyes fixed on the glowing coals.

He bade her good evening in a low voice; she turned her charming head and nodded, and he drew a chair to the fender and stretched out his wet shoes to the warmth.

"Is Victor still out?" he inquired.

She said that her husband had not yet returned. Her eyes were on the fire, Recklow's rested on her shadowy face.

"Benton got his man in Chicago," he said. "It was not Togrul Kahn."

"Who was it?"

"Only a Swami *fakir* who'd been preaching sedition to a little group of greasy Bengalese from Seattle. . . . I've heard from

169

Selden, too."

She nodded listlessly and lifted her eyes.

"Neither Sanang nor Togrul have appeared in Boston," he said. "I think they're here in New York."

The girl said nothing.

After a silence:

"Are you worried about your husband?" he asked abruptly.

"I am always uneasy when he is absent," she said quietly.

"Of course. . . . But I don't suppose he knows that."

"I suppose not."

Recklow leaned over, took a coal in the tongs and lighted a cigar. Leaning back in his armchair, he said in a musing voice:

"No, I suppose your husband does not realise that you are so deeply concerned over his welfare."

The girl remained silent.

"I suppose," said Recklow softly, "he doesn't dream you are in love with him."

Tressa Cleves did not stir a muscle. After a long silence she said in her even voice:

"Do you think I am in love with my husband, Mr. Recklow?"

"I think you fell in love with him the first evening you met him."

"I did."

Neither of them spoke again for some minutes. Recklow's cigar went wrong; he rose and found another and returned to the fire, but did not light it.

"It's a rotten day, isn't it?" he said with a shiver, and dumped a scuttle of coal on the fire.

They watched the blue flames playing over the grate.

Tressa said: "I could no more help falling in love with him than I could stop my heart beating. . . . But I did not dream that anybody knew."

"Don't you think he ought to know?"

"Why? He is not in love with me."

"Are you sure, Mrs. Cleves?"

170

"Yes. He is wonderfully sweet and kind. But he could not fall in love with a girl who has been what I have been."

Recklow smiled. "What have you been, Tressa Norne?"

"You know."

"A temple-girl at Yian?"

"And at the Lake of the Ghosts," she said in a low voice.

"What of it?"

"I cannot tell you, Mr. Recklow. . . . Only that I lost my soul in the Yezidee Temple—"

"That is untrue !"

"I wish it were untrue. . . . My husband tells me that nothing can really harm the soul. I try to believe him. . . . But Erlik lives. And when my soul at last shall escape my body, it shall not escape the Slayer of Souls."

"That is monstrously untrue—"

"No. I tell you that Prince Sanang slew my soul. And my soul's ghost belongs to Erlik. How can any man fall in love with such a girl?"

"Why do you say that Sanang slew your soul?" asked Recklow, peering at her averted face through the reddening firelight.

She lay still in her chair for a moment, then turned suddenly on him:

"He *did* slay it! He came to the Lake of the Ghosts as my lover; he meant to have done it there; but I would not have him—would not listen, nor suffer his touch!—I mocked at him and his passion. I laughed at his Tchortchas. They were afraid of me!—"

She half rose from her chair, grasped the arms, then seated herself again, her eyes ablaze with the memory of wrongs.

"How dare I show my dear lord that I am in love with him when Sanang's soul caught my soul out of my body one day-surprised my soul while my body lay asleep in the Yezidee Temple!—and bore it in his arms to the very gates of hell!"

"Good God," whispered Recklow, "what do you mean? Such things can't happen."

"Why not? They do happen. I was caught unawares. . . . It was

171

one golden afternoon, and Yulan and Sansa and I were eating oranges by the fountain in the inner shrine. And I lay down by the pool and *made the effort*—you understand?"

"Yes."

"Very well. My soul left my body asleep and I went out over the tops of the flowers—idly, without aim or intent—as the winds blow in summer. ... It was in the Wood of the White Moth that I saw Sanang's soul flash downward like a streak of fire and wrap my soul in flame! . . . And, in a flash, we were at the gates of hell before I could free myself from his embrace. . . . Then, by the Temple pool, among the oranges, I cried out asleep; and my terrified body sat up sobbing and trembling in Yulun's arms. But the Slayer of Souls had slain mine in the Wood of the White Moth—slain it as he caught me in his flaming arms. . . . And now you know why such a woman as I dare not bend to kiss the dust from my dear Lord's feet—*Aie-a! Aie-a!* I who have lost my girl's soul to him who slew it in the Wood of the White Moth!"

She sat rocking in her chair in the red firelight, her hands framing her lovely face, her eyes staring straight ahead as though they saw opening before them through the sombre shadows of that room all the dread magic of the East where the dancing flame of Sanang's blazing soul lighted their path to hell through the enchanted forest.

Recklow had grown pale, but his voice was steady.

"I see no reason," he said, "why your husband should not love you."

"I tell you my girl's soul belonged to Sanang—was part of his, for an instant."

"It is burned pure of dross."

"It is *burned*."

Recklow remained silent. Tressa lay deep in her armchair, twisting her white fingers.

"What makes him so late?" she said . . . "I sent my soul out twice to look for him, and could not find him."

"Send it again," said Recklow, fearfully.

For ten minutes the girl lay as though asleep, then her eyes unclosed and she said drowsily: "I cannot find him."

"Did—did you learn anything while—while you were-away?" asked Recklow cautiously.

"Nothing. There is a thick darkness out there—I mean a darkness gathering over the whole land. It is like a black fog. When the damned pray to Erlik there is a darkness that gathers like a brown mist—"

Her voice ceased; her hands tightened on the arms of her chair.

"*That* is what Sanang is doing!" she said in a breathless voice.

"What?" demanded Recklow.

"*Praying*! That is what he is doing! A million perverted minds which he has seized and obsessed are being concentrated on blasphemous prayers to Erlik! Sanang is directing them. Do you understand the terrible power of a million minds all *willing*, in unison, the destruction of good and the triumph of evil? A million human minds! More! For that is what he is doing. That is the thick darkness that is gathering over the entire Western world. It is the terrific materialisation of evil power from evil minds, all focussed upon the single thought that evil must triumph and good die !"

She sat, gripping the arms of her chair, pale, rigid, terribly alert, dreadfully enlightened, now, concerning the awful and new menace threatening the sanity of mankind.

She said in her steady, emotionless voice: "When the Yezidee Sorcerers desire to overwhelm a nomad people—some *yort* perhaps that has resisted the Sheiks of the Eight Towers, then the Slayer of Souls rides with his Black Banners to the Namaz-Ga or Place of Prayer.

"Two marble bridges lead to it. There are fourteen hundred mosques there. Then come the Eight, each with his shroud, chanting the prayers for those dead in hell. And there the Yezidees pray blasphemously, all their minds in ferocious unison. . . . And I have seen a little *yort* full of Broad Faces with their

173

slanting eyes and sparse beards, sicken and die, and turn black in the sun as though the plague had breathed on them. And I have seen the Long Noses and bushy beards of walled towns wither and perish in the blast and blight from the Namaz-Ga where the Slayer of Souls sat his saddle and prayed to Erlik, and half a million Yezidees prayed in blasphemous unison."

Recklow's head rested on his left hand. The other, unconsciously, had crept toward his pistol—the weapon which had become so useless in this awful struggle between this girl and the loosened forces of hell.

"Is that what you think Sanang is about?" he asked heavily.

"Yes. I know it. He has seized the minds of a million men in America. Every anarchist is today concentrating in one evil and supreme mental effort, under Sanang's direction, to will the triumph of evil and the doom of civilisation. . . . I wish my husband would come home."

"Tressa?"

She turned her pallid face in the firelight: "If Sanang has appointed a Place of Prayer," she said, "he himself will pray on that spot. That will be the Namaz-Ga for the last two Yezidee Sorcerers still alive in the Western World."

"That's what I wished to ask you," said Recklow softly. "Will you try once more, Tressa?"

"Yes. I will send out my soul again to look for the Namaz-Ga."

She lay back in her armchair and closed her eyes.

"Only," she added, as though to herself, "I wish my dear lord were safe in this room beside me. . . . May God's warriors be his escort. And surely they are well armed, and can prevail over demons. *Aie-a!* I wish my lord would come home out of the darkness. . . . Mr. Recklow?"

"Yes, Tressa."

"I thought I heard him on the stairs."

"Not yet."

"*Aie-a!*" she sighed and closed her eyes again.

She lay like one dead. There was no sound in the room save

the soft purr of the fire.

Suddenly from the sleeping girl a frightened voice burst: "Yulun! Yulun! Where is that yellow maid of the Baroulass? . . . What is she doing? That sleek young thing belongs to Togrul Kahn? Yulun! I am afraid of her! Tell Sansa to watch that she does not stir from the Lake of the Ghosts! . . . Warn that young Baroulass Sorceress that if she stirs I slay her. And know how to do it in spite of Sanang and all the prayers from the Namaz-Gal Yulun! Sansa! Watch her, follow her, hearts of flame! My soul be ransom for yours! *Tokhta!*"

The girl's eyes unclosed. Presently she stirred slightly, passed one hand across her forehead, turned her head toward Recklow.

"I could not discover the Namaz-Ga," she said wearily. "I wish my husband would return."

CHAPTER 16
THE PLACE OF PRAYER

Her husband called her on the telephone a few minutes later:

"Fifty-three, Six-twenty-six speaking! Who is this?"

"V-sixty-nine," replied his young wife happily. "Are you all right?"

"Yes. Is M.H. 2479 there?"

"He is here."

"Very well. An hour ago I saw Togrul Khan in a limousine and chased him in a taxi. His car got away in the fog but it was possible to make out the number. An empty Cadillac limousine bearing that number is now waiting outside the 44th Street entrance to the Hotel Astor. The doorman will hold it until I finish telephoning. Tell M. H. 2479 to send men to cover this matter—"

"Victor!"

"Be careful! Yes, what is it?"

"I beg you not to stir in this affair until I can join you—"

"Hurry then. It's just across the street from Westover Court—"

His voice ceased; she heard another voice, faintly, and an exclamation from her husband; then his hurried voice over the wire: "The doorman just sent word to hurry. The car number is N.Y. 015 F 0379! I've got to run! Goodb—"

He left the booth at the end of Peacock Alley, ran down the marble steps to the left and out to the snowy sidewalk, passing on his way a young girl swathed to the eyes in chinchilla who was hurrying into the hotel. As he came to where the limousine was standing, he saw that it was still empty although the door stood open and the engine was running. Around the chauffeur stood the gold laced doorman, the gorgeously uniformed carriage porter and a mounted policeman.

"Hey!" said the latter when he saw Cleves,—"what's the matter here? What are you holding up this car for?"

Cleves beckoned him, whispered, then turned to the doorman.

"Why did you send for me? Was the chauffeur trying to pull out?"

"Yes, sir. A lady come hurrying out an' she jumps in, and the shawfur he starts her humming—"

"A lady! Where did she go?"

"It was that young lady in chinchilla fur. The one you just met when you run out. Yessir! Why, as soon as I held up the car and called this here cop, she opens the door and out she jumps and beats it into the hotel again—"

"Hold that car, officer!" interrupted Cleves. "Keep it standing here and arrest anybody who gets into it! I'll be back again—"

He turned and hurried into the hotel, traversed Peacock Alley scanning every woman he passed, searching for a slim shape swathed in chinchilla. There were no chinchilla wraps in Peacock Alley; none in the dining-room where people already were beginning to gather and the orchestra was now playing; no young girl in chinchilla in the waiting room, or in the north dining-room.

Then, suddenly, far across the crowded lobby, he saw a slender, bare-headed girl in a chinchilla cloak turn hurriedly away from the room-clerk's desk, holding a key in her white gloved hand.

Before he could take two steps in her direction she had disappeared in the crowd.

He made his way through the packed lobby as best he could amid throngs of people dressed for dinner, theatre, or other gaiety awaiting them somewhere out there in the light-smeared winter fog; but when he arrived at the room clerk's desk he looked for a chinchilla wrap in vain.

Then he leaned over the desk and said to the clerk in a low voice: "I am a Federal agent from the Department of Justice. Here are my credentials. Now, who was that young woman in chinchilla furs to whom you gave her door key a moment ago?"

The clerk leaned over his counter and, dropping his voice, answered that the lady in question had arrived only that morning from San Francisco; had registered as Madame Aoula Baroulass; and had been given a suite on the fourth floor numbered from 408 to 414.

"Do you mean to arrest her?" added the clerk in a weird whisper.

"I don't know. Possibly. Have you the master-key?"

The clerk handed it to him without a word; and Cleves hurried to the elevator.

On the fourth floor the matron on duty halted him, but when he murmured an explanation she nodded and laid a finger on her lips.

"*Madame* has gone to her apartment," she whispered.

"Has she a servant? Or friends with her?"

"No, sir. . . . I did see her speak to two foreign looking gentlemen in the elevator when she arrived this morning."

Cleves nodded; the matron pointed out the direction in silence, and he went rapidly down the carpeted corridor, until he came to a door numbered 408.

For a second only he hesitated, then swiftly fitted the master-key and opened the door.

The room—a bedroom—was brightly lighted; but there was nobody there. The other rooms—dressing closet, bathroom and parlour, all were brilliantly lighted by ceiling fixtures and wall brackets; but there was not a person to be seen in any of the rooms—nor, save for the illumination, was there any visible sign that anybody inhabited the apartment.

Swiftly he searched the apartment from end to end. There was no baggage to be seen, no garments, no toilet articles, no flowers in the vases, no magazines or books, not one article of feminine apparel or of personal bric-a-brac visible in the entire place.

Nor had the bed even been turned down—nor any preparation for the night's comfort been attempted. And, except for the blazing lights, it was as though the apartment had not been entered by anybody for a month.

All the windows were closed, all shades lowered and curtains drawn. The air, though apparently pure enough, had that vague flatness which one associates with an unused guest-chamber when opened for an airing.

Now, deliberately, Cleves began a more thorough search of the apartment, looking behind curtains, under beds, into clothes presses, behind sofas.

Then he searched the bureau drawers, dressers, desks for any sign or clew of the girl in the chinchillas. There was no dust anywhere,—the hotel management evidently was particular-but there was not even a pin to be found.

Presently he went out into the corridor and looked again at the number on the door. He had made no mistake.

Then he turned and sped down the long corridor to where the matron was standing beside her desk preparing to go off duty as soon as the other matron arrived to relieve her.

To his impatient question she replied positively that she had seen the girl in chinchillas unlock 408 and enter the apartment less than five minutes before he had arrived in pursuit.

"And I saw her lights go on as soon as she went in," added the matron, pointing to the distant illuminated transom.

"Then she went out through into the next apartment," insisted Cleves.

"The fire-tower is on one side of her; the scullery closet on the other," said the matron. "She could not have left that apartment without coming out into the corridor. And if she had come out I should have seen her."

"I tell you she isn't in those rooms!" protested Cleves.

"She must be there, sir. I saw her go in a few seconds before you came up."

At that moment the other matron arrived. There was no use arguing. He left the explanation of the situation to the woman who was going off duty, and, hastening his steps, he returned to apartment 408.

The door, which he had left open, had swung shut. Again he fitted the ·master-key, entered, paused on the threshold, looked around nervously, his nostrils suddenly filled with a puff of perfume.

And there on the table by the bed he saw a glass bowl filled with a mass of Chinese orchids—great odorous clusters of orange and snow-white bloom that saturated all the room with their freshening scent.

So astounded was he that he stood stock still, one hand still on the door-knob; then in a trice he had closed and locked the door from inside.

Somebody was in that apartment. There could be no doubt about it. He dropped his right hand into his overcoat pocket and took hold of his automatic pistol.

For ten minutes he stood so, listening, peering about the room from bed to curtains, and out into the parlour. There was not a sound in the place. Nothing stirred.

Now, grasping his pistol but not drawing it, he began another stealthy tour of the apartment, exploring every nook and cranny. And, at the end, had discovered nothing new.

When at length he realised that, as far as he could discover, there was not a living thing in the place excepting himself, a very faint chill grew along his neck and shoulders, and he caught his breath suddenly, deeply.

He had come back to the bedroom, now. The perfume of the orchids saturated the still air.

And, as he stood staring at them, all of a sudden he saw, where their twisted stalks rested in the transparent bowl of water, something moving—something brilliant as a live ember gliding out from among the mass of submerged stems—a living fish glowing in scarlet hues and winnowing the water with grotesquely trailing fins as delicate as filaments of scarlet lace.

To and fro swam the fish among the maze of orchid stalks. Even its eyes were hot and red as molten rubies; and as its crimson gills swelled and relaxed and swelled, tints of cherry-fire waxed and waned over its fat and glowing body.

And vaguely, now, in the perfume saturated air, Cleves seemed to sense a subtle taint of evil,—something sinister in the intense stillness of the place—in the jewelled fish gliding so silently in and out among the pallid convolutions of the drowned stems.

As he stood staring at the fish, the drugged odour of the orchids heavy in his throat and lungs, something stirred very lightly in the room.

Chills crawling over every limb, he looked around across his shoulder.

There was a figure seated cross-legged in the middle of the bed!

Then, in the perfumed silence, the girl laughed.

For a full minute neither of them moved. No sound had echoed her low laughter save the deadened pulsations of his own heart. But now there grew a faint ripple of water in the bowl where the scarlet fish, suddenly restless, was swimming hither and thither as though pursued by an invisible hand.

With the slight noise of splashing water in his ears, Cleves stood staring at the figure on the bed. Under her chinchilla cloak the girl seemed to be all a pale golden tint—hair, skin, eyes. The scant shred of an evening gown she wore, the jewels at her throat and breast, all were yellow and amber and saffron-gold.

And now, looking him in the eyes, she leisurely disengaged

the robe of silver fur from her naked shoulders and let it fall around her on the bed. For a second the lithe, willowy golden thing gathered there as gracefully as a coiled snake filled him with swift loathing. Then, almost instantly, the beauty of the lissome creature fascinated him.

She leaned forward and set her elbows on her two knees, and rested her face between her hands—like a gold rose-bud between two ivory petals, he thought, dismayed by this young thing's beauty, shaken by the dull confusion of his own heart battering his breast like the blows of a rising tide.

"What do you wish?" she inquired in her soft young voice. "Why have you come secretly into my rooms to search—and clasping in your hand a loaded pistol deep within your pocket?"

"Why have you hidden yourself until now?" he retorted in a dull and laboured voice.

"I have been here."

"Where?"

"Here! . . . Looking at you. . . . And watching my scarlet fish. His name is Dzelim. He is nearly a thousand years old and as wise as a magician. Look upon him, my lord! See how rapidly he darts around his tiny crystal world! like a comet through outer star-dust, running the eternal race with Time. . . . And—yonder is a chair. Will my lord be seated—at his new servant's feet?"

A strange, physical weariness seemed to weight his limbs and shoulders. He seated himself near the bed, never taking his heavy gaze from the smiling, golden thing which squatted there watching him so intently.

"Whose limousine was that which you entered and then left so abruptly?" he asked.

"My own."

"What was the Yezidee Togrul Kahn doing in it?"

"Did you see anybody in my car?" she asked, veiling her eyes a little with their tawny lashes.

"I saw a man with a thick beard dyed red with henna, and the bony face and slant eyes of Togrul the Yezidee."

"May my soul be ransom for yours, my lord, but you lie!" she said softly. Her lips parted in a smile; but her half-veiled eyes were brilliant as two topazes.

"Is that your answer?"

She lifted one hand and with her forefinger made signs from right to left and then downward as though writing in Turkish and in Chinese characters.

"It is written," she said in a low voice, "that we belong to God and we return to him. Look out what you are about, my lord!"

He drew his pistol from his overcoat and, holding it, rested his hand on his knee.

"Now," he said hoarsely, "while we await the coming of Togrul Kahn, you shall remain exactly where you are, and you shall tell me exactly who you are in order that I may decide whether to arrest you as an alien enemy inciting my countrymen to murder, or to let you go as a foreigner who is able to prove her honesty and innocence."

The girl laughed:

"Be careful," she said. "My danger lies in your youth and mine—somewhere between your lips and mine lies my only danger from you, my lord."

A dull flush mounted to his temples and burned there.

"I am the golden comrade to Heavenly-Azure," she said, still smiling. "I am the Third Immaum in the necklace Keuke wears where Yulun hangs as a rose-pearl, and Sansa as a pearl on fire.

"Look upon me, my lord!"

There was a golden light in his eyes which seemed to stiffen the muscles and confuse his vision. He heard her voice again as though very far away:

"It is written that we shall love, my lord—thou and I—this night—this night. Listen attentively. I am thy slave. My lips shall touch thy feet. Look upon me, my lord!"

There was a dazzling blindness in his eyes and in his brain. He swayed a little still striving to fix her with his failing gaze. t His pistol hand slipped sideways from his knee, fell limply, and the weapon dropped to the thick carpet. He could still see the glimmering golden shape of her, still hear her distant voice:

"It is written that we belong to God . . . *Tokhta!* . . ."

Over his knees was settling a snow-white sheet; on it, in his lap, lay a naked knife. There was not a sound in the room save the rushing and splashing of the scarlet fish in its crystal bowl.

Bending nearer, the girl fixed her yellow eyes on the man who looked back at her with dying gaze, sitting upright and knee deep in his shroud.

Then, noiselessly she uncoiled her supple golden body, extending her right arm toward the knife.

"Throw back thy head, my lord, and stretch thy throat to the knife's sweet edge," she whispered caressingly. "No!—do not close your eyes. Look upon me. Look into my eyes. I am Aoula, temple girl of the Baroulass! I am mistress to the Slayer of Souls! I am a golden plaything to Sanang Noïane, Prince of the Yezidees. Look upon me attentively, my lord!"

Her smooth little hand closed on the hilt; the scarlet fish splashed furiously in the bowl, dislodging a blossom or two which fell to the carpet and slowly faded into mist.

Now she grasped the knife, and she slipped from the bed to the floor and stood before the dazed man.

"This is the Namaz-Ga," she said in her silky voice. "Behold, this is the appointed Place of Prayer. Gaze around you, my lord. These are the shadows of mighty men who come here to see you die in the Place of Prayer."

Cleves's head had fallen back, but his eyes were open. The Baroulass girl took his head in both hands and turned it hither and thither. And his glazing eyes seemed to sweep a throng of shadowy white-robed men crowding the room. And he saw the bloodless, symmetrical visage of Sanang among them, and the great red beard of Togrul; and his stiffening lips parted in an uttered cry, and sagged open, flaccid and soundless.

The Baroulass sorceress lifted the shroud from his knees and spread it on the carpet, moving with leisurely grace about her business and softly intoning the Prayers for the Dead.

Then, having made her arrangements, she took her knife into her right hand again and came back to the half-conscious man, and stood close in front of him, bending near and looking curiously into his dimmed eyes.

"Ayah!" she said smilingly. "This is the Place of Prayer. And you shall add your prayer to ours before I use my knife. So! I give you back your power of speech. Pronounce the name of Erlik!"

Very slowly his dry lips moved and his dry tongue trembled. The word they formed was,

"Tressa!"

Instantly the girl's yellow eyes grew incandescent and her lovely mouth became distorted. With her left hand she caught his chin, forced his head back, exposing his throat, and using all her strength drew the knife's edge across it.

But it was only her clenched fingers that swept the taut throat—clenched and empty fingers in which the knife had vanished.

And when the Baroulass girl saw that her clenched hand was empty, felt her own pointed nails cutting into the tender flesh of her own palm, she stared at her blood-stained fingers in sudden terror—stared, spread them, shrieked where she stood, and writhed there trembling and screaming as though gripped in an invisible trap.

But she fell silent when the door of the room opened noiselessly behind her;—and it was as though she dared not turn her head to face the end of all things which had entered the room and was drawing nearer in utter silence.

Suddenly she saw its shadow on the wall; and her voice burst from her lips in a last shuddering scream.

Then the end came slowly, without a sound, and she sank at the knees, gently, to a kneeling posture, then backward, extending her supple golden shape across the shroud; and lay there limp as a dead snake.

Tressa went to the bowl of water and drew from it every blossom. The scarlet fish was now thrashing the water to an iridescent spume; and Tressa plunged in her hands and seized it and flung it out—squirming and wheezing crimson foam—on the shroud beside the golden girl of the Baroulass. Then, very slowly, she drew the shroud over the dying things; stepped back to the chair where her husband lay unconscious; knelt down beside him and took his head on her shoulder, gazing, all the while, at the outline of the dead girl under the snowy shroud.

After a long while Cleves stirred and opened his eyes. Presently he turned his head sideways on her shoulder.

"Tressa," he whispered.

"Hush," she whispered, "all is well now." But she did not move her eyes from the shroud, which now outlined the still shapes of *two* human figures.

"John Recklow!" she called in a low voice.

Recklow entered noiselessly with drawn pistol. She motioned to him; he bent and lifted the edge of the shroud, cautiously. A bushy red beard protruded.

"Togrul!" he exclaimed. . . . "But who is this young creature lying dead beside him?"

Then Tressa caught the collar of her tunic in her left hand and flung back her lovely face looking upward out of eyes like sapphires wet with rain:

"In the name of the one and only God," she sobbed—"if there be no resurrection for dead souls, then I have slain this night in vain!

"For what does it profit a girl if her soul be lost to a lover and her body be saved for her husband?"

She rose from her knees, the tears still falling, and went and looked down at the outlined shapes beneath the shroud.

Recklow had gone to the telephone to summon his own men and an ambulance. Now, turning toward Tressa from his chair:

"God knows what we'd do without you, Mrs. Cleves. I believe this accounts for all the Yezidees except Sanang."

"Excepting Prince Sanang," she said drearily. Then she went slowly to where her husband lay in his armchair, and sank down on the floor, and laid her cheek across his feet.

Chapter 17
The Slayer of Souls

In that great blizzard which, on the 4th of February, struck the eastern coast of the United States from Georgia to Maine, John Recklow and his men hunted Sanang, the last of the Yezidees.

And Sanang clung like a demon to the country which he had doomed to destruction, imbedding each claw again as it was torn loose, battling for the supremacy of evil with all his dreadful psychic power, striving still to seize, cripple, and slay the bodies and souls of a hundred million Americans.

Again he scattered the uncounted myriads of germs of the Black Plague which he and his Yezidees had brought out of Mongolia a year before; and once more the plague swept over the country, and thousands on thousands died.

But now the National, State and City governments were fighting, with physicians, nurses, and police, this gruesome epidemic which had come into the world from they knew not where. And National, State and City governments, aroused at last, were fighting the more terrible plague of anarchy.

Nationwide raids were made from the Atlantic to the Pacific, and from the Gulf to the Lakes. Thousands of terrorists of all shades and stripes whose minds had been seized and poisoned by the Yezidees were being arrested. Deportations had begun; government agents were everywhere swarming to clean out the foulness that had struck deeper into the body of the Republic than anyone had supposed.

And it seemed, at last, as though the Red Plague, too, was about to be stamped out along with the Black Death called Influenza.

But only a small group of Secret Service men knew that a resurgence of these horrors was inevitable unless Sanang, the Slayer of Souls, was destroyed. And they knew, too, that only one person in America could hope to destroy Sanang, the last of the

Yezidees, and that was Tressa Cleves.

Only by the sudden onset of the plague in various cities of the land had Recklow any clew concerning the whereabouts of Sanang.

In Boston, then Washington, then Kansas City, and then New York the epidemic suddenly blazed up. And in these places of death the Secret Service men always found a clew, and there they hunted Sanang, the Yezidee, to kill him without mercy where they might find him.

But they never found Sanang Noïane; only the ghastly marks of his poisoned claws on the body of the sickened nation—only minds diseased by the Red Plague and bodies dying of the Black Death—civil and social centres disorganized, disrupted, depraved, dying.

When the blizzard burst upon New York, struggling in the throes of the plague, and paralysed the metropolis for a week, John Recklow sent out a special alarm, and New York swarmed with Secret Service men searching the snow-buried city for a graceful, slender, dark young man whose eyes slanted a trifle in his amber-tinted face; who dressed fashionably, lived fastidiously, and spoke English perfectly in a delightfully modulated voice.

And to New York, thrice stricken by anarchy, by plague, and now by God, hurried, from all parts of the nation, thousands of secret agents who had been hunting Sanang in distant cities or who had been raiding the traitorous and secret gatherings of his mental dupes.

Agent ZB-303, who was volunteer agent James Benton, came from Boston with his new bride who had just arrived by way of England—a young girl named Yulun who landed swathed in sables, and stretched out both lovely little hands to Benton the instant she caught sight of him on the pier. Where upon he took the slim figure in furs into his arms, which was interesting because they had never before met in the flesh.

So,—their honeymoon scarce begun, Benton and Yulun came from Boston in answer to Recklow's emergency call.

And all the way across from San Francisco came volunteer

agent XLY-37I, otherwise Alek Selden, bringing with him a girl named Sansa whom he had gone to the coast to meet, and whom he had immediately married after she had landed from the Japanese steamer *Nan-yang Maru*. Which, also, was remarkable, because, although they recognised each other instantly, and their hands and lips clung as they met, neither had ever before beheld the living body of the other.

The third man who came to New York at Recklow's summons was volunteer agent 53-6-26, otherwise Victor Cleyes.

His young wife, suffering from nervous shock after the deaths of Togrul Khan and of the Baroulass girl, Aoula, had been convalescing in a private sanatorium in Westchester.

Until the summons came to her husband from Recklow, she had seen him only for a few moments every day. But the call to duty seemed to have effected a miraculous cure in the slender, blue-eyed girl who had lain all day long, day after day, in her still, sunny room scarcely unclosing her eyes at all save only when her husband was permitted to enter for the few minutes allowed them every day.

The physician had just left, after admitting that Mrs. Cleves seemed to be well enough to travel if she insisted; and she and her maid had already begun to pack when her husband came into her room.

She looked around over her shoulder, then rose from her knees, flung an armful of clothing into the trunk before which she had been kneeling, and came across the room to him. Then she dismissed her maid from the room. And when the girl had gone:

"I am well, Victor," she said in a low voice. "Why are you troubled?"

"I can't bear to have you drawn into this horrible affair once more."

"Who else is there to discover and overcome Sanang?" she asked calmly.

He remained silent.

So, for a few moments they stood confronting each other

there in the still, sunny chamber—husband and wife who had never even exchanged the first kiss—two young creatures more vitally and intimately bound together than any two on earth—yet utterly separated body and soul from each other—two solitary spirits which had never merged; two bodies virginal and inviolate.

Tressa spoke first: "I must go. That was our bargain."

The word made him wince as though it had been a sudden blow. Then his face flushed red.

"Bargain or no bargain," he said, "I don't want you to go because I'm afraid you cannot endure another shock like the last one. . . . And every time you have thrown your own mind and body between this Nation and destruction you have nearly died of it"

"And if I die?" she said in a low voice.

What answer she awaited—perhaps hoped for—was not the one he made. He said: "If you die in what you believe to be your line of duty, then it will be I who have killed you."

"That would not be true. It is you who have saved me."

"I have not. I have done nothing except to lead you Into danger of death since I first met you. If you mean spiritually, that also is untrue. You have saved yourself—if that indeed were necessary. You have redeemed yourself—if it is true you needed redemption—which I never believed—"

"Oh," she sighed swiftly, "Sanang surprised my soul when it was free of my body—followed my soul into the Wood of the White Moth—caught it there all alone—and—slew it!"

His lips and throat had gone dry as he watched the pallid terror grow in her face.

Presently he recovered his voice: "You call that Yezidee the Slayer of Souls," he said, "but I tell you there is no such creature, no such power!

"I suppose I—I know what you mean—having seen what we call souls dissociated from their physical bodies—but that this Yezidee could do you any spiritual damage I do not for one instant believe. The idea is monstrous, I tell you—"

189

"I—I fought him—soul battling against soul—" she stammered, breathing faster and irregularly. "I struggled with Sanang there in the Wood of the White Moth. I called on God! I called on my two great dogs, Bars and Alaga! I recited the *Fatha* with all my strength—fighting convulsively whenever his soul seized mine; I cried out the name of Khidr, begging for wisdom! I called on the Ten Imaums, on Ali the Lion, on the Blessed Companions. Then I tore my spirit out of the grasp of his soul—but there was no escape!—no escape," she wailed. "For on every side I saw the cloud-topped rampart of Gog and Magog, and the woods rang with Erlik's laughter—the dissonant mirth of hell—"

She began to shudder and sway a little, then with an effort she controlled herself in a measure.

"There never has been," she began again with lips that quivered in spite of her—"there never has been one moment in our married lives when my soul dared forget the Wood of the White Moth—dared seek yours. . . . God lives. But so does Erlik. There are angels; but there are as many demons. . . . My soul is ashamed. . . . And very lonely . . . very lonely . . . but no fit companion-for yours—"

Her hands dropped listlessly beside her and her chin sank.

"So you believe that Yezidee devil caught your soul when it was wandering somewhere out of your body, and destroyed it," he said.

She did not answer, did not even lift her eyes until he had stepped close to her—closer than he had ever come. Then she looked up at him, but closed her eyes as he swept her into his arms and crushed her face and body against his own.

Now her red lips were on his; now her face and heart and limbs and breast melted into his her breath, her pulse, her strength flowed into his and became part of their single being and single pulse and breath. And she felt their two souls flame and fuse together, and burn together in one heavenly blaze—felt the swift conflagration mount, overwhelm, and sweep her clean of the last lingering taint; felt her soul, unafraid, clasp her husband's spirit in its white embrace—clung to him, uplifted out of hell, rising into the blinding light of Paradise.

Far—far away she heard her own voice in singing whispers-heard her lips pronounce *The Name*—"*Ata!—Ata! Allahou*—"

Her blue eyes unclosed; through a mist, in which she saw her husband's face, grew a vast metallic clamour in her ears.

Her husband kissed her, long, silently; then, retaining her hand, he turned and lifted the receiver from the clamouring telephone.

"Yes! Yes, this is 53-6-26. Yes, V-69 is with me. . . . When? . . . Today? . . . Very well. . . . Yes, we'll come at once. . . . Yes, we can get a train in a few minutes. . . . All right. Goodbye."

He took his wife into his arms again.

"Dearest of all in the world," he said, "Sanang is cornered in a row of houses near the East River, and Recklow has flung a cordon around the entire block. Good God! I *can't* take you there !"

Then Tressa smiled, drew his head down, looked into his face till the clear blue splendour of her gaze stilled the tumult in his brain.

"I alone know how to deal with Prince Sanang," she said quietly. "And if John Recklow, or you, or Mr. Benton or Mr. Selden should kill him with your pistols, it would be only his body you slay, not the evil thing that would escape you and re-turn to Erlik."

"*Must* you do this thing, Tressa?"

"Yes, I must do it."

"But—if our pistols cannot kill this sorcerer, how are you going to deal with him?"

"I know how."

"Have you the strength?"

"Yes—the bodily and the spiritual. Don't you know that I am already part of you?"

"We shall be nearer still," he murmured.

She flushed but met his gaze.

"Yes. . . . We shall be but one being. . . . Utterly. . . . For already our hearts and souls are one. And we shall become of one mind and one body.

"I am no longer afraid of Sanang Noïane !"

"No longer afraid to slay him?" he asked quietly.

A blue light flashed in her eyes and her face grew still and white and terrible.

"Death to the body? That is nothing, my lord!" she said, in a hard, sweet voice. "It is written that we belong to God and that we return to Him. All living things must die, Heart of the World! It is only the death of souls that matters. And it has arrived at a time in the history of mankind, I think, when the Slayer of Souls shall slay no more."

She looked at him, flushed, withdrew her hand and went slowly across the room to the big bay window where potted flowers were in bloom.

From a window-box she took a pinch of dry soil and dropped it into the bosom of her gown.

Then, facing the East, with lowered arms and palms turned outward:

"There is no god but God," she whispered—"the merciful, the long-suffering, the compassionate, the just.

"For it is written that when the heavens are rolled together like a scroll, every soul shall know what it hath wrought.

"And those souls that are dead in Jehannum shall arise from the dead, and shall have their day in court. Nor shall Erlik stay them till all has been said.

"And on that day the soul of a girl that hath been put to death shall ask for what reason it was slain.

"Thus it has been written."

Then Tressa dropped to her knees, touched the carpet with her forehead, straightened her lithe body and, looking over her shoulder, clapped her hands together sharply.

Her maid opened the door. "Hasten with my lord's luggage!" she cried happily; and, still kneeling, lifted her head to her husband and laughed up into his eyes.

"You should call the porter for we are nearly ready. Shall we

192

go to the station in a sleigh? Oh, wonderful!"

She leaped to her feet, extended her hand and caught his.

"Horses for the lord of the Yiort!" she cried, laughingly. "*Kosh*! Take me out into this new white world that has been born today of the ten purities and the ten thousand felicities! It has been made anew for you and me who also have been born this day!"

He scarcely knew this sparkling, laughing girl with her quick grace and her thousand swift little moods and gaieties.

Porters came to take his luggage from his own room; and then her trunk and bags were ready, and were taken away.

The baggage sleigh drove off. Their own jingling sleigh followed; and Tressa, buried in furs, looked out upon a dazzling, unblemished world, lying silvery white under a sky as azure as her eyes.

"Keuke Mongol—Heavenly Azure," he whispered close to her crimsoned cheek, "do you know how I have loved you—always—always?"

"No, I did not know that," she said.

"Nor I, in the beginning. Yet it happened, also, from the beginning when I first saw you."

"That is a delicious thing to be told. Within me a most heavenly glow is spreading. . . . Unglove your hand."

She slipped the glove from her own white fingers and felt for his under the furs.

"*Aie*," she sighed, "you are more beautiful than Ali; more wonderful than the Flaming Pearl. Out of ice and fire a new world has been made for us."

"Heavenly Azure—my darling!"

"Oh-h," she sighed, "your words are sweeter than the breeze in Yian I—I shall be a bride to you such as there never has been since the days of the Blessed Companions—may their names be perfumed and sweet-scented! . . . Shall I truly be one with you, my lord?"

"Mind, soul, and body, one being, you and I, little Heavenly Azure."

"Between your two hands you hold me like a burning rose, my lord."

"Your sweetness and fire penetrate my soul."

"We shall burn together then till the sky-carpet be rolled up. *Kosh!* We shall be one, and on that day I shall not be afraid."

The sleigh came to a clashing, jingling halt; the train ploughed into the depot buried in vast clouds of snowy steam.

But when they had taken the places reserved for them, and the train was moving swifter and more swiftly toward New York, fear suddenly overwhelmed Victor Cleves, and his face grew grey with the menacing tumult of his thoughts.

The girl seemed to comprehend him, too, and her own features became still and serious as she leaned forward in her chair.

"It is in God's hands, Heart of the World," she said in a low voice. "We are one, thou and I,—or nearly so. Nothing can harm my soul."

"No. . . . But the danger—to your life—"

"I fear no Yezidee."

"The beast will surely try to kill you. And what can I do? You say my pistol is useless."

"Yes. . . . But I want you near me."

"Do you imagine I'd leave you for a second? Good God," he added in a strangled voice, "isn't there any way I can kill this wild beast? With my naked hands—?"

"You must leave him to me, Victor."

"And you believe you can slay him? *Do* you?"

She remained silent for a long while, bent forward in her armchair, and her hands clasped tightly on her knees.

"My husband," she said at last, "what your astronomers have but just begun to suspect is true, and has long, long been known to the Sheiks-el-Djebel.

"For, near to this world we live in, are other worlds—planets that do not reflect light. And there is a dark world called Yrimid, close to the earth—a planet wrapped in darkness—a black star. . . . And upon it Erlik dwells. . . . And it is peopled by demons. . . .

194

And from it comes sickness and evil—"

She moistened her lips; sat for a while gazing vaguely straight before her.

"From this black planet comes all evil upon earth," she resumed in a hushed voice. "For it is very near to the earth. It is not a hundred miles away. All strange phenomena for which our scientists cannot account are due to this invisible planet,— all new and sudden pestilences; all convulsions of nature; the newly noticed radio disturbances; the new, so-called inter-planetary signals—all—all have their hidden causes within that black and demon-haunted planet long known to the Yezidees, and by them called Yrimid, or Erlik's World.

"And—it is to this black planet that I shall send Sanang, Slayer of Souls. I shall tear him from this earth, though he cling to it with every claw; and I shall fling his soul into darkness—out across the gulf—drive his soul forth—hurl it toward Erlik like a swift rocket charred and falling from the sky into endless night.

"So shall I strive to deal with Prince Sanang, Sorcerer of Mount Alamout, the last of the Assassins, Sheik-el-Djebel, and Slayer of Souls. . . . May God remember him in hell."

Already their train was rolling into the great terminal.

Recklow was awaiting them. He took Tressa's hands in his and gazed earnestly into her face.

"Have you come to show us how to conclude this murderous business?" he asked grimly.

"I shall try," she said calmly. "Where have you cornered Sanang?"

"Could you and Victor come at once?"

"Yes." She turned and looked at her husband, who had become quite pale.

Recklow saw the look they exchanged. There could be no misunderstanding what had happened to these two. Their tragedy had ended. They were united at last. He understood it instantly,—realised how terrible was this new and tragic situation for them both.

Yet, he knew also that the salvation of civilisation itself now depended upon this girl. She must face Sanang. There was nothing else possible.

"The streets are choked with snow," he said, "but I have a coupe and two strong horses waiting."

He nodded to one of his men standing near. Cleves gave him the hand luggage and checks.

"All right," he said in a low voice to Recklow; and passed one arm through Tressa's.

The *coupé* was waiting on Forty-second Street, guarded by a policeman. When they had entered and were seated, two mounted policemen rode ahead of the lurching vehicle, picking a way amid the monstrous snow-drifts, and headed for the East River.

"We've got him somewhere in a wretched row of empty houses not far from East River Park. I'm taking you there. I've drawn a cordon of my men around the entire block. He can't get away. But I dared take no chances with this Yezidee sorcerer dared not let one of my men go in to look for him—go anywhere near him,—until I could lay the situation before you, Mrs. Cleves."

"Yes," she said calmly, "it was the only way, Mr. Recklow. There would have been no use shooting him—no use taking him prisoner. A prisoner, he remains as deadly as ever; dead, his mind still lives and breeds evil. You are quite right; it is for me to deal with Sanang."

Recklow shuddered in spite of himself. "Can you tear his claws from the vitals of the world, and free the sick brains of a million people from the slavery of this monster's mind?"

The girl said seriously:

"Even Satan was stoned. It is so written. And was cast out. And dwells forever and ever in Abaddon. No star lights that Pit. None lights the Black Planet, Yrimid. It is where evil dwells. And there Sanang Noïane belongs."

And now, beyond the dirty edges of the snow-smothered city, under an icy mist they caught sight of the river where ships lay blockaded by frozen floes.

Gulls circled over it; ghostly factory chimneys on the further shore loomed up gigantic, ranged like minarettes.

The *coupé*, jolting along behind the mounted policemen, struggled up toward the sidewalk and stopped. The two horses stood steaming, knee deep in snow. Recklow sprang out; Tressa gave him one hand and stepped lithely to the sidewalk. Then Cleves got out and came and took hold of his wife's arm again.

"Well," he said harshly to Recklow, "where is this damned Yezidee hidden?"

Recklow pointed in silence, but he and Tressa had already lifted their gaze to the stark, shabby row of abandoned three-story houses where every dirty blind was closed.

"They're to be demolished and model tenements built," he said briefly.

A man muffled in a fur overcoat came up and took Tressa's hand and kissed it.

She smiled palely at Benton, spoke of Yulun, wished him happiness. While she was yet speaking Selden approached and bent over her gloved hand. She spoke to him very sweetly of Sansa, expressing pleasure at the prospect of seeing her again in the body.

"The Seldens and ourselves have adjoining apartments at the Ritz," said Benton. "We have reserved a third suite for you and Victor."

She inclined her lovely head, gravely, then turned to Recklow, saying that she was ready.

"It makes no difference which front door I unlock," he said. "All these tenements are connected by human rat-holes and hidden runways leading from one house to another. . . . How many men do you want?"

"I want you four men,—nobody else."

Recklow led the way up a snow-covered stoop, drew a key from his pocket, fitted it, and pulled open the door.

A musty chill struck their faces as they entered the darkened and empty hallway. Involuntarily every man drew his pistol.

"I must ask you to do exactly what I tell you to do," she said calmly.

197

"Certainly," said Recklow, caressing his white moustache and striving to pierce the gloom with his keen eyes.

Then Tressa took her husband's hand. "Come," she said. They mounted the stairway together; and the three others followed with pistols lifted.

There was a vague grey light on the second floor; the broken rear shutters let it in.

As though she seemed to know her way, the girl led them forward, opened a door in the wall, and disclosed a bare, dusty room in the next house.

Through this she stepped; the others crept after her with weapons ready. She opened a second door, turned to the four men.

"Wait here for me. Come only when I call," she whispered.

"For God's sake take me with you," burst out Cleves.

"In God's name stay where you are till you hear me call your name!" she said almost breathlessly.

Then, suddenly she turned, swiftly retracing her steps; and they saw her pass through the first door and disappear into the first house they had entered.

A terrible silence fell among them. The sound of her steps on the bare boards had died away. There was not a sound in the chilly dusk.

Minute after minute dragged by. One by one the men peered fearfully at Cleves. His visage was ghastly and they could see his pistol-hand trembling.

Twice Recklow looked at his wrist watch. The third time he said, unsteadily: "She has been gone three-quarters of an hour."

Then, far away, they heard a heavy tread on the stairs. Nearer and nearer came the footsteps. Every pistol was levelled at the first door as a man's bulky form darkened it.

"It's one of my men," said Recklow in a voice like a low groan. "Where on earth is Mrs. Cleves?"

"I came to tell you," said the agent, "Mrs. Cleves came out of the first house nearly an hour ago. She got into the *coupé* and told the driver to go to the Ritz."

"What!" gasped Recklow.

"She's gone to the Ritz," repeated the agent. "No one else has come out. And I began to worry—hearing nothing of you, Mr. Recklow. So I stepped in to see—"

"You say that Mrs. Cleves went out of the house we entered, got into the *coupé*, and told the driver to go to the Ritz?" demanded Cleves, astounded.

"Yes, sir."

"Where is that *coupé*? Did it return?"

"It had not returned when I came in here."

"Go back and look for it. Look in the other street," said Recklow sharply.

The agent hurried away over the creaking boards. The four men gazed at one another.

"The thing to do is to obey her and stay where we are," said Recklow grimly. "Who knows what peril we may cause her if we move from—"

His words froze on his lips as Tressa's voice rang out from the darkness beyond the door they were guarding:

"Victor! I—I need you! Come to me, my husband!"

As Cleves sprang through the door into the darkness beyond, Benton smashed a window sash with all the force of his shoulder, and, reaching out through the shattered glass, tore the rotting blinds from their hinges, letting in a flood of sickly light.

Against the bare wall stood Tressa, both arms extended, her hands flat against the plaster, and each hand transfixed and pinned to the wall by a knife.

A white sheet lay at her feet. On it rested a third knife. And, bending on one knee to pick it up, they caught a glimpse of a slender young man in fashionable afternoon attire, who, as they entered with the crash of the shattered window in their ears, sprang to his nimble feet and stood confronting them, knife in hand.

Instantly every man fired at him and the bullets whipped the plaster to a smoke behind him, but the slender, dark skinned young man stood motionless, looking at them out of brilliant eyes that slanted a trifle.

Again the racket of the fusillade swept him and filled the room with plaster dust.

Cleves, frantic with horror, laid hold of the knives that pinned his wife's hands to the wall, and dragged them out.

But there was no blood, no wound to be seen on her soft palms. She took the murderous looking blades from him, threw one terrible look at Sanang, kicked the shroud across the floor toward him, and flung both knives upon it.

The place was still dim with plaster dust and pistol fumes as she stepped forward through the acrid mist, motioning the four men aside.

"Sanang!" she cried in a clear voice, "may God remember you in hell, for my feet have spurned your shroud, and your knives, which could not scar my palms, shall never pierce my heart I Look out for yourself, Prince Sanang!"

"*Tòkhta* !" he said, calmly. "My soul be ransom for yours!"

"That is a lie! My soul is already ransomed! My mind is the more powerful. It has already halted yours. It is conquering yours. It is seizing your mind and enslaving it. It is mastering your will, Sanang! Your mind bends before mine. You know it! You know it is bending. You feel it is breaking down!"

Sanang's eyes began to glitter but his pale brown face had grown almost white.

"I slew you once—in the Wood of the White Moth," he said huskily. "There is no resurrection from such a death, little Heavenly Azure. Look upon me! My soul and yours are one !"

"You are looking upon my soul," she said.

"A lie! You are in your body !"

The girl laughed. "My body lies asleep in the Ritz upon my husband's bed," she said. "My body is his, my mind belongs to him, my soul is already one with his. Do you not know it, dog of a Yezidee? Look upon me, Sanang Noïane! Look upon my un-wounded hands! My shroud lies at your feet. And there lie the knives that could not pierce my heart! I am thrice clean! Listen to my words, Sanang! There is no other god but God!"

The young man's visage grew pasty and loose and horrible; his lips became flaccid like dewlaps; but out of these sagging folds of livid skin his voice burst whistling, screaming, as though wrenched from his very belly:

"May Erlik strangle you! May you rot where you stand! May your face become a writhing mass of maggots and your body a corruption of living worms!

"For what you are doing to me this day may every demon in hell torment you!

"Have a care what you are about!" he screeched. "You are slaying my mind, you sorceress! You have seized my mind and are crushing it! You are putting out its light, you Yezidee witch!- you are quenching the last spark—of reason—in—me—"

"Sanang!"

His knife fell clattering to the floor. But he stood stock still, his hands clutching his head—stood motionless, while scream on scream tore through the loose and gaping lips, blowing them into ghastly, distorted folds.

"Sanang Noïane!" she cried in her clear voice, "the Eight Towers are darkened! The Rampart of Gog and Magog is fallen! On Mount Alamoul nothing is living. The minds of mankind are free again!"

She stepped forward, slowly, and stood near him; chanting in a low voice the Prayers for the Dead.

She bent down and unrolled the shroud, laid it on his shoulders and drew it up and across his face, covering his dying eyes, and swathed him so, slowly, from head to foot.

Then she gathered up the three knives, cast them upward into the air. They did not fall again. They disappeared. And all the while, under her breath, the girl was chanting the Prayers for the Dead as she moved silently about her business.

Shrouded to the forehead in its white cerements, the muffled figure of Sanang stood upright, motionless as a swathed and frozen corpse.

Outside, the daylight had become greyer. It had begun to snow again, and a few flakes blew in through the shattered windows and clung to the winding sheet of Sanang.

And now Tressa drew close to the shrouded shape and stood before it, gazing intently upon the outlined features of the last of the Yezidees.

"Sanang," she said very softly, "I hear your soul bidding your body farewell. *Tòkhta!*"

Then, under the strained gaze of the four men gathered there, the shroud fell to the floor in a loose heap of white folds. There was nobody under it; no trace of Sanang. The human shape of the Yezidee had disappeared; but a greyish mist had filled the room, wavering up like smoke from the shroud, and, like smoke, blowing in a long streamer toward the window where the draught drew it out through the falling snow and scattered the last shred of it against the greying sky.

In the room the mist thinned swiftly; the four men could now see one another. But Tressa was no longer in the room. And in place of the white shroud a piece of filthy tattered carpet lay on the floor. And a dead rat, flattened out, dry and dusty, lay upon it.

"For God's sake," whispered Recklow hoarsely, "let us get out of this!"

Cleves, his pistol clutched convulsively, stared at him in terror. But Recklow took him by the arm and drew him away, muttering that Tressa was waiting for him, and might be ill, and that there was nothing further to expect in this ghastly spot.

They went with Cleves to the Ritz. At the desk the clerk said that Mrs. Cleves had the keys and was in her apartment.

The three men entered the corridor with him; watched him try the door; saw him open it; lingered a moment after it had closed; heard the key turn.

At the sound of the door closing the maid came.

"*Madame* is asleep in her room," she whispered.

"When did she come in?"

"More than two hours ago, sir. I have drawn her bath, but when I opened the door a few moments ago, *Madame* was still asleep."

He nodded; he was trembling when he put off his overcoat and dropped hat and gloves on the carpet.

From the little rose and ivory reception room he could see the closed door of his wife's chamber. And for a while he stood staring at it.

Then, slowly, he crossed this room, opened the door; entered.

In her bedroom the tinted twilight was like ashes of roses. He went to the bed and looked down at her shadowy face; gazed intently; listened; then, in sudden terror, bent and laid his hand on her heart. It was beating as tranquilly as a child's; but as she stirred, turned her head, and unclosed her eyes, under his hand her heart leaped like a wild thing caught unawares and the snowy skin glowed with an exquisite and deepening tint as she lifted her arms and clasped them around her husband's neck, drawing his quivering face against her own.

In the Court of the Dragon

(A Story from The King in Yellow.)

Oh, thou who burn'st in heart for those who burn
In Hell, whose fires thyself shall feed in turn;
How long be crying— 'Mercy on them.' God!
Why, who art thou to teach and He to learn?

In the Church of St. Barnabé vespers were over; the clergy left the altar; the little choir-boys flocked across the chancel and settled in the stalls. A Suisse in rich uniform marched down the south aisle, sounding his staff at every fourth step on the stone pavement; behind him came that eloquent preacher and good man, Monseigneur C——.

My chair was near the chancel rail, I now turned toward the west end of the church. The other people between the altar and the pulpit turned too. There was a little scraping and rustling while the congregation seated itself again; the preacher mounted the pulpit stairs, and the organ voluntary ceased.

I had always found the organ-playing at St. Barnabé highly interesting. Learned and scientific it was, too much so for my small knowledge, but expressing a vivid if cold intelligence. Moreover, it possessed the French quality of taste: taste reigned supreme, self-controlled, dignified and reticent.

Today, however, from the first chord I had felt a change for the worse, a sinister change. During vespers it had been chiefly the chancel organ which supported the beautiful choir, but now and again, quite wantonly as it seemed, from the west gallery where the great organ stands, a heavy hand had struck across the

church at the serene peace of those clear voices. It was something more than harsh and dissonant, and it betrayed no lack
of skill. As it recurred again and again, it set me thinking of
what my architect's books say about the custom in early times
to consecrate the choir as soon as it was built, and that the nave,
being finished sometimes half a century later, often did not get
any blessing at all: I wondered idly if that had been the case at
St. Barnabé, and whether something not usually supposed to be
at home in a Christian church might have entered undetected
and taken possession of the west gallery. I had read of such things
happening, too, but not in works on architecture.

Then I remembered that St. Barnabé was not much more
than a hundred years old, and smiled at the incongruous association of mediaeval superstitions with that cheerful little piece of
eighteenth-century *rococo*.

But now vespers were over, and there should have followed a
few quiet chords, fit to accompany meditation, while we waited
for the sermon. Instead of that, the discord at the lower end of
the church broke out with the departure of the clergy, as if now
nothing could control it.

I belong to those children of an older and simpler generation
who do not love to seek for psychological subtleties in art; and
I have ever refused to find in music anything more than melody
and harmony, but I felt that in the labyrinth of sounds now is-
suing from that instrument there was something being hunted.
Up and down the pedals chased him, while the manuals blared
approval. Poor devil! whoever he was, there seemed small hope
of escape!

My nervous annoyance changed to anger. Who was doing
this? How dare he play like that in the midst of divine service?
I glanced at the people near me: not one appeared to be in
the least disturbed. The placid brows of the kneeling nuns, still
turned towards the altar, lost none of their devout abstraction
under the pale shadow of their white head-dress. The fashionable lady beside me was looking expectantly at Monseigneur
C——. For all her face betrayed, the organ might have been

singing an *Ave Maria*.

But now, at last, the preacher had made the sign of the cross, and commanded silence. I turned to him gladly. Thus far I had not found the rest I had counted on when I entered St. Barnabé that afternoon.

I was worn out by three nights of physical suffering and mental trouble: the last had been the worst, and it was an exhausted body, and a mind benumbed and yet acutely sensitive, which I had brought to my favourite church for healing. For I had been reading *The King in Yellow*.

"The sun ariseth; they gather themselves together and lay them down in their dens." Monseigneur C—— delivered his text in a calm voice, glancing quietly over the congregation. My eyes turned, I knew not why, toward the lower end of the church. The organist was coming from behind his pipes, and passing along the gallery on his way out, I saw him disappear by a small door that leads to some stairs which descend directly to the street. He was a slender man, and his face was as white as his coat was black. "Good riddance!" I thought, "with your wicked music! I hope your assistant will play the closing voluntary."

With a feeling of relief—with a deep, calm feeling of relief, I turned back to the mild face in the pulpit and settled myself to listen. Here, at last, was the ease of mind I longed for.

"My children," said the preacher, "one truth the human soul finds hardest of all to learn: that it has nothing to fear. It can never be made to see that nothing can really harm it."

"Curious doctrine!" I thought, "for a Catholic priest. Let us see how he will reconcile that with the Fathers."

"Nothing can really harm the soul," he went on, in, his coolest, clearest tones, "because——"

But I never heard the rest; my eye left his face, I knew not for what reason, and sought the lower end of the church. The same man was coming out from behind the organ, and was passing along the gallery *the same way*. But there had not been time for him to return, and if he had returned, I must have seen him. I felt a faint chill, and my heart sank; and yet, his going and coming were no affair of mine. I looked at him: I could not look away from his black figure and his white face. When he was exactly opposite to me, he turned and sent across the church straight into my eyes, a look of hate, intense and deadly: I have never seen any other like it; would to God I might never see it again! Then he disappeared by the same door through which I had watched him depart less than sixty seconds before.

I sat and tried to collect my thoughts. My first sensation was like that of a very young child badly hurt, when it catches its breath before crying out.

To suddenly find myself the object of such hatred was exquisitely painful: and this man was an utter stranger. Why should he hate me so?—me, whom he had never seen before? For the moment all other sensation was merged in this one pang: even fear was subordinate to grief, and for that moment I never doubted; but in the next I began to reason, and a sense of the incongruous came to my aid.

As I have said, St. Barnabé is a modern church. It is small and well lighted; one sees all over it almost at a glance. The organ gallery gets a strong white light from a row of long windows in the clerestory, which have not even coloured glass.

The pulpit being in the middle of the church, it followed that, when I was turned toward it, whatever moved at the west end could not fail to attract my eye. When the organist passed it was no wonder that I saw him: I had simply miscalculated the interval between his first and his second passing. He had come in that last time by the other side-door. As for the look which had so upset me, there had been no such thing, and I was a nervous fool.

I looked about. This was a likely place to harbour supernatural horrors! That clear-cut, reasonable face of Monseigneur C——, his collected manner and easy, graceful gestures, were they not just a little discouraging to the notion of a gruesome mystery? I glanced above his head, and almost laughed. That flyaway lady supporting one corner of the pulpit canopy, which looked like a fringed damask tablecloth in a high wind, at the first attempt of a basilisk to pose up there in the organ loft, she would point her gold trumpet at him, and puff him out of existence! I laughed to myself over this conceit, which, at the time, I thought very amusing, and sat and chaffed myself and everything else, from the old harpy outside the railing, who had made me pay ten *centimes* for my chair, before she would let me in (she was more like a *basilisk*, I told myself, than was my organist with the anaemic complexion): from that grim old dame, to, yes, alas! Monseigneur C—— himself. For all devoutness had fled. I had never yet done such a thing in my life, but now I felt a desire to mock.

As for the sermon, I could not hear a word of it for the jingle in my ears of

> *The skirts of St. Paul has reached.*
> *Having preached us those six Lent lectures,*
> *More unctuous than ever he preached,*

keeping time to the most fantastic and irreverent thoughts.

It was no use to sit there any longer: I must get out of doors and shake myself free from this hateful mood. I knew the rudeness I was committing, but still I rose and left the church.

A spring sun was shining on the Rue St. Honoré, as I ran down the church steps. On one corner stood a barrow full of yellow jonquils, pale violets from the Riviera, dark Russian violets, and white Roman hyacinths in a golden cloud of mimosa. The street was full of Sunday pleasure-seekers. I swung my cane and laughed with the rest. Someone overtook and passed me. He never turned, but there was the same deadly malignity in his white profile that there had been in his eyes. I watched him as long as I could see him. His lithe back expressed the same menace; every step that carried him away from me seemed to bear him on some errand connected with my destruction.

I was creeping along, my feet almost refusing to move. There began to dawn in me a sense of responsibility for something long forgotten. It began to seem as if I deserved that which he threatened: it reached a long way back—a long, long way back.

It had lain dormant all these years: it was there, though, and presently it would rise and confront me. But I would try to escape; and I stumbled as best I could into the Rue de Rivoli, across the Place de la Concorde and on to the Quai. I looked with sick eyes upon the sun, shining through the white foam of the fountain, pouring over the backs of the dusky bronze river-gods, on the far-away Arc, a structure of amethyst mist, on the countless vistas of grey stems and bare branches faintly green. Then I saw him again coming down one of the chestnut alleys of the Cours la Reine.

I left the riverside, plunged blindly across to the Champs Elysées and turned toward the Arc. The setting sun was sending its rays along the green sward of the Rond-point: in the full glow he sat on a bench, children and young mothers all about him. He was nothing but a Sunday lounger, like the others, like myself. I said the words almost aloud, and all the while I gazed on the malignant hatred of his face. But he was not looking at me. I crept past and dragged my leaden feet up the Avenue. I knew that every time I met him brought him nearer to the accomplishment of his purpose and my fate. And still I tried to save myself.

The last rays of sunset were pouring through the great Arc. I passed under it, and met him face to face. I had left him far down the Champs Elysées, and yet he came in with a stream of people who were returning from the Bois de Boulogne. He came so close that he brushed me. His slender frame felt like iron inside its loose black covering. He showed no signs of haste, nor of fatigue, nor of any human feeling. His whole being expressed one thing: the will, and the power to work me evil.

In anguish I watched him where he went down the broad crowded avenue, that was all flashing with wheels and the trappings of horses and the helmets of the Garde Republicaine.

He was soon lost to sight; then I turned and fled. Into the *Bois*, and far out beyond it—I know not where I went, but after a long while as it seemed to me, night had fallen, and I found myself sitting at a table before a small café. I had wandered back into the *Bois*. It was hours now since I had seen him. Physical fatigue and mental suffering had left me no power to think or feel. I was tired, so tired! I longed to hide away in my own den. I resolved to go home. But that was a long way off.

I live in the Court of the Dragon, a narrow passage that leads from the Rue de Rennes to the Rue du Dragon.

It is an "*impasse*"; traversable only for foot passengers. Over the entrance on the Rue de Rennes is a balcony, supported by an iron dragon. Within the court tall old houses rise on either side, and close the ends that give on the two streets. Huge gates, swung back during the day into the walls of the deep archways, close this court, after midnight, and one must enter then by ringing at certain small doors on the side. The sunken pavement collects unsavoury pools. Steep stairways pitch down to doors that open on the court. The ground floors are occupied by shops of second-hand dealers, and by iron workers. All day long the place rings with the clink of hammers and the clang of metal bars.

Unsavoury as it is below, there is cheerfulness, and comfort, and hard, honest work above.

Five flights up are the ateliers of architects and painters, and the hiding-places of middle-aged students like myself who want to live alone. When I first came here to live I was young, and not alone.

I had to walk a while before any conveyance appeared, but at last, when I had almost reached the Arc de Triomphe again, an empty cab came along and I took it.

From the *Arc* to the Rue de Rennes is a drive of more than half an hour, especially when one is conveyed by a tired cab horse that has been at the mercy of Sunday fete-makers.

There had been time before I passed under the Dragon's wings to meet my enemy over and over again, but I never saw him once, and now refuge was close at hand.

Before the wide gateway a small mob of children were playing. Our concierge and his wife walked among them, with their black poodle, keeping order; some couples were waltzing on the side-walk. I returned their greetings and hurried in.

All the inhabitants of the court had trooped out into the street. The place was quite deserted, lighted by a few lanterns hung high up, in which the gas burned dimly.

My apartment was at the top of a house, halfway down the court, reached by a staircase that descended almost into the street, with only a bit of passage-way intervening, I set my foot on the threshold of the open door, the friendly old ruinous stairs rose before me, leading up to rest and shelter. Looking back over my right shoulder, I saw *him,* ten paces off. He must have entered the court with me.

He was coming straight on, neither slowly, nor swiftly, but straight on to me. And now he was looking at me. For the first time since our eyes encountered across the church they met now again, and I knew that the time had come.

Retreating backward, down the court, I faced him. I meant to escape by the entrance on the Rue du Dragon. His eyes told me that I never should escape.

It seemed ages while we were going, I retreating, he advancing, down the court in perfect silence; but at last I felt the shadow of the archway, and the next step brought me within it. I had meant to turn here and spring through into the street. But the shadow was not that of an archway; it was that of a vault. The great doors on the Rue du Dragon were closed. I felt this by the blackness which surrounded me, and at the same instant I read it in his face. How his face gleamed in the darkness, drawing swiftly nearer! The deep vaults, the huge closed doors, their cold iron clamps were all on his side. The thing which he had threatened had arrived: it gathered and bore down on me from the fathomless shadows; the point from which it would strike was his infernal eyes. Hopeless, I set my back against the barred doors and defied him.

There was a scraping of chairs on the stone floor, and a rustling as the congregation rose. I could hear the Suisse's staff in the south aisle, preceding Monseigneur C—— to the sacristy.

The kneeling nuns, roused from their devout abstraction,

made their reverence and went away. The fashionable lady, my neighbour, rose also, with graceful reserve. As she departed her glance just flitted over my face in disapproval.

Half dead, or so it seemed to me, yet intensely alive to every trifle, I sat among the leisurely moving crowd, then rose too and went toward the door.

I had slept through the sermon. Had I slept through the sermon? I looked up and saw him passing along the gallery to his place. Only his side I saw; the thin bent arm in its black covering looked like one of those devilish, nameless instruments which lie in the disused torture-chambers of mediaeval castles.

But I had escaped him, though his eyes had said I should not. *Had* I escaped him? That which gave him the power over me came back out of oblivion, where I had hoped to keep it. For I knew him now. Death and the awful abode of lost souls, whither my weakness long ago had sent him—they had changed him for every other eye, but not for mine. I had recognized him almost from the first; I had never doubted what he was come to do; and now I knew while my body sat safe in the cheerful little church, he had been hunting my soul in the Court of the Dragon.

I crept to the door: the organ broke out overhead with a blare. A dazzling light filled the church, blotting the altar from my eyes. The people faded away, the arches, the vaulted roof vanished. I raised my seared eyes to the fathomless glare, and I saw the black stars hanging in the heavens: and the wet winds from the lake of Hali chilled my face.

And now, far away, over leagues of tossing cloud-waves, I saw the moon dripping with spray; and beyond, the towers of Carcosa rose behind the moon.

Death and the awful abode of lost souls, whither my weakness long ago had sent him, had changed him for every other eye but mine. And now I heard *his voice*, rising, swelling, thundering through the flaring light, and as I fell, the radiance increasing, increasing, poured over me in waves of flame. Then I sank into the depths, and I heard the King in Yellow whispering to my soul:

It is a fearful thing to fall into the hands of the living God!

Passeur

(A Story from Mystery of Choice.)

O friends, I've served ye food and bed;
O Friends, the mist is rising wet;
Then bide a moment, O my dead,
Where, lonely, I must linger yet!...

Because man goeth to his long home,
And the mourners go about the streets.

When he had finished his pipe he tapped the brier bowl
against the chimney until the ashes powdered the charred log
smouldering across the andirons. Then he sank back in his chair,
absently touching the hot pipe-bowl with the tip of each finger
until it grew cool enough to be dropped into his coat pocket.

Twice he raised his eyes to the little American clock ticking
upon the mantel. He had half an hour to wait.

The three candles that lighted the room might be trimmed to
advantage; this would give him something to do. A pair scissors
lay open upon the bureau, and he rose and picked them up. For
a while he stood dreamily shutting and opening the scissors, his
eyes roaming about the room. There was an easel in the corner,
and a pile of dusty canvases behind it; behind the canvases there
was a shadow—that gray, menacing shadow that never moved.

When he had trimmed each candle he wiped the smoky
scissors on a paint rag and flung them on the bureau again. The
clock pointed to ten; he had been occupied exactly three minutes.

The bureau was littered with neckties, pipes, combs and

brushes, matches, reels and fly-books, collars, shirt studs, a new pair of Scotch shooting stockings, and a woman's workbasket.

He picked out all the neckties, folded them once, and hung them over a bit of twine that stretched across the looking-glass; the shirt studs he shovelled into the top drawer along with brushes, combs, and stockings; the reels and fly-books he dusted with his handkerchief and placed methodically along the mantel shelf. Twice he stretched out his hand toward the woman's workbasket, but his hand fell to his side again, and he turned away into the room staring at the dying fire.

Outside the snow-sealed window a shutter broke loose and banged monotonously, until he flung open the panes and fastened it. The soft, wet snow, that had choked the window-panes all day, was frozen hard now, and he had to break the polished crust before he could find the rusty shutter hinge.

He leaned out for a moment, his numbed hands resting on the snow, the roar of a rising snow-squall in his ears; and out across the desolate garden and stark hedgerow he saw the flat black river spreading through the gloom.

A candle sputtered and snapped behind him; a sheet of drawing-paper fluttered across the floor, and he closed the panes and turned back into the room, both hands in his worn pockets.

The little American clock on the mantel ticked and ticked, but the hands lagged, for he had not been occupied five minutes in all. He went up to the mantel and watched the hands of the clock. A minute—longer than a year to him—crept by.

Around the room the furniture stood ranged—a chair or two of yellow pine, a table, the easel, and in one corner the broad curtained bed; and behind each lay shadows, menacing shadows that never moved.

A little pale flame started up from the smoking log on the andirons; the room sang with the sudden hiss of escaping wood gases. After a little the back of the log caught fire; jets of blue flame flared up here and there with mellow sounds like the lighting of gas-burners in a row, and in a moment a thin sheet of yellow flame wrapped the whole charred log.

Then the shadows moved; not the shadows behind the furniture—they never moved—but other shadows, thin, gray, confusing, that came and spread their slim patterns all around him, and trembled and trembled.

He dared not step or tread upon them, they were too real; they meshed the floor around his feet, they ensnared his knees, they fell across his breast like ropes. Some night, in the silence of the moors, when wind and river were still, he feared these strands of shadow might tighten—creep higher around his throat and tighten. But even then he knew that those other shadows would never move, those gray shapes that knelt crouching in every corner.

When he looked up at the clock again ten minutes had straggled past. Time was disturbed in the room; the strands of shadow seemed entangled among the hands of the clock, dragging them back from their rotation. He wondered if the shadows would strangle Time, some still night when the wind and the flat river were silent.

There grew a sudden chill across the floor; the cracks of the boards let it in. He leaned down and drew his *sabots* toward him from their place near the andirons, and slipped them over his *chaussons*; and as he straightened up, his eyes mechanically sought the mantel above, where in the dusk another pair of *sabots* stood, little, slender, delicate *sabots*, carved from red beach. A year's dust grayed their surface; a year's rust dulled the silver bank across the instep. He said this to himself aloud, knowing that it was within a few minutes of the year.

His own *sabots* came from Mort-Dieu; they were shaved square and banded with steel. But in days past he had thought that no *sabot* in Mort-Dieu was delicate enough to touch the instep of the Mort-Dieu *passeur*. So he sent to the shore lighthouse, and they sent to Lorient, where the women are coquettish and show their hair under the *coiffe*, and wear dainty *sabots*; and in this town, there vanity corrupts and there is much lace in coiffe and collarette, a pair of delicate *sabots* was found, banded with silver and chiselled in red beach. The *sabots* stood on the

215

mantel above the fire now, dusty and tarnished.

There was a sound from the window, the soft murmur of snow blotting glass panes. The wind, too, muttered under the roof eaves. Presently it would begin to whisper to him from the chimney—he knew it—and he held his hands over his ears and stared at the clock.

In the hamlet of Mort-Dieu the pines sing all day of the sea secrets, but in the night the ghosts of little gray birds fill the branches, singing of the sunshine of past years. He heard the song as he sat, and he rushed his hands over his ears; but the gray birds joined with the wind in the chimney, and he heard all that he dared not hear, and he thought all that he dared not hope or think, and the swift tears scalded his eyes.

In Mort-Dieu the nights are longer than anywhere on earth; he knew it—why should he not know? This had been so for a year; it was different before. There were so many things different before; days and nights vanished like minutes then; the pines told no secrets of the sea, and the gray birds had not yet come to Mort-Dieu. Also, thee Jeanne, *passeur* at the Carmes.

When he first saw her she was poling the square, flat-bottomed ferry skiff from the Carmes to Mort-Dieu, a red handkerchief bound across her silky black hair, a red skirt fluttering just below her knees. The next time he saw her he had to call to her across the placid river, "*Ohé! Ohé, passeur!*" She came, poling the flat skiff, her deep blue eyes fixed pensively on him, the scarlet skirt and kerchief idly flapping in the April wind. Then day followed day when the far call "*Passeur!*" grew clearer and more joyous, and the faint answering cry, "I come! rippled across the water like music tinged with laughter. Then spring came, and with spring came love—love, carried free across the ferry from the Carmes to Mort-Dieu.

The flame above the scarred log whistled, flickered, and went out in a jet of wood vapour, only to play like lightning above the gas and relight again. The clock ticked more loudly, and the song from the pines filled the room. But in his straining eyes a summer landscape was reflected, where white clouds sailed and white foam curled under the square bow of a little skiff. And he pressed his numbed hands tighter to his ears to drown the cry, "*Passeur! Passeur!*"

And now for a moment the clock ceased ticking. It was time to go—who but he should know it, he who went out into the night swinging his lantern? And he went. He had gone each night from the first—from that first strange winter evening when a strange voice had answered him across the river, the voice of the new *passeur*. He had never heard *her* voice again.

So he passed down the windy wooden stairs, lantern hanging lighted in his hand, and stepped out into the storm. Through sheets of drifting snow, over heaps of frozen seaweed and icy drift he moved, shifting the lantern right and left, until its glimmer on the water warned him. Then he called out into the night, "*Passeur!*" The frozen spray spattered his face and crusted the lantern; he heard the distant boom of breakers beyond the bar, and the noise of mighty winds among the seaward cliffs.

"*Passeur!*"

Across the broad flat river, black as a sea of pitch, a tiny light sparkled a moment. Again he cried, "*Passeur!*"

"I come!"

He turned ghastly white, for it was her voice—or was he crazy?—and he sprang waist deep into the icy current and cried out again, but his voice ended in a sob.

Slowly through the snow the flat skiff took shape, creeping nearer and nearer. But she was not at the pole—he saw that; there was only a tall, thin man, shrouded to the eyes in oilskins; and he leaped into the boat and bade the ferryman hasten.

Halfway across he rose in the skiff, and called, "Jeanne!" But the roar of the storm and the thrashing of icy waves drowned his voice. Yet he heard her again, and she called to him by name.

When at last the boat grated upon the invisible shore, he lifted his lantern, trembling, stumbling among the rocks, and calling to her as though his voice could silence the voice that had spoken a year ago that night. And it could not. He sank shivering upon his knees, and looked out into the darkness, where an ocean rolled across the world. Then his stiff lips moved, and he repeated her name; but the hand of the ferryman fell gently upon his head.

And when he raised his eyes he saw that the ferryman was Death.

The Key to Grief

The wild hawk to the wind-swept sky
The deer to the wholesome wold,
And the heart of a man to the heart of a maid,
As it was in the days of old.

—Kipling

1

They were doing their work very badly. They got the rope around his neck, and tied his wrists with moose-bush withes, but again he fell, sprawling, turning, twisting over the leaves, tearing up everything around him like a trapped panther.

He got the rope away from them; he clung to it with bleeding fists; he set his white teeth in it, until the jute strands relaxed, unravelled, and snapped, gnawed through by his white teeth.

Twice Tully struck him with a gum hook. The dull blows fell on flesh rigid as stone.

Panting, foul with forest mould and rotten leaves, hands and face smeared with blood, he sat up on the ground, glaring at the circle of men around him.

"Shoot him!" gasped Tully, dashing the sweat from his bronzed brow; and Bates, breathing heavily, sat down on a log and dragged a revolver from his rear pocket. The man on the ground watched him; there was froth in the corners of his mouth.

"Git back!" whispered Bates, but his voice and hand trembled. "Kent," he stammered, "won't ye hang?"

The man on the ground glared.

"Y'eve got to die, Kent," he urged; "they all say so. Ask Lefty

Sawyer; ask Dyce; ask Carrots. He's got to swing fur it—ain't he, Tully?—Kent, fur God's sake, swing fur these here gents!"

The man on the ground panted; his bright eyes never moved.

After a moment Tully sprang on him again. There was a flurry of leaves, a crackle, a gasp and a grunt, then the thumping and thrashing of two bodies writhing in the brush. Dyce and Carrots jumped on the prostrate men. Lefty Sawyer caught the rope again, but the jute strands gave way and he stumbled. Tully began to scream "He's chokin' me !" Dyce staggered out into the open, moaning over a broken wrist.

"Shoot!" shouted Lefty Sawyer, and dragged Tully aside. "Shoot Jim Bates! Shoot straight, b'God!"

"Git back!" gasped Bates, rising from the fallen log.

The crowd parted right and left; a quick report rang out—another—another. Then from the whirl of smoke a tall form staggered, dealing blows-blows that sounded sharp as the crack of a whip.

"He's off! Shoot straight!" they cried.

There was a gallop of heavy boots in the woods. Bates, faint and dazed, turned his head.

"Shoot!" shrieked Tully.

But Bates was sick; his smoking revolver fell to the ground; his white face and pale eyes contracted. It lasted only a moment; he started after the others, plunging, wallowing through thickets of osier and hemlock underbrush.

Far ahead he heard Kent crashing on like a young moose in November, and he knew he was making for the shore. The others knew too. Already the gray gleam of the sea cut a straight line along the forest edge; already the soft clash of the surf on the rocks broke faintly through the forest silence.

"He's got a canoe there!" bawled Tully. "He'll be into it!"

And he was into it, kneeling in the bow, driving his paddle to the handle. The rising sun gleamed like red lightning on the flashing blade; the canoe shot to the crest of a wave, hung, bows dripping in the wind, dropped into the depths, glided, tipped, rolled, shot up again, staggered, and plunged on.

Tully ran straight out into the cove surf; the water broke against his chest, bare and wet with sweat. Bates sat down on a worn black rock and watched the canoe listlessly.

The canoe dwindled to a speck of gray and silver; and when Carrots, who had run back to the gum camp for a rifle, returned, the speck on the water might have been easier to hit than a loon's head at twilight. So Carrots, being thrifty by nature, fired once, and was satisfied to save the other cartridges. The canoe was still visible, making for the open sea. Somewhere beyond the horizon lay the keys, a string of rocks bare as skulls, black and slimy where the sea cut their base, white on the crests with the excrement of sea birds.

"He's makin' fur the Key to Grief!" whispered Bates to Dyce.

Dyce, moaning, and nursing his broken wrist, turned a sick face out to sea.

The last rock seaward was the Key to Grief, a splintered pinnacle polished by the sea. From the Key to Grief, seaward a day's paddle, if a man dared, lay the long wooded island in the ocean known as Grief on the charts of the bleak coast.

In the history of the coast, two men had made the voyage to the Key to Grief, and from there to the island. One of these was a rum-crazed pelt hunter, who lived to come back; the other was a college youth; they found his battered canoe at sea, and a day later his battered body was flung up in the cove.

So, when Bates whispered to Dyce, and when Dyce called to the others, they knew that the end was not far off for Kent and his canoe; and they turned away into the forest, sullen, but satisfied that Kent would get his dues when the devil got his.

Lefty spoke vaguely of the wages of sin. Carrots, with an eye to thrift, suggested a plan for an equitable division of Kent's property.

When they reached the gum camp they piled Kent's personal effects on a blanket.

Carrots took the inventory: a revolver, two gum hooks, a fur cap, a nickel-plated watch, a pipe, a pack of new cards, a gum sack, forty pounds of spruce gum, and a frying pan.

Carrots shuffled the cards, picked out the joker, and flipped it pensively into the fire. Then he dealt cold decks all around.

When the goods and chattels of their late companion had been divided by chance for there was no chance to cheat-somebody remembered Tully.

"He's down there on the coast, starin' after the canoe," said Bates huskily.

He rose and walked toward a heap on the ground covered by a blanket. He started to lift the blanket, hesitated, and finally turned away. Under the blanket lay Tully's brother, shot the night before by Kent.

"Guess we'd better wait till Tully comes," said Carrots uneasily. Bates and Kent had been campmates. An hour later Tully walked into camp.

He spoke to no one that day. In the morning Bates found him down on the coast digging, and said: "Hello, Tully! Guess we ain't much hell on lynchin'!"

"Naw," said Tully. "Git a spade."

"Goin' to plant him there?"

"Yep."

"Where he kin hear them waves?"

"Yep."

"Purty spot."

"Yep."

"Which way will he face?"

"Where he kin watch fur that damned canoe!" cried Tully fiercely.

"He-he can't see," ventured Bates uneasily. "He's dead, ain't he?"

"He'll heave up that there sand when the canoe comes back! An' it's a-comin'! An' Bud Kent'll be in it, dead or alive! Git a spade!"

The pale light of superstition flickered in Bate's eyes. He hesitated.

"The-the dead can't see," he began; "kin they?"

Tully turned a distorted face toward him.

"Yer lie!" he roared. "My brother kin see, dead or livin'! An' he'll see the hangin' of Bud Kent! An' he'll git up outer the grave fur to see it, Bill Bates! I'm tellin' ye! I'm tellin' ye! Deep as I'll plant him, he'll heave that there sand and call to me, when the canoe comes in! I'll hear him; I'll be here! An' we'll live to see the hangin' of Bud Kent!"

About sundown they planted Tully's brother, face to the sea.

2.

On the Key to Grief the green waves rub all day. White at the summit, black at the base, the shafted rocks rear splintered pinnacles, slanting like channel buoys. On the polished pillars sea birds brood—white-winged, bright-eyed sea birds, that nestle and preen and flap and clatter their orange-coloured beaks when the sifted spray drives and drifts across the reef.

As the sun rose, painting crimson streaks criss-cross over the waters, the sea birds sidled together, huddling row on row, steeped in downy drowse.

Where the sun of noon burnished the sea, an opal wave washed, listless, noiseless; a sea bird stretched one listless wing.

And into the silence of the waters a canoe glided, bronzed by the sunlight, jewelled by the salt drops stringing from prow to thwart, seaweed a-trail in the diamond-flashing wake, and in the bow a man dripping with sweat.

Up rose the gulls, sweeping in circles, turning, turning over rock and sea, and their clamour filled the sky, starting little rippling echoes among the rocks.

The canoe grated on a shelf of ebony; the seaweed rocked and washed; the little sea crabs sheered sideways, down, down into limpid depths of greenest shadows. Such was the coming of Bud Kent to the Key to Grief.

He drew the canoe halfway up the shelf of rock and sat down, breathing heavily, one brown arm across the bow. For an hour he sat there. The sweat dried under his eyes. The sea birds came back, filling the air with soft querulous notes.

There was a livid mark around his neck, a red, raw circle. The salt wind stung it; the sun burned it into his flesh like a collar of redhot steel. He touched it at times; once he washed it with cold salt water.

Far in the north a curtain of mist hung on the sea, dense, motionless as the fog on the Grand Banks. He never moved his eyes from it; he knew what it was. Behind it lay the Island of Grief.

All the year round the Island of Grief is hidden by the banks of mist, ramparts of dead white fog encircling it on every side. Ships give it wide berth. Some speak of warm springs on the island whose waters flow far out to sea, rising in steam eternally.

The pelt hunter had come back with tales of forests and deer and flowers everywhere; but he had been drinking much, and much was forgiven him.

The body of the college youth tossed up in the cove on the mainland was battered out of recognition, but some said, when found, one hand clutched a crimson blossom half wilted, but broad as a sap pan.

So Kent lay motionless beside his canoe, burned with thirst, every nerve vibrating, thinking of all these things. It was not fear that whitened the firm flesh under the tan; it was the fear of fear. He must not think-he must throttle dread; his eyes must never falter, his head never turn from that wall of mist across the sea. With set teeth he crushed back terror; with glittering eyes he looked into the hollow eyes of fright. And so he conquered fear.

He rose. The sea birds whirled up into the sky, pitching, tossing, screaming, till the sharp flapping of their pinions set the snapping echoes flying among the rocks.

Under the canoe's sharp prow the kelp bobbed and dipped and parted; the sunlit waves ran out ahead, glittering, dancing. Splash! splash! bow and stern! And now he knelt again, and the polished paddle swung and dipped, and swept and swung and dipped again.

Far behind, the clamour of the sea birds lingered in his ears, till the mellow dip of the paddle drowned all sound and the sea was a sea of silence.

No wind came to cool the hot sweat on cheek and breast. The sun blazed a path of flame before him, and he followed out into the waste of waters. The still ocean divided under the bows and rippled innocently away on either side, tinkling, foaming, sparkling like the current in a woodland brook. He looked around at the world of flattened water, and the fear of fear rose up and gripped his throat again. Then he lowered his head, like a tortured bull, and shook the fear of fear from his throat, and drove the paddle into the sea as a butcher stabs, to the hilt.

So at last he came to the wall of mist. It was thin at first, thin and cool, but it thickened and grew warmer, and the fear of fear dragged at his head, but he would not look behind.

Into the fog the canoe shot; the gray water ran by, high as the gunwales, oily, silent. Shapes flickered across the bows, pillars mist that rode the waters, robed in films of tattered shadows. Gigantic forms towered to dizzy heights above him, shaking out shredded shrouds of cloud. The vast draperies of the fog swayed and hung at trembled as he brushed them; the white twilight deepened to sombre gloom. And now it grew thinner; the fog became a mist, at the mist a haze, and the haze floated away and vanished into the blue of the heavens.

All around lay a sea of pearl and sapphire, lapping, lapping on silver shoal.

So he came to the Island of Grief.

3

On the silver shoal the waves washed and washed, breaking like crushed opals where the sands sang with the humming froth.

Troops of little shore birds, wading on the shoal, tossed their sun tipped wings and scuttled inland, where, dappled with shadow from the fringing forest, the white beach of the island stretched.

The water all around was shallow, limpid as crystal, and he

saw the ribbed sand shining on the bottom, where purple sea-weed floats and delicate sea creatures darted and swarmed and scattered again at the dip of his paddle.

Like velvet rubbed on velvet the canoe brushed across the sun He staggered to his feet, stumbled out, dragged the canoe high under the trees, turned it bottom upward, and sank beside it, face downward in the sand. Sleep came to drive away the fear of fear but hunger, thirst, and fever fought with sleep, and he dreamed of a rope that sawed his neck, of the fight in the woods, a the shots. He dreamed, too, of the camp, of his forty pounds spruce gum, of Tully, and of Bates. He dreamed of the fire and the smoke-scorched kettle, of the foul odour of musty bedding, of the greasy cards, and of his own new pack, hoarded for weeks to please the others. All this he dreamed, lying there face down-ward in the sand; but he did not dream of the face of the dead.

The shadows of the leaves moved on his blond head, crisp with clipped curls. A butterfly flitted around him, alighting now on his legs, now on the back of his bronzed hands. All the af-ternoon the bees hung droning among the wildwood blossoms; the leaves above scarcely rustled; the shore birds brooded along the water's edge; the thin tide, sleeping on the sand, mirrored the sky.

Twilight paled the zenith; a breeze moved in the deeper woods; a star glimmered, went out, glimmered again, faded, and glimmered.

Night came. A moth darted to and fro under the trees; a bee-tle hummed around a heap of seaweed and fell scrambling in the sand. Somewhere among the trees a sound had become distinct, the song of a little brook, melodious, interminable. He heard it in his dream it threaded all his dreams like a needle of silver, and like a needle it pricked him pricked his dry throat and cracked lips. It could not awake him; the cool night swathed him head and foot.

Toward dawn a bird woke up and piped. Other birds stirred, restless, half awakened; a gull spread a cramped wing on the shore, preened its feathers, scratched its tufted neck, and took two drowsy steps toward the sea.

The sea breeze stirred out behind the mist bank; it raised the feathers on the sleeping gulls; it set the leaves whispering. A twig snapped, broke off and fell. Kent stirred, sighed, trembled, and awoke.

The first thing he heard was the song of the brook, and he stumbled straight into the woods. There it lay, a thin, deep stream in the gray morning light, and he stretched himself beside it and laid his cheek in it. A bird drank in the pool, too—a little fluffy bird, bright-eyed and fearless.

His knees were firmer when at last he rose, heedless of the drops that beaded lips and chin. With his knife he dug and scraped at some white roots that hung half meshed in the bank of the brook, and when he had cleaned them in the pool he ate them.

The sun stained the sky when he went down to the canoe, but the eternal curtain of fog, far out at sea, hid it as yet from sight.

He lifted the canoe, bottom upwards, to his head, and, paddle and pole in either hand, carried it into the forest.

After he had set it down he stood a moment, opening and shutting his knife. Then he looked up into the trees. There were birds there, if he could get at them. He looked at the brook. There were prints of his fingers in the sand; there, too, was the print of something else—a deer's pointed hoof.

He had nothing but his knife. He opened it again and looked at it.

That day he dug for clams and ate them raw. He waded out into the shallows, too, and jabbed at fish with his setting pole, but hit nothing except a yellow crab.

Fire was what he wanted. He hacked and chipped at flinty-looking pebbles, and scraped tinder from a stick of sun-dried driftwood. His knuckles bled, but no fire came.

That night he heard deer in the woods, and could not sleep for thinking, until the dawn came up behind the wall of mist, and he rose with it to drink his fill at the brook and tear raw clams with his white teeth. Again he fought for fire, craving it as he had never craved water, but his knuckles bled, and the knife scraped on the flint in vain.

His mind, perhaps, had suffered somewhat. The white beach seemed to rise and fall like a white carpet on a gusty hearth. The birds, too, that ran along the sand, seemed big and juicy, like partridges; and he chased them, hurling shells and bits of drift-wood at them till he could scarcely keep his feet for the rising, plunging beach or carpet, whichever it was. That night the deer aroused him at intervals. He heard them splashing and grunting and crackling along the brook. Once he arose and stole after them, knife in hand, till a false step into the brook awoke him to his folly, and he felt his way back to the canoe, trembling.

Morning came, and again he drank at the brook, lying on the sand where countless heart-shaped hoofs had passed leaving clean imprints; and again he ripped the raw clams from their shells and swallowed them, whimpering.

All day long the white beach rose and fell and heaved and flattened under his bright dry eyes. He chased the shore birds at times, till the unsteady beach tripped him up and he fell full length in the sand. Then he would rise moaning, and creep into the shadow of the wood, and watch the little song-birds in the branches, moaning, always moaning.

His hands, sticky with blood, hacked steel and flint together, but so feebly that now even the cold sparks no longer came.

He began to fear the advancing night; he dreaded to hear the big warm deer among the thickets. Fear clutched him suddenly, and he lowered his head and set his teeth and shook fear from his throat again.

Then he started aimlessly into the woods, crowding past bushes, scraping trees, treading on moss and twig and mouldy stump, his bruised hands swinging, always swinging.

The sun set in the mist as he came out of the woods on to another beach—a warm, soft beach, crimsoned by the glow in the evening clouds.

And on the sand at his feet lay a young girl asleep, swathed in the silken garment of her own black hair, round limbed, brown, smooth as the bloom on the tawny beach.

A gull flapped overhead, screaming. Her eyes, deeper than night, unclosed. Then her lips parted in a cry, soft with sleep, "*Ihó!*"

She rose, rubbing her velvet eyes. "*Ihó!*" she cried in wonder; "*Inâh!*"

The gilded sand settled around her little feet. Her cheeks crimsoned. "*E-hó! E-hó!*" she whispered, and hid her face in her hair.

<h1 style="text-align:center">4</h1>

The bridge of the stars spans the sky seas; the sun and the moon are the travellers who pass over it. This was also known in the lodges of the Isantee, hundreds of years ago. Chaské told it to Harpam, and when Harpam knew he told it to Hapeda; and so the knowledge spread to Harka, and from Winona to Wehârka, up and down, across and ever across, woof and web, until it came to the Island of Grief. And how? God knows!

Wehârka, prattling in the tules, may have told Ne-kâ; and Ne-kâ, high in the November clouds, may have told Kay-óshk, who told it to Shinge-bis, who told it to Skeé-skah, who told it to Sé-só-Kah.

Ihó! Inâh! Behold the wonder of it! And this is the fate of all knowledge that comes to the Island of Grief.

As the red glow died in the sky, and the sand swam in shadows, the girl parted the silken curtains of her hair and looked at him.

"*Ehó!*" she whispered again in soft delight.

For now it was plain to her that he was the sun! He had crossed the bridge of stars in the blue twilight; he had come!

"*E-tó!*"

She stepped nearer, shivering, faint with the ecstasy of this holy miracle wrought before her.

He was the Sun! His blood streaked the sky at dawn; his blood stained the clouds at even. In his eyes the blue of the sky still lingered, smothering two blue stars; and his body was as white as the breast of the Moon.

She opened both arms, hands timidly stretched, palm upward. Her face was raised to his, her eyes slowly closed; the deep-fringed lids trembled.

Like a young priestess she stood, motionless save for the sudden quiver of a limb, a quick pulse-flutter in the rounded throat. And so she worshipped, naked and unashamed, even after he, reeling, fell heavily forward on his face; even when the evening breeze stealing over the sands stirred the hair on his head, as winds stir the fur of a dead animal in the dust.

When the morning sun peered over the wall of mist, and she saw it was the sun, and she saw him, flung on the sand at her feet, then she knew that he was a man, only a man, pallid as death and smeared with blood.

And yet—miracle of miracles—the divine wonder in her eyes deepened, and her body seemed to swoon, and fall a-trembling, and swoon again.

For, although it was but a man who lay at her feet, it had been easier for her to look upon a god.

He dreamed that he breathed fire—fire, that he craved as he had never craved water. Mad with delirium, he knelt before the flames. rubbing his torn hands, washing them in the crimson-scented flames. He had water, too, cool scented water, that sprayed his burning flesh, that washed in his eyes, his hair, his throat. After that came hunger, a fierce rending agony, that scorched and clutched and tore at his entrails; but that, too, died away, and he dreamed that he had eaten and all his flesh was warm. Then he dreamed that he slept and when he slept he dreamed no more.

One day he awoke and found her stretched beside him, soft palm tightly closed, smiling, asleep.

5

Now the days began to run more swiftly than the tide along the tawny beach; and the nights, star-dusted and blue, came and vanished and returned, only to exhale at dawn like perfume from a violet.

They counted hours as they counted the golden bubbles, winking with a million eyes along the foam-flecked shore; and the hours ended: and began, and glimmered, iridescent, and ended as bubbles end in a tiny rainbow haze.

There was still fire in the world; it flashed up at her touch and where she chose. A bow strung with the silk of her own hair, an arrow winged like a sea bird and tipped with shell, a line from the silver tendon of a deer, a hook of polished bone—these were the mysteries he learned, and learned them laughing, her silken head bent close to his.

The first night that the bow was wrought and the glossy string attuned, she stole into the moonlit forest to the brook; and there they stood, whispering, listening, and whispering, though neither understood the voice they loved.

In the deeper woods, Kaug, the porcupine, scraped and snuffed. They heard Wabóse, the rabbit, pit-a-pat, pit-a-pat, loping across dead leaves in the moonlight. Skeé-skah, the wood-duck, sailed past, noiseless, gorgeous as a floating blossom.

Out on the ocean's placid silver, Shinge-bis, the diver, shook the scented silence with his idle laughter, till Kay-óshk, the gray gull, stirred in his slumber. There came a sudden ripple in the stream, a mellow splash, a soft sound on the sand.

"*Ihó!* Behold!"

"I see nothing."

The beloved voice was only a wordless melody to her.

"*Ihó!* Ta-hinca, the red deer! *E-hó!* The buck will follow!"

"Ta-hinca," he repeated, notching the arrow.

"*E-tó!* Ta-mdóka!"

So he drew the arrow to the head, and the gray gull feathers brushed his ear, and the darkness hummed with the harmony of the singing string.

Thus died Ta-mdóka, the buck deer of seven prongs.

As an apple tossed spinning into the air, so spun the world above the hand that tossed it into space.

And one day in early spring, Sé-só-Kah, the robin, awoke at dawn, and saw a girl at the foot of the blossoming tree holding a babe cradled in the silken sheets of her hair.

At its feeble cry, Kaug, the porcupine, raised his quilled head. Wabosé, the rabbit, sat still with palpitating sides. Kay-óshk, the gray gull, tiptoed along the beach.

Kent knelt with one bronzed arm around them both.

"*Ihó! Inâh!*" whispered the girl, and held the babe up in the rosy flames of dawn.

But Kent trembled as he looked, and his eyes filled. On the pale green moss their shadows lay-three shadows. But the shadow of the babe was white as froth.

Because it was the firstborn son, they named it Chaské; and the girl sang as she cradled it there in the silken vestments of her hair; all day long in the sunshine she sang:

Wâ-wa, wâ-wa, wâ-we--yeá;
Kah-wéen, nee-zheéka Ke-diaus-âi,
Ka-gâh nau-wâi, ne-mé-go S'weén,
Ne-bâun, ne-bâun, ne-dâun-is âis.
E-we wâ-wa, wâ-we-yeá;
E-we wâ-wa, wâ-we-yeá.

Out in the calm ocean, Shinge-bis, the diver, listened, preening his satin breast in silence. In the forest, Ta-hinca, the red deer, turned her delicate head to the wind.

That night Kent thought of the dead, for the first time since he had come to the Key of Grief.

"*Aké-u! aké-u!*" chirped Sé-só-Kah, the robin. But the dead never come again.

"Beloved, sit close to us," whispered the girl, watching his troubled eyes. *Ma-cânte maséca.*"

But he looked at the babe and its white shadow on the moss, and he only sighed: "*Ma-cânte maséca*, beloved! Death sits watching us across the sea."

Now for the first time he knew more than the fear of fear; he knew fear. And with fear came grief.

He never before knew that grief lay hidden there in the forest. Now he knew it. Still, that happiness, eternally reborn when two small hands reached up around his neck, when feeble fingers clutched his hand—that happiness that Sé-só-Kah understood, chirping to his brooding mate—that Ta-mdóka knew, licking his dappled fawns—that happiness gave him heart to meet grief calmly, in dreams or in the forest depths, and it helped him to look into the hollow eyes of fear.

He often thought of the camp now; of Bates, his blanket mate; of Dyce, whose wrist he had broken with a blow; of Tully, whose brother he had shot. He even seemed to hear the shot, the sudden report among the hemlocks; again he saw the haze of smoke, he caught a glimpse of a tall form falling through the bushes.

He remembered every minute incident of the trial: Bates's hand laid on his shoulder; Tully, red-bearded and wild-eyed, demanding his death; while Dyce spat and spat and smoked and kicked at the blackened log-ends projecting from the fire. He remembered, too, the verdict, and Tully's terrible laugh; and the new jute rope that they stripped off the market-sealed gum packs.

He thought of these things, sometimes wading out on the shoals, shell-tipped fish spear poised: at such times he would miss his fish. He thought of it sometimes when he knelt by the forest stream listening for Ta-hinca's splash among the cresses: at such moments the feathered shaft whistled far from the mark, and Tamdóka stamped and snorted till even the white fisher, stretched on a rotting log, flattened his whiskers and stole away into the forest's blackest depths.

When the child was a year old, hour for hour notched at sunset and sunrise, it prattled with the birds, and called to Ne-Kâ, the wild goose, who called again to the child from the sky: "Northward! northward, beloved!"

When winter came—there is no frost on the Island of Grief—Ne-Kâ, the wild goose, passing high in the clouds, called: "Southward! southward, beloved!" And the child answered in a soft whisper of an unknown tongue, till the mother shivered, and covered it with her silken hair.

"O beloved!" said the girl, "Chaské calls to all things living-to Kaug, the porcupine, to Wabóse, to Kay-óshk, the gray gull-he calls, and they understand."

Kent bent and looked into her eyes.

"Hush, beloved; it is not *that* I fear."

"Then what, beloved?"

"His shadow. It is white as surf foam. And at night—I—I have seen—"

"Oh, what?"

"The air about him aglow like a pale rose."

"*Ma cânté maséca.* The earth alone lasts. I speak as one dying—I know, O beloved!"

Her voice died away like a summer wind.

"Beloved!" he cried.

But there before him she was changing; the air grew misty, and her hair wavered like shreds of fog, and her slender form swayed, and faded, and swerved, like the mist above a pond.

In her arms the babe was a figure of mist, rosy, vague as a breath on a mirror.

"The earth alone lasts. *Inâh!* It is the end, O beloved!"

The words came from the mist—a mist as formless as the ether—a mist that drove in and crowded him, that came from the sea, from the clouds, from the earth at his feet. Faint with terror, he staggered forward calling, "Beloved! And thou, Chaské, O beloved! *Aké u! Aké u!*"

Far out at sea a rosy star glimmered an instant in the mist and went out.

A sea bird screamed, soaring over the waste of fog—smothered waters. Again he saw the rosy star; it came nearer; its reflection glimmered in the water.

"Chaské!" he cried.

234

He heard a voice, dull in the choking mist.

"O beloved, I am here!" he called again.

There was a sound on the shoal, a flicker in the fog, the flare of a torch, a face white, livid, terrible—the face of the dead.

He fell upon his knees; he closed his eyes and opened them. Tully stood beside him with a coil of rope.

★ ★ ★ ★ ★

Ihó! Behold the end! The earth alone lasts. The sand, the opal wave on the golden beach, the sea of sapphire, the dusted starlight, the wind, and love, shall die. Death also shall die, and lie on the shores of the skies like the bleached skull there on the Key to Grief, polished, empty, with its teeth embedded in the sand.

The Man at the Next Table

(Adapted from excerpts chapters 22 to 25 in the novel In Search of the Unknown.)

The caricaturist is a freebooter. Public tolerance grants him letters of marque. . . .

Marmaduke Humphrey.

Ainsi rien ne se passe, rien de vraiment immortel et d'éternellement doux que dans notre âme.

1

It was high noon in the city of Antwerp. From slender steeples floated the mellow music of the Flemish bells, and in the spire of the great cathedral across the square the cracked chimes clashed discords until my ears ached.

When the fiend in the cathedral had jerked the last tuneless clang from the chimes, I removed my fingers from my ears and sat down at one of the iron tables in the court. A waiter with his face shaved blue, brought me a bottle of Rhine wine, a tumbler of cracked ice, and a siphon.

"Does *Monsieur* desire anything else?" he inquired.

"Yes—the head of the cathedral bell-ringer; bring it with vinegar and potatoes," I said, bitterly. Then I began to ponder on my great-aunt and the Crimson Diamond.

The white walls of the Hotel St. Antoine rose in a rectangle around the sunny court, casting long shadows across the basin of the fountain. The strip of blue overhead was cloudless. Sparrows twittered under the eaves; the yellow awnings fluttered, the flowers swayed in the summer breeze, and the jet of the fountain

236

splashed among the water plants. On the sunny side of the *piazza* the tables were vacant; on the shady side, I was lazily aware that the tables behind me were occupied, but I was indifferent as to their occupants, partly because I shunned all tourists, partly because I was thinking of my great-aunt.

Most old ladies are eccentric, but there is a limit, and my great-aunt had overstepped it. I had believed her to be wealthy; she died bankrupt. Still, I knew there was one thing she did possess, and that was the famous "Crimson Diamond." Now, of course, you know who my great-aunt was.

Excepting the Koh-i-noor, and the Regent, this enormous and unique stone was, as everybody knows, the most valuable gem in existence. Any ordinary person would have placed that diamond in a safe-deposit. My great-aunt did nothing of the kind. She kept it in a small velvet bag, which she carried about her neck. She never took it off, but wore it dangling openly on her heavy silk gown.

In this same bag she also carried dried catnip leaves of which she was inordinately fond. Nobody but myself, her only living relative, knew that the Crimson Diamond lay among the sprigs of catnip in the little velvet bag.

"Harold," she would say, "do you think I m a fool? If I place the Crimson Diamond in any safe-deposit vault in New York, somebody would steal it sooner or later." Then she would nibble a sprig of catnip and peer cunningly at me. I loathed the odour of catnip and she knew it. I also loathed cats. This also she knew and of course surrounded herself with a dozen. Poor old lady! On the 1st day of March, 1896, she was found dead in her bed in her apartments at the Waldorf. The doctor said she died from natural causes. The only other occupant of her sleeping room was a cat. The cat fled when we broke open the door, and I heard that she was received and cherished by some people in a neighbouring apartment.

Now, although my great-aunt's death was due to purely natural causes, there was one very startling and disagreeable feature of the case. The velvet bag, containing the Crimson Diamond, had disappeared. Every inch of the apartment was searched, the floors torn up, the walls dismantled, but the Crimson Diamond had vanished. Chief of Police Conlin detailed four of his best men on the case, and as I had nothing better to do, I enrolled myself as a volunteer. I also offered $25,000 reward for the recovery of the gem. All New York was agog.

The case seemed hopeless enough, although there were five of us after the thief. McFarlane was in London, and had been for a month, but Scotland Yard could give him no help, and the last I heard of him he was roaming through Surrey after a man with a white spot in his hair. Harrison had gone to Paris. He kept writing me that clues were plenty and the scent hot, but as Dennet, in Berlin, and Clancy, in Vienna, wrote me the same thing, I began to doubt these gentle men s ability.

"You say," I answered Harrison, "that the fellow is a Frenchman, and that he is now concealed in Paris; but Dennet writes me by the same mail that the thief is undoubtedly a German, and was seen yesterday in Berlin. Today I received a letter from Clancy, assuring me that Vienna holds the culprit, and that he is an Austrian from Trieste. Now for Heaven's sake," I ended, "let me alone and stop writing me letters until you have something to write about."

The night clerk of the Waldorf had furnished us with our first clue. On the night of my aunt's death he had seen a tall, grave-faced man, hurriedly leave the hotel. As the man passed the desk, he removed his hat and mopped his forehead, and the night clerk noticed that in the middle of his head there was a patch of hair, as white as snow.

We worked this clue for all it was worth, and, a month later, I received a cable dispatch from Paris, saying that a man, answering to the description of the Waldorf suspect, had offered an enormous crimson diamond for sale to a jeweller in the Palais Royal. Unfortunately the fellow took fright and disappeared before the jeweller could send for the police, and since that time, McFarlane in London, Harrison in Paris, Dennet in Berlin, and Clancy in Vienna, had been chasing men with white patches on their hair until no gray-headed patriarch in Europe was free from suspicion. I myself had sleuthed it through England, France, Holland and Belgium, and now I found myself in Antwerp at the Hotel St. Antoine without a clue that promised anything except another outrage on some respectable white-haired citizen. The case seemed hopeless enough, unless the thief tried again to sell the gem.

Here was our only hope, for, unless he cut the stone into smaller ones, he had no more chance of selling it than he would have had if he had stolen the Venus of Milo and peddled her about the *rue de* Seine. Even were he to cut up the stone, no respectable gem collector or jeweller would buy a crimson diamond without first notifying me; for although a few red stones are known to collectors, the colour of the Crimson Diamond was absolutely unique, and there was little probability of an honest mistake.

Thinking of all these things I sat sipping my Rhine wine in the shadow of the yellow awnings. A large white cat came sauntering by and stopped in front of me to perform her toilet until I wished she would go away. After a while she sat up, licked her whiskers, yawned once or twice, and was about to stroll on, when, catching sight of me, she stopped short and looked me squarely in the face. I returned the attention with a scowl because I wished to discourage any advances towards social intercourse which she might contemplate; but after a while her steady gaze disconcerted me, and I turned to my Rhine wine. A few minutes later I looked up again. The cat was still eyeing me.

"Now what the devil is the matter with the animal," I muttered, "does she recognize in me a relative?"

"Perhaps," observed a man at the next table.

"What do you mean by that?" I demanded.

"What I say," replied the man at the next table.

I looked him full in the face. He was old and bald and appeared weak-minded. His age protected his impudence. I turned my back on him. Then my eyes fell on the cat again. She was still gazing earnestly at me.

Disgusted that she should take such pointed public notice of me, I wondered whether other people saw it; I wondered whether there was anything peculiar in my own personal appearance. How hard the creature stared. It was most embarrassing.

"What has got into that cat?" I thought.

"It's sheer impudence. It's an intrusion, and I won't stand it!" The cat did not move. I tried to stare her out of countenance. It was useless. There was aggressive inquiry in her yellow eyes. A sensation of uneasiness began to steal over me—a sensation of embarrassment not unmixed with awe. All cats looked alike to me, and yet there was something about this one that bothered me—something that I could not explain to myself, but which began to occupy me.

She looked familiar—this Antwerp cat. An odd sense of having seen her before—of having been well acquainted with her in former years slowly settled in my mind, and, although I could never remember the time when I had not detested cats, I was almost convinced that my relations with this Antwerp tabby had once been intimate if not cordial. I looked more closely at the animal.

Then an idea struck me,—an idea which persisted and took definite shape in spite of me. I strove to escape from it, to evade it, to stifle and smother it; an inward struggle ensued which brought the perspiration in beads upon my cheeks,—a struggle short, sharp, decisive. It was useless—useless to try to put it from me,—this idea so wretchedly bizarre, so grotesque and fantastic, so utterly inane,—it was useless to deny that the cat bore a distinct resemblance to my great-aunt!

I gazed at her in horror. What enormous eyes the creature had!

"Blood is thicker than water," said the man at the next table.

"What does he mean by that?" I muttered, angrily swallowing a tumbler of Rhine wine and seltzer. But I did not turn. What was the use?

"Chattering old imbecile," I added to myself, and struck a match, for my cigar was out; but as I raised the match to relight it, I encountered the cat's eyes again. I could not enjoy my cigar with the animal staring at me, but I was justly indignant, and I did not intend to be routed. "The idea! forced to leave for a cat!" I sneered, "we will see who will be the one to go!" I tried to give her a jet of seltzer from the siphon, but the bottle was too nearly empty to carry far. Then I attempted to lure her nearer, calling her in French, German, and English, but she did not stir. I did not know the Flemish for "cat."

"She's got a name, and won't come," I thought. "Now, what under the sun can I call her?"

"Aunty," suggested the man at the next table.

I sat perfectly still. Could that man have answered my thoughts?—for I had not spoken aloud. Of course not—it was a coincidence,—but a very disgusting one.

"Aunty," I repeated mechanically, "aunty, aunty—good gracious, how horribly human that cat looks!" Then somehow or other, Shakespeare's words crept into my head and I found myself repeating:

"the soul of his grandam might happily inhabit a bird; the soul of his grandam might happily inhabit a bird; the soul of—nonsense!" I growled "it isn't printed correctly! One might possibly say, speaking in poetical metaphor, that the soul of a bird might happily inhabit one's grandam—" I stopped short, flushing painfully.

"What awful rot!" I murmured, and lighted another cigar. The cat was still staring; the cigar went out. I grew more and more nervous. "What rot!" I repeated. "Pythagoras must have been an ass, but I do believe that there are plenty of asses alive today who swallow that sort of thing."

"Who knows," sighed the man at the next table, and I sprang to my feet and wheeled about. But I only caught a glimpse of a pair of frayed coat-tails and a bald head vanishing into the dining-room. I sat down again, thoroughly indignant. A moment later the cat got up and went away.

2

Daylight was fading in the city of Antwerp. Down into the sea sank the sun, tinting the vast horizon with flakes of crimson, and touching with rich deep undertones the tossing waters of the Scheldt. Its glow fell like a rosy mantle over red-tiled roofs and meadows; and through the haze the spires of twenty churches pierced the air like sharp, gilded flames. To the west and south the green plains, over which the Spanish armies tramped so long ago, stretched away until they met the sky; the enchantment of the afterglow had turned old Antwerp into fairyland; and sea and sky and plain were beautiful and vague as the night mists floating in the moats below.

Along the sea-wall from the Rubens Gate, all Antwerp strolled, and chattered, and flirted and sipped their Flemish wines from slender Flemish glasses or gossiped over *krugs* of foaming beer.

From the Scheldt came the cries of sailors, the creaking of cordage, and the puff! puff! of the ferryboats. On the bastions of the fortress opposite a bugler was standing. Twice the mellow notes of the bugle came faintly over the water, then a great gun thundered from the ramparts, and the Belgian flag fluttered along the lanyards to the ground.

I leaned listlessly on the sea-wall and looked down at the Scheldt below. A battery of artillery was embarking for the fortress. The tub-like transport lay hissing and whistling in the slip, and the stamping of horses, the rumbling of gun and caisson, and the sharp cries of the officers came plainly to the ear.

When the last *caisson* was aboard and stowed, and the last trooper had sprung jingling to the deck, the transport puffed out into the Scheldt, and I turned away through the throng of promenaders, and found a little table on the terrace, just outside of the pretty *café*. And as I sat down, I became aware of a girl at the next table—a girl all in white—the most ravishingly and distractingly pretty girl that I had ever seen. In the agitation of the moment I forgot that I was a woman-hater, I forgot my name, my fortune, my aunt, and the Crimson Diamond—all these I forgot in a purely human impulse to see clearly; and to that end

I removed my monocle from my left eye. Some moments later I came to myself and feebly replaced it. It was too late; the mischief was done. I was not aware at first of the exact state of my feelings,—for I had never before been in love—but I did know that at her request I would have been proud to stand on my head, or turn a flip-flap into the Scheldt.

I did not stare at her, but I managed to see her most of the time when her eyes were in another direction. I found myself drinking something which a waiter brought presumably upon an order which I did not remember having given. Later I noticed that it was a loathsome drink which the Belgians call American Grog, but I swallowed it and lighted a cigarette. As the fragrant cloud rose in the air, a voice, which I recognized with a chill, broke into my dream of enchantment. Could *he* have been there all the while,—there sitting beside that vision in white? His hat was off, and the ocean breezes whispered about his bald head. His frayed coat-tails were folded carefully over his knees, and between the thumb and forefinger of his left hand he balanced a bad cigar. He looked at me in a mildly cheerful way, and said, "I know now."

"Know what?" I asked, thinking it better to humour him, for I was convinced that he was mad.

"I know why cats bite."

This was startling. I hadn't the vaguest idea what to say.

"I know why," he repeated; "can you guess why?" There was a covert tone of triumph in his voice and he smiled encouragement. "Come, try and guess," he urged.

I was uneasy, but I told him with stiff civility that I was unequal to problems.

"Listen, young man," he continued, folding his coat-tails closely about his legs—"try to reason it out; why should cats bite? Don't you know? I do."

He looked at me anxiously.

"You take no interest in this problem?" he demanded.

"Oh, yes."

"Then why do you not ask me why?" he said, looking vaguely disappointed.

"Well," I said in desperation, "why do cats bite?—hang it all!" I thought, "it's like a burnt-cork show, and I'm Mr. Bones and he's Tambo!"

Then he smiled gently. "Young man," he said, "cats bite because they feed on catnip. I have reasoned it out."

I stared at him in blank astonishment. Was this benevolent looking old party poking fun at me? Was he paying me up for the morning's snub? Was he a malignant and revengeful old party, or was he merely feeble-minded? Who might he be? What was he doing here in Antwerp—what was he doing now!—for the bald one had turned familiarly to the beautiful girl in white.

"Elsie," he said, "do you feel chilly?" The girl shook her head.

"Not in the least, papa."

"Good Lord!" I thought"—her father!"

"I have been to the Zoo today," announced the bald one, turning toward me.

"Ah, indeed," I observed,—"er—I trust you enjoyed it."

"I have been contemplating the apes," he continued, dreamily. "Yes, contemplating the apes."

I said nothing, but tried to look interested.

"Yes, the apes," he murmured, fixing his mild eyes on me. Then he leaned toward me confidentially and whispered; "can you tell me what a monkey thinks?"

"I cannot," I replied, sharply.

"Ah," he sighed, sinking back in his chair, and patting the slender hand of the girl beside him, "ah, who can tell what a monkey thinks?" His gentle face lulled my suspicions, and I replied very gravely; "who can tell whether they think at all?"

"True, true! Who can tell whether they think at all; and if they do think, ah! who can tell what they think?"

"But," I began, "if you can't tell whether they think at all, what's the use of trying to conjecture what they *would* think if they *did* think?"

He raised his hand in deprecation. "Ah, it is exactly that which is of such absorbing interest, exactly that! It is the abstruseness of the proposition which stimulates research—which stirs profoundly the brain of the thinking world. The question is of vital and instant importance. Possibly you have already formed an opinion."

I admitted that I had thought but little on the subject.

"I doubt," he continued, swathing his knees in his coat-tails,—"I doubt whether you have given much attention to the subject lately discussed by the Boston Dodo Society of Pythagorean Research."

"I am not sure," I said politely, "that I recall that particular discussion. May I ask what was the question brought up?"

"The *Felis Domesticus* question."

"Ah, that must indeed be interesting! And—er what may be the *Felis Do—do—*"

"*Domesticus*—not Dodo. *Felis Domesticus*, the common or garden cat."

"Indeed," I murmured.

"You are not listening," he said.

I only half heard him; I could not turn my eyes from her face.

"Cat!" shouted the bald one, and I almost leaped from my chair. "Are you deaf?" he inquired, sympathetically.

"No—oh no!" I replied, colouring with confusion; "you were—pardon me—you were—er—speaking of the Dodo. Extraordinary bird that—"

"I was not discussing the Dodo," he sighed "I was speaking of cats."

"Of course," I said.

"The question is, he continued, twisting his frayed coat-tails into a sort of rope" the question is, how are we to ameliorate the present condition and social status of our domestic cats——"

"Feed 'em," I suggested.

He raised both hands. They were eloquent with patient expostulation. "I mean their spiritual condition," he said.

I nodded, but my eyes reverted to that exquisite face. She

245

sat silent, her eyes fixed on the waning flecks of colour in the western sky.

"Yes," repeated the bald one, "the spiritual welfare of our domestic cats——"

"Toms and Tabbies?" I murmured.

"Exactly," he said, tying a large knot in his coat-tails.

"You will ruin your coat," I observed.

"Papa!" exclaimed the girl, turning in dismay, as that gentleman gave a guilty start, "stop it at once!"

He smiled apologetically and made a feeble attempt to conceal his coat-tails.

"My dear," he said, with gentle deprecation, "I am so absent-minded—I always do it in the heat of argument."

The girl rose, and, bending over her untidy parent, deftly untied the knot in his flapping coat. When he was disentangled, she sat down and said, with a ghost of a smile; "he is so very absent-minded."

"Your father is evidently a great student," I said, pleasantly. How I pitied her, tied to this lunatic!

"Yes, he is a great student," she said, quietly.

"I am," he murmured, "that's what makes me so absent-minded. I often go to bed and forget to sleep." Then looking at me he asked me my name, adding, with a bow, that his name was P. Royal Wyeth, Professor of Pythagorean Research and Abstruse Paradox.

"My first name is Penny—named after Professor Penny of Harvard, he said, but I seldom use my first name in connection with my second, as the combination suggests a household remedy of penetrating odour.

"My name is Kensett," I said, "Harold Kensett of New York."

"Student?"

"Er—a little—"

"Student of diamonds?"

I smiled. "Oh, I see you know who my great-aunt was," I said.

"I know her," he said.

"Ah,—perhaps you are unaware that my great-aunt is not now living—"

"I know her," he repeated, obstinately.

I bowed. What a crank he was!

"What do you study? You don't fiddle away all your time, do you?" he asked.

Now that was just what I did, but I was not pleased to have Miss Wyeth know it. Although my time was chiefly spent in shooting and fishing, I had once, in a fit of energy, succeeded in stuffing and mounting a woodcock, so I evaded a humiliating confession by saying that I had done a little work in ornithology.

"Good!" cried the Professor, beaming all over. "I knew you were a fellow scientist. Possibly you are a brother member of the Boston Dodo Society of Pythagorean Research. Are you a Dodo?"

I shook my head. "No, I am not a Dodo."

"Only a jay?"

"A—what?" I said, angrily.

"A jay. We call the members of the Junior Ornithological Jay Society of New York, jays, just as we refer to ourselves as Dodos. Are you not even a jay?"

"I am not," I said, watching him suspiciously.

"I must convert you, I see," said the Professor, smiling.

"I'm afraid I do not approve of Pythagorean research," I began, but the beautiful Miss Wyeth turned to me very seriously, and looking me frankly in the eyes, said:

"I trust you will be open to conviction."

"Good Lord!" I thought, "can she be another crank." I looked at her steadily. What a little beauty she was. She also then belonged to the Pythagoreans—a sect I despised. Everybody knows all about the Pythagorean craze, its rise in Boston, its rapid spread, and its subsequent consolidation with Theosophy, Hypnotism, the Salvation Army, the Shakers, the Dunkards, and the Mind Cure Cult, upon a business basis.

I had hitherto regarded all Pythagoreans with the same scornful indifference which I accorded to the Faith Curists; being a member of the Catholic Church I was scarcely prepared to take any of them seriously. Least of all did I approve of the "business basis," and I looked very much askance indeed at the "Scientific and Religious Trust Company," duly incorporated and generally known as the Pythagorean Trust, which, consolidating with Mind Curists, Faith Curists, and other nourishing Salvation Syndicates, actually claimed a place among ordinary Trusts, and at the same time pretended to a control over man s future life. No, I could never listen—I was ashamed of even entertaining the notion, and I shook my head.

"No, Miss Wyeth, I am afraid I do not care to listen to any reasoning on this subject."

"Don't you believe in Pythagoras?" demanded the Professor, subduing his excitement with difficulty, and adding another knot to his coat-tails.

"No," I said, "I do not."

"How do you know you don't?" enquired the Professor.

"Because," I said, firmly, "it is nonsense to say that the soul of a human being can inhabit a hen!"

"Put it in a more simplified form!" insisted the Professor; "do you believe that the soul of a hen can inhabit a human being?"

"No, I don't!"

"Did you ever hear of a hen-pecked man?" cried the Professor, his voice ending in a shout.

I nodded, intensely annoyed.

"Will you listen to reason, then?" he continued, eagerly.

"No," I began, but I caught Miss Wyeth s blue eyes fixed on mine with an expression so sad, so sweetly appealing, that I faltered.

"Yes, I will listen," I said, faintly.

Will you become my pupil? insisted the Professor.

I was shocked to find myself wavering, but my eyes were looking into hers, and I could not disobey what I read there. The longer I looked the greater inclination I felt to waver. I saw that

I was going to give in, and, strangest of all, my conscience did not trouble me. I felt it coining a sort of mild exhilaration took possession of me. For the first time in my life I became reckless I even gloried in my recklessness.

"Yes, yes," I cried, leaning eagerly across the table, "I shall be glad delighted! Will you take me as your pupil?" My single eye-glass fell from its position unheeded. "Take me! Oh, will you take me?" I cried. Instead of answering, the Professor blinked rapidly at me for a moment. I imagined his eyes had grown bigger, and were assuming a greenish tinge. The corners of his mouth began to quiver, emitting queer, caressing little noises, and he rapidly added knot after knot to his twitching coat-tails. Suddenly he bent forward across the table until his nose almost touched mine. The pupils of his eyes expanded, the iris assuming a beautiful changing golden-green tinge, and his coat-tails switched violently. Then he began to mew.

I strove to rouse myself from my paralysis—I tried to shrink back, for I felt the end of his cold nose touch mine. I could not move. The cry of terror died in my straining throat, my hands tight ened convulsively; I was incapable of speech or motion. At the same time my brain became won derfully clear. I began to remember everything that had ever happened to me—eve-rything that I had ever done or said. I even remembered things that I had neither done nor said, I recalled distinctly much that had never happened. How fresh and strong my memory! The past was like a mirror, crystal clear, and there, in glorious tints and hues, the scenes of my childhood grew and glowed and faded, and gave place to newer and more splendid scenes.

For a moment the episode of the cat at the Hotel St. Anto-ine flashed across my mind. When it vanished, a chilly stupor slowly clouded my brain; the scenes, the memories, the brilliant colours, faded, leaving me enveloped in a grey vapour, through which the two great eyes of the Professor twinkled with a murky light. A peculiar longing stirred me,—a strange yearning for something—I knew not what—but, oh! how I longed and yearned for it! Slowly this indefinite, incomprehensible longing became a living pain. Ah, how I suffered!—and how the vapours seemed to crowd around me. Then, as at a great distance, I heard her voice, sweet, imperative:

"Mew!" she said.

For a moment I seemed to see the interior of my own skull, lighted as by a flash of fire; the rolling eye-balls, veined in scarlet, the glistening muscles quivering along the jaw, the humid masses of the convoluted brain,—then awful darkness—a darkness almost tangible—an utter blackness, through which now seemed to creep a thin silver thread, like a river crawling across a world—like a thought gliding to the brain—like a song, a thin, sharp song which some distant voice was singing—which I was singing.

And I knew that I was mewing!

I threw myself back in my chair and mewed with all my heart. Oh, that heavy load which was lifted from my breast! How good, how satisfying it was to mew! And how I did mew!

I gave myself up to it, heart and soul; my whole being thrilled with the passionate outpourings of a spirit freed. My voice trembled in the upper bars of a feline love song, quavered, descended, swelling again into an intimation that I brooked no rival, and ended with a magnificent *crescendo*.

I finished, somewhat abashed, and glanced askance at the Professor and his daughter, but the one sat nonchalantly disentangling his coat-tails, and the other was apparently absorbed in the distant landscape. Evidently they did not consider me ridiculous. Flushing painfully, I turned in my chair to see how my gruesome solo had affected the people on the terrace. Nobody even looked at me. This, however, gave me little comfort, for, as I began to realize what I had done, my mortification and rage knew no bounds. I was ready to die of shame. What on earth had induced me to mew? I looked wildly about for escape—I would leap up—rush home to bury my burning face in my pillows, and later in the friendly cabin of a homeward-bound steamer. I would fly—fly at once! Woe to the man who blocked my way! I started to my feet, but at that moment I caught Miss Wyeth's eyes fixed on mine.

"Don't go," she said.

What in Heaven's name lay in those blue eyes! I slowly sank back into my chair.

Then the Professor spoke. "Elsie, I have just received a dispatch."

"Where from, Papa?"

"From India. I'm going at once."

She nodded her head, without turning her eyes from the sea. "Is it important, papa?

"I should say so. The cashier of the Trust has eloped with an Astral body, and has taken all our funds, including a lot of first mortgages on Nirvana. I suppose he s been dabbling in futures, and was short in his accounts. I shan't be gone long."

"Then goodnight, papa," she said, kissing him, "try to be back by eleven." I sat stupidly staring at them.

"Oh, it's only to Bombay—I shan't go to Thibet tonight,— goodnight, my dear," said the Professor.

Then a singular thing occurred. The Professor had at last succeeded in disentangling his coat tails, and now, jamming his hat over his ears, and waving his arms with a bat-like motion, he climbed upon the seat of his chair, and ejaculated the word "Presto!" Then I found my voice.

"Stop him!" I cried, in terror.

"Presto! Presto!" shouted the Professor, balancing himself on the edge of his chair and waving his arms majestically, as if preparing for a sudden flight across the Scheldt; and, firmly convinced that he not only meditated it but was perfectly capable of attempting it, I covered my eyes with my hands.

"Are you ill, Mr. Kensett?" said the girl, quietly.

I raised my head indignantly. "Not at all, Miss Wyeth, only I'll bid you good-evening, for this is the 19th century, and I'm a Christian."

"So am I," she said. "So is my father."

"The devil he is," I thought. Her next words made me jump.

"Please do not be profane, Mr. Kensett."

How did she know I was profane? I had not spoken a word! Could it be possible she was able to read my thoughts? This was too much, and I rose and bowed stiffly.

"I have the honour to bid you good-evening, I began," and reluctantly turned to include the Professor, expecting to see that gentleman balancing himself on his chair. The Professor's chair was empty.

"Oh," said the girl, faintly, "my father has gone."

"Gone! Where?"

"To—to India, I believe."

I sank helplessly into my own chair.

"I do not think he will stay very long—he promised to return by eleven, she said, timidly.

I tried to realize the purport of it all. Gone to India? Gone! How? On a broomstick? Good Heavens!" I murmured, "am I sane?"

"Perfectly," she said, "and I am tired; you may take me back to the hotel."

I scarcely heard her; I was feebly attempting to gather up my numbed wits. Slowly I began to comprehend the situation, to review the start ling and humiliating events of the day. At noon, in the court of the Hotel St. Antoine, I had been annoyed by a man and a cat. I had retired to my own room and had slept until dinner. In the evening I met two tourists on the sea-wall promenade. I had been beguiled into conversation—yes, into intimacy with these two tourists! I had had the intention of embracing the faith of Pythagoras! Then I had mewed like a cat with all the strength of my lungs. Then the male tourist vanishes—and leaves me in charge of the female tourist, alone and at night in a strange city! And now the female tourist proposes that I take her home!

With a remnant of self-possession I groped for my eye-glass, seized it, screwed it firmly into my eye, and looked long and earnestly at the girl. As I looked, my eyes softened, my monocle dropped, and I forgot everything in the beauty and purity of the face before me. My heart began to beat against my stiff white waistcoat. Had I dared—yes, dared to think of this wondrous little beauty, as a female tourist? Her pale sweet face, turned toward the sea, seemed to cast a spell upon the night. How loud my heart was beating.

The yellow moon floated, half dipping in the sea, flooding land and water with enchanted lights. Wind and wave seemed to feel the spell of her eyes, for the breeze died away, the heaving Scheldt tossed noiselessly, and the dark Dutch *luggers* swung idly on the tide with every sail adroop.

A sudden hush fell over land and water, the voices on the promenade were stilled; little by little the shadowy throng, the terrace, the sea itself vanished, and I only saw her face, shadowed against the moon.

It seemed as if I had drifted miles above the earth, through all space and eternity, and there was nought between me and high Heaven but that white face. Ah, how I loved her! I knew it—I never doubted it. Could years of passionate adoration touch her heart—her little heart, now beating so calmly with no thought of love to startle it from its quiet and send it fluttering against the gentle breast? In her lap her clasped hands tightened,—her eyelids drooped as though some pleasant thought was passing. I saw the colour dye her temples, I saw the blue eyes turn, half-frightened to my own,—I saw and I knew she had read my thoughts.

Then we both rose, side by side, and she was weeping softly, yet for my life I dared not speak. She turned away, touching her eyes with a bit of lace, and I sprang to her side and offered her my arm.

"You cannot go back alone," I said.

She did not take my arm.

"Do you hate me, Miss Wyeth?"

"I am very tired," she said, "I must go home."

"You cannot go alone."

"I do not care to accept your escort."

"Then—you send me away?"

"No," she said, in a hard voice. "You can come if you like." So I humbly attended her to the Hotel St. Antoine.

3

As we reached the Place Verte and turned into the court of the hotel, the sound of the midnight bells swept over the city, and a horse-car jingled slowly by on its last trip to the railroad station.

We passed the fountain, bubbling and splashing in the moonlit court, and, crossing the square, entered the southern wing of the hotel. At the foot of the stairway she leaned for an instant against the banisters.

I am afraid we have walked too fast, I said. She turned to me coldly. "No,—conventionalities must be observed. You were quite right in escaping as soon as possible."

"But," I protested, "I assure you——"

She gave a little movement of impatience. "Don't," she said, "you tire me—conventionalities tire me. Be satisfied,—nobody has seen you."

"You are cruel," I said, in a low voice—"what do you think I care for conventionalities——"

"You care everything,—you care what people think, and you try to do what they say is good form. You never did such an original thing in your life as you have just done."

"You read my thoughts", I exclaimed, bitterly—"it is not fair——"

"Fair or not, I know what you consider me,—ill-bred, common, pleased with any sort of attention. Oh! Why should I waste one word—one thought on you!"

"Miss Wyeth,—" I began, but she interrupted me.

"Would you dare tell me what you think of me?—Would you dare tell me what you think of my father?"

I was silent. She turned and mounted two steps of the stairway, then faced me again.

"Do you think it was for my own pleasure that I permitted myself to be left alone with you? Do you imagine that I am flat-

254

tered by your attention—do you venture to think I ever could be? How dared you think what you did think there on the sea-wall?"

"I cannot help my thoughts!" I replied.

"You turned on me like a tiger when you awoke from your trance. Do you really suppose that you mewed? Are you not aware that my father hypnotized you?"

"No—I did not know it," I said. The hot blood tingled in my finger tips, and I looked angrily at her.

"Why do you imagine that I waste my time on you?" she said. "Your vanity has answered that question,—now let your intelligence answer it. I am a Pythagorean; I have been chosen to bring in a convert, and you were the convert selected for me by the Mahatmas of the Consolidated Trust Company. I have followed you from New York to Antwerp, as I was bidden, but now my courage fails, and I shrink from fulfilling my mission, knowing you to be the type of man you are. If I could give it up—if I could only go away,—never, never again to see you! Ah, I fear they will not permit it!—until my mission is accomplished. Why was I chosen,—I, with a woman's heart and a woman's pride. I—I hate you!"

"I love you," I said, slowly.

She paled and looked away.

"Answer me," I said.

Her wide blue eyes turned back again, and I held them with mine. At last she slowly drew a long-stemmed rose from the bunch at her belt, turned, and mounted the shadowy staircase. For a moment I thought I saw her pause on the landing above, but the moonlight was uncertain. After waiting for a long time in vain, I moved away, and in going raised my hand to my face, but I stopped short, and my heart stopped too, for a moment. In my hand I held a long-stemmed rose.

With my brain in a whirl I crept across the court and mounted the stairs to my room. Hour after hour I walked the floor, slowly at first, then more rapidly, but it brought no calm to the fierce tumult of my thoughts, and at last I dropped into a chair before the empty fireplace, burying my head in my hands.

Uncertain, shocked, and deadly weary, I tried to think,—I strove to bring order out of the chaos in my brain, but I only sat staring at the long-stemmed rose. Slowly I began to take a vague pleasure in its heavy perfume, and once I crushed a leaf between my palms, and, bending over, drank in the fragrance.

Twice my lamp flickered and went out, and twice, treading softly, I crossed the room to relight it. Twice I threw open the door, thinking that I heard some sound without. How close the air was,—how heavy and hot! And what was that strange, subtle odour which had insensibly filled the room? It grew stronger and more penetrating, and I began to dislike it, and to escape it I buried my nose in the half-opened rose. Horror! The odour came from the rose,—and the rose itself was no longer a rose- not even a flower now, it was only a bunch of catnip; and I dashed it to the floor and ground it under my heel.

"Mountebank!" I cried in a rage. My anger grew cold—and I shivered, drawn perforce to the curtained window. Something was there—outside. I could not hear it, for it made no sound, but I knew it was there, watching me. What was it? The damp hair stirred on my head. I touched the heavy curtains. What- ever was outside them sprang up, tore at the window, and then rushed away.

Feeling very shaky, I crept to the window, opened it, and leaned out. The night was calm. I heard the fountain splashing in the moonlight and the sea winds soughing through the palms. Then I closed the window and turned back into the room; and as I stood there a sudden breeze, which could not have come from without, blew sharply in my face, extinguishing the can- dle and sending the long curtains bellying out into the room. The lamp on the table flashed and smoked and sputtered; the room was littered with flying papers and catnip leaves. Then the strange wind died away, and somewhere in the night a cat snarled.

I turned desperately to my trunk and flung it open. Into it I threw everything I owned, pell-mell, closed the lid, locked it, and seizing my mackintosh and travelling bag, ran down the stairs, crossed the court and entered the night office of the hotel. There I called up the sleepy clerk, settled my reckoning, and sent a porter for a cab.

"Now," I said, "what time does the next train leave?"

"The next train for where?"

"Anywhere!"

The clerk locked the safe, and carefully keeping the desk between himself and me, motioned the office boy to look at the timetables.

"Next train, 2.10. Brussels—Paris," read the boy.

At that moment the cab rattled up by the kerbstone, and I sprang in while the porter tossed my traps on top. Away we bumped over the stony pavement, past street after street lighted dimly by tall gas-lamps, and alley after alley brilliant with the glare of villainous all-night *café*-concerts, and then, turning, we rumbled past the Circus and the Eldorado, and at last stopped with a jolt before the Brussels Station.

I had not a moment to lose. "Paris!" I cried,—"first-class!" and, pocketing the book of coupons, hurried across the platform to where the Brussels train lay. A guard came running up, flung open the door of a first-class carriage, slammed and locked it, after I had jumped in, and the long train glided from the arched station out into the starlit morning.

I was all alone in the compartment. The wretched lamp in the roof flickered dimly, scarcely lighting the stuffy box. I could not see to read my time-table, so I wrapped my legs in the travelling rug and lay back, staring out into the misty morning. Trees, walls, telegraph poles, flashed past, and the cinders drove in showers against the rattling windows. I slept at times, fitfully, and once, springing up, peered sharply at the opposite seat, possessed with the idea that somebody was there.

When the train reached Brussels, I was sound asleep, and the guard awoke me with difficulty.

"Breakfast, sir?" he asked.

"Anything," I sighed, and stepped out to the platform, rubbing my legs and shivering. The other passengers were already breakfasting in the station cafe, and I joined them and managed to swallow a cup of coffee and a roll.

The morning broke, grey and cloudy, and I bundled myself into my mackintosh for a tramp along the platform Up and down I stamped, puffing a cigar, and digging my hands deep in my pockets, while the other passengers huddled into the warmer compartments of the train or stood watching the luggage being lifted into the forward mail carriage. The wait was very long; the hands of the great clock pointed to six, and still the train lay motionless along the platform. I approached a guard, and asked him whether anything was wrong.

"Accident on the line," he replied; "*Monsieur* had better go to his compartment and try to sleep, for we may be delayed until noon."

I followed the guard's advice, and crawling into my corner, wrapped myself in the rug and lay back watching the rain-drops spattering along the window-sill. At noon, the train had not moved, and I lunched in the compartment. At four o clock in the afternoon the station-master came hurrying along the platform, crying *"montez! montez! Messieurs—Dames, s'il vous plait,"*—and the train steamed out of the station and whirled away through the flat, treeless Belgian plains. At times I dozed, but the shaking of the car always awoke me, and I would sit blinking out at the endless stretch of plain, until a sudden flurry of rain blotted the landscape from my eyes.

At last, a long, shrill whistle from the engine, a jolt, a series of bumps, and an apparition of red trousers and bayonets warned me that we had arrived at the French frontier. I turned out with the others, and opened my valise for inspection, but the customs officials merely chalked it without examination, and I hurried back to my compartment amid the shouting of guards and the clanging of station bells. Again I found that I was alone in the compartment, so I smoked a cigarette, thanked Heaven, and fell into a dream less sleep.

How long I slept I do not know, but when I awoke, the train

was roaring through a tunnel. When again it flashed out into the open country, I peered through the grimy rain-stained window and saw that the storm had ceased and stars were twinkling in the sky. I stretched my legs, yawned, pushed my travelling cap back from my forehead, and stumbling to my feet, walked up and down the compartment until my cramped muscles were relieved. Then I sat down again, and, lighting a cigar, puffed great rings and clouds of fragrant smoke across the aisle.

The train was flying; the cars lurched and shook, and the windows rattled accompaniment to the creaking panels. The smoke from my cigar dimmed the lamp in the ceiling and hid the opposite seat from view. How it curled and writhed in the corners, now eddying upward, now floating across the aisle like a veil. I lounged back in my cushioned seat watching it with interest. What queer shapes it took. How thick it was becoming—how strangely luminous! Now it had filled the whole compartment, puff after puff crowding upward, waving, wavering, clouding the windows, and blotting the lamp from sight.

It was most interesting. I had never before smoked such a cigar. What an extraordinary brand! I examined the end, flicking the ashes away. The cigar was out. Fumbling for a match to relight it, my eyes fell on the drifting smoke curtain, which swayed across the corner opposite. It seemed almost tangible. How like a real curtain it hung, grey, impenetrable. A man might hide behind it. Then an idea came into my head, and it persisted until my uneasiness amounted to a vague terror. I tried to fight it off—I strove to resist—but the conviction slowly settled upon me that something was behind that smoke veil,—something which had entered the compartment while I slept.

"It can't be," I muttered, my eyes fixed on the misty drapery, "the train has not stopped."

The car creaked and trembled. I sprang to my feet, and swept my arm through the veil of smoke. Then my hair slowly rose on my head. For my hand touched another hand, and my eyes had met two other eyes.

My senses reeled. I heard a voice in the gloom, low and sweet, calling me by name; I saw the eyes again, tender and blue; soft fingers touched my own.

"Are you afraid?" she said.

My heart began to beat again, and my face warmed with returning blood.

"It is only I," she said, gently.

I seemed to hear my own voice speaking as if at a great distance; "you here—alone?"

"How cruel of you," she faltered, "I am not alone." At the same instant my eyes fell upon the Professor, calmly seated by the further window. His hands were thrust into the folds of a corded and tasselled dressing-gown, from beneath which peeped two enormous feet encased in car pet slippers. Upon his head towered a yellow night cap. He did not pay the slightest attention to either me or his daughter, and, except for the lighted cigar which he kept shifting between his lips, he might have been taken for a wax dummy.

Then I began to speak, feebly, hesitating like a child.

"How did you come into this compartment? You—you do not possess wings, I suppose. You could not have been here all the time. Will you explain—explain to me? See, I ask you very humbly, for I do not understand. This is the 19th century, and these things don't fit in. I'm wearing a Dunlap hat—I've got a copy of the *New York Herald* in my bag,—President Cleveland is alive and everything is so very commonplace in the world! Is this real magic? Perhaps I'm filled with hallucinations. Perhaps I'm asleep and dreaming. Perhaps you are not really here—nor I—nor anybody, nor anything!"—

The train plunged into a tunnel, and when again it dashed out from the other end, the cold wind blew furiously in my face from the further window. It was wide open; the Professor was gone.

"Papa has changed to another compartment," she said, quietly; "I think perhaps you were beginning to bore him."

Her eyes met mine and she smiled faintly.

"Are you very much bewildered?"

I looked at her in silence. She sat very quietly, her white hands clasped above her knee, her curly hair glittering to her girdle. A long robe, almost silvery in the twilight, clung to her young figure; her bare feet were thrust deep into a pair of shimmering eastern slippers.

"When you fled," she sighed, "I was asleep and there was no time to lose. I barely had a moment to go to Bombay, to find Papa, and return in time to join you. This is an East Indian costume.

Still I was silent.

"Are you shocked?" she asked simply

"No," I replied in a dull voice, "I m past that."

"You are very rude," she said, with the tears starting to her eyes.

"I do not mean to be. I only wish to go away—away somewhere and find out what my name is."

"Your name is Harold Kensett."

"Are you sure?" I asked, eagerly.

"Yes,—what troubles you?"

"Is everything plain to you? Are you a sort of prophet and second sight medium? Is nothing hidden from you?" I asked.

"Nothing,"—she faltered. My head ached and I clasped it in my hand.

A sudden change came over her. "I am human,—believe me!"—she said with piteous eagerness; "indeed I do not seem strange to those who understand. You wonder, because you left me at midnight in Antwerp and you wake to find me here. If, because I find myself reincarnated, endowed with senses and capabilities which few at present possess;—if I am so made, why should it seem strange? It is all so natural to me. If I appear to you——"

"Appear!!!"

"Yes—"

"Elsie!" I cried, "can you vanish?"

"Yes," she murmured,—"does it seem to you unwomanly?"

"Great Heaven!" I groaned.

"Don't," she cried, with tears in her voice,—"oh, please don't! Help me to bear it! If you only knew how awful it is to be different from other girls,—how mortifying it is to me to be able to vanish,—oh, how I hate and detest it all!"

"Don't cry," I said, looking at her pityingly.

"Oh dear me!" she sobbed. "You shudder at the sight of me because I can vanish."

"I don't!" I cried.

"Yes you do! You abhor me,—you shrink away! Oh why did I ever see you,—why did you ever come into my life,—what have I done in ages past, that now, reborn, I suffer cruelly-cruelly!"

"What do you mean!" I whispered. My voice trembled with happiness.

"I?—nothing—but you think me a fabled monster."

"Elsie,—my sweet Elsie," I said, "I don't think you a fabled monster;—I love you, see—see—I am at your feet,—listen to me, my darling,"—

She turned her blue eyes to mine. I saw tears sparkling on the curved lashes.

"Elsie, I love you," I said again.

Slowly she raised her white hands to my head and held it a moment, looking at me strangely. Then her face grew nearer to my own, her glittering hair fell over my shoulders, her lips rested on mine.

In that long sweet kiss, the beating of her heart answered mine, and I learned a thousand truths, wonderful, mysterious, splendid,—but when our lips fell apart,—the memory of what I learned departed also.

"It was so very simple and beautiful," she sighed, "and I—I never saw it. But the Mahatmas knew—ah, they knew that my mission could only be accomplished through love."

"And it is," I whispered, "for you shall teach me,—me your husband."

"And—and you will not be impatient? You will try to believe?"

"I will believe what you tell me, my sweet heart."

"Even about—cats?"

Before I could reply the further window opened and a yellow nightcap, followed by the Professor, entered from somewhere without. Elsie sank back on her sofa, but the Professor needed not to be told, and we both knew he was already busily reading our thoughts.

For a moment there was dead silence,—long enough for the Professor to grasp the full significance of what had passed. Then he uttered a single exclamation; "Oh!"

After a while, however, he looked at me for the first time that evening, saying; "Congratulate you, Mr. Kensett, I'm sure;"—tied several knots in the cord of his dressing-gown, lighted a cigar, and paid no further attention to either of us. Some moments later he opened the window again and disappeared. I looked across the aisle at Elsie.

"You may come over beside me," she said, shyly.

4

It was nearly ten o clock and our train was rapidly approaching Paris. We passed village after village wrapped in mist, station after station hung with twinkling red and blue and yellow lanterns, then sped on again with the echo of the switch bells ringing in our ears.

When at length the train slowed up and stopped, I opened the window and looked out upon a long wet platform, shining under the electric lights.

A guard came running by, throwing open the doors of each compartment, and crying, "Paris next! Tickets, if you please."

I handed him my book of coupons from which he tore several and handed it back. Then he lifted his lantern and peered into the compartment saying: "Is *Monsieur* alone?"

I turned to Elsie.

"He wants your ticket—give it to me."

"What's that?" demanded the guard. I looked anxiously at Elsie.

"If your father has the tickets—" I began, but was interrupted by the guard who snapped, "*Monsieur* will give himself the trouble to remember that I do not understand English."

"Keep quiet!" I said sharply in French, "I am not speaking to you."

The guard stared stupidly at me, then at my luggage, and finally, entering the car, knelt down and peered under the seats. Presently he got up, very red in the face, and went out slamming the door. He had not paid the slightest attention to Elsie, but I distinctly heard him say, "only Englishmen and idiots talk to themselves!"

"Elsie," I faltered, "do you mean to say that guard could not see you?

She began to look so serious again that I merely added, "never mind, I don't care whether you are invisible or not, dearest. "

"I am not invisible to you," she said; "why should you care?"

A great noise of bells and whistles drowned our voices, and amid the whirring of switch bells, the hissing of steam, and the cries of "Paris! All out!" our train glided into the station.

It was the Professor who opened the door of our carriage. There he stood, calmly adjusting his yellow nightcap and drawing his dressing-gown closer with the corded tassels.

"Where have you been?" I asked.

"On the engine."

"*In* the engine I suppose you mean," I said.

"No I don't; I mean *on* the engine,—on the pilot. It was very refreshing. Where are we going now?"

"Do you know Paris?" asked Elsie, turning to me.

"Yes. I think your father had better take you to the Hotel Normandie on the *rue de l'Echelle*—"

"But you must stay there too!"

"Of course—if you wish—"

She laughed nervously.

"Don't you see that my father and I could not take rooms-now? You must engage three rooms for yourself."

"Why?" I asked stupidly.

"Oh dear—why because we are invisible."

I tried to repress a shudder. The Professor gave Elsie his arm and, as I studied his ensemble, I thanked Heaven that he was invisible.

At the gate of the station I hailed a four-seated cab, and we rattled away through the stony streets, brilliant with gas jets, and in a few moments rolled smoothly across the Avenue de l'Opera, turned into the *rue de l'Echelle*, and stopped. A bright little page, all over buttons, came out, took my luggage, and preceded us into the hallway.

I, with Elsie on my arm and the Professor shuffling along beside me, walked over to the desk.

"Room?" said the clerk, "we have a very desirable room on the second fronting the rue St. Honoré—"

"But we—that is I want three rooms—three separate rooms!" I said.

The clerk scratched his chin. "*Monsieur* is expecting friends?"

"Say yes," whispered Elsie, with a suspicion of laughter in her voice.

"Yes," I repeated feebly.

"Gentlemen of course?" said the clerk looking at me narrowly.

"One lady."

"Married, of course?"

"What's that to you?" I said sharply, "what do you mean by speaking to us—"

"Us!"

"I mean to me," I said, badly rattled; "give me the rooms and let me get to bed, will you?"

"*Monsieur* will remember," said the clerk coldly, "that this is an old and respectable hotel."

"I know it," I said, smothering my rage.

The clerk eyed me suspiciously.

"Front!" he called with irritating deliberation, "show this gentleman to apartment ten."

"How many rooms are there!" I demanded.

"Three sleeping rooms and a parlour."

"I will take it," I said with composure.

"On probation," muttered the clerk insolently.

Swallowing the insult I followed the bell-boy up the stairs, keeping between him and Elsie, for I dreaded to see him walk through her as if she were thin air. A trim maid rose to meet us and conducted us through a hallway into a large apartment. She threw open all the bedroom doors and said, "Will *Monsieur* have the goodness to choose?"

"Which will you take," I began, turning to Elsie.

"I! *Monsieur*!" cried the startled maid.

That completely upset me. "Here," I muttered, slipping some silver into her hand, "now for the love of Heaven run away!"

When she had vanished with a doubtful "*Merci, Monsieur*," I handed the Professor the keys and asked him to settle the thing with Elsie.

Elsie took the corner room, the Professor rambled into the next one, and I said good night and crept wearily into my own chamber. I sat down and tried to think. A great feeling of fatigue weighted my spirits.

"I can think better with my clothes off," I said, and slipped the coat from my shoulders. How tired I was. "I can think better in bed," I muttered, flinging my cravat on the dresser and tossing my shirt studs after it. I was certainly very tired. "Now," I yawned, grasping the pillow and drawing it under my head, "now, I can think a bit," but before my head fell on the pillow, sleep closed my eyes.

I began to dream at once. It seemed as though my eyes were wide open and the Professor was standing beside my bed.

"Young man," he said, "you've won my daughter and you must pay the piper!"

"What piper?" I said.

"The pied piper of Hamlin, I don't think," replied the Professor vulgarly, and before I could realise what he was doing he had drawn a reed pipe from his dressing-gown and was playing a strangely annoying air. Then an awful thing occurred. Cats began to troop into the room, cats by the hundred, toms and tabbies, grey, yellow, Maltese, Persian, Manx, all purring and all marching round and round, rubbing against the furniture, the Professor, and even against me. I struggled with the nightmare.

"Take them away!" I tried to gasp.

"Nonsense," he said, "here is an old friend."

I saw the white tabby cat of the Hotel St. Antoine.

"An old friend," he repeated, and played a dismal melody on his reed.

I saw Elsie enter the room, lift the white tabby in her arms and bring her to my side.

"Shake hands with him," she commanded.

To my horror the tabby deliberately extended a paw and tapped me on the knuckles.

"Oh!" I cried in agony, "this is a horrible dream! Why, oh, why can't I wake!"

"Yes," she said, dropping the cat, "it is partly a dream but some of it is real. Remember what I say, my darling; you are to go tomorrow morning and meet the twelve o clock train from Antwerp at the Gare du Nord. Papa and I are coming to Paris on that train. Don't you know that we are not really here now, you silly boy? Goodnight then. I shall be very glad to see you."

I saw her glide from the room, followed by the Professor, playing a gay quickstep, to which the cats danced two and two.

"Goodnight sir," said each cat, as it passed my bed; and I dreamed no more.

When I awoke, the room, the bed had vanished; I was in the street, walking rapidly; the sun shone down on the broad white pavements of Paris, and the streams of busy life flowed past me on either side. How swiftly I was walking! Where the devil was I going? Surely I had business somewhere that needed immediate attention. I tried to remember when I had awakened, but I could not. I wondered where I had dressed myself; I had apparently taken great pains with my toilet, for I was immaculate, monocle and all, even down to a long-stemmed rose nestling in my button-hole.

I knew Paris and recognized the streets through which I was hurrying. Where could I be going? What was my hurry? I glanced at my watch and found I had not a moment to lose. Then as the bells of the city rang out midday, I hastened into the railroad station on the Rue Lafayette and walked out to the platform. And as I looked down the glittering track, around the distant curve shot a locomotive followed by a long line of cars. Nearer and nearer it came while the station gongs sounded and the switch-bells began ringing all along the track.

"Antwerp express!" cried the *Sous-Chef de Gare*, and as the train slipped along the tiled platform I sprang upon the steps of a first-class carriage and threw open the door.

"How do you do, Mr. Kensett," said Elsie Wyeth, springing lightly to the platform. "Really it is very nice of you to come to the train." At the same moment a bald, mild-eyed gentleman emerged from the depths of the same compartment carrying a large covered basket.

"How are you, Kensett?" he said. "Glad to see you again. Rather warm in that compartment—no I will not trust this basket to an expressman; give Miss Wyeth your arm and I'll follow. We go to the Normandie I believe?"

All the morning I had Elsie to myself, and at dinner I sat beside her with the Professor opposite. The latter was cheerful enough, but he nearly ruined my dinner for he smelled strongly of catnip. After dinner he became restless and fidgeted about in his chair until coffee was brought, and we went up to the parlour of our apartment. Here his restlessness increased to such an extent that I ventured to ask him if he was in good health.

"It s that basket—the covered basket which I have in the next room," he said.

"What's the trouble with the basket?" I asked.

"The basket s all right—but the contents worry me."

"May I inquire what the contents are?" I ventured.

The Professor rose.

"Yes," he said, "you may inquire of my daughter." He left the room but reappeared shortly, carrying a saucer of milk.

I watched him enter the next room which was mine.

"What on earth is he taking that into my room for?" I asked Elsie. "I don't keep cats."

"But you will," she said.

"I? never!"

"You will if I ask you to."

"But—but you won't ask me."

"But I do."

"Elsie!"

"Harold!"

"I detest cats."

"You must not."

"I can't help it."

"You will when I ask it. Have I not given myself to you? Will you not make a little sacrifice for me?

"I don't understand—"

"Would you refuse my first request?"

"No," I said miserably, "I will keep dozens of cats——"

"I do not ask that; I only wish you to keep one."

"Was that what your father had in that basket?" I asked suspiciously.

"Yes, the basket came from Antwerp."

"What! The white Antwerp cat!" I cried.

"Yes."

"And you ask me to keep that cat? Oh Elsie!"

"Listen!" she said, "I have a long story to tell you; come nearer, close to me. You say you love me?"

I bent and kissed her.

"Then I shall put you to the proof," she murmured.

"Prove me!"

"Listen. That cat is the same cat that ran out of the apartment in the Waldorf when your great-aunt ceased to exist—in human shape. My father and myself, having received word from the Mahatmas of the Trust Company, sheltered and cherished the cat. We were ordered by the Mahatmas to convert you. The task was appalling—but there is no such thing as refusing a command, and we laid our plans. That man with a white spot in his hair was my father—"

"What! Your father is bald."

"He wore a wig then. The white spot came from dropping chemicals on the wig while experimenting with a substance which you could not comprehend."

"Then—then that clue was useless; but who could have taken the Crimson Diamond? And who was the man with the white spot on his head who tried to sell the stone in Paris?"

"That was my father."

"He—he—st—took the Crimson Diamond?!" I cried aghast.

"Yes and no. That was only a paste stone that he had in Paris. It was to draw you over here. He had the real Crimson Diamond also."

"Your father?"

"Yes. He has it in the next room now. Can you not see how it disappeared, Harold? Why, the cat swallowed it!"

"Do you mean to say that the white tabby swallowed the Crimson Diamond?"

"By mistake. She tried to get it out of the velvet bag, and, as the bag was also full of catnip, she could not resist a mouthful, and unfortunately just then you broke in the door and so startled the cat that she swallowed the Crimson Diamond."

There was a painful pause. At last I said;

"Elsie, as you are able to vanish, I suppose you also are able to converse with cats."

"I am," she replied, trying to keep back the tears of mortification.

"And that cat told you this?"

"She did."

"And my Crimson Diamond is inside that cat? "

"It is."

"Then," said I firmly, "I am going to chloroform the cat."

"Harold!" she cried in terror, "that cat is your great-aunt!"

I don't know to this day how I stood the shock of that announcement, or how I managed to listen, while Elsie tried to explain the transmigration theory, but it was all Chinese to me. I only knew that I was a blood relation of a cat, and the thought nearly drove me mad.

"Try, my darling, try to love her," whispered Elsie, "she must be very precious to you—"

"Yes, with my diamond inside her," I replied faintly.

"You must not neglect her," said Elsie.

"Oh no, I'll always have my eye on her—I mean I will surround her with luxury—er, milk and bones and catnip and books—er—does she read?"

"Not the books that human-beings read. Now go and speak to your aunt, Harold."

"Eh! How the deuce—"

"Go, for my sake try to be cordial."

She rose and led me unresistingly to the door of my room.

"Good Heavens!" I groaned, "this is awful."

"Courage, my darling!" she whispered, "be brave for love of me."

I drew her to me and kissed her. Beads of cold perspiration started in the roots of my hair, but I clenched my teeth and entered the room alone. The room was dark and I stood silent, not knowing where to turn, fearful lest I step on the cat, my aunt! Then through the dreary silence I called; "Aunty!"

A faint noise broke upon my ear, and my heart grew sick, but I strode into the darkness calling hoarsely: —

"Aunt Tabby! it is your nephew!"

Again the faint sound. Something was stirring there among the shadows,—a shape moving softly along the wall, a shade which glided by me, paused, wavered, and darted under the bed. Then I threw myself on the floor, profoundly moved, begging, imploring my aunt to come to me.

"Aunty! Aunty!" I murmured, "your nephew is waiting to take you to his heart!"

And at last I saw my great-aunt's eyes, shining in the dark.

★ ★ ★ ★ ★ ★

271

Close the door. That meeting is not for the eyes of the world! Close the door upon that sacred scene where great-aunt and nephew are united at last.

A Pleasant Evening

(A story from The Maker of Moons.)

Et pis, doucett ment on's endort,
On fait sa carne, on fait sa sorgue,
On ronfle, et, comme un tuyau'd orgue,
L'tuyan s'met à ronfler pus fort. . . ."

Aristide Bruant.

1

As I stepped upon the platform of a Broadway cable-car at Forty-second Street, somebody said; "hello, Hilton, Jamison's looking for you."

"Hello, Curtis," I replied, "what does Jamison want?"

"He wants to know what you've been doing all the week, said Curtis, hanging desperately to the railing as the car lurched forward; he says you seem to think that the *Manhattan Illustrated Weekly* was created for the sole purpose of providing salary and vacations for you."

"The shifty old tom-cat!" I said, indignantly, "he knows well enough where I've been. Vacation! Does he think the State Camp in June is a snap?"

"Oh," said Curtis," you've been to Peekskill?"

"I should say so," I replied, my wrath rising as I thought of my assignment.

"Hot?" inquired Curtis, dreamily.

"One hundred and three in the shade," I answered. "Jamison wanted three full pages and three half pages, all for process work, and a lot of line drawings into the bargain. I could have faked them I wish I had. I was fool enough to hustle and break my neck to get some honest drawings, and that's the thanks I get!"

"Did you have a camera?"

"No. I will next time—I'll waste no more conscientious work on Jamison," I said sulkily.

"It doesn't pay," said Curtis. "When I have military work assigned me, I don't do the dashing sketch-artist act, you bet; I go to my studio, light my pipe, pull out a lot of old *Illustrated London News*, select several suitable battle scenes by Caton Woodville-and use 'em too."

The car shot around the neck-breaking curve at Fourteenth Street.

"Yes," continued Curtis, as the car stopped in front of the Morton House for a moment, then plunged forward again amid a furious clanging of gongs, "it doesn't pay to do decent work for the fat-headed men who run the *Manhattan Illustrated*. They don't appreciate it."

"I think the public does," I said, "but I'm sure Jamison doesn't. It would serve him right if I did what most of you fellows do-take a lot of Caton Woodville's and Thulstrup's drawings, change the uniforms, chic a figure or two, and turn in a drawing labelled from life. I m sick of this sort of thing anyway. Almost every day this week I've been chasing myself over that tropical camp, or galloping in the wake of those batteries. I've got a full page of the camp by moonlight, full pages of 'artillery drill' and 'light battery in action', and a dozen smaller drawings that cost me more groans and perspiration than Jamison ever knew in all his lymphatic life!"

"Jamison's got wheels," said Curtis,—"more wheels than there are bicycles in Harlem. He wants you to do a full page by Saturday."

"A what?" I exclaimed, aghast.

"Yes he does he was going to send Jim Crawford, but Jim expects to go to California for the winter fair, and you've got to do it."

"What is it?" I demanded savagely.

"The animals in Central Park," chuckled Curtis.

I was furious. The animals! Indeed! I'd show Jamison that I was entitled to some consideration! This was Thursday; that gave me a day and a half to finish a full-page drawing for the paper, and, after my work at the State Camp I felt that I was entitled to a little rest. Anyway I objected to the subject. I intended to tell Jamison so—I intended to tell him firmly. However, many of the things that we often intended to tell Jamison were never told. He was a peculiar man, fat-faced, thin-lipped, gentle-voiced, mild-mannered, and soft in his movements as a pussy cat. Just why our firmness should give way when we were actually in his presence, I have never quite been able to determine. He said very little—so did we, although we often entered his presence with other intentions.

The truth was that the *Manhattan Illustrated Weekly* was the best paying, best illustrated paper in America, and we young fellows were not anxious to be cast adrift. Jamison's knowledge of art was probably as extensive as the knowledge of any 'Art editor' in the city. Of course that was saying nothing, but the fact merited careful consideration on our part, and we gave it much consideration.

This time, however, I decided to let Jamison know that drawings are not produced by the yard, and that I was neither a floorwalker nor a hand-me-down. I would stand up for my rights; I'd tell old Jamison a few things to set the wheels under his silk hat spinning, and if he attempted any of his pussy-cat ways on me, I'd give him a few plain facts that would curl what hair he had left.

Glowing with a splendid indignation I jumped off the car at the City Hall, followed by Curtis, and a few minutes later entered the office of the *Manhattan Illustrated News*.

"Mr. Jamison would like to see you, sir," said one of the compositors as I passed into the long hallway. I threw my drawings on the table and passed a handkerchief over my forehead.

"Mr. Jamison would like to see you, sir," said a small freckle-faced boy with a smudge of ink on his nose.

"I know it," I said, and started to remove my gloves.

"Mr. Jamison would like to see you, sir," said a lank messenger who was carrying a bundle of proofs to the floor below.

"The deuce take Jamison," I said to myself. I started toward the dark passage that leads to the abode of Jamison, running over in my mind the neat and sarcastic speech which I had been composing during the last ten minutes.

Jamison looked up and nodded softly as I entered the room. I forgot my speech.

"Mr. Hilton," he said, "we want a full page of the Zoo before it is removed to Bronx Park. Saturday afternoon at three o clock the drawing must be in the engraver's hands. Did you have a pleasant week in camp?"

"It was hot," I muttered, furious to find that I could not re-member my little speech.

"The weather," said Jamison, with soft courtesy, "is oppressive everywhere. Are your drawings in, Mr. Hilton?"

"Yes. It was infernally hot and I worked like a nigger—"

"I suppose you were quite overcome. Is that why you took a two days trip to the Catskills? I trust the mountain air re-stored you—but was it prudent to go to Cranston's for the *cotillion* Tuesday? Dancing in such uncomfortable weather is really unwise. Good-morning, Mr. Hilton, remember the engraver should have your drawings on Saturday by three."

I walked out, half hypnotized, half enraged. Curtis grinned at me as I passed—I could have boxed his ears.

"Why the mischief should I lose my tongue whenever that old tom-cat purrs!" I asked myself as I entered the elevator and was shot down to the first floor. "I'll not put up with this sort of thing much longer—how in the name of all that's foxy did he know that I went to the mountains? I suppose he thinks I m lazy because I don't wish to be boiled to death. How did he know about the dance at Cranston's? Old cat!"

The roar and turmoil of machinery and busy men filled my ears as I crossed the avenue and turned into the City Hall Park.

From the staff on the tower the flag drooped in the warm

sunshine with scarcely a breeze to lift its crimson bars. Overhead stretched a splendid cloudless sky, deep, deep blue, thrilling, scintillating in the gemmed rays of the sun.

Pigeons wheeled and circled about the roof of the grey Post Office or dropped out of the blue above to flutter around the fountain in the square.

On the steps of the City Hall the unlovely politician lounged, exploring his heavy under jaw with wooden toothpick, twisting his drooping black moustache, or distributing tobacco juice over marble steps and close-clipped grass.

My eyes wandered from these human vermin to the calm scornful face of Nathan Hale, on his pedestal, and then to the grey-coated Park policeman whose occupation was to keep little children from the cool grass.

A young man with thin hands and blue circles under his eyes was slumbering on a bench by the fountain, and the policeman walked over to him and struck him on the soles of his shoes with a short club.

The young man rose mechanically, stared about, dazed by the sun, shivered, and limped away. I saw him sit down on the steps of the white marble building, and I went over and spoke to him. He neither looked at me, nor did he notice the coin I offered.

"You're sick," I said, "you had better go to the hospital."

"Where?" he asked vacantly—"I've been, but they wouldn't receive me."

He stooped and tied the bit of string that held what remained of his shoe to his foot.

"You are French," I said.

"Yes."

"Have you no friends? Have you been to the French Consul?"

"The Consul!" he replied; "no, I haven't been to the French Consul."

After a moment I said, "You speak like a gentleman."

He rose to his feet and stood very straight, looking me, for the first time, directly in the eyes.

"Who are you?" I asked abruptly.

"An outcast," he said, without emotion, and limped off thrusting his hands into his ragged pockets.

"Huh!" said the Park policeman who had come up behind me in time to hear my question and the vagabond's answer; "don't you know who that hobo is?—An' you a newspaper man!"

"Who is he, Cusick?" I demanded, watching the thin shabby figure moving across Broadway toward the river.

"On the level you don't know, Mr. Hilton?" repeated Cusick, suspiciously.

"No, I don't; I never before laid eyes on him."

"Why," said the sparrow policeman, "that's 'Soger Charlie';—you remember—that French officer what sold secrets to the Dutch Emperor."

"And was to have been shot? I remember now, four years ago—and he escaped—you mean to say that is the man?"

"Everybody knows it," sniffed Cusick, "I'd a-thought you newspaper gents would have knowed it first."

"What was his name?" I asked after a moment's thought.

"Soger Charlie—"

"I mean his name at home."

"Oh, some French *dago* name. No Frenchman will speak to him here; sometimes they curse him and kick him. I guess he's dyin by inches."

I remembered the case now. Two young French cavalry officers were arrested, charged with selling plans of fortifications and other military secrets to the Germans. On the eve of their conviction, one of them, Heaven only knows how, escaped and turned up in New York. The other was duly shot. The affair had made some noise, because both young men were of good families. It was a painful episode, and I had hastened to forget it. Now that it was recalled to my mind, I remembered the newspaper accounts of the case, but I had forgotten the names of the miserable young men.

"Sold his country," observed Cusick, watching a group of children out of the corner of his eyes—"you can't trust no

278

Frenchman nor *dagoes* nor Dutchmen either. I guess Yankees are about the only white men."

I looked at the noble face of Nathan Hale and nodded.

"Nothin' sneaky about us, eh, Mr. Hilton?"

I thought of Benedict Arnold and looked at my boots.

Then the policeman said, "Well, solong, Mr. Hilton," and went away to frighten a pasty-faced little girl who had climbed upon the railing and was leaning down to sniff the fragrant grass.

"Cheese it, de cop!" cried her shrill-voiced friends, and the whole bevy of small ragamuffins scuttled away across the square.

With a feeling of depression I turned and walked toward Broadway, where the long yellow cable-cars swept up and down, and the din of gongs and the deafening rumble of heavy trucks echoed from the marble walls of the Court House to the granite mass of the Post Office.

Throngs of hurrying busy people passed up town and down town, slim sober-faced clerks, trim cold-eyed brokers, here and there a red-necked politician linking arms with some favourite heeler, here and there a City Hall lawyer, sallow-faced and saturnine. Sometimes a fireman, in his severe blue uniform, passed through the crowd, sometimes a blue-coated policeman, mopping his clipped hair, holding his helmet in his white-gloved hand. There were women too, pale-faced shop girls with pretty eyes, tall blonde girls who might be typewriters and might not, and many, many older women whose business in that part of the city no human being could venture to guess, but who hurried up town and down town, all occupied with *something* that gave to the whole restless throng a common likeness—the expression of one who hastens toward a hopeless goal.

I knew some of those who passed me. There was little Jocelyn of the *Mail and Express*; there was Hood, who had more money than he wanted and was going to have less than he wanted when he left Wall Street; there was Colonel Tidmouse of the 45th Infantry, N.G.S.N.Y., probably coming from the office of the *Army and Navy Journal*, and there was Dick Harding who wrote the best stories of New York life that have been printed. People said his hat no longer fitted,—especially people who also wrote stories of New York life and whose hats threatened to fit as long as they lived.

I looked at the statue of Nathan Hale, then at the human stream that flowed around his pedestal.

"*Quand même*," I muttered and walked out into Broadway, signalling to the gripman of an uptown cable-car.

2

I passed into the Park by the Fifth Avenue and 59th Street gate; I could never bring myself to enter it through the gate that is guarded by the hideous pigmy statue of Thorwaldsen.

The afternoon sun poured into the windows of the New Netherlands Hotel, setting every orange-curtained pane a-glitter, and tipping the wings of the bronze dragons with flame.

Gorgeous masses of flowers blazed in the sun shine from the grey terraces of the Savoy, from the high grilled court of the Vanderbilt palace, and from the balconies of the *Plaza* opposite.

The white marble *façade* of the Metropolitan Club was a grateful relief in the universal glare, and I kept my eyes on it until I had crossed the dusty street and entered the shade of the trees.

Before I came to the Zoo I smelled it. Next week it was to be removed to the fresh cool woods and meadows in Bronx Park, far from the stifling air of the city, far from the infernal noise of the Fifth Avenue omnibuses.

A noble stag stared at me from his enclosure among the trees as I passed down the winding asphalt walk. "Never mind, old fellow," said I, "you will be splashing about in the Bronx River next week and cropping maple shoots to your heart's content."

On I went, past herds of staring deer, past great lumbering elk, and moose, and long-faced African antelopes, until I came to the dens of the great *carnivora*.

The tigers sprawled in the sunshine, blinking and licking their paws; the lions slept in the shade or squatted on their haunches, yawning gravely. A slim panther travelled to and fro behind her barred cage, pausing at times to peer wistfully out into the free sunny world. My heart ached for caged wild things, and I walked on, glancing up now and then to encounter the blank stare of a tiger or the mean shifty eyes of some ill-smelling hyena.

Across the meadow I could see the elephants swaying and swinging their great heads, the sober bison solemnly slobbering over their cuds, the sarcastic countenances of camels, the wicked little zebras, and a lot more animals of the camel and llama tribe, all resembling each other, all equally ridiculous, stupid, deadly uninteresting.

Somewhere behind the old arsenal an eagle was screaming, probably a Yankee eagle; I heard the "tchug! tchug!" of a blowing hippopotamus, the squeal of a falcon, and the snarling yap! of quarrelling wolves.

"A pleasant place for a hot day!" I pondered bitterly, and I thought some things about Jamison that I shall not insert in this volume. But I lighted a cigarette to deaden the aroma from the hyenas, unclasped my sketching block, sharpened my pencil, and fell to work on a family group of hippopotami.

They may have taken me for a photographer, for they all wore smiles as if welcoming a friend, and my sketch block presented a series of wide open jaws, behind which shapeless bulky bodies vanished in alarming perspective.

The alligators were easy; they looked to me as though they had not moved since the founding of the Zoo, but I had a bad time with the big bison, who persistently turned his tail to me, looking stolidly around his flank to see how I stood it. So I pretended to be absorbed in the antics of two bear cubs, and the dreary old bison fell into the trap, for I made some good sketches of him and laughed in his face as I closed the book.

There was a bench by the abode of the eagles, and I sat down on it to draw the vultures and condors, motionless as mummies among the piled rocks. Gradually I enlarged the sketch, bringing in the gravel *plaza*, the steps leading up to Fifth Avenue, the sleepy park policeman in front of the arsenal—and a slim, white-browed girl, dressed in shabby black, who stood silently in the shade of the willow trees.

After a while I found that the sketch, instead of being a study of the eagles, was in reality a composition in which the girl in black occupied the principal point of interest. Unwittingly I had subordinated everything else to her, the brooding vultures, the trees and walks, and the half indicated groups of sun-warmed loungers.

She stood very still, her pallid face bent, her thin white hands loosely clasped before her. "Rather dejected reverie," I thought, "probably she's out of work." Then I caught a glimpse of a sparkling diamond ring on the slender third finger of her left hand.

"She'll not starve with such a stone as that about her," I said to myself, looking curiously at her dark eyes and sensitive mouth. They were both beautiful, eyes and mouth—beautiful, but touched with pain.

After a while I rose and walked back to make a sketch or two of the lions and tigers. I avoided the monkeys—I can't stand them, and they never seem funny to me, poor dwarfish, degraded caricatures of all that is ignoble in ourselves.

"I've enough now," I thought; "I'll go home and manufacture a full page that will probably please Jamison." So I strapped the elastic band around my sketching block, replaced pencil and rubber in my waistcoat pocket, and strolled off toward the Mall to smoke a cigarette in the evening glow before going back to my studio to work until midnight, up to the chin in charcoal grey and Chinese white.

Across the long meadow I could see the roofs of the city faintly looming above the trees. A mist of amethyst, ever deepening, hung low on the horizon, and through it, steeple and dome, roof and tower, and the tall chimneys where thin fillets of smoke curled idly, were transformed into pinnacles of beryl and flaming minarets, swimming in filmy haze. Slowly the enchantment deepened; all that was ugly and shabby and mean had fallen away from the distant city, and now it towered into the evening sky, splendid, gilded, magnificent, purified in the fierce furnace of the setting sun.

The red disk was half hidden now; the tracery of trees, feathery willow and budding birch, darkened against the glow; the fiery rays shot far across the meadow, gilding the dead leaves, staining with soft crimson the dark moist tree trunks around me.

Far across the meadow a shepherd passed in the wake of a huddling flock, his dog at his heels, faint moving blots of grey.

A squirrel sat up on the gravel walk in front of me, ran a few feet, and sat up again, so close that I could see the palpitation of his sleek flanks.

Somewhere in the grass a hidden field insect was rehearsing last summer's solos; I heard the tap! tap! tat-tat-t-t-tat! of a woodpecker among the branches overhead and the querulous note of a sleepy robin.

The twilight deepened; out of the city the music of bells floated over wood and meadow; faint mellow whistles sounded from the river craft along the north shore, and the distant thunder of a gun announced the close of a June day.

The end of my cigarette began to glimmer with a redder light; shepherd and flock were blotted out in the dusk, and I only knew they were still moving when the sheep bells tinkled faintly.

Then suddenly that strange uneasiness that all have known—that half-awakened sense of having seen it all before, of having been through it all, came over me, and I raised my head and slowly turned.

A figure was seated at my side. My mind was struggling with the instinct to remember. Something so vague and yet so familiar—something that eluded thought yet challenged it, something—God knows what! troubled me. And now, as I looked, without interest, at the dark figure beside me, an apprehension, totally involuntary, an impatience to *understand*, came upon me, and I sighed and turned restlessly again to the fading west.

I thought I heard my sigh re-echoed—I scarcely heeded; and in a moment I sighed again, dropping my burned-out cigarette on the gravel beneath my feet.

"Did you speak to me?" said someone in a low voice, so close that I swung around rather sharply.

"No," I said after a moment's silence.

It was a woman. I could not see her face clearly, but I saw on her clasped hands, which lay listlessly in her lap, the sparkle of a great diamond. I knew her at once. It did not need a glance at the shabby dress of black, the white face, a pallid spot in the twilight, to tell me that I had her picture in my sketch-book.

"Do—do you mind if I speak to you?" she asked timidly.

The hopeless sadness in her voice touched me, and I said: "Why, no, of course not. Can I do anything for you?"

"Yes," she said, brightening a little, "if you—you only would."

"I will if I can," said I, cheerfully; "what is it? Out of ready cash?"

"No, not that," she said, shrinking back.

I begged her pardon, a little surprised, and withdrew my hand from my change pocket.

"It is only—only that I wish you to take these,"—she drew a thin packet from her breast,—"these two letters."

"I?" I asked astonished.

"Yes, if you will."

"But what am I to do with them?" I demanded.

"I can't tell you; I only know that I must give them to you. Will you take them?"

"Oh, yes, I'll take them," I laughed, "am I to read them?" I added to myself, "It's some clever begging trick."

"No," she answered slowly, "you are not to read them; you are to give them to somebody."

"To whom? Anybody?"

"No, not to anybody. You will know whom to give them to when the time comes."

"Then I am to keep them until further instructions?"

"Your own heart will instruct you," she said, in a scarcely audible voice. She held the thin packet toward me, and to humour her I took it. It was wet.

"The letters fell into the sea," she said; "There was a photograph which should have gone with them but the salt water washed it blank. Will you care if I ask you something else?"

"I? Oh, no."

"Then give me the picture that you made of me today."

I laughed again, and demanded how she knew I had drawn her.

"Is it like me?" she said.

"I think it is very like you," I answered truthfully.

"Will you not give it to me?"

Now it was on the tip of my tongue to refuse, but I reflected that I had enough sketches for a full page without that one, so I handed it to her, nodded that she was welcome, and stood up. She rose also, the diamond flashing on her finger.

"You are sure that you are not in want?" I asked, with a tinge of good-natured sarcasm.

"Hark!" she whispered; "listen!—do you hear the bells of the convent?"

I looked out into the misty night.

"There are no bells sounding," I said, "and anyway there are no convent bells here. We are in New York, *mademoiselle*"—I had noticed her French accent—"we are in Protestant Yankeeland, and the bells that ring are much less mellow than the bells of France."

I turned pleasantly to say goodnight. She was gone.

3

"Have you ever drawn a picture of a corpse?" inquired Jamison next morning as I walked into his private room with a sketch of the proposed full page of the Zoo.

"No, and I don't want to," I replied, sullenly.

"Let me see your Central Park page," said Jamison in his gentle voice, and I displayed it. It was about worthless as an artistic production, but it pleased Jamison, as I knew it would.

"Can you finish it by this afternoon?" he asked, looking up at me with persuasive eyes.

"Oh, I suppose so," I said, wearily; "anything else, Mr. Jamison?"

"The corpse," he replied, "I want a sketch by tomorrow—finished."

"What corpse?" I demanded, controlling my indignation as I met Jamison's soft eyes.

There was a mute duel of glances. Jamison passed his hand across his forehead with a slight lifting of the eyebrows.

"I shall want it as soon as possible," he said in his caressing voice.

What I thought was, "Damned purring pussy cat!" What I said was, "Where is this corpse?"

"In the Morgue—have you read the morning papers? No? Ah,—as you very rightly observe you are too busy to read the morning papers. Young men must learn industry first, of course, of course. What you are to do is this : the San Francisco police have sent out an alarm regarding the disappearance of a Miss Tufft—the millionaire's daughter, you know. Today a body was brought to the Morgue here in New York, and it has been identified as the missing young lady,—by a diamond ring. Now I am convinced that it isn't, and I'll show you why, Mr. Hilton."

He picked up a pen and made a sketch of a ring on a margin of that morning's *Tribune*.

"That is the description of her ring as sent on from San Francisco. You notice the diamond is set in the centre of the ring where the two gold serpents *tails* cross! Now the ring on the finger of the woman in the Morgue is like this," and he rapidly sketched another ring where the diamond rested in the *fangs* of the two gold serpents.

"That is the difference," he said in his pleasant, even voice.

"Rings like that are not uncommon," said I, remembering that I had seen such a ring on the finger of the white-faced girl in the park the evening before. Then a sudden thought took shape—perhaps that was the girl whose body lay in the Morgue!

"Well," said Jamison, looking up at me, "what are you think-ing about?"

"Nothing," I answered, but the whole scene was before my eyes, the vultures brooding among the rocks, the shabby black dress, and the pallid face,—and the ring, glittering on that slim white hand!

"Nothing," I repeated, "when shall I go, Mr. Jamison? Do you want a portrait—or what?"

"Portrait,—careful drawing of the ring, and,—er—a centre piece of the Morgue at night. Might as well give people the horrors while we're about it."

"But," said I, "the policy of this paper—"

"Never mind, Mr. Hilton," purred Jamison, "I am able to di-rect the policy of this paper."

"I don't doubt you are," I said angrily.

"I am," he repeated, undisturbed and smiling; "you see this Tufft case interests society. I am—er—also interested."

He held out to me a morning paper and pointed to a head-ing.

I read:

Miss Tufft Dead! Her Fiancé was Mr. Jamison, the well known Editor.

"What!" I cried in horrified amazement. But Jamison had left the room, and I heard him chatting and laughing softly with some visitors in the press-room outside.

I flung down the paper and walked out.

"The cold-blooded toad!" I exclaimed again and again;— "making capital out of his *fiancée's* disappearance! Well, I—I'm d—nd! I knew he was a bloodless, heartless, grip-penny, but I never thought—I never imagined—" Words failed me.

Scarcely conscious of what I did I drew a *Herald* from my pocket and saw the column entitled:

Miss Tufft Found! Identified by a Ring. Wild Grief of Mr. Jamison, her Fiancé.

That was enough. I went out into the street and sat down

in City Hall Park. And, as I sat there, a terrible resolution came to me; I would draw that dead girl's face in such a way that it would chill Jamison's sluggish blood, I would crowd the black shadows of the Morgue with forms and ghastly faces, and every face should bear something in it of Jamison. Oh, I'd rouse him from his cold snaky apathy! I'd confront him with Death in such an awful form, that, passionless, base, inhuman as he was, he'd shrink from it as he would from a dagger thrust.

Of course I'd lose my place, but that did not bother me, for I had decided to resign anyway, not having a taste for the society of human reptiles. And, as I sat there in the sunny park, furious, trying to plan a picture whose sombre horror should leave in his mind an ineffaceable scar, I suddenly thought of the pale black-robed girl in Central Park. Could it be her poor slender body that lay among the shadows of the grim Morgue! If ever brooding despair was stamped on any face, I had seen its print on hers when she spoke to me in the Park and gave me the letters. The letters! I had not thought of them since, but now I drew them from my pocket and looked at the addresses.

"Curious," I thought, "the letters are still damp; they smell of salt water too."

I looked at the address again, written in the long fine hand of an educated woman who had been bred in a French convent. Both letters bore the same address, in French:

Captain'd Ynioi,
(Kindness of a Stranger.)

"Captain'd Yniol," I repeated aloud "confound it, I've heard that name! Now, where the deuce where in the name of all that's queer —" Somebody who had sat down on the bench beside me placed a heavy hand on my shoulder.

It was the Frenchman, "Soger Charlie."

"You spoke my name," he said in apathetic tones.

"Your name!"

"Captain'd Yniol," he repeated; "it is my name."

I recognized him in spite of the black goggles he was wearing, and, at the same moment, it flashed into my mind that'd Yniol was the name of the traitor who had escaped. Ah, I remembered now!

"I am Captain'd Yniol," he said again, and I saw his fingers closing on my coat sleeve.

It may have been my involuntary movement of recoil, I don't know, but the fellow dropped my coat and sat straight up on the bench.

"I am Captain'd Yniol," he said for the third time, "charged with treason and under sentence of death."

"And innocent!" I muttered, before I was even conscious of having spoken. What was it that wrung those involuntary words from my lips, I shall never know, perhaps—but it was I, not he, who trembled, seized with a strange agitation, and it was I, not he, whose hand was stretched forth impulsively, touching his.

Without a tremor he took my hand, pressed it almost imperceptibly, and dropped it. Then I held both letters toward him, and, as he neither looked at them nor at me, I placed them in his hand. Then he started.

"Read them," I said, "they are for you."

"Letters!" he gasped in a voice that sounded like nothing human.

"Yes, they are for you,—I know it now—"

"Letters!—letters directed to *me*?"

"Can you not see?" I cried.

Then he raised one frail hand and drew the goggles from his eyes, and, as I looked, I saw two tiny white specks exactly in the centre of both pupils.

"Blind!" I faltered.

"I have been unable to read for two years," he said.

After a moment he placed the tip of one finger on the letters.

"They are wet," I said; "shall—would you like to have me read them?" For a long time he sat silently in the sunshine, fumbling with his cane, and I watched him without speaking.

At last he said, "Read, *Monsieur*," and I took the letters and broke the seals.

The first letter contained a sheet of paper, damp and discoloured, on which a few lines were written:

"My darling, I knew you were innocent—" Here the writing ended, but, in the blur beneath, I read:

Paris shall know France shall know, for at last I have the proofs and I am coming to find you, my soldier, and to place them in your own dear brave hands. They know, now, at the War Ministry—they have a copy of the traitor's confession but they dare not make it public—they dare not withstand the popular astonishment and rage. Therefore I sail on Monday from Cherbourg by the Green Cross Line, to bring you back to your own again, where you will stand before all the world, without fear, without reproach.

"This—this is terrible!" I stammered; "God live and see such things done!"

But with his thin hand he gripped my arm again, bidding me read the other letter; and I shuddered at the menace in his voice.

Then, with his sightless eyes on me, I drew the other letter from the wet, stained envelope. And before I was aware before I understood the purport of what I saw, I had read aloud these half effaced lines:

The *Lorient* is sinking—an iceberg mid-ocean—goodbye you are innocent I love—

"The *Lorient*!" I cried; "it was the French steamer that was never heard from—the *Lorient* of the Green Cross Line! I had forgotten—I—"

The loud crash of a revolver stunned me; my ears rang and ached with it as I shrank back from a ragged dusty figure that collapsed on the bench beside me, shuddered a moment, and tumbled to the asphalt at my feet.

The trampling of the eager hard-eyed crowd, the dust and

taint of powder in the hot air, the harsh alarm of the ambulance clattering up Mail Street,—these I remember, as I knelt there, helplessly holding the dead man's hands in mine.

"Soger Charlie," mused the sparrow police man, "shot hisself, didn't he, Mr. Hilton? You seen him, sir,—blowed the top of his head off, didn't he, Mr. Hilton?"

"Soger Charlie," they repeated, "a French *dago* what shot hisself;" and the words echoed in my ears long after the ambulance rattled away, and the increasing throng dispersed, sullenly, as a couple of policemen cleared a space around the pool of thick blood on the asphalt.

They wanted me as a witness, and I gave my card to one of the policemen who knew me. The rabble transferred its fascinated stare to me, and I turned away and pushed a path between frightened shop girls and ill-smelling loafers, until I lost myself in the human torrent of Broadway.

The torrent took me with it where it flowed—East? West?—I did not notice nor care, but I passed on through the throng, listless, deadly weary of attempting to solve God's justice—striving to understand His purpose—His laws—His judgements which are "true and righteous altogether."

4

"More to be desired are they than gold, yea, than much fine gold. Sweeter also than honey and the honey-comb!"

I turned sharply toward the speaker who shambled at my elbow. His sunken eyes were dull and lustreless, his bloodless face gleamed pallid as a death mask above the blood-red jersey—the emblem of the soldiers of Christ.

I don't know why I stopped, lingering, but, as he passed, I said, "Brother, I also was meditating upon God's wisdom and His testimonies."

The pale fanatic shot a glance at me, hesitated, and fell into my own pace, walking by my side. Under the peak of his Salvation Army cap his eyes shone in the shadow with a strange light.

"Tell me more," I said, sinking my voice below the roar of traffic, the clang! clang! of the cable-cars, and the noise of feet on the worn pavements—"tell me of His testimonies."

"*Moreover by them is Thy servant warned and in keeping of them there is great reward. Who can understand His errors? Cleanse Thou me from secret faults. Keep back Thy servant also from presumptuous sins. Let them not have dominion over me. Then shall I be upright and I shall be innocent from the great transgression. Let the words of my mouth and the meditation of my heart be acceptable in Thy sight, O Lord! My strength and my Redeemer!*"

"It is Holy Scripture that you quote, I said; I also can read that when I choose. But it cannot clear for me the reasons—it cannot make me understand—"

"What?" he asked, and muttered to himself.

"That, for instance," I replied, pointing to a cripple, who had been *born* deaf and dumb and horridly misshapen,—a wretched diseased lump on the sidewalk below St. Paul's Churchyard,—a sore-eyed thing that mouthed and mowed and rattled pennies in a tin cup as though the sound of copper could stem the human pack that passed hot on the scent of gold.

Then the man who shambled beside me turned and looked long and earnestly into my eyes. And after a moment a dull recollection stirred within me—a vague something that seemed like the awakening memory of a past, long, long forgotten, dim, dark, too subtle, too frail, too indefinite—ah! the old feeling that all men have known—the old strange uneasiness, that useless struggle to remember when and where it all occurred before.

And the man's head sank on his crimson jersey, and he muttered, muttered to himself of God and love and compassion, until I saw that the fierce heat of the city had touched his brain, and I went away and left him prating of mysteries that none but such as he dare name.

So I passed on through dust and heat; and the hot breath of men touched my cheek and eager eyes looked into mine. Byes, eyes, that met my own and looked through them, beyond far beyond to where gold glittered amid the mirage of eternal hope.

Gold! It was in the air where the soft sunlight gilded the floating moats, it was under foot in the dust that the sun made gilt, it glimmered from every window pane where the long red beams struck golden sparks above the gasping gold-hunting hordes of Wall Street.

High, high, in the deepening sky the tall buildings towered, and the breeze from the bay lifted the sun-dyed flags of commerce until they waved above the turmoil of the hives below—waved courage and hope and strength to those who lusted after gold.

The sun dipped low behind Castle William as I turned listlessly into the Battery, and the long straight shadows of the trees stretched away over greensward and asphalt walk.

Already the electric lights were glimmering among the foliage although the bay shimmered like polished brass and the topsails of the ships glowed with a deeper hue, where the red sun rays fall athwart the rigging.

Old men tottered along the sea-wall, tapping the asphalt with worn canes, old women crept to and fro in the coming twilight,—old women who carried baskets that gaped for charity or bulged with mouldy stuffs,—food, clothing?—I could not tell; I did not care to know.

The heavy thunder from the parapets of Castle William died away over the placid bay, the last red arm of the sun shot up out of the sea, and wavered and faded into the sombre tones of the afterglow. Then came the night, timidly at first, touching sky and water with grey fingers, folding the foliage into soft massed shapes, creeping on ward, onward, more swiftly now, until colour and form had gone from all the earth and the world was a world of shadows.

And, as I sat there on the dusky sea-wall, gradually the bitter thoughts faded and I looked out into the calm night with something of that peace that comes to all when day is ended.

The death at my very elbow of the poor blind wretch in the Park had left a shock, but now my nerves relaxed their tension and I began to think about it all,—about the letters and the strange woman who had given them to me. I wondered where she had found them, whether they really were carried by some vagrant current in to the shore from the wreck of the fated *Lorient*.

Nothing but these letters had human eyes encountered from the *Lorient*, although we believed that fire or berg had been her portion; for there had been no storms when the *Lorient* steamed away from Cherbourg.

And what of the pale-faced girl in black who had given these letters to me, saying that my own heart would teach me where to place them?

I felt in my pockets for the letters where I had thrust them all crumpled and wet. They were there, and I decided to turn them over to the police. Then I thought of Cusick and the City Hall Park and these set my mind running on Jamison and my own work,—ah! I had forgotten that, I had forgotten that—I had sworn to stir Jamison's cold, sluggish blood! Trading on his *fiancée's* reported suicide,—or murder! True, he had told me that he was satisfied that the body at the Morgue was not Miss Tufft's because the ring did not correspond with his *fiancée's* ring. But what sort of a man was that!—to go crawling and nosing about morgues and graves for a full-page illustration which might sell a few extra thousand papers. I had never known he was such a man. It was strange too—for that was not the sort of illustration that the *Weekly* used; it was against all precedent against the whole policy of the paper. He would lose a hundred subscribers where he would gain one by such work.

"The callous brute!" I muttered to myself, "I'll wake him up—I'll—"

I sat straight up on the bench and looked steadily at a figure which was moving toward me under the spluttering electric light.

It was the woman I had met in the park.

She came straight up to me, her pale face gleaming like marble in the dark, her slim hands outstretched.

"I have been looking for you all day—all day," she said, in the same low thrilling tones,—"I want the letters back; have you them here?"

"Yes," I said, "I have them here,—take them in Heaven's name; they have done enough evil for one day!"

She took the letters from my hand; I saw the ring, made of the double serpents, flashing on her slim finger, and I stepped closer, and looked her in the eyes.

"Who are you?" I asked.

"I? My name is of no importance to you," she answered.

"You are right," I said, "I do not care to know your name. That ring of yours—"

"What of my ring?" she murmured.

"Nothing,—a dead woman lying in the Morgue wears such a ring. Do you know what your letters have done? No? Well I read them to a miserable wretch and he blew his brains out!"

"You read them to a man!"

"I did. He killed himself."

"Who was that man?"

"Captain'd Yniol—"

With something between a sob and a laugh she seized my hand and covered it with kisses, and I, astonished and angry, pulled my hand away from her cold lips and sat down on the bench.

"You needn't thank me," I said sharply; "if I had known that,—but no matter. Perhaps after all the poor devil is better off somewhere in other regions with his sweetheart who was drowned,—yes, I imagine he is. He was blind and ill,—and broken-hearted."

"Blind?" she asked gently.

"Yes. Did you know him?"

"I knew him."

"And his sweetheart, Aline? "

"Aline," she repeated softly,—"she is dead. I come to thank you in her name."

"For what?—for his death?"

"Ah, yes, for that."

"Where did you get those letters?" I asked her, suddenly.

She did not answer, but stood fingering the wet letters.

Before I could speak again she moved away into the shadows of the trees, lightly, silently, and far down the dark walk I saw her diamond flashing.

Grimly brooding, I rose and passed through the Battery to the steps of the Elevated Road. These I climbed, bought my ticket, and stepped out to the damp platform. When a train came I crowded in with the rest, still pondering on my vengeance, feeling and believing that I was to scourge the conscience of the man who speculated on death.

And at last the train stopped at 28th Street, and I hurried out and down the steps and away to the Morgue.

When I entered the Morgue, Skelton, the keeper, was standing before a slab that glistened faintly under the wretched gas jets. He heard my footsteps, and turned around to see who was coming. Then he nodded, saying: "Mr. Hilton, just take a look at this here stiff—I'll be back in a moment this is the one that all the papers take to be Miss Tufft,—but they're all off, because this stiff has been here now for two weeks."

I drew out my sketching-block and pencils.

"Which is it, Skelton?" I asked, fumbling for my rubber.

"This one, Mr. Hilton, the girl what's smilin'. Picked up off Sandy Hook, too. Looks as if she was asleep, eh?"

"What's she got in her hand—clenched tight? Oh,—a letter. Turn up the gas, Skelton, I want to see her face."

The old man turned the gas jet, and the flame blazed and whistled in the damp, fetid air. Then suddenly my eyes fell on the dead.

Rigid, scarcely breathing, I stared at the ring, made of two twisted serpents set with a great diamond,—I saw the wet letters crushed in her slender hand,—I looked, and—God help me!—I looked upon the dead face of the girl with whom I had been speaking on the Battery!

"Dead for a month at least," said Skelton, calmly.

Then, as I felt my senses leaving me, I screamed out, and at

296

the same instant somebody from behind seized my shoulder and shook me savagely—shook me until I opened my eyes again and gasped and coughed.

"Now then, young feller!" said a Park police man bending over me, "if you go to sleep on a bench, somebody'll lift your watch!"

I turned, rubbing my eyes desperately.

Then it was all a dream—and no shrinking girl had come to me with damp letters,—I had not gone to the office—there was no such person as Miss Tufft,—Jamison was not an unfeeling villain,—no, indeed!—he treated us all much better than we deserved, and he was kind and generous too. And the ghastly suicide! Thank God that also was a myth,—and the Morgue and the Battery at night where that pale-faced girl had—ugh!

I felt for my sketch-block, found it; turned the pages of all the animals that I had sketched, the hippopotami, the buffalo, the tigers—ah! where was that sketch in which I had made the woman in shabby black the principal figure, with the brooding vultures all around and the crowd in the sunshine—? It was gone.

I hunted everywhere, in every pocket. It was gone.

At last I rose and moved along the narrow asphalt path in the falling twilight.

And as I turned into the broader walk, I was aware of a group, a policeman holding a lantern, some gardeners, and a knot of loungers gathered about something,—a dark mass on the ground.

"Found 'em just so," one of the gardeners was saying, "better not touch 'em until the coroner comes."

The policeman shifted his bull's-eye a little; the rays fell on two faces, on two bodies, half supported against a park bench. On the finger of the girl glittered a splendid diamond, set between the fangs of two gold serpents. The man had shot himself; he clasped two wet letters in his hand. The girl's clothing and hair were wringing wet, and her face was the face of a drowned person.

"Well, sir," said the policeman, looking at me; "you seem to know these two people—by your looks—"

"I never saw them before," I gasped, and walked on, trembling in every nerve.

For among the folds of her shabby black dress I had noticed the end of a paper, my sketch that I had missed!

Rue Barrée

(*A story from The King in Yellow.*)

For let Philosopher and Doctor preach
Of what they will and what they will not,—each
Is but one link in an eternal chain
That none can slip nor break nor over-reach.

Crimson nor yellow roses nor
The savour of the mounting sea
Are worth the perfume I adore
That clings to thee.
The languid-headed lilies tire,
The changeless waters weary me;
I ache with passionate desire
Of thine and thee.
There are but these things in the world—
Thy mouth of fire,
Thy breasts, thy hands, thy hair upcurled
And my desire.

1

One morning at Julian's, a student said to Selby, "That is Fox-hall Clifford," pointing with his brushes at a young man who sat before an easel, doing nothing.

Selby, shy and nervous, walked over and began: "My name is Selby,—I have just arrived in Paris, and bring a letter of introduction—" His voice was lost in the crash of a falling easel, the owner of which promptly assaulted his neighbour, and for a time the noise of battle rolled through the studios of MM.

299

Boulanger and Lefebvre, presently subsiding into a scuffle on the stairs outside. Selby, apprehensive as to his own reception in the studio, looked at Clifford, who sat serenely watching the fight.

"It's a little noisy here," said Clifford, "but you will like the fellows when you know them." His unaffected manner delighted Selby. Then with a simplicity that won his heart, he presented him to half a dozen students of as many nationalities. Some were cordial, all were polite. Even the majestic creature who held the position of Massier, unbent enough to say: "My friend, when a man speaks French as well as you do, and is also a friend of Monsieur Clifford, he will have no trouble in this studio. You expect, of course, to fill the stove until the next new man comes?"

"Of course."

"And you don't mind chaff?"

"No," replied Selby, who hated it.

Clifford, much amused, put on his hat, saying, "You must expect lots of it at first."

Selby placed his own hat on his head and followed him to the door.

As they passed the model stand there was a furious cry of "*Chapeau! Chapeau!*" and a student sprang from his easel menacing Selby, who reddened but looked at Clifford.

"Take off your hat for them," said the latter, laughing.

A little embarrassed, he turned and saluted the studio.

"*Et moi?*" cried the model.

"You are charming," replied Selby, astonished at his own audacity, but the studio rose as one man, shouting: "He has done well! he's all right!" while the model, laughing, kissed her hand to him and cried: "*À demain beau jeune homme!*"

All that week Selby worked at the studio unmolested. The French students christened him "*l'Enfant Prodigue*," which was freely translated, "The Prodigious Infant," "The Kid," "Kid Selby," and "Kidby." But the disease soon ran its course from "Kidby" to "Kidney," and then naturally to "Tidbits," where it was arrested by Clifford's authority and ultimately relapsed to "Kid."

Wednesday came, and with it M. Boulanger. For three hours the students writhed under his biting sarcasms,—among the others Clifford, who was informed that he knew even less about a work of art than he did about the art of work. Selby was more fortunate. The professor examined his drawing in silence, looked at him sharply, and passed on with a non-committal gesture. He presently departed arm in arm with Bouguereau, to the relief of Clifford, who was then at liberty to jam his hat on his head and depart.

The next day he did not appear, and Selby, who had counted on seeing him at the studio, a thing which he learned later it was vanity to count on, wandered back to the Latin Quarter alone.

Paris was still strange and new to him. He was vaguely troubled by its splendour. No tender memories stirred his American bosom at the Place du Châtelet, nor even by Notre Dame. The Palais de Justice with its clock and turrets and stalking sentinels in blue and vermilion, the Place St. Michel with its jumble of omnibuses and ugly water-spitting griffins, the hill of the Boulevard St. Michel, the tooting trams, the policemen dawdling two by two, and the table-lined terraces of the Café Vacehett were nothing to him, as yet, nor did he even know, when he stepped from the stones of the Place St. Michel to the asphalt of the Boulevard, that he had crossed the frontier and entered the student zone,—the famous Latin Quarter.

A cabman hailed him as "*bourgeois*," and urged the superiority of driving over walking. A *gamin*, with an appearance of great concern, requested the latest telegraphic news from London, and then, standing on his head, invited Selby to feats of strength. A pretty girl gave him a glance from a pair of violet eyes. He did not see her, but she, catching her own reflection in a window, wondered at the colour burning in her cheeks. Turning to resume her course, she met Foxhall Clifford, and hurried on. Clifford, open-mouthed, followed her with his eyes; then he looked after Selby, who had turned into the Boulevard St. Germain toward the rue de Seine. Then he examined himself in the shop window. The result seemed to be unsatisfactory.

"I'm not a beauty," he mused, "but neither am I a hobgoblin. What does she mean by blushing at Selby? I never before saw her look at a fellow in my life,—neither has anyone in the Quarter. Anyway, I can swear she never looks at me, and goodness knows I have done all that respectful adoration can do."

He sighed, and murmuring a prophecy concerning the salvation of his immortal soul swung into that graceful lounge which at all times characterized Clifford. With no apparent exertion, he overtook Selby at the corner, and together they crossed the sunlit Boulevard and sat down under the awning of the Café du Cercle. Clifford bowed to everybody on the terrace, saying, "You shall meet them all later, but now let me present you to two of the sights of Paris, Mr. Richard Elliott and Mr. Stanley Rowden."

The "sights" looked amiable, and took vermouth.

"You cut the studio today," said Elliott, suddenly turning on Clifford, who avoided his eyes.

"To commune with nature?" observed Rowden.

"What's her name this time?" asked Elliott, and Rowden answered promptly, "Name, Yvette; nationality, Breton—"

"Wrong," replied Clifford blandly, "it's Rue Barrée."

The subject changed instantly, and Selby listened in surprise to names which were new to him, and eulogies on the latest Prix de Rome winner. He was delighted to hear opinions boldly expressed and points honestly debated, although the vehicle was mostly slang, both English and French. He longed for the time when he too should be plunged into the strife for fame.

The bells of St. Sulpice struck the hour, and the Palace of the Luxembourg answered chime on chime. With a glance at the sun, dipping low in the golden dust behind the Palais Bourbon, they rose, and turning to the east, crossed the Boulevard St. Germain and sauntered toward the École de Médecine. At the corner a girl passed them, walking hurriedly. Clifford smirked, Elliot and Rowden were agitated, but they all bowed, and, without raising her eyes, she returned their salute. But Selby, who had lagged behind, fascinated by some gay shop window, looked up to meet two of the bluest eyes he had ever seen. The eyes were dropped in an instant, and the young fellow hastened to overtake the others.

"By Jove," he said, "do you fellows know I have just seen the prettiest girl—" An exclamation broke from the trio, gloomy, foreboding, like the chorus in a Greek play.

"Rue Barrée!"

"What!" cried Selby, bewildered.

The only answer was a vague gesture from Clifford.

Two hours later, during dinner, Clifford turned to Selby and said, "You want to ask me something; I can tell by the way you fidget about."

"Yes, I do," he said, innocently enough; "it's about that girl. Who is she?"

In Rowden's smile there was pity, in Elliott's bitterness.

"Her name," said Clifford solemnly, "is unknown to any one, at least," he added with much conscientiousness, "as far as I can learn. Every fellow in the Quarter bows to her and she returns the salute gravely, but no man has ever been known to obtain more than that. Her profession, judging from her music-roll, is that of a pianist. Her residence is in a small and humble street which is kept in a perpetual process of repair by the city authorities, and from the black letters painted on the barrier which defends the street from traffic, she has taken the name by which we know her,—Rue Barrée. Mr. Rowden, in his imperfect knowledge of the French tongue, called our attention to it as Roo Barry—"

"I didn't," said Rowden hotly.

"And Roo Barry, or Rue Barrée, is today an object of adoration to every rapin in the Quarter—"

"We are not rapins," corrected Elliott.

"*I* am not," returned Clifford, "and I beg to call to your attention, Selby, that these two gentlemen have at various and apparently unfortunate moments, offered to lay down life and limb at the feet of Rue Barrée. The lady possesses a chilling smile which she uses on such occasions and," here he became gloomily impressive, "I have been forced to believe that neither the scholarly grace of my friend Elliott nor the buxom beauty of my friend Rowden have touched that heart of ice."

Elliott and Rowden, boiling with indignation, cried out, "And you!"

"I," said Clifford blandly, "do fear to tread where you rush in."

2

Twenty-four hours later Selby had completely forgotten Rue Barrée. During the week he worked with might and main at the studio, and Saturday night found him so tired that he went to bed before dinner and had a nightmare about a river of yellow ochre in which he was drowning. Sunday morning, apropos of nothing at all, he thought of Rue Barrée, and ten seconds afterwards he saw her. It was at the flower-market on the marble bridge. She was examining a pot of pansies. The gardener had evidently thrown heart and soul into the transaction, but Rue Barrée shook her head.

It is a question whether Selby would have stopped then and there to inspect a cabbage-rose had not Clifford unwound for him the yarn of the previous Tuesday. It is possible that his curiosity was piqued, for with the exception of a hen-turkey, a boy of nineteen is the most openly curious biped alive. From twenty until death he tries to conceal it. But, to be fair to Selby, it is also true that the market was attractive. Under a cloudless sky the flowers were packed and heaped along the marble bridge to the parapet. The air was soft, the sun spun a shadowy lacework among the palms and glowed in the hearts of a thousand roses.

Spring had come,—was in full tide. The watering carts and sprinklers spread freshness over the Boulevard, the sparrows had become vulgarly obtrusive, and the credulous Seine angler anxiously followed his gaudy quill floating among the soapsuds of the *lavoirs*. The white-spiked chestnuts clad in tender green vibrated with the hum of bees. Shoddy butterflies flaunted their winter rags among the heliotrope. There was a smell of fresh earth in the air, an echo of the woodland brook in the ripple of the Seine, and swallows soared and skimmed among the anchored river craft. Somewhere in a window a caged bird was singing its heart out to the sky.

Selby looked at the cabbage-rose and then at the sky. Something in the song of the caged bird may have moved him, or perhaps it was that dangerous sweetness in the air of May.

At first he was hardly conscious that he had stopped then he was scarcely conscious why he had stopped, then he thought he would move on, then he thought he wouldn't, then he looked at Rue Barrée.

The gardener said, "*Mademoiselle*, this is undoubtedly a fine pot of pansies."

Rue Barrée shook her head.

The gardener smiled. She evidently did not want the pansies. She had bought many pots of pansies there, two or three every spring, and never argued. What did she want then? The pansies were evidently a feeler toward a more important transaction. The gardener rubbed his hands and gazed about him.

"These tulips are magnificent," he observed, "and these hyacinths—" He fell into a trance at the mere sight of the scented thickets.

"That," murmured Rue, pointing to a splendid rose-bush with her furled parasol, but in spite of her, her voice trembled a little. Selby noticed it, more shame to him that he was listening, and the gardener noticed it, and, burying his nose in the roses, scented a bargain. Still, to do him justice, he did not add a *centime* to the honest value of the plant, for after all, Rue was probably poor, and anyone could see she was charming.

"Fifty *francs, Mademoiselle*."

The gardener's tone was grave. Rue felt that argument would be wasted. They both stood silent for a moment. The gardener did not eulogize his prize,—the rose-tree was gorgeous and any one could see it.

"I will take the pansies," said the girl, and drew two francs from a worn purse. Then she looked up. A tear-drop stood in the way refracting the light like a diamond, but as it rolled into a little corner by her nose a vision of Selby replaced it, and when a brush of the handkerchief had cleared the startled blue eyes, Selby himself appeared, very much embarrassed. He instantly looked up into the sky, apparently devoured with a thirst for astronomical research, and as he continued his investigations for fully five minutes, the gardener looked up too, and so did a policeman. Then Selby looked at the tips of his boots, the gardener looked at him and the policeman slouched on. Rue Barrée had been gone some time.

"What," said the gardener, "may I offer *Monsieur?*"

Selby never knew why, but he suddenly began to buy flowers. The gardener was electrified. Never before had he sold so many flowers, never at such satisfying prices, and never, never with such absolute unanimity of opinion with a customer. But he missed the bargaining, the arguing, the calling of Heaven to witness. The transaction lacked spice.

"These tulips are magnificent!"

"They are!" cried Selby warmly.

"But alas, they are dear."

"I will take them."

"*Dieu!*" murmured the gardener in a perspiration, "he's madder than most Englishmen."

"This cactus—"

"Is gorgeous!"

"Alas—"

"Send it with the rest."

The gardener braced himself against the river wall.

"That splendid rose-bush," he began faintly.

"That is a beauty. I believe it is fifty *francs*—"

He stopped, very red. The gardener relished his confusion. Then a sudden cool self-possession took the place of his momentary confusion and he held the gardener with his eye, and bullied him.

"I'll take that bush. Why did not the young lady buy it?"

"*Mademoiselle* is not wealthy."

"How do you know?"

"*Dame*, I sell her many pansies; pansies are not expensive."

"Those are the pansies she bought?"

"These, *Monsieur*, the blue and gold."

"Then you intend to send them to her?"

"At midday after the market."

"Take this rose-bush with them, and"—here he glared at the gardener—"don't you dare say from whom they came." The gardener's eyes were like saucers, but Selby, calm and victorious, said: "Send the others to the Hôtel du Sénat, 7 rue de Tournon. I will leave directions with the concierge."

Then he buttoned his glove with much dignity and stalked off, but when well around the corner and hidden from the gardener's view, the conviction that he was an idiot came home to him in a furious blush. Ten minutes later he sat in his room in the Hôtel du Sénat repeating with an imbecile smile: "What an ass I am, what an ass!"

An hour later found him in the same chair, in the same position, his hat and gloves still on, his stick in his hand, but he was silent, apparently lost in contemplation of his boot toes, and his smile was less imbecile and even a bit retrospective.

3

About five o'clock that afternoon, the little sad-eyed woman who fills the position of concierge at the Hôtel du Sénat held up her hands in amazement to see a wagon-load of flower-bearing shrubs draw up before the doorway. She called Joseph, the intemperate *garçon*, who, while calculating the value of the flowers in *petits verres*, gloomily disclaimed any knowledge as to their destination.

"*Voyons*," said the little concierge, "*cherchons la femme!*"

"You?" he suggested.

The little woman stood a moment pensive and then sighed. Joseph caressed his nose, a nose which for gaudiness could vie with any floral display.

Then the gardener came in, hat in hand, and a few minutes

later Selby stood in the middle of his room, his coat off, his shirt-sleeves rolled up. The chamber originally contained, besides the furniture, about two square feet of walking room, and now this was occupied by a cactus. The bed groaned under crates of pansies, lilies and heliotrope, the lounge was covered with hyacinths and tulips, and the washstand supported a species of young tree warranted to bear flowers at some time or other.

Clifford came in a little later, fell over a box of sweet peas, swore a little, apologized, and then, as the full splendour of the floral *fête* burst upon him, sat down in astonishment upon a geranium. The geranium was a wreck, but Selby said, "Don't mind," and glared at the cactus.

"Are you going to give a ball?" demanded Clifford.

"N—no,—I'm very fond of flowers," said Selby, but the statement lacked enthusiasm.

"I should imagine so." Then, after a silence, "That's a fine cactus."

Selby contemplated the cactus, touched it with the air of a connoisseur, and pricked his thumb.

Clifford poked a pansy with his stick. Then Joseph came in with the bill, announcing the sum total in a loud voice, partly to impress Clifford, partly to intimidate Selby into disgorging a *pourboire* which he would share, if he chose, with the gardener. Clifford tried to pretend that he had not heard, while Selby paid bill and tribute without a murmur. Then he lounged back into the room with an attempt at indifference which failed entirely when he tore his trousers on the cactus.

Clifford made some commonplace remark, lighted a cigarette and looked out of the window to give Selby a chance. Selby tried to take it, but getting as far as—"Yes, spring is here at last," froze solid. He looked at the back of Clifford's head. It expressed volumes. Those little perked-up ears seemed tingling with suppressed glee. He made a desperate effort to master the situation, and jumped up to reach for some Russian cigarettes as an incentive to conversation, but was foiled by the cactus, to whom again he fell a prey. The last straw was added.

"Damn the cactus." This observation was wrung from Selby against his will,—against his own instinct of self-preservation, but the thorns on the cactus were long and sharp, and at their repeated prick his pent-up wrath escaped. It was too late now; it was done, and Clifford had wheeled around.

"See here, Selby, why the deuce did you buy those flowers?"

"I'm fond of them," said Selby.

"What are you going to do with them? You can't sleep here."

"I could, if you'd help me take the pansies off the bed."

"Where can you put them?"

"Couldn't I give them to the concierge?"

As soon as he said it he regretted it. What in Heaven's name would Clifford think of him! He had heard the amount of the bill. Would he believe that he had invested in these luxuries as a timid declaration to his concierge? And would the Latin Quarter comment upon it in their own brutal fashion? He dreaded ridicule and he knew Clifford's reputation.

Then somebody knocked.

Selby looked at Clifford with a hunted expression which touched that young man's heart. It was a confession and at the same time a supplication. Clifford jumped up, threaded his way through the floral labyrinth, and putting an eye to the crack of the door, said, "Who the devil is it?"

This graceful style of reception is indigenous to the Quarter.

"It's Elliott," he said, looking back, "and Rowden too, and their bulldogs." Then he addressed them through the crack.

"Sit down on the stairs; Selby and I are coming out directly."

Discretion is a virtue. The Latin Quarter possesses few, and discretion seldom figures on the list. They sat down and began to whistle.

Presently Rowden called out, "I smell flowers. They feast within!"

"You ought to know Selby better than that," growled Clifford behind the door, while the other hurriedly exchanged his torn trousers for others.

"*We* know Selby," said Elliott with emphasis.

"Yes," said Rowden, "he gives receptions with floral decorations and invites Clifford, while we sit on the stairs."

"Yes, while the youth and beauty of the Quarter revel," suggested Rowden; then, with sudden misgiving; "Is Odette there?"

"See here," demanded Elliott, "is Colette there?"

Then he raised his voice in a plaintive howl, "Are you there, Colette, while I'm kicking my heels on these tiles?"

"Clifford is capable of anything," said Rowden; "his nature is soured since Rue Barrée sat on him."

Elliott raised his voice: "I say, you fellows, we saw some flowers carried into Rue Barrée's house at noon."

"Posies and roses," specified Rowden.

"Probably for her," added Elliott, caressing his bulldog.

Clifford turned with sudden suspicion upon Selby. The latter hummed a tune, selected a pair of gloves and, choosing a dozen cigarettes, placed them in a case. Then walking over to the cactus, he deliberately detached a blossom, drew it through his buttonhole, and picking up hat and stick, smiled upon Clifford, at which the latter was mightily troubled.

4

Monday morning at Julian's, students fought for places; students with prior claims drove away others who had been anxiously squatting on coveted *tabourets* since the door was opened in hopes of appropriating them at roll-call; students squabbled over palettes, brushes, portfolios, or rent the air with demands for *Ciceri* and bread. The former, a dirty ex-model, who had in palmier days posed as Judas, now dispensed stale bread at one *sou* and made enough to keep himself in cigarettes. Monsieur Julian walked in, smiled a fatherly smile and walked out. His disappearance was followed by the apparition of the clerk, a foxy creature who flitted through the battling hordes in search of prey.

Three men who had not paid dues were caught and summoned. A fourth was scented, followed, outflanked, his retreat towards the door cut off, and finally captured behind the stove. About that time, the revolution assuming an acute form, howls rose for "Jules!"

Jules came, umpired two fights with a sad resignation in his big brown eyes, shook hands with everybody and melted away in the throng, leaving an atmosphere of peace and good-will. The lions sat down with the lambs, the *massiers* marked the best places for themselves and friends, and, mounting the model stands, opened the roll-calls.

The word was passed, "They begin with C this week."

They did.

"Clisson!"

Clisson jumped like a flash and marked his name on the floor in chalk before a front seat.

"Caron!"

Caron galloped away to secure his place. Bang! went an easel. "*Nom de Dieu!*" in French,—"Where in h—l are you goin'!" in English. Crash! a paintbox fell with brushes and all on board. "*Dieu de Dieu de—*" spat! A blow, a short rush, a clinch and scuffle, and the voice of the *massier*, stern and reproachful:

"*Cochon!*"

Then the roll-call was resumed.

"Clifford!"

The *massier* paused and looked up, one finger between the leaves of the ledger.

"Clifford!"

Clifford was not there. He was about three miles away in a direct line and every instant increased the distance. Not that he was walking fast,—on the contrary, he was strolling with that leisurely gait peculiar to himself. Elliott was beside him and two bulldogs covered the rear. Elliott was reading the "*Gil Blas*," from which he seemed to extract amusement, but deeming boisterous mirth unsuitable to Clifford's state of mind, subdued his amusement to a series of discreet smiles. The latter, moodily aware of this, said nothing, but leading the way into the Luxembourg Gardens installed himself upon a bench by the northern terrace and surveyed the landscape with disfavour. Elliott, according to the Luxembourg regulations, tied the two dogs and then, with an interrogative glance toward his friend, resumed the *Gil Blas* and the discreet smiles.

The day was perfect. The sun hung over Notre Dame, setting the city in a glitter. The tender foliage of the chestnuts cast a shadow over the terrace and flecked the paths and walks with tracery so blue that Clifford might here have found encouragement for his violent "impressions" had he but looked; but as usual in this period of his career, his thoughts were anywhere except in his profession. Around about, the sparrows quarrelled and chattered their courtship songs, the big rosy pigeons sailed from tree to tree, the flies whirled in the sunbeams and the flowers exhaled a thousand perfumes which stirred Clifford with languorous wistfulness. Under this influence he spoke.

"Elliott, you are a true friend—"

"You make me ill," replied the latter, folding his paper. "It's just as I thought,—you are tagging after some new petticoat again. And," he continued wrathfully, "if this is what you've kept me away from Julian's for,—if it's to fill me up with the perfections of some little idiot—"

"Not idiot," remonstrated Clifford gently.

"See here," cried Elliott, "have you the nerve to try to tell me that you are in love again?"

"Again?"

"Yes, again and again and again and—by George have you?"

"This," observed Clifford sadly, "is serious."

For a moment Elliott would have laid hands on him, then he laughed from sheer helplessness. "Oh, go on, go on; let's see, there's Clémence and Marie Tellec and Cosette and Fifine, Colette, Marie Verdier—"

"All of whom are charming, most charming, but I never was serious—"

"So help me, Moses," said Elliott, solemnly, "each and every one of those named have separately and in turn torn your heart with anguish and have also made me lose my place at Julian's in this same manner; each and every one, separately and in turn. Do you deny it?"

"What you say may be founded on facts—in a way—but give me the credit of being faithful to one at a time—"

"Until the next came along."

"But this,—this is really very different. Elliott, believe me, I am all broken up."

Then there being nothing else to do, Elliott gnashed his teeth and listened.

"It's—it's Rue Barrée."

"Well," observed Elliott, with scorn, "if you are moping and moaning over *that* girl,—the girl who has given you and myself every reason to wish that the ground would open and engulf us,—well, go on!"

"I'm going on,—I don't care; timidity has fled—"

"Yes, your native timidity."

"I'm desperate, Elliott. Am I in love? Never, never did I feel so d—n miserable. I can't sleep; honestly, I'm incapable of eating properly."

"Same symptoms noticed in the case of Colette."

"Listen, will you?"

"Hold on a moment, I know the rest by heart. Now let me ask you something. Is it your belief that Rue Barrée is a pure girl?"

"Yes," said Clifford, turning red.

"Do you love her,—not as you dangle and tiptoe after every pretty inanity—I mean, do you honestly love her?"

"Yes," said the other doggedly, "I would—"

"Hold on a moment; would you marry her?"

Clifford turned scarlet. "Yes," he muttered.

"Pleasant news for your family," growled Elliott in suppressed fury. "'Dear father, I have just married a charming *grisette* whom I'm sure you'll welcome with open arms, in company with her mother, a most estimable and cleanly washlady.' Good heavens!

This seems to have gone a little further than the rest. Thank your stars, young man, that my head is level enough for us both. Still, in this case, I have no fear. Rue Barrée sat on your aspirations in a manner unmistakably final."

"Rue Barrée," began Clifford, drawing himself up, but he suddenly ceased, for there where the dappled sunlight glowed in spots of gold, along the sun-flecked path, tripped Rue Barrée. Her gown was spotless, and her big straw hat, tipped a little from the white forehead, threw a shadow across her eyes.

Elliott stood up and bowed. Clifford removed his head-covering with an air so plaintive, so appealing, so utterly humble that Rue Barrée smiled.

The smile was delicious and when Clifford, incapable of sustaining himself on his legs from sheer astonishment, toppled slightly, she smiled again in spite of herself. A few moments later she took a chair on the terrace and drawing a book from her music-roll, turned the pages, found the place, and then placing it open downwards in her lap, sighed a little, smiled a little, and looked out over the city. She had entirely forgotten Foxhall Clifford.

After a while she took up her book again, but instead of reading began to adjust a rose in her corsage. The rose was big and red. It glowed like fire there over her heart, and like fire it warmed her heart, now fluttering under the silken petals. Rue Barrée sighed again. She was very happy. The sky was so blue, the air so soft and perfumed, the sunshine so caressing, and her heart sang within her, sang to the rose in her breast. This is what it sang: "Out of the throng of passers-by, out of the world of yesterday, out of the millions passing, one has turned aside to me."

So her heart sang under his rose on her breast. Then two big mouse-coloured pigeons came whistling by and alighted on the terrace, where they bowed and strutted and bobbed and turned until Rue Barrée laughed in delight, and looking up beheld Clifford before her. His hat was in his hand and his face was wreathed in a series of appealing smiles which would have touched the heart of a Bengal tiger.

For an instant Rue Barrée frowned, then she looked curiously at Clifford, then when she saw the resemblance between his bows and the bobbing pigeons, in spite of herself, her lips parted in the most bewitching laugh. Was this Rue Barrée? So changed, so changed that she did not know herself; but oh! that song in her heart which drowned all else, which trembled on her lips, struggling for utterance, which rippled forth in a laugh at nothing,—at a strutting pigeon,—and Mr. Clifford.

"And you think, because I return the salute of the students in the Quarter, that you may be received in particular as a friend? I do not know you, *Monsieur*, but vanity is man's other name;—be content, Monsieur Vanity, I shall be punctilious—oh, most punctilious in returning your salute."

"But I beg—I implore you to let me render you that homage which has so long—"

"Oh dear; I don't care for homage."

"Let me only be permitted to speak to you now and then,—occasionally—very occasionally."

"And if *you*, why not another?"

"Not at all,—I will be discretion itself."

"Discretion—why?"

Her eyes were very clear, and Clifford winced for a moment, but only for a moment. Then the devil of recklessness seizing him, he sat down and offered himself, soul and body, goods and chattels. And all the time he knew he was a fool and that infatuation is not love, and that each word he uttered bound him in honour from which there was no escape. And all the time Elliott was scowling down on the fountain plaza and savagely checking both bulldogs from their desire to rush to Clifford's rescue,—for even they felt there was something wrong, as Elliott stormed within himself and growled maledictions.

When Clifford finished, he finished in a glow of excitement, but Rue Barrée's response was long in coming and his ardour cooled while the situation slowly assumed its just proportions. Then regret began to creep in, but he put that aside and broke out again in protestations. At the first word Rue Barrée checked him.

"I thank you," she said, speaking very gravely. "No man has ever before offered me marriage." She turned and looked out over the city. After a while she spoke again. "You offer me a great deal. I am alone, I have nothing, I am nothing." She turned again and looked at Paris, brilliant, fair, in the sunshine of a perfect day. He followed her eyes.

"Oh," she murmured, "it is hard,—hard to work always—always alone with never a friend you can have in honour, and the love that is offered means the streets, the *boulevard*—when passion is dead. I know it,—*we* know it,—we others who have nothing,—have no one, and who give ourselves, unquestioning—when we love,—yes, unquestioning—heart and soul, knowing the end."

She touched the rose at her breast. For a moment she seemed to forget him, then quietly—"I thank you, I am very grateful." She opened the book and, plucking a petal from the rose, dropped it between the leaves. Then looking up she said gently, "I cannot accept."

5

It took Clifford a month to entirely recover, although at the end of the first week he was pronounced convalescent by Elliott, who was an authority, and his convalescence was aided by the cordiality with which Rue Barrée acknowledged his solemn salutes. Forty times a day he blessed Rue Barrée for her refusal, and thanked his lucky stars, and at the same time, oh, wondrous heart of ours!—he suffered the tortures of the blighted.

Elliott was annoyed, partly by Clifford's reticence, partly by the unexplainable thaw in the frigidity of Rue Barrée. At their frequent encounters, when she, tripping along the rue de Seine, with music-roll and big straw hat would pass Clifford and his familiars steering an easterly course to the Café Vachette, and at the respectful uncovering of the band would colour and smile at Clifford, Elliott's slumbering suspicions awoke. But he never found out anything, and finally gave it up as beyond his comprehension, merely qualifying Clifford as an idiot and reserving his opinion of Rue Barrée. And all this time Selby was jealous.

At first he refused to acknowledge it to himself, and cut the studio for a day in the country, but the woods and fields of course aggravated his case, and the brooks babbled of Rue Barrée and the mowers calling to each other across the meadow ended in a quavering "Rue Bar-rée-e!" That day spent in the country made him angry for a week, and he worked sulkily at Julian's, all the time tormented by a desire to know where Clifford was and what he might be doing. This culminated in an erratic stroll on Sunday which ended at the flower-market on the Pont au Change, began again, was gloomily extended to the morgue, and again ended at the marble bridge. It would never do, and Selby felt it, so he went to see Clifford, who was convalescing on mint juleps in his garden.

They sat down together and discussed morals and human happiness, and each found the other most entertaining, only Selby failed to pump Clifford, to the other's unfeigned amusement. But the juleps spread balm on the sting of jealousy, and trickled hope to the blighted, and when Selby said he must go, Clifford went too, and when Selby, not to be outdone, insisted on accompanying Clifford back to his door, Clifford determined to see Selby back half way, and then finding it hard to part, they decided to dine together and "flit." To flit, a verb applied to Clifford's nocturnal prowls, expressed, perhaps, as well as anything, the gaiety proposed. Dinner was ordered at Mignon's, and while Selby interviewed the chef, Clifford kept a fatherly eye on the butler. The dinner was a success, or was of the sort generally termed a success. Toward the dessert Selby heard someone say as at a great distance, "Kid Selby, drunk as a lord."

A group of men passed near them; it seemed to him that he shook hands and laughed a great deal, and that everybody was very witty. There was Clifford opposite swearing undying confidence in his chum Selby, and there seemed to be others there, either seated beside them or continually passing with the swish of skirts on the polished floor. The perfume of roses, the rustle of fans, the touch of rounded arms and the laughter grew vaguer and vaguer. The room seemed enveloped in mist. Then, all in a moment each object stood out painfully distinct, only forms and visages were distorted and voices piercing. He drew himself up, calm, grave, for the moment master of himself, but very drunk.

He knew he was drunk, and was as guarded and alert, as keenly suspicious of himself as he would have been of a thief at his elbow. His self-command enabled Clifford to hold his head safely under some running water, and repair to the street considerably the worse for wear, but never suspecting that his companion was drunk. For a time he kept his self-command. His face was only a bit paler, a bit tighter than usual; he was only a trifle slower and more fastidious in his speech. It was midnight when he left Clifford peacefully slumbering in somebody's armchair, with a long suede glove dangling in his hand and a plumy boa twisted about his neck to protect his throat from drafts. He walked through the hall and down the stairs, and found himself on the sidewalk in a quarter he did not know. Mechanically he looked up at the name of the street.

The name was not familiar. He turned and steered his course toward some lights clustered at the end of the street. They proved farther away than he had anticipated, and after a long quest he came to the conclusion that his eyes had been mysteriously removed from their proper places and had been reset on either side of his head like those of a bird. It grieved him to think of the inconvenience this transformation might occasion him, and he attempted to cock up his head, hen-like, to test the mobility of his neck. Then an immense despair stole over him,—tears gathered in the tear-ducts, his heart melted, and he collided with a tree. This shocked him into comprehension; he stifled the violent tenderness in his breast, picked up his hat and moved on more briskly.

His mouth was white and drawn, his teeth tightly clinched. He held his course pretty well and strayed but little, and after an apparently interminable length of time found himself passing a line of cabs. The brilliant lamps, red, yellow, and green annoyed him, and he felt it might be pleasant to demolish them with his cane, but mastering this impulse he passed on. Later an idea struck him that it would save fatigue to take a cab, and he started back with that intention, but the cabs seemed already so far away and the lanterns were so bright and confusing that he gave it up, and pulling himself together looked around.

A shadow, a mass, huge, undefined, rose to his right. He recognized the Arc de Triomphe and gravely shook his cane at it. Its size annoyed him. He felt it was too big. Then he heard something fall clattering to the pavement and thought probably it was his cane but it didn't much matter. When he had mastered himself and regained control of his right leg, which betrayed symptoms of insubordination, he found himself traversing the Place de la Concorde at a pace which threatened to land him at the Madeleine. This would never do.

He turned sharply to the right and crossing the bridge passed the Palais Bourbon at a trot and wheeled into the Boulevard St. Germain. He got on well enough although the size of the War Office struck him as a personal insult, and he missed his cane, which it would have been pleasant to drag along the iron railings as he passed. It occurred to him, however, to substitute his hat, but when he found it he forgot what he wanted it for and replaced it upon his head with gravity. Then he was obliged to battle with a violent inclination to sit down and weep.

This lasted until he came to the *rue de Rennes*, but there he became absorbed in contemplating the dragon on the balcony overhanging the Cour du Dragon, and time slipped away until he remembered vaguely that he had no business there, and marched off again. It was slow work. The inclination to sit down and weep had given place to a desire for solitary and deep reflection. Here his right leg forgot its obedience and attacking the left, outflanked it and brought him up against a wooden board which seemed to bar his path. He tried to walk around it, but found the street closed. He tried to push it over, and found he couldn't.

Then he noticed a red lantern standing on a pile of paving-stones inside the barrier. This was pleasant. How was he to get home if the *boulevard* was blocked? But he was not on the *boulevard*. His treacherous right leg had beguiled him into a detour, for there, behind him lay the boulevard with its endless line of lamps,—and here, what was this narrow dilapidated street piled up with earth and mortar and heaps of stone? He looked up. Written in staring black letters on the barrier was

Rue Barrée.

He sat down. Two policemen whom he knew came by and advised him to get up, but he argued the question from a standpoint of personal taste, and they passed on, laughing. For he was at that moment absorbed in a problem. It was, how to see Rue Barrée. She was somewhere or other in that big house with the iron balconies, and the door was locked, but what of that? The simple idea struck him to shout until she came. This idea was replaced by another equally lucid,—to hammer on the door until she came; but finally rejecting both of these as too uncertain, he decided to climb into the balcony, and opening a window politely inquire for Rue Barrée.

There was but one lighted window in the house that he could see. It was on the second floor, and toward this he cast his eyes. Then mounting the wooden barrier and clambering over the piles of stones, he reached the sidewalk and looked up at the façade for a foothold. It seemed impossible. But a sudden fury seized him, a blind, drunken obstinacy, and the blood rushed to his head, leaping, beating in his ears like the dull thunder of an ocean. He set his teeth, and springing at a window-sill, dragged himself up and hung to the iron bars. Then reason fled; there surged in his brain the sound of many voices, his heart leaped up beating a mad tattoo, and gripping at cornice and ledge he worked his way along the *façade*, clung to pipes and shutters, and dragged himself up, over and into the balcony by the lighted window. His hat fell off and rolled against the pane. For a moment he leaned breathless against the railing—then the window was slowly opened from within.

They stared at each other for some time. Presently the girl

320

took two unsteady steps back into the room. He saw her face,—all crimsoned now,—he saw her sink into a chair by the lamplit table, and without a word he followed her into the room, closing the big door-like panes behind him. Then they looked at each other in silence.

The room was small and white; everything was white about it,—the curtained bed, the little wash-stand in the corner, the bare walls, the china lamp,—and his own face,—had he known it, but the face and neck of Rue were surging in the colour that dyed the blossoming rose-tree there on the hearth beside her. It did not occur to him to speak. She seemed not to expect it. His mind was struggling with the impressions of the room. The whiteness, the extreme purity of everything occupied him—began to trouble him.

As his eye became accustomed to the light, other objects grew from the surroundings and took their places in the circle of lamplight. There was a piano and a coal-scuttle and a little iron trunk and a bathtub. Then there was a row of wooden pegs against the door, with a white chintz curtain covering the clothes underneath. On the bed lay an umbrella and a big straw hat, and on the table, a music-roll unfurled, an inkstand, and sheets of ruled paper. Behind him stood a wardrobe faced with a mirror, but somehow he did not care to see his own face just then. He was sobering.

The girl sat looking at him without a word. Her face was expressionless, yet the lips at times trembled almost imperceptibly. Her eyes, so wonderfully blue in the daylight, seemed dark and soft as velvet, and the colour on her neck deepened and whitened with every breath. She seemed smaller and more slender than when he had seen her in the street, and there was now something in the curve of her cheek almost infantine. When at last he turned and caught his own reflection in the mirror behind him, a shock passed through him as though he had seen a shameful thing, and his clouded mind and his clouded thoughts grew clearer.

For a moment their eyes met then his sought the floor, his

lips tightened, and the struggle within him bowed his head and strained every nerve to the breaking. And now it was over, for the voice within had spoken. He listened, dully interested but already knowing the end,—indeed it little mattered;—the end would always be the same for him;—he understood now—always the same for him, and he listened, dully interested, to a voice which grew within him. After a while he stood up, and she rose at once, one small hand resting on the table.

Presently he opened the window, picked up his hat, and shut it again. Then he went over to the rosebush and touched the blossoms with his face. One was standing in a glass of water on the table and mechanically the girl drew it out, pressed it with her lips and laid it on the table beside him. He took it without a word and crossing the room, opened the door. The landing was dark and silent, but the girl lifted the lamp and gliding past him slipped down the polished stairs to the hallway. Then unchaining the bolts, she drew open the iron wicket.

Through this he passed with his rose.

The Immortal

(A story from Police.)

1

As everybody knows, the great majority of Americans, upon reaching the age of natural selection, are elected to the American Institute of Arts and Ethics, which is, so to speak, the Ellis Island of the Academy.

Occasionally a general mobilization of the Academy is ordered and, from the teeming population of the Institute, a new Immortal is selected for the American Academy of Moral Endeavor by the simple process of blindfolded selection from *Who's Which.*

The motto of this most stately of earthly institutions is a peculiarly modest, truthful, and unintentional epigram by Tupper:

Unknown, I became Famous; Famous, I remain Unknown.

And so I found it to be the case; for, when at last I was privileged to write my name, "Smith, Academician," I discovered to my surprise that I knew none of my brother Immortals, and, more amazing still, none of them had ever heard of me.

This latter fact became the more astonishing to me as I learned the identity of the other Immortals.

Even the President of our great republic was numbered among these Olympians. I had every right to suppose that he had heard of me. I had happened to hear of him, because his Secretary of State once mentioned him at Chautauqua.

It was a wonderfully meaningless sensation to know nobody and to discover myself equally unknown amid that matchless companionship. We were like a mixed bunch of gods, Greek, Norse, Hindu, Hottentot—all gathered on Olympus, having never heard of each other but taking it for granted that we were all gods together and all members of this club.

My initiation into the Academy had been fixed for April first, and I was much worried concerning the address which I was of course expected to deliver on that occasion before my fellow members.

It had to be an exciting address because slumber was not an infrequent phenomenon among the Immortals on such solemn occasions. Like dozens of dozing Joves a dull discourse always set them nodding.

But always under such circumstances the pretty ushers from Barnard College passed around refreshments; a suffragette orchestra struck up; the ushers uprooted the seated Immortals and fox-trotted them into comparative consciousness.

But I didn't wish to have my inaugural address interrupted, therefore I was at my wits' ends to discover a subject of such exciting scientific interest that my august audience could not choose but listen as attentively as they would listen from the front row to some deathless stunt in vaudeville.

That morning I had left the Bronx rather early, hoping that a long walk might compose my thoughts and enable me to think of some sufficiently entertaining and unusual subject for my inaugural address.

I walked as far as Columbia University, gazed with rapture upon its magnificent architecture until I was as satiated as though I had arisen from a banquet at Childs'.

To aid mental digestion I strolled over to the noble home of the Academy and Institute adjoining Mr. Huntington's Hispano-Moresque Museum.

It was a fine, sunny morning, and the Immortals were being exercised by a number of pretty ushers from Barnard.

I gazed upon the impressive procession with pride unutterable; very soon I also should walk two and two in the sunshine, my dome crowned with figurative laurels, cracking scientific witticisms with my fellow inmates, or, perhaps, squeezing the pretty fingers of some—But let that pass.

I was, as I say, gazing upon this inspiring scene on a beautiful morning in February, when I became aware of a short and visibly vulgar person beside me, plucking persistently at my elbow.

"Are you the great Academician, Perfessor Smith?" he asked, tipping his pearl-coloured and somewhat soiled bowler.

"Yes," I said condescendingly. "Your description of me precludes further doubt. What can I do for you, my good man?"

"Are you this here Perfessor Smith of the Department of Anthropology in the Bronx Park Zoological Society?" he persisted.

"What do you desire of me?" I repeated, taking another look at him. He was exceedingly ordinary.

"Prof, old sport," he said cordially, "I took a slant at the papers yesterday, an' I seen all about the big time these guys had when you rode the goat—"

"Rode—*what?*"

"When you was elected. Get me?"

I stared at him. He grinned in a friendly way.

"The privacy of those solemn proceedings should remain sacred. It were unfit to discuss such matters with the world at large," I said coldly.

"I get you," he rejoined cheerfully.

"What do you desire of me?" I repeated. "Why this unseemly apropos?"

"I was comin' to it. Perfessor, I'll be frank. I need money—"

"You need brains!"

"No," he said good-humouredly, "I've got 'em; plenty of 'em; I'm overstocked with idees. What I want to do is to sell *you* a few—"

"Do you know you are impudent!"

"Listen, friend. I seen a piece in the papers as how you was to make the speech of your life when you ride the goat for these here guys on April first—"

"I decline to listen—"

"*One* minute, friend! I want to ask you one thing! *What* are you going to talk about?"

I was already moving away but I stopped and stared at him.

"That's the question," he nodded with unimpaired cheerfulness, "*what* are you going to talk about on April *the* first? Remember it's the hot-air party of your life. *Ree*-member that each an' every paper in the United States will print what you say. Now, how about it, friend? Are you up in your lines?"

Swallowing my repulsion for him I said: "Why are you concerned as to what may be the subject of my approaching address?"

"There you are, Prof!" he exclaimed delightedly; "I want to do business with you. That's me! I'm frank about it. Say, there ought to be a wad of the joyful in it for us both—"

"What?"

"Sure. We can work it any old way. Take Tyng, Tyng and Company, the typewriter people. I'd be ashamed to tell you what I can get out o' them if you'll mention the Tyng-Tyng typewriter in your speech—"

"What you suggest is infamous!" I said haughtily.

"Believe *me* there's enough in it to make it a financial coup, and I ask you, Prof, isn't a financial coup respectable?"

"You seem to be morally unfitted to comprehend—"

"Pardon *me*! I'm fitted up regardless with all kinds of fixtures. I'm fixed to undertake anything. Now if you'd prefer the Bunsen Baby Biscuit bunch—why old man Bunsen would come across—"

"I won't do such things!" I said angrily.

"Very well, very well. Don't get riled, sir. That's only one way to build on Fifth Avenoo. I've got one hundred thousand other ways—"

"I don't want to talk to you—"

"They're honest—some of them. Say, if you want a stric'ly honest deal I've got the goods. Only it ain't as easy and the money ain't as big—"

"I don't want to talk to you—"

"Yes you do. You don't reelize it but you do. Why you're fixin' to make the holler of your life, ain't you? What are you goin' to say? Hey? What you aimin' to say to make those guys set up? What's the use of up-stagin'? Ain't you willin' to pay me a few plunks if I *dy*-vulge to you the most startlin' phenomena that has ever electrified civilization sense the era of P. T. Barnum!"

I was already hurrying away when the mention of that great scientist's name halted me once more.

The little flashy man had been tagging along at my heels, talking cheerfully and volubly all the while; and now, as I halted again, he struck an attitude, legs apart, thumbs hooked in his arm-pits, and his head cocked knowingly on one side.

"Prof," he said, "if you'd work in the Tyng-Tyng Company, or fix it up with Bunsen to mention his Baby Biscuits as the most nootritious of condeements, there'd be more in it for you an' me. But it's up to you."

"Well I won't!" I retorted.

"Very well, ve-ry well," he said soothingly. "Then look over another line o' samples. No trouble to show 'em—none at all, sir! Now if P. T. Barnum was alive—"

I said very seriously: "The name of that great discoverer falling from your illiterate lips has halted me a second time. His name alone invests your somewhat suspicious conversation with a dignity and authority heretofore conspicuously absent. If, as you hint, you have any scientific information for sale which P. T. Barnum might have considered worth purchasing, you may possibly find in me a client. Proceed, young sir."

"Say, listen, Bo—I mean, Prof. I've got the goods. Don't worry. I've got information in my think-box that would make your kick-in speech the event of the century. The question remains, do I get mine?"

"What is this scientific information?"

We had now walked as far as Riverside Drive. There were plenty of unoccupied benches. I sat down and he seated himself beside me.

For a few moments I gazed upon the magnificent view. Even

he seemed awed by the proportions of the superb iron gas tank dominating the prospect.

I gazed at the colossal advertisements across the Hudson, at the freight trains below; I gazed upon the lordly Hudson itself, that majestic sewer which drains the Empire State, bearing within its resistless flood millions of tons of insoluble matter from that magic fairyland which we call "up-state," to the sea. And, thinking of disposal plants, I thought of that sublime paraphrase—"From the Mohawk to the Hudson, and from the Hudson to the Sea."

"Bo," he said, "I gotta hand it to you. Them guys might have got wise if you had worked in the Tyng-Tyng Company or the Bunsen stuff. There was big money into it, but it might not have went."

I waited curiously.

"But this here dope I'm startin' in to cook for you is a straight, reelible, an' hones' pill. P.T. Barnum he would have went a million miles to see what I seen last January down in the Coquina country—"

"Where is that?"

"Say; that's what costs money to know. When I put you wise I'm due to retire from actyve business. Get me?"

"Go on."

"Sure. I was down to the Coquina country, a-doin'—well, I was doin' rubes. I gotta be hones' with *you*, Prof. That's what I was a-doin' of—sellin' farms under water to suckers. Bee-u-tiful Florida! Own your own orange grove. Seven crops o' strawberries every winter in Gawd's own country—get me?"

He bestowed upon me a loathsome wink.

"Well, it went big till I made a break and got in Dutch with the Navy Department what was surveyin' the Everglades for a safe and sane harbour of refuge for the navy in time o' war.

"Sir, they was a-dredgin' up the farms I was sellin', an' the suckers heard of it an' squealed somethin' fierce, an' I had to hustle! Yes, sir, I had to git up an' mosey cross-lots. And what with the Federal Gov'ment chasin' me one way an' them rubes an' the sheriff of Pickalocka County racin' me t'other, I got lost for fair—yes, sir."

He smiled reminiscently, produced from his pockets the cold and offensive remains of a partly consumed cigar, and examined it critically. Then he requested a match.

"I shall now pass over lightly or in subdood silence the painful events of my flight," he remarked, waving his cigar and expelling a long squirt of smoke from his unshaven lips. "Surfice it to say that I got everythin' that was comin' to me, an' then some, what with snakes and murskeeters, an' briers an' mud, an' hunger an' thirst an' heat. Wasn't there a *wop* named Pizarro or somethin' what got lost down in Florida? Well, he's got nothin' on me. I never want to see the dam' state again. But I'll go back if *you* say so!"

His small rat eyes rested musingly upon the river; he sucked thoughtfully at his cigar, hooked one soiled thumb into the armhole of his fancy vest and crossed his legs.

"To resoom," he said cheerily; "I come out one day, half nood, onto the banks of the Miami River. The rest was a pipe after what I had went through.

"I trimmed a guy at Miami, got clothes and railroad fare, an' ducked.

"Now the valyble portion of my discourse is this here partial information concernin' what I seen—or rather what I run onto durin' my crool flight from my ree-lentless persecutors.

"An' these here is the facts: There is, contrary to maps, Coast Survey guys, an' general opinion, a range of hills in Florida, made entirely of coquina.

"It's a good big range, too, fifty miles long an' anywhere from one to five miles acrost.

"An' what I've got to say is this: Into them there Coquina hills there still lives the expirin' remains of the cave-men—"

"What!" I exclaimed incredulously.

"Or," he continued calmly, "to speak more stric'ly, the few individools of that there expirin' race is now totally reduced to a few women."

"Your statement is wild—"

"No; but they're wild. I seen 'em. Bein' extremely bee-utiful I approached nearer, but they hove rocks at me, they did, an' they run into the rocks like squir'ls, they did, an' I was too much on the blink to stick around whistlin' for dearie.

"But I seen 'em; they was all dolled up in the skins of wild annermals. When I see the first one she was eatin' onto a ear of corn, an' I nearly ketched her, but she run like hellnall—yes, sir. Just like that.

"So next I looked for some cave guy to waltz up an' paste me, but no. An' after I had went through them dam' Coquina mountains I realized that there was nary a guy left in this here expirin' race, only women, an' only about a dozen o' them."

He ceased, meditatively expelled a cloud of pungent smoke, and folded his arms.

"Of course," said I with a sneer, "you have proofs to back your pleasant tale?"

"Sure. I made a map."

"I see," said I sarcastically. "You propose to have me pay you for that map?"

"Sure."

"How much, my confiding friend?"

"Ten thousand plunks."

I began to laugh. He laughed, too: "You'll pay 'em if you take my map an' go to the Coquina hills," he said.

I stopped laughing: "Do you mean that I am to go there and investigate before I pay you for this information?"

"Sure. If the goods ain't up to sample the deal is off."

"Sample? What sample?" I demanded derisively.

He made a gesture with one soiled hand as though quieting a balky horse.

"I took a snapshot, friend. You wanta take a slant at it?"

"You took a photograph of one of these alleged cave-dwellers?"

"I took ten but when these here cave-ladies hove rocks at me the fillums was put on the blink—all excep' this one which

I dee-veloped an' printed."

He drew from his inner coat pocket a photograph and handed it to me—the most amazing photograph I ever gazed upon. Astounded, almost convinced I sat looking at this irrefutable evidence in silence. The smoke of his cigar drifting into my face aroused me from a sort of dazed inertia.

"Listen," I said, half strangled, "are you willing to wait for payment until I personally have verified the existence of these—er—creatures?"

"You betcher! When you have went there an' have saw the goods, just let me have mine if they're up to sample. Is that right?"

"It seems perfectly fair."

"It is fair. I wouldn't try to do a scientific guy—no, sir. Me without no eddycation, only brains? Fat chance I'd have to put one over on a Academy sport what's chuck-a-block with Latin an' Greek an' scientific stuff an' all like that!"

I admitted to myself that he'd stand no chance.

"Is it a go?" he asked.

"Where is the map?" I inquired, trembling internally with excitement.

"Ha—ha!" he said. "Listen to my mirth! The map is inside here, old sport!" and he tapped his retreating forehead with one nicotine-stained finger.

"I see," said I, trying to speak carelessly; "you desire to pilot me."

"I don't desire to but I gotta go with you."

"An accurate map—"

"Can it, old sport! A accurate map is all right when it's pasted over the front of your head for a face. But I wear the other kind of map *inside* me conk. Get me?"

"I confess that I do not."

"Well, get *this*, then. It's a cash deal. If the goods is up to sample you hand me mine then an' there. I don't deliver no goods f.o.b. I shows 'em to you. After you have saw them it's up to you to round 'em up. That's all, as they say when our great President pulls a gun. There ain't goin' to be no shootin'; walk out quietly, ladies!"

After I had sat there for fully ten minutes staring at him I came to the only logical conclusion possible to a scientific mind.

I said: "You are, admittedly, unlettered; you are confessedly a chevalier of industry; personally you are exceedingly distasteful to me. But it is useless to deny that you are the most extraordinary man I ever saw.... How soon can you take me to these Coquina hills?"

"Gimme twenty-four hours to—fix things," he said gaily.

"Is that all?"

"It's plenty, I guess. An'—say!"

"What?"

"It's a stric'ly cash deal. Get me?"

"I shall have with me a certified check for ten thousand dollars. Also a pair of automatics."

He laughed: "Huh!" he said, "I could loco your cabbage-palm soup if I was *that* kind! I'm on the level, Perfessor. If I wasn't I could get you in about a hundred styles while you was blinkin' at what you was a-thinkin' about. But I ain't no gun-man. You hadn't oughta pull that stuff on me. I've give you your chanst; take it or leave it."

I pondered profoundly for another ten minutes. And at last my decision was irrevocably reached.

"It's a bargain," I said firmly. "What is your name?"

"Sam Mink. Write it Samuel onto that there certyfied check—if you can spare the extra seconds from your valooble time."

2

On Monday, the first day of March, 1915, about 10:30 a.m., we came in sight of something which, until I had met Mink, I never had dreamed existed in southern Florida—a high range of hills.

It had been an eventless journey from New York to Miami, from Miami to Fort Coquina; but from there through an absolutely pathless wilderness as far as I could make out, the journey had been exasperating.

Where we went I do not know even now: saw-grass and water, hammock and shell mound, palm forests, swamps, wildernesses of water-oak and live-oak, vast stretches of pine, lagoons, sloughs, branches, muddy creeks, reedy reaches from which wild fowl rose in clouds where alligators lurked or lumbered about after stranded fish, horrible mangrove thickets full of moccasins and water-turkeys, heronry more horrible still, out of which the heat from a vertical sun distilled the last atom of nauseating effluvia—all these choice spots we visited under the guidance of the wretched Mink. I seemed to be missing nothing that might discourage or disgust me.

He appeared to know the way, somehow, although my compass became mysteriously lost the first day out from Fort Coquina.

Again and again I felt instinctively that we were travelling in a vast circle, but Mink always denied it, and I had no scientific instruments to verify my deepening suspicions.

Another thing bothered me: Mink did not seem to suffer from insects or heat; in fact, to my intense annoyance, he appeared to be having a comfortable time of it, eating and drinking with gusto, sleeping snugly under a mosquito bar, permitting me to do all camp work, the paddling as long as we used a canoe, and all the cooking, too, claiming, on his part, a complete ignorance of culinary art.

Sometimes he condescended to catch a few fish for the common pan; sometimes he bestirred himself to shoot a duck or two. But usually he played on his concertina during his leisure moments which were plentiful.

I began to detest Samuel Mink.

At first I was murderously suspicious of him, and I walked about with my automatic arsenal ostentatiously displayed. But he looked like such a miserable little shrimp that I became ashamed of my precautions. Besides, as he cheerfully pointed out, a little *koonti* soaked in my drinking water, would have done my business for me if he had meant me any physical harm. Also he had a horrid habit of noosing moccasins for sport; and it would have been easy for him to introduce one to me while I slept.

Really what most worried me was the feeling which I could not throw off that somehow or other we were making very little progress in any particular direction.

He even admitted that there was reason for my doubts, but he confided to me that to find these Coquina hills, was like traversing a maze. Doubling to and fro among forests and swamps, he insisted, was the only possible path of access to the undiscovered Coquina hills of Florida. Otherwise, he argued, these Coquina hills would long ago have been discovered.

And it seemed to me that he had been right when at last we came out on the edge of a palm forest and beheld that astounding blue outline of hills in a country which has always been supposed to lie as flat as a flabby flap-jack.

A desert of saw-*palmetto* stretched away before us to the base of the hills; game trails ran through it in every direction like sheep paths; a few moth-eaten Florida deer trotted away as we appeared.

Into one of these trails stepped Samuel Mink, burdened only with his concertina and a box of cigars. I, loaded with seventy pounds of impedimenta including a moving-picture apparatus, reeled after him.

He walked on jauntily toward the hills, his pearl-coloured bowler hat at an angle. Occasionally he played upon his concertina as he advanced; now and then he cut a pigeon wing. I hated him. At every toilsome step I hated him more deeply. He played "Tipperary" on his concertina.

"See 'em, old top?" he inquired, nodding toward the hills. "I'm a man of my word, I am. Look at 'em! Take 'em in, old sport! An' reemember, each an' every hill is guaranteed to contain one bony fidy cave-lady what is the last vanishin' traces of a extinc' an' dissappeerin' race!'"

We toiled on—that is, I did, bowed under my sweating load of paraphernalia. He skipped in advance like some degenerate twentieth century faun, playing on his pipes the unmitigated melodies of George Cohan.

"Watch your step!" he cried, nimbly avoiding the attentions of a ground-rattler which tried to caress his ankle from under a saw-palmetto.

With a shudder I gave the deadly little reptile room and floundered forward a prey to exhaustion, melancholy, and red-bugs. A few buzzards kept pace with me, their broad, black shadows gliding ominously over the sun-drenched earth; blue-tail lizards went rustling and leaping away on every side; floppy soft-winged butterflies escorted me; a strange bird which seemed to be dressed in a union suit of checked gingham, flew from tree to tree as I plodded on, and squealed at me persistently.

At last I felt the hard *coquina* under foot; the cool blue shadow of the hills enveloped me; I slipped off my pack, dumped it beside a little rill of crystal water which ran sparkling from the hills, and sat down on a soft and fragrant carpet of hound's-tongue.

After a while I drank my fill at the rill, bathed head, neck, face and arms, and, feeling delightfully refreshed, leaned back against the fern-covered slab of coquina.

"What are you doing?" I demanded of Mink who was un-packing the kit and disengaging the moving-picture machine.

"Gettin' ready," he replied, fussing busily with the camera.

"You don't expect to see any cave people here, do you?" I asked with a thrill of reviving excitement.

"Why not?"

"*Here?*"

"Cert'nly. Why the first one I seen was a-drinkin' into this brook."

"Here! Where I'm sitting?" I asked incredulously.

"Yes, sir, right there. It was this way; I was lyin' down, tryin' to figure the shortes' way to Fort Coquina, an' wishin' I was nearer Broadway than I was to the Equator, when I heard a voice say, 'Blub-blub, muck-a-muck!' an' then I seen two cave-ladies come sof'ly stealin' along."

"W-where?"

"Right there where you are a-sittin'. Say, they was lookers!

An' they come along quiet like two big-eyed deer, kinder nosin' the air and listenin'.

"'Gee whiz,' thinks I, 'Longacre ain't got so much on them dames!' An' at that one o' them wore a wild-cat's skin an' that's all—an' a wild-cat ain't big. And t'other she sported pa'm-leaf pyjamas.

"So when they don't see nothin' around to hinder, they just lays down flat and takes a drink into that pool, lookin' up every swallow like little birds listenin' and kinder thankin' God for a good square drink.

"I knowed they was wild girls soon as I seen 'em. Also they sez to one another, 'Blub-blub!' Kinder sof'ly. All the same I've seen wilder ladies on Broadway so I took a chanst where I was squattin' behind a rock.

"So sez I, 'Ah there, sweetie Blub-blub! Have a taxi on me!' An' with that they is on their feet, quiverin' all over an' nosin' the wind. So first I took some snapshots at 'em with my Bijoo camera.

"I guess they scented me all right for I seen their eyes grow bigger, an' then they give a bound an' was off over the rocks; an' me after 'em. Say, that was some steeple-chase until a few more cave-ladies come out on them rocks above us an' hove chunks of coquina at me.

"An' with all that dodgin' an' duckin' of them there rocks the cave-girls got away; an' I seen 'em an' the other cave-ladies scurryin' into little caves—one whisked into this hole, another scuttled into that—bing! all over!

"All I could think of was to light a cigar an' blow the smoke in after the best-lookin' cave-girl. But I couldn't smoke her out, an' I hadn't time to starve her out. So that's all I know about this here pree-historic an' extinc' race o' vanishin' cave-ladies."

As his simple and illiterate narrative advanced I became pro-portionally excited; and, when he ended, I sprang to my feet in an uncontrollable access of scientific enthusiasm:

"Was she really pretty?" I asked.

"Listen, she was that peachy—"

"Enough!" I cried. "Science expects every man to do his duty! Are your films ready to record a scene without precedent in the scientific annals of creation?"

"They sure is!"

"Then place your camera and your person in a strategic position. This is a magnificent spot for an ambush! Come over beside me!"

He came across to where I had taken cover among the ferns behind the parapet of *coquina*, and with a thrill of pardonable joy I watched him unlimber his photographic artillery and place it in battery where my every posture and action would be recorded for posterity if a cave-lady came down to the water-hole to drink.

"It were futile," I explained to him in a guarded voice, "for me to attempt to cajole her as you attempted it. Neither playful nor moral suasion could avail, for it is certain that no cave-lady understands English."

"I thought o' that, too," he remarked. "I said, 'Blub-blub! muck-a-muck!' to 'em when they started to run, but it didn't do no good."

I smiled: "Doubtless," said I, "the spoken language of the cave-dweller is made up of similarly primitive exclamations, and you were quite right in attempting to communicate with the cave-ladies and establish a cordial entente. Professor Garner has done so among the Simian population of Gaboon. Your attempt is most creditable and I shall make it part of my record.

"But the main idea is to capture a living specimen of cave-lady, and corroborate every detail of that pursuit and capture upon the films.

"And believe me, Mr. Mink," I added, my voice trembling with emotion, "no Academician is likely to go to sleep when I illustrate my address with such pictures as you are now about to take!"

"The police might pull the show," he suggested.

"No," said I, "Science is already immune; art is becoming so. Only nature need fear the violence of prejudice; and doubtless

337

she will continue to wear pantalettes and common-sense night-ies as long as our great republic endures."

I unslung my field-glasses, adjusted them and took a penetrating squint at the hillside above.

Nothing stirred up there except a buzzard or two wheeling on tip-curled pinions above the palms.

Presently Mink inquired whether I had "lamped" anything, and I replied that I had not.

"They may be snoozin' in their caves," he suggested. "But don't you fret, old top; you'll get what's comin' to you and I'll get mine."

"About that check—" I began and hesitated.

"Sure. What about it?"

"I suppose I'm to give it to you when the first cave-woman appears."

"That's what!"

I pondered the matter for a while in silence. I could see no risk in paying him this draft on sight.

"All right," I said. "Bring on your cave-dwellers."

Hour succeeded hour, but no cave-dwellers came down to the pool to drink. We ate luncheon—a bit of cold duck, some koonti-bread, and a dish of palm-cabbage. I smoked an inexpensive cigar; Mink lit a more pretentious one. Afterward he played on his concertina at my suggestion on the chance that the music might lure a cave-girl down the hill. Nymphs were sometimes caught that way, and modern science seems to be reverting more and more closely to the simpler truths of the classics which, in our ignorance and arrogance, we once dismissed as fables unworthy of scientific notice.

However this Broadway faun piped in vain: no white-footed dryad came stealing through the ferns to gaze, perhaps to dance to the concertina's plaintive melodies.

So after a while he put his concertina into his pocket, cocked his derby hat on one side, gathered his little bandy legs under his person, and squatted there in silence, chewing the wet and bitter end of his extinct cigar.

Toward mid-afternoon I unslung my field-glasses again and surveyed the hill.

At first I noticed nothing, not even a buzzard; then, of a sudden, my attention was attracted to something moving among the fern-covered slabs of coquina just above where we lay concealed—a slim, graceful shape half shadowed under a veil of lustrous hair which glittered like gold in the sun.

"Mink!" I whispered hoarsely. "One of them is coming! This—this indeed is the stupendous and crowning climax of my scientific career!"

His comment was incredibly coarse: "Gimme the dough," he said without a tremor of surprise. Indeed there was a metallic ring of menace in his low and entirely cold tones as he laid one hand on my arm. "No welchin'," he said, "or I put the whole show on the bum!"

The overwhelming excitement of the approaching crisis neutralized my disgust; I fished out the certified check from my pocket and flung the miserable scrap of paper at him. "Get your machine ready!" I hissed. "Do you understand what these moments mean to the civilized world!"

"I sure do," he said.

Nearer and nearer came the lithe white figure under its glorious crown of hair, moving warily and gracefully amid the great coquina slabs—nearer, nearer, until I no longer required my glasses.

She was a slender red-lipped thing, blue-eyed, dainty of hand and foot.

The spotted pelt of a wild-cat covered her, or attempted to.

I unfolded a large canvas sack as she approached the pool. For a moment or two she stood gazing around her and her close-set ears seemed to be listening. Then, apparently satisfied, she threw back her beautiful young head and sent a sweet wild call floating back to the sunny hillside.

"Blub-blub!" rang her silvery voice; "blub-blub! Muck-a-muck!" And from the fern-covered hollows above other voices replied joyously to her reassuring call, "Blub-blub-blub!"

The whole bunch was coming down to drink—the entire remnant of a prehistoric and almost extinct race of human creatures was coming to quench its thirst at this water-hole. How I wished for James Barnes at the camera's crank! He alone could do justice to this golden girl before me.

One by one, clad in their simple yet modest gowns of pelts and garlands, five exquisitely superb specimens of cave-girl came gracefully down to the water-hole to drink.

Almost swooning with scientific excitement I whispered to the unspeakable Mink: "Begin to crank as soon as I move!" And, gathering up my big canvas sack I rose, and, still crouching, stole through the ferns on tip-toe.

They had already begun to drink when they heard me; I must have made some slight sound in the ferns, for their keen ears detected it and they sprang to their feet.

It was a magnificent sight to see them there by the pool, tense, motionless, at gaze, their dainty noses to the wind, their beautiful eyes wide and alert.

For a moment, enchanted, I remained spellbound in the presence of this prehistoric spectacle, then, waving my sack, I sprang out from behind the rock and cantered toward them.

Instead of scattering and flying up the hillside they seemed paralyzed, huddling together as though to get into the picture. Delighted I turned and glanced at Mink; he was cranking furiously.

With an uncontrollable shout of triumph and delight I pranced toward the huddling cave-girls, arms outspread as though heading a horse or concentrating chickens. And, totally forgetting the uselessness of urbanity and civilized speech as I danced around that lovely but terrified group, "Ladies!" I cried, "do not be alarmed, because I mean only kindness and proper respect. Civilization calls you from the wilds! Sentiment, pity, piety propel my legs, not the ruthless desire to injure or enslave you! Ladies! You are under the wing of science. An anthropologist is speaking to you! Fear nothing! Rather rejoice! Your wonderful race shall be rescued from extinction—even if I have to do it myself! Ladies, don't run!" They had suddenly scattered and were now beginning to dodge me. "I come among you bearing the precious promises of education, of religion, of equal franchise, of fashion!"

"Blub-blub!" they whimpered continuing to dodge me.

"Yes!" I cried in an excess of transcendental enthusiasm. "Blub-blub! And though I do not comprehend the exquisite simplicity of your primeval speech, I answer with all my heart, 'Blub-blub!'"

Meanwhile, they were dodging and eluding me as I chased first one, then another, one hand outstretched, the other invitingly clutching the sack.

A hasty glance at Mink now and then revealed him industriously cranking away.

Once I fell into the pool. That section of the film should never be released, I determined, as I blew the water out of my mouth, gasped, and started after a lovely, ruddy-haired cave-girl whose curiosity had led her to linger beside the pool in which I was floundering.

But run as fast as I could and skip hither and thither with all the agility I could muster I did not seem to be able to seize a single cave-girl.

Every few minutes, baffled and breathless, I rested; and they always clustered together uttering their plaintively musical "blub-blub," not apparently very much afraid of me, and even exhibiting curiosity. Now and then they cast glances toward Mink who was grinding away steadily, and I could scarcely retain a shout of joy as I realized what wonderful pictures he was taking. Indeed luck seemed to be with me, so far, for never once did these beautiful prehistoric creatures retire out of photographic range.

But otherwise the problem was becoming serious. I could not catch one of them; they eluded me with maddening swiftness and grace; my pauses to recover my breath became more frequent.

At last, dead beat, I sat down on a slab of coquina. And when I was able to articulate I turned around toward Mink.

341

"You'll have to drop your camera and come over and help me," I panted. "I'm all in!"

"Not quite," he said.

For a moment I did not understand him; then under my outraged eyes, and within the hearing of my horrified ears a terrible thing occurred.

"Now, ladies!" yelled Mink, "all on for the fine-ally! Upstage there, you red-headed little spot-crabber! Mabel! Take the call! Now smile the whole bloomin' bunch of you!"

What was he saying? I did not comprehend. I stared dully at the six cave-girls as they grouped themselves in a semi-circle behind me.

Then, as one of them came up and unfolded a white strip of cloth behind my head, the others drew from concealed pockets in their kilts of cat-fur, little silk flags of all nations and began to wave them.

Paralysed I turned my head. On the strip of white cloth, which the tallest cave-girl was holding directly behind my head, was printed in large black letters:

SUNSET SOAP

For one cataclysmic instant I gazed upon this hideous spectacle, then with an unearthly cry I collapsed into the arms of the nicest looking one.

There is little more to say. Contrary to my fears the release of this outrageous film did not injure my scientific standing. Modern science, accustomed to proprietary testimonials, has become reconciled to such things.

My appearance upon the films in the movies in behalf of Sunset Soap, oddly enough, seemed to enhance my scientific reputation. Even such austere purists as Guilford, the Cubist poet, congratulated me upon my fearless independence of ethical tradition.

And I had lived to learn a gentler truth than that, for, the pretty girl who had been cast for Cave-girl No. 3—But let that pass. *Adhibenda est in jocando moderatio.*

Sweet are the uses of advertisement.

The Silent Land

(A story from The Maker of Moons.)

And the woman fled into the wilderness, where she hath a place prepared of God.

1

Ferris and I had had a dispute, a bitter one, and, as usual, Ferris had pushed his cap over his eyes until the hair on the back of his head stuck out.

"You can't do it," he said, shoving both hands up to the wrists in his canvas fishing-coat.

"I'll prove it," said I. "What a stubborn mule you are, Ferris!"

"Stubborn nothing," he retorted, "you and your theories must have your little airing, I suppose, but I don't intend to assist."

"I'm right sometimes," I said.

"Sometimes you're wrong, too," said Ferris. Then he walked off toward the cliffs, whistling, uncompromising, untidy.

"There's a hole in your leggings!" I called after him, but he did not deign to answer me. "Obstinate ass," I thought, for we were very fond of each other, "if he wastes his time with the Silver Doctor he'll rue it." Then I looked at Solomon and lighted a cigarette.

Solomon was a bird, an enervating bird of the Ibis species, wrinkled and wizened, like the mummies of his native land, which was Egypt. The bird was mine, a sarcastic tribute from Ferris, and the bird and the sarcasm both bore directly on the

343

only disputes which ever arose between Ferris and myself. The cause of these disputes was a trout-fly, an innocent toy of scarlet and tinsel, known to anglers as the "Red Ibis." I swore by it, Ferris swore at it. In the long winter nights when the streams gurgled under the frozen forests and the lake was a sheet of soggy snow, Ferris and I loafed before the fire pulling tangled masses of leaders and flies about and dragging the silken lines over the rugs to hear the reels click.

Every fly known to the brethren of the angle was discussed—every fly except the Red Ibis. We both honestly tried to avoid this bone of contention. We talked of Duns and Hackles, and Spinners and Gnats, but in spite of every precaution the Red Ibis would occasionally rise like a fiery spectre between us, and then we disputed vehemently.

"No angler with a rag of self-respect would use the Ibis," said Ferris, with that obstinate shrug which added gall to the insult, and I—well, the crowning insult came when Ferris sent to Cairo and imported a live Egyptian Ibis for me.

"Pull out his tail feathers when you're short of Red Ibis," gasped Ferris, weak with laughter, as I stood silently inspecting the bird in my studio.

"I'll send him to Central Park," said I, swallowing my wrath; but I thought better of it, and Solomon, the wizened, became an important member of my household.

The bird was a mystery. I never cared to encounter his filmy eyes. Centuries seemed to roll away when he unclosed them, visions of tombs and obelisks filled my mind—glimpses of desert sunsets and the warm waters of lazy rivers. His black shrivelled head, bare as a skull, lay like a withered gourd among the garish flame-coloured feathers on his breast.

"Solly," said I, when Ferris disappeared below the cliff, "do you want a frog?"

The bird unclosed one eye. I went to a pail of water in which I kept minnows, and Solomon followed me, solemnly hopping.

"Help yourself, Solly," said I, uncovering the pail.

I called him Solly because I wished to put myself at ease with this relic of Egyptian Royalty. The splendour of Pharo's court had not dimmed this hoary prophet's eye, which was piercing when the sleepy film left it—piercing enough to make me feel thousands of years young, and very *bourgeois*. In vain I addressed him as Solly, in vain I gave him chocolate creams,—he was the aristocrat, the venerable high-priest of an Empire dead—and I was his man-servant, his ass, and his ox.

Solomon dabbed once or twice at a sportive minnow, pecked pensively at the handle of the pail, swallowed a pebble or two, and then, ruffling his scarlet feathers, sidled aimlessly back into the sedge by the frog-pond. I watched him for awhile, brooding dreamily among the rushes, but he paid no further attention either to me or to the small green frogs that squatted on the lily-pads or floated half submerged, watching him with enormous eyes.

A noisy blue-jay flitted through the orchard and alighted on a crab-apple tree solely to insult Solomon. He of course was unsuccessful, and his language became so utterly unfit for publication that I moved away, shocked and annoyed.

The sun was very hot. It glittered with a blinding light across the rippling pond, where dragonflies darted and sailed and chased each other over the water, or flitted among the clouds of dancing midges, searching for prey.

A sweet smell came to me from orchard and sedge; there was an odour of scented rushes in the air, and the lingering summer wind bore puffs of perfume from clover-fields and meadows fragrant with flowering mint. I looked again toward the cliffs. Ferris was not in sight.

"Obstinate mule," I thought, and, picking up my rod and fly-book, I sauntered toward the forest.

"Ferris," said I to myself, "is after that big trout by the Red Rock Rapids, but he'll never raise him with a Silver Doctor, and he'll come home in a devil of a temper."

I sat down in a clump of sweet fern and joined my rod. When I had run the silk through the guides and had fastened the nine-foot leader, I opened my fly-book and sought for a Red Ibis fly.

There was not one in the book.

I must send to New York tomorrow, I thought, turning the aluminium leaves impatiently; fancy my being out of Red Ibis! I selected a yellow Oak fly for the dropper and a nameless Gnat for the hand-fly, and, drawing the leader down to the reel, started on again, carrying my rod with the tip behind me.

The forest was dim and moist and silent. Where the sunshine fell among the ferns a few flies buzzed in the gilded warmth; but except for this and a strange grey bird which flitted before me silently as I walked, there was no sign of life, nothing stirring, not a rustle among the leaves, not a movement, not a bird-note.

Over moss and dead leaves aglisten in the pale forest light I passed,—over crumbling logs, damp and lichen-covered, half submerged in little pools; and the musty fragrance of the forest mould set me dreaming of dryads, and fauns, and lost altars, whose marbles, stained with tender green, glimmer in ancient forests.

This belt of woods was always silent; I often wondered why. There were no birds—none except this strange grey creature which kept flitting ahead of me, uttering no note. It was the first bird I had ever seen in the western forest belt—the first bird except Solomon, who occasionally accompanied me on my trips to the long pool in the river which borders the wooded belt on the west.

It was an unknown bird to me,—I could catch fleeting glimpses of it,—and its long slender wings and dark eyes brought no recollections to my mind.

To the north, south, and east the woods were full of thrushes and wood-peckers; full of game, too—grouse, deer, foxes, and an occasional mink and otter, but the shy wood creatures left the western forest belt alone, and even the trout seemed to shun the dark pools where the river swept the edges of the wood until it curved out again by Lynx Peak. I say the trout shunned it, but there was one, a monstrous fish, wily and subtile, that lived in the long amber pool below. Early in the season Ferris had raised him with a Silver Doctor, and Ferris's madness on the Silver Doctor

346

dated from that moment. His mania for this fly lead him to use it in season and out, and no amount of persuasion or of ridicule moved him.

"Because," said I, "you had a Silver Doctor snapped off by a big fish, do you imagine it's the only fly in the world?"

"It's good enough for me," he said.

There were two things which Ferris used to say that maddened me. One was, "The Silver Doctor's good enough for me;" the other was, "New York's good enough for me."

We never discussed the latter question after Ferris had alluded to me as a "Latin Quarter Nondescript," but the battle still raged over the merits of the Silver Doctor and the Red Ibis.

When I came to the wooded slope which over hung the river I buttoned my shooting coat and began a cautious descent, trailing my rod carefully. I headed for the foot of the pool, for one of my theories, which ruffled Ferris, was that certain pools should be fished up stream. This was one of those pools, according to my theory; and when I had reached the rocks and had waded into the rushing water, I faced upstream and cast straight out into the rapids which curled among the boulders at the foot of the pool.

At the second cast I hooked a snag and waded out to disengage it. Fumbling about under the foaming water I found my fly imbedded in something which refused to give way. I tugged cautiously and gently; it was useless. Then I rolled up my sleeve and plunged my arm into the water up to the shoulder. This time it did give way; I drew out my arm and held up something glistening and dripping, in which my hook was firmly imbedded. It was a shoe, small, pointed, high-heeled, and buckled with a silver buckle.

"This," said I, "is most extraordinary," and I sat down on a flat rock, holding the shoe close to my eyes.

"Besnard—Paris," I read stamped on the lining over the heel. And the buckle was of sterling silver. I sat for a moment, thinking.

Our cottage, Ferris's and mine, was the only house in the

whole region that I knew of, except the old house in the glade by the White Moss Spring. That was unoccupied and had been for yearsa crumbling, abandoned farm, tottering among the young growth of an advancing forest. But as I sat thinking I remembered early in the season having seen smoke above the trees once when we were in the neighbourhood of the White Moss Spring, and I recollected that Ferris had spoken of poachers. We had been too lazy to investigate, too lazy even to remember it until, as I sat there holding the small shoe, the incident came back to me, and I wondered whether anybody had taken up an abode in the abandoned farm.

I didn't like it. The forests and streams be longed to Ferris and me, and although up to the present moment it had not been necessary to employ many keepers, I began to fear that our woods were being invaded and that we should soon be obliged to find protection.

I looked at the shoe, turning it over carefully in my hands. It was new—had scarcely been worn at all.

"Pooh," I thought, "the owner of this could scarcely do much damage among the game, but of course there may be bigger shoes in company with this, and those bigger shoes had better look out!"

My first impulse was to throw the shoe into the underbrush. I started to do this, and then carefully laid it down on a sun-warmed rock.

"Let it dry," I muttered; "it's evidence for Ferris." But as it happened, Ferris was not destined to see the shoe.

2

I fished the pool twice, once up and once down, and heaven knows I fished it conscientiously; but no trout rose to the flies, although I changed the cast half a dozen times and even violated my feelings by tying a Silver Doctor. It was true I glanced up and down the river to see whether Ferris was in sight before I did so.

"The wily old devil won't come up," said I to myself, meaning the trout; "I'll give him a rest for a while." And I sat down on the rock where the pointed shoe was drying in the sun, laying my rod beside me.

"What's the use of speculating about this shoe," I thought, and straightway began to speculate.

The strange grey bird with the slender wings and dark eyes slipped through the undergrowth along the opposite side of the pool, but it uttered no call, and I caught only fleeting glimpses of it at intervals. Once, for a moment, it flitted quite near, and a sudden sense of having seen it before came over me, but after a little thinking I found myself associating it with a rare bird I had once noticed in Northern France, and of course it was impossible that this could be a French bird.

"It was an association of ideas," said I to myself, looking at the mark in the slim shoe. "Besnard—Paris." And I began speculating upon the owner of the shoe.

"Young? Probably. Slender? Probably. Pretty? The deuce take the shoe," I muttered, picking up my rod. Presently I laid it down again, softly.

"Now, perhaps," said I to myself, "this little shoe has tapped the gravel of the Luxembourg, patted the asphalt of the Boulevard des Italiens, brushed the lawns of the Bois—ah me! ah me!—the devil take the shoe!"

The sun beat down upon the rock; the little shoe in my hand was nearly dry.

"No," said I to myself, "I'll not show it to Ferris. And I'll not shove it into my pocket—no—for if Ferris finds it he'll rag me to death. I'll throw it away." I stood up.

"I'll just throw it away," I repeated aloud to encourage myself, for I didn't want to throw it away.

"One, two, three," said I, with an attempt at carelessness which changed to astonishment as I raised my eyes to the bank above whither I had intended to hurl the shoe.

For an instant I stood rigid, my right hand clutching the shoe, arrested in mid air. Then I placed the shoe very carefully upon the rock beside me and took off my shooting-cap.

"I beg your pardon," said I, "I did not see you."

349

I stood silent, politely holding my shooting-cap against my stomach. But I was confused, for she had answered me in French, pure Parisian French, and my ideas were considerably unbalanced.

I am afraid I stared a little. I tried not to. She was slender and very young. Her dark eyes, half shadowed under black lashes, made me think of the strange, dark-eyed bird that had followed me. She sat on the crooked trunk of a tree over hanging the bank, her feet negligently crossed, her hands in the pockets of a leather shooting-jacket. I'm afraid to say how short her skirts were,—but of course this is the age of bicycles and shooting-kilts.

"*Madame*," I said, trying to keep my eyes from one small stockinged foot, I have found a shoe—"

"My shoe, *Monsieur*," she said, serenely.

"Permit me, *madame*," said I—

"*Mademoiselle*—" said she—

"Permit me,—a thousand pardons, *Mademoiselle*,—to return to you your shoe."

"It was very stupid of me to lose it," said she.

"It is nearly dry," said I; "will *Mademoiselle* pardon the un-committed stupidity of which I was nearly guilty."

"You were going to throw it away," said she.

"I almost perpetrated that unpardonable crime—"

"Give it to me," she said, with a gracious gesture.

Now when she smiled I smiled too, and picking up the shoe waded across the pool to the bank under her.

"May I come up?" I asked.

"*Pardi, Monsieur*, how else am I to get my shoe?"

I clambered up, hanging to limbs and branches. It was a miracle I did not break my neck.

"Why do you not take the path?" she asked. "Do you not know you might fall—and all for a shoe?"

"But such a shoe—"

"True, the buckle is silver"

"Which I claim the privilege of buckling," said I, dragging

myself up beside her.

She deliberately held out her slim stockinged foot, and I slipped the shoe on it.

The silver buckle was not easily buckled. There were difficulties—for the tongue had become bent and needed straightening.

"You might take the shoe off again to arrange the buckle," she said.

"I can straighten it without that," said I.

When at last the buckle was clasped we had been talking so long that I had told her my name, my residence, my profession, and more or less about Ferris. I don't know why I told her all this. She seemed to be interested. Then I asked her if she lived at the "Brambles."

"The Brambles?" she repeated, looking at her shoes.

"The deserted Farm by the White Moss Spring—"

"Yes—not alone; I have a housekeeper."

"Aged?"

"Very—and fierce. But I shall do as I please."

"Did you buy the house?"

"No. It was empty, and I walked in. Next day they sent my twelve trunks from Lynne Centre. The furniture was good."

"And you have been there for two months?"

"Yes. I have a horse and dog cart too. Rose drives to Lynne Centre twice a week for the marketing. I think I shall keep a cow—I generally do what I please. I choose to amuse myself with you just now."

"This," said I, "is a very strange history; did you know that Mr. Ferris and myself—existed?"

"It is not a strange history,—no, I once saw your house as I passed through the forest belt, but there was nobody there on the lawn except an ordinary person with little side whiskers."

"Howlett!" I exclaimed.

"*Comment?*" she asked.

"A servant, an Englishman."

"Probably," said she, looking dreamily at me.

351

Then I told her all about Ferris and myself; how we came every spring to the Clover Cottage with Howlett, a cook, and three dogs as retinue, how we fished in summer and shot in the autumn, how twice a year men came all the way from Lynne Center to house our hay and repair dam ages, how the game-keepers lurked at the mouth of the valley, miles to the south, to prevent poachers from entering, but we concluded it was not necessary for keepers to patrol the woods inside the valley.

"Now," I said, "the poachers are in our very midst—here established—and such dangerous poachers, too! What shall we do with them, *Mademoiselle*?"

"You mean me," she said, with wide open eyes.

"No," said I, "I do not mean you—you are very welcome in our valley."

"But I am sure you do mean me," she said, smiling.

Then we talked of other things, of Paris and France; of trout, and flies, and Ferris, of Normandy, and the beauty of the world; but it was nearly five o clock before we spoke of love.

"I have never loved," she said, looking at me calmly.

"Oh, how unnecessary!" I thought, for I had believed her clever.

"But," she continued, gravely, "I think it is time that I did."

"I think so too," said I.

"I should like to fall in love," said she; "I have nothing else to do."

"I also am very idle," I said.

"Then," said she, "the opportunity only is lacking."

I think I muttered something about poachers—I was not perfectly cool.

"Now," said she, "I know you mean me!"

"Ah," said I, "I mean a keener poacher than you or I, a free rover more to be dreaded than an army of riflemen."

"Then you don't mean me," she said.

I shook my head.

"Do you know," said she, "I should very much like to be the heroine of a romance."

"I will aid you to be one!" I said, hastily. We had known each other nearly three hours.

"Let us," said she, "pretend that this is the forest of Versailles in the time of Louis Quinze."

"Let us indeed!" I cried, enthusiastically.

"And you are a Count—"

"And you a Marquise—"

"Named Diane; it is my real name."

"Diane."

"And you—"

"My real name is Louis—"

"It will do; you may kiss my hand."

I wondered just where she was going to draw the line. Then, the devil prompting, I entered recklessly into this most extraordinary adventure.

And what an adventure! Words, thoughts even failed me as I looked at her. This woodland maid with the wonderful eyes! There was no mistaking the challenge in her eyes, the half- innocent smile, the utter disregard for every human conventionality.

"How," thought I—"how can such a woman wear a child-like face!" I had known *coquettes*,—many,—but the depth of this strange girl's recklessness I feared to sound—I dreaded almost to understand.

"She is too deep," said I to myself—"too deep for me, " and I looked her questioningly in the eyes.

I don't know why or how,—I never shall know probably, but a sudden conviction seized me that she was as innocent as she looked. Imagine a man coming to such a conclusion! I felt inclined to laugh, and yet I was as firmly convinced as though I had known her all my life.

"You may kiss my hand," she said, and held it out to me.

I did. I wished I hadn't a moment later, for I tumbled head over heels in love with her and fairly gasped at the idea.

"Lovers in the Court of Louis Quinze resembled us, I think," she said, after a long silence.

"We will try to make the resemblance perfect," said I, taking both her hands in mine.

She bent her head a little,—there was just a shadow of resistance,—then I kissed her on the lips.

There are moments in a man's life when he does not know whether he is a-foot or a-horseback. I remember that I sat down on the bank and carefully uprooted several ferns. When I had regained control of my voice,—the little maid was very silent,—I asked her to tell me of herself, if it might please her to do so.

"I was born," said the little maid, resting her small head on one hand, "in Rouen. Do you know Rouen?"

"Yes."

"Papa was an officer, and he killed his general when I was seven years old. It was something about Mama; I never saw her again. Then we went to Canada very quickly; Papa died there. I had been in a convent school; I ran away, and went to New York. I am nineteen, and very reckless."

"Yes, Diane."

"I have a great deal of money in banknotes. It was Papa's. I have never counted it—it is in a big trunk. I understand English, but do not care to speak it. I do not care what becomes of me; I wish it were over—this life. You are the first man who ever kissed me. Do you believe me?"

"Yes, Diane."

"I wonder you do. let us go down to the river where the sunlight falls. The descent is easy——"

"Diane—you must not go—"

"With you—will you give me your hand?"

"Come."

"Did you see that shy grey bird?" said the little maid, hesitating on the slope, her hand in mine.

I could not see it, for we had already begun the descent.

3

"Where the mischief have you been all day?" demanded Ferris that evening as we sat on the veranda after dinner.

"Well," said I lighting a pipe, "when you had your fit of sulks I went off for a brace of trout."

"Did you see anything worth seeing?"

"I saw no trout," said I.

"Unfortunate, eh?"

"Oh not very," I said, looking at Solomon.

"Not very?"

"Look at that ridiculous bird, Ferris."

"Swallowed a frog the wrong way," said Ferris, watching the solemn contortions of Solomon; "he looks like a little Jew in a crimson overcoat with a stomach ache. What fly did you use, Louis?"

"Everything; couldn't raise a fin."

"Oh, you've been trying that old devil down by the west woods! I should think you'd let him alone; it's useless," yawned Ferris.

"I'm going to try for him every day till I get him," said I, trying not to lie more than necessary: "Of course you'll not infringe?"

"Infringe! Not much! You can have the whole west woods to your own sweet self; but you're an idiot!"

"Not at all," said I, thankfully; and in a burst of confidence I confessed that I had used a Silver Doctor.

There was a momentary gleam of triumph in Ferris's eyes, but he was very decent about it and asked me most politely for the loan of a Red Ibis. Oh men of the busy world, learn courtesy from the angler! There are other things you need not learn from anglers.

"My dear fellow," said I, more touched than I had been for a long time, "I haven't a Red Ibis left. I shall write Conroy tonight before I retire. If you really do want an Ibis I will catch Solomon and pluck a plume from his tail feathers."

"I don't want it enough to inconvenience you or hurt Solomon's feelings," said Ferris, laughing.

After a long interval of silent smoking Ferris rose and yawned at the moon.

"Do you know what a Spirit-bird is," Ferris? I asked, rapping my pipe on the arm of my chair.

"Spirit-bird—the French one—the Oiseau Saint-Esprit? Yes, I've seen one—in the Vosges."

"Grey—with slim wings and big dark eyes?"

"That's the bird," said Ferris; "why?"

"Well, I thought I saw one today. Of course that's impossible."

"Of course," said Ferris, yawning again! "I'm going to turn in; goodnight, old chap."

"Goodnight," said I, tapping nervously on the veranda with my pipe.

Howlett came out a few moments later with my wading-shoes which he had been oiling.

"Well," said I, "are the hob-nails all right?"

"Seving 'ob nails is h'out, sir," replied Howlett, holding up the shoes for my inspection.

"Put them in as soon as they re dry. Did you oil the bamboo? Good. Is my lamp lighted? Put it out—and you need not sit up, Howlett ; I m going for a stroll."

"Thank you sir," said Howlett,—"and Solomon, sir?"

Now it was one of my delights to see Howlett house Solomon. The wily Ibis loved to snoop about in the moonlight, and he was always ready for Howlett when that dignified servant came to round him up.

I looked at Solomon, who stood gloomily brooding among the water-lilies.

"He ought to be in bed," said I.

Howlett descended the veranda steps with arms extended, but Solomon sidled out into the pond. Howlett pleaded earnestly. He flattered and cajoled, but Solomon was obdurate.

"Nothink I say do move 'im, sir!" said Howlett, stiffly; "he is vicious tonight, sir."

"Then take the boat," I said.

Howlett in a boat chasing a sulky Ibis was one of those rare spectacles that few are permitted to witness. Once a week Solomon turned "vicious" and then, at Ferris's and my suggestion, Howlett took to the boat. A terrestrial Howlett was solemnly ludicrous, but an aquatic Howlett was impossible. Of course Ferris and I never laughed—that is, aloud, but we usually felt rather weak after it was over.

In the course of half an hour Solomon, mad, wet, and rumpled was cornered by Howlett and clasped to his stiff shirt front, muddy, bedraggled, and kicking.

"Are you not mortified, you bad bird?" said I, as Howlett passed toward the kitchen where Kitty the cook was airing his straw-thatched house.

"A vicious bird, sir, goodnight, sir," murmured Howlett.

"Goodnight, Howlett; breakfast at seven tomorrow," said I, and sauntered out into the moonlit valley.

I had been walking almost half an hour when it occurred to me that I should be in bed.

"What the deuce am I sprinting about the valley at this hour for?" I thought, looking around.

Over the shadowy meadows the night mist hung, silvered by the moonlight, and I heard the meadow-brook rippling through the sedge. Slender birches glimmered among the alders, and all the little poplar leaves were quivering, but I felt no breath of air.

Where the dark forest fringed the meadow I saw the moonbeams sparkling on lonely pools, but the depths of the woodland were black and impenetrable, and the forest itself was vague as the mist that shrouded it.

For a long time I stood, looking at the stars and the mist, and little by little I came to understand why I was there alone.

I knew I should go on, I wished to, but I lingered in the moonlight staring at earth and sky until something moved in the thicket beside me, and I followed it, knowing it was the Spirit-bird.

When I entered the forest I could scarcely see my hand, but I felt a trodden path beneath my feet, and I heard before me the whisper of soft wings, and presently I heard the river, rushing through rocks of the western forest, and when I came to the wooded bank the moonlight fell all around me.

There was a narrow strip in the forest, over grown with silver birch and poplar and lighted by the moon, but I searched it in vain, up and down, up and down, always with the whisper of soft wings in my ears.

At last I called, "Diane," and before I called again, her hands lay close in mine.

★ ★ ★ ★ ★

"I came," said the little maid, "because you were coming."

"Who told you I was coming?"

"Told me? No one told me. Rose is asleep. Why did you come?"

"Why did you, Diane?"

"I? Because you came. How did you find my bower?"

"Your bower, Diane?"

"It is yours I know; I call it mine; I call it the Silent Land."

"It is very silent," I said.

"It is always silent—no birds, not even the noise of the water. Do you think it is sad? There are times when sounds,—the song of living creatures and the countless movements of things that live, trouble me. Then I come here. There are flowers."

"The air is very sweet, too sweet. What is the perfume? The trees are heavy with fragrance. Ah!—are you tired, Diane?"

"No—it is the odour of blossoms; I sleep here sometimes."

"Your hair is loose—how long it is! Is it the perfume from your hair—is it your breath—"

"The blossoms are very sweet; the moon has gone."

"There is a star,—how soft your breath is."

"I do not see the star; where, Louis?"

"It is there;—clouds are veiling it;—there is a mist over all—"

"It is my hair—over your eyes."

4

"Howlett," said I, one warm afternoon, "Solomon is unendurable: he follows me everywhere, and I wish you to see that he minds his own business."

"A hobstinate bird, sir," said Howlett, "and vicious when crossed, which I scorn is h'anger,—beg pardon sir,—for 'e's took to biting wen is vittles disagrees."

"Has he bitten you?"

"Twice, sir,—which 'appily my h'eyes is huninjured, though h'aimed at by 'is beak."

"This is intolerable," said I; "you must punish him, Howlett."

"'Ow, sir?"

"Tie him up when he bites. Have those flies come from Conroy's?"

"Nothink 'as came, sir."

"Where is Mr. Ferris?"

"Mr. Ferris is a whipping of the h'Amber Pool sir, with three sea-trout to the good and a brace of square tails. Solomon followed 'im, sir, and is h'observing the sport."

"Then I can get away without that red feathered Paul Pry tiptoeing after me," I thought, and sent Howlett for my rod-case.

"Tell Mr. Ferris, when he returns, that I may not be back until dinner," I said, when Howlett brought the case.

I selected a four-ounce split bamboo, pocketed my fly-book and a tin box of floating flies for dry fishing, picked up a land-ing-net, and walked away toward the western woodland, whis-tling. I had not fished for three weeks, although every day I went away into the western woods with rod and creel. Ferris laughed at my infatuation for the long pool where the great fish lay and jeered at me when I returned evening after evening with no trout, although the river, except the western stretch, was full of trout. He had never come to the pool, I should have seen him from the Silent Land if he had,—but Solomon sneaked after me on several occasions. Once I caught him craning his neck and peering into the bower,—our bower—and as I did not care to have him pilot Ferris thither, I hustled him off.

The woods were fragrant and warm, stained by the afternoon

sun; the quiet murmur of the brook came to me from leafy thickets as I walked, and I heard the river rushing in the distance and the summer wind among the pines. White clouds shimmered in the blue above, sailing, sailing God knows where, but they passed across the azure, one by one, drifting to the south, and I watched them with the vague longing that comes to men who watch white sails at sea.

I had turned my steps toward the long pool, for I had decided to fish that afternoon, wishing to redeem my words to Ferris—at least in part; but as I stepped across the trail I heard the sound of wings, and a shadow glided in front of me toward the forest. It was always so from the first, and now, as always, I turned away, following unquestioningly the Spirit-bird. The noise of the river ceased as I entered the Silent Land. For an instant the grey bird hovered high in the sun shine, then left me alone.

I threw myself full length upon the blossoming bank and waited, chin on hand. And as I waited, she came noiselessly across the moss, so quietly, so silently that I saw her only when her fingers touched mine.

"It has been a long time," we said; and; "Did you sleep?" and; "When did you awake?"

Then we asked each other a thousand little questions which are asked when lovers meet, and we answered as lovers answer. We spoke of the Spirit-bird as we always did, wondering, and she told me how that morning it had tapped upon her window as the day broke.

"Rose did not hear it," she said, "but I was already awake and thinking."

"I awoke at sunrise too," I said; "for a moment I thought it was a swallow in the chimney that fluttered so—"

"*The Spirit-bird flies swiftly when Love is dreaming,*—that is a very old proverb of Normandy. What shall we do, Louis there is so much to do and so little time in life!—I brought my lute—ah! you are laughing!"

"The lute is such an old-fashioned toy; I didn't know you played. Will you sing too, Diane? Something very old, older than the lute."

"I learned a song this morning because I thought you would care for it. That is why I dared to bring my lute into the Silent Land. The song is called, "Tristesse.""

Then the little maid sat up among the blossoms and touched the soft strings, singing:

J'ai perdu ma force et ma vie,
Et mes amis et ma gaité;
J'ai perdu jusqu' à la fierté
Qui faisait croire a mon génie.

Quand j'ai connu la Vérité
J'ai cru que c'était une amie;
Quand je 1'ai comprise et sentie,
J'en etais déjà dégoûte.

Et pourtant elle est éternelle
Et ceux qui se sont passés d elle
Ici-bas ont tout ignore

Dieu parle, il faut qu'on lui réponde;
Le seul bien qui me reste au monde
Est d'avoir quelquefois pleuré.

"That is all," said the little maid.

"Sing, Diane," I said, but I scarcely heard my own voice.

She laughed and bent above me with a graceful gesture. "Not that," she said, "for you at least are not sad. There is a *chansonnette*,—shall I sing again?—then be very still, here at my feet. Do you not think my lute is sweet?"

Je voudrais pour moi qu'il fut toujours fête
Et tourner la tête

Aux plus orgueilleux
Être en même temps de glace et de flamme,
La haine dans l'âme,
L' amour dans les yeux.

"You, Diane?" I whispered; but she smiled, and the mystery of love veiled her dark eyes; and she sang:

Je ne voudrais pas à la contredanse,
Sans quelque prudence
Livrer mon bras nu
Puis, au cotillion, laisser ma main blanche
Trainer sur la manche
Du premier venu.

Si mon fin corset, si souple et si juste,
D'un bras trop robuste
Se sentait serré,
J'aurais, je 1'avoue, une peur mortelle
Qu'un bout de dentelle
N'en fut déchiré.

She looked at me with soft, unfathomable eyes and touched the lute. When I moved she started from her reverie with a gay little nod to me:

Quand on est coquette, il faut être sage,
L'oiseau de passage
Qui vole à plein cœur
Ne dort pas en l'air comme une hirondelle,
Et peut, d'un coup d'aile
Briser une fleur!

"Sing," I said in a changed voice.

"I have sung," she said, and laid her lute in my hands. But I knew nothing of minstrelsy and lay silent, idly touching the strings.

She had fashioned for her fair head a wreath of sweet-fern twined with clustered buds, white as snow and faintly perfumed.

"So I am crowned," she said, "a princess in the Silent Land. Where I step, all things green shall flourish; where I turn my eyes, blossoms shall open in the summer wind;—am I not queen?"

"Will you not sing again, Diane?"

"No, it pleases me to hear a legend now. You may begin, Louis."

"Which—the Werewolf or the Man in Purple Tatters or

362

the—"

"No, no—something new."

"The Seventh Seal?"

"Begin it."

"And when he opened the Seventh Seal there was silence in Heaven—"

"Dear Saints, have we not silence enough in the Silent Land? Tell me about battles."

"And the sound of their wings was as the sound of chariots of many horses running to battle. I could tell you about battles, Diane."

"Tell me,—don't move your arm,—tell me of battles, Louis."

"There was once a King in Carcosa," I began. But the little maid was already asleep.

I thought I heard a step in the undergrowth and listened.

The forest was silent.

5

When we awoke it was night. Down from the dark heavens a great star fell, burning like a lamp. Above the low-hanging branches, sombre, drooping, heavy with fragrance, a misty darkness lay like a vast veil spread.

In the stillness I heard her quiet breathing, but we did not speak.

Silence is a Prophet, unveiling mysteries.

Then, through the forest, we heard the sound of wings, and as we moved, stepping together into the shadows, the moon rose above Lynx Peak, gigantic, golden, splendid.

So we passed out of the forest into the starlit night.

6

The skies were leaden, the watery clouds hung low over the valley, and a wet wind blew from the west, ruffling the long pool where Diane stood. Kilted and capped in tweeds, creel swinging with every movement of the rod which swayed and bent with her bending wrist, she moved from ripple to shallow, wading noiselessly while the silken line whistled and the gay flies chased each other across the wind-lashed pool.

We spoke in a low voice, glancing at each other when the light cast struck the water.

"Under the alders Diane—" I said; "have you changed the Grey Dun for the Royal?"

"No, what is your new cast?"

"Emerald and Orange Miller I shall tie an Alder-fly in place of the Miller. Do you think the water warrants a cast of three?"

"It is rough; I don't know,—Louis, was that an offer?"

"I think it was the spray from the rapids. Shall we move up a little? Do you feel the chill of the water?"

"I am cold to my knees," said the little maid, "the river is rising I think—ah, what was that?"

"Nothing,—you touched a floating leaf in the swirl."

"Splash!" A great fish flopped over in the pool, a trout, lazy, unwieldy, monstrous.

"Oh! he missed it!" cried Diane, turning a little white.

"Cast again," I whispered, tossing my rod onto the sandy beach and unslinging my landing-net.

Trembling a little with excitement she cast across the swirl, once, twice, twenty times, but the monster was invisible. Somewhere in the dusky depths of that amber well the fierce fish lay watching the lightly dropping flies, unmoved. Then we changed the cast; I emptied my fly-book, but nothing stirred except the hurrying water, curling, gurgling, tumbling through the rocks. Finally I broke the silence.

"Diane, it was the spinner that he rose to. He's after something redder. Have you a Scarlet Ibis?"

"No—have you?"

I almost groaned, for Conroy's flies had not arrived, and I hadn't an Ibis in the world.

After a while she reeled in her silken line, and we waded to the sandy beach and sat down.

"Oh, the pity of it," sighed Diane; "never have I seen such a trout before. I suppose it is useless, Louis."

I sat moodily poking holes in the sand with the butt of my landing-net.

We spoke of other things for a time, sinking our voices below the roar of the river. Presently a sunbeam stole through the vapour above, lighting the depths of the dark pool. And all at once we saw the trout, hanging just above the pebbly bottom; we saw the scarlet fins move, the great square tail waving gently in the current, the mottled spotted back, the round staring eyes. The swelling of the gills was scarcely perceptible, the broad mouth hardly moved.

For a long time we sat silent, fascinated; then something stirred behind us on the beach and we slowly turned. It was Solomon.

"*Ciel!*" faltered Diane, "what is that?"

"My bird—an Egyptian Ibis," I whispered, laughing silently; he has followed me, after all."

Solomon ruffled his scarlet plumes, blinked at me, scratched his head with his broad foot, pecked at a bit of mica, and took two solemn steps nearer.

"Diane," said I, suddenly, "I'll get a red fly for you; don't move—the bird will come close to us."

But Solomon was in no hurry. Inch by inch he sidled nearer, dallying with bits of moss and shining pebbles, often pausing to reflect, but gradually approaching, for his curiosity concerning Diane was great.

"He looks as if he had stepped off an obelisk," murmured Diane; "I have seen hieroglyphics that resembled him. Oh, what a prehistoric head—so old, so old!"

"His name is Solomon," I whispered. "Solomon in all his glory was not arrayed like one of these. I'm going to have a small bit of Solomon's glory—sh—h! ah! I've got him!"

It was over in a second, and I do not believe it was painful. There was a flurry of sand, a furious flapping of flame-coloured wings, a squawk! a smothered laugh—nothing more.

Mortified, furious, Solomon marched off, shaking the river sand from wing and foot, and Diane and I, with tears of laughter in our eyes, wound the scarlet feather about a spare hook, tied it close with a thread from my coat, and whipped it firmly to the shank. I looped the improvised fly to Diane's leader, and she shook the line free. The reel sang a sweet tune as she drew the silk through the guides, and presently she motioned me to follow her out into the rippling shallows, and I went, swinging my landing-net to my shoulder.

She cast once. The fly struck the swirl and sank a little, but she drew it to the surface and the current swept it under the alders. For a moment it sank again; then the ripples parted, and a broad crimson-flecked side rolled just below the surface of the water. At the same moment the light rod curved, deeply quivering, the reel screamed like the wind in the chimney, and the straining line cut through the water, moving up the pool with lightning speed.

"Strike!" I cried, and she struck heavily, but the reel sang out like a whistling buoy, and the fish tumbled into the churning water under the falls at the head of the pool.

"Now," said Diane, with a strange quiet in her voice, "I suppose he is gone, Louis."

But the vicious tug and long, fierce strain contradicted her, and I stepped back a pace or two to let her fight the battle to the bitter end.

The struggle was splendid. Once I believe she became a little frightened,—the rod was staggering under the furious fish,- and she spoke in a queer, small voice: "Are you there, Louis?"

"I am here, Diane."

"Close behind?"

"Close behind."

She said nothing more until the great fish lay floating within reach of my net.

"Now!" she gasped.

It was done in a second; and, as I bore the deep-laden net to the beach, I caught a fleeting glimpse of a figure among the trees on the bank above. Diane was kneeling breathlessly on a rock beside me; she did not see the figure. I did, for an instant.

It was Ferris.

Dinner was over. Ferris and I lingered silently over the Burgundy, and Howlett hovered in the corner with a decanter of port until Ferris shook his head.

It had been a silent dinner. Ferris tried to be cordial, and failed. Then he tried to be indifferent, with better success. We exchanged a word or two concerning a new keeper who was to be stationed at the notch in the north, and I spoke to Howlett about cleaning the lamps.

Neither of us mentioned rods or trout, although Howlett had served us a delicious sea-trout that evening which had fallen to Ferris's rod, over which we ordinarily should have exulted.

Ferris of course knew that I had seen him among the trees on the bank above the long pool. It was my place to speak; we both understood that, but I did not. What was there to say? Suppose I should go back to the beginning and tell him—not all, but all that I was bound in honour to tell him. What would he think if I spoke of the Spirit-bird, of the Silent Land, of my long deception? An explanation was due him—I felt that with a vague sense of anger and humiliation. For weeks I had abandoned him; I never thought about his being lonely, but I knew now that he had felt it deeply.

Oh, it was the underhand part of the business that sickened me, the daily deceit, the double dealing. Ferris was no infant. A word would have been enough. I had never by sign or speech spoken that word which would at least have set me right with him, and which I could have spoken honourably. And moreover, if I had spoken that word,—no, not a word even, a look would have been enough,—Ferris would never have entered the western forest belt.

We sat dawdling over our wine in the glow of the long candles while the fire crackled in the chimney place; for the evening was chilly, and Solomon brooded sullenly before the blaze . Howlett, noiseless and pompous, glided from side-board to table, decorously avoiding the evil jabs from Solomon's curved bill, until Ferris woke up and told him he might retire, which he did with a modest goodnight, sir, and a haughty glance at Solomon. A half hour of strained silence followed. I leaned on the table, my head on my hands, watching the candle light reflected on the fragile wine glasses. Myriads of little flames glistened on the crystal bowls, deep stained with the red wine's glow. The fire snapped and sparkled on the hearth, and Solomon slept, his wizened head buried in the depths of his flaming plumage.

And as we sat there, there came a faint tapping at the curtained window. Ferris did not hear it I did, for it was the Spirit-bird.

"I must go," said I, rising suddenly.

"Where?" said Ferris.

I looked at him stupidly for a moment, then sank back into my chair.

Solomon stirred in his slumber and I heard the wind rising in the chimney.

Ferris leaned across the table and touched my sleeve.

I looked at him silently.

"I must speak," he said; "are you ready?"

I did not reply.

"Sadness and silence have no place here, between you and me. Shall I tell you a story I once read?"

"I am half asleep," I muttered.

"This is the story," he said, unheeding my words. "There was once a King in Carcosa—"

My hand fell heavily upon the table.

"—And there was given unto him a mouth speaking great things and blasphemies—"

"For God's sake, Ferris—"

"Yes," he said, "for God's sake."

We sat staring at each other across the table, and if my face was as white as his I do not know, but my hand trembled among the glasses till they tinkled.

"I was born in France," he said at last. "You did not know

it, for I never told you. What do you know about me after all? Nothing. What have years of friendship taught you about my past? Nothing. Now learn. My father was shot dead by an inferior officer in Rouen. The assassin escaped to Canada—where I found him. He died by his own hand—from choice. I did not know he had a child."

The dull fear at my heart must have looked from my eyes. Ferris nodded.

"Yes, you know the rest," he said; "the shame and disgrace of the suicide drove the child away—anywhere to escape it—anywhere—here, into the wilderness the woman fled where she hath a place prepared of God."

The Spirit-bird was tapping on the window, I heard the noise of wings beating against the pane.

"I must go," I said, and my voice sounded within me as from a great distance.

"Vengeance is God's," said Ferris, quietly: "I am guilty."

"I must go," I repeated, steadying myself with my hand on the table.

The noise of wings filled my ears. I knew the summons.

"Do you not hear?" I cried.

"The wind," said Ferris.

Then the door slowly opened from without, the long candles flared in the wind, and the ashes stirred and drifted among the embers on the hearth. And out of the night came a slender figure, with dark eyes wide, and timid hands outstretched outstretched until they fell into my own and lay there.

"I came from the Silent Land," she said; "the bird lead me; see, it has entered with me, Louis."

"It is my wife who has entered," I said quietly to Ferris, and the little maid clung close to me, holding out one slim hand to Ferris.

There was an interval of silence.

"Father Gregory will breakfast with us tomorrow," said Ferris to me.

"A Priest?"

369

Open the window," smiled Ferris; "there is a small grey bird here."

So I opened the window and it flew away.

"Goodnight," whispered the little maid, and kissed her hand to the open window.

"Diane!"

She came to me quietly. Ferris had vanished; Solomon peered dreamily at us with filmy eyes.

"The Spirit-bird has gone," she said.

Then, with her arms about my neck, I raised her head, touching her white brow with my lips.

★ ★ ★ ★ ★

When my wife read as far as you have read, she picked up the embroidery which she had dropped beside her on the table.

"Do you like my story?" I asked.

But she only smiled at me from under her straight eyebrows.

The next morning I received her ultimatum; I am to cease writing about beautiful women of doubtful antecedents who inhabit forest glades, I am to stop making fun of Howlett , I am to curb my passion for rod and gun, and, if I insist on writing about my wife, I am to tell the truth concerning her. This I have promised Ysonde to do, and I shall try to.

The Carpet of Belshazzar

(A story from The Tree of heaven.)

We all were glad to see him; on his return he had found us all his friends. Nobody had spoken to him about his abrupt departure from New York; nobody had mentioned Westover; nothing connected with that episode was even hinted at by any of us, I believe, during his short sojourn among us. It was he himself who spoke of it first.

Of course during his absence we had followed his career; many among us had read and tried to understand what he had written in his three world- famous volumes, Occult Philosophy, The Weight of Human Souls, and *The Interstellar Laws of Psychic Phenomena*.

It seemed, at times, here to us in America, that it was impossible that the man we had known so well could have become the great Psychic Scientist who had written these three astounding works—who now occupied the Chair of Psychical Philosophy in the great University of Trebizond—the man who was the confidential adviser of the *Shah* of Persia, the mentor of the *Ameer* of Afghanistan, the inspirer of the greatest diplomat of all the East—the late Akhound of Swat.

As he sat there in his immaculate evening dress, bronzed, youthful looking, presiding so quietly at the little dinner which he had given to us as a half-formal, half-intimate leave-taking before he sailed, it seemed to us incredible that this man, now on his return journey to Trebizond *via* Lhassa, could be the beloved and dreaded arbiter of Asiatic politics—the one white man in all

371

the Orient who had ever been wholly respected, and absolutely feared by the temporal and spiritual heads of nations, religions, clans, and sects.

That, of course, he was what is popularly known as an adept, we supposed. What his wisdom, his insight, his amazing knowledge of the occult might include, we preferred, rather uncomfortably, not to conjecture.

There is, naturally, in all of us a childlike de sire to hear of marvels; there is also a stronger and more childish desire to see miracles performed.

I am quite sure that we all hoped he might perhaps care to do something for us—merely to convince us. And at first, I know that many among us, seated there in the private room at the Lenox Club, felt a trifle ill at ease and a little in awe of this man with whom we were at such close quarters.

There was nothing particularly remarkable about the dinner; it was the usual excellent affair one might expect at the Lenox; the wines perfect, the service flawless.

And now, smoking our cigars, lounging in groups over the flower-laden table, we fell into the old, intimate, easy channels of conversation, chat ting of past days, of our hopes and ambitions.

And our host, quiet, self-contained, pushed back his chair, looking somewhat curiously, I thought, from one to the other. And I thought, too, as his pleasant bronzed features changed from a faint smile to a graver expression, and then reverted to the smile for a moment, that he seemed to see something in each of us that was perhaps hidden from ourselves—that, as his eyes swept us, he was not only capable of reading much of what was not understood by us, but also something in the hid den future which awaited each of us.

So strongly did this idea begin to take hold of me that it began to make me uneasy. I felt, too, that others among us harboured that same idea—for the conversation was less accented now, and intermittent; voices had fallen to a lower, quieter pitch; and after a little nobody spoke.

Then I saw that we all were looking straight at our host, as though under some subtle and fascinated compulsion.

He sat very still; his composure appeared a trifle forced, as though he had voicelessly summoned us to concentrate upon him our attention, and was now searching for the exact words for some statement which he had meant to make to us all.

After a moment a slight flush crept over his handsome face. He said:

"You fellows are very good to come here and let me take leave of you so pleasantly. You have been very kind to me since I have come again among you. The sort of friendship that asks nothing but takes a man for granted is a good sort. Helmer,"—he looked at the sculptor Helmer—"I shall see you soon again." We all turned in surprise to Helmer, who seemed as surprised as we were. "I shall see you sooner than you expect. . . . Smith!"—he smiled at J. Abingdon Smith, 3rd—"someday you will uproot a Tree of Dreams, but not the dream, Smith; that will become very real when you awake—as true"—and he turned to the man on his left—"as true as a dream which you shall dream under the Sign of Venus."

We sat there breathless, expectant. He was doing something after all; he was prophesying, in a curious sort of manner, probably speaking in symbols. And though we could not understand, we listened while the little shivers fluttered our pulses.

Then he looked at Edgerton, smiling; and Edgerton flushed up and looked back at him, almost defiantly.

"Edgerton," he said, "don't worry too much. What is not to be settled in court can sometimes be settled—*ex curia*" And to the young man on his right: "Doctor, don't overwork. If you do you will learn a stranger truth than is locked up among the molecules and atoms in your laboratory!"

Then he leaned across the table and laid one hand on Leeds's shoulder. "I congratulate you," he said, smiling; "you've got a good-natured ghost following you about. But he'll leave you if you turn idle. And don't be afraid, my boy."

"I'm not afraid," said young Leeds, rather pallid, but straightening up in his chair.

Our host laughed; then his face changed, and he raised his eyes to Shannon:

"Where is Harrod?" he asked slowly.

"At Bar Harbor," replied Shannon, "I believe."

"I thought so. And—remember one thing—there is a certain law which governs the validity of a check drawn to a man's order when that check has been signed by a man no longer living. But, Shannon, the intention is the important thing in such a matter."

"What, exactly, do you mean?" asked Shannon, astonished.

But our host had already turned to Escourt:

"Captain," he said, "you sail—when?"

"I have no sailing orders," laughed Escourt.

"Not yet?" Our host looked quietly at the young officer. "Well, it isn't the length of a voyage that counts, Escourt—nor the size of the troopship. No; you will anchor, some day, in a smaller craft than you started in, in the Port of the Golden Pool."

Escourt, still smiling, waited; but our host sat silent, head bent, one hand on the edge of the table cloth.

"Not one of you," he said, without raising his eyes, "not one among you but who shall come face to face with what you still consider miracles. . . . Even Hildreth, yonder"—Hildreth jumped—"even Hildreth shall learn from the Swastika."

"Swa—swat? What—what?" stammered Hildreth.

"Nothing to alarm you," smiled the other; then again the swift shadow fell across his face.

"Not one man among you who has not proven his friendship for me," he said, looking up and around. And to me he added: "You must prove it still further by telling fearlessly to the world what there will be to tell after I have gone, and after my words have been proven—the words I have spoken here tonight—and which no one among you understands. . . . But you all will understand them. And when the last man among you has understood"—turning again to me—"you must bear witness to the world, bear witness in printed page and over your own signature. Do you promise?"

"Yes," I said.

Then very quietly he looked around the table, and leaned forward, regarding each man in turn.

"I think," he said, "that it is time you understood exactly the facts about which you have for borne to question me. And I mean to tell you before we part; I mean to tell you the truth concerning Westover and—all that happened. . . . And when you know these facts, then you may begin to surmise why I went to Trebizond, why I remain, and—and—*what miracle of happiness I have found there—for the third time reincarnated.*"

He leaned back in his chair; his clear eyes became fixed and dreamy. Then he began to speak, in a low voice, as though to himself:

★ ★ ★ ★ ★ ★

Time, and the funeral of Time, alas!—and the Old Year's passing-bell! Whistles from city and river, deep horns sounding from the foggy docks; and under my window a voice and a song—ah! that young voice in the street below calling me through the falling snow!

If it be true that Time makes all hurts well, I do not know; and "a thousand years in Thy sight is but as yesterday when it is passed, and as a watch in the night"; a thousand years! And this also is true; the flames of love make hot the furnace of Abaddon.

We were in the gallery as usual, Geraldine and I—the gallery where the carpets of the East were hung along the shadowy walls. For lately it was my pleasure to acquire rare rugs, and it was my profession to furnish expert opinion upon the age and origin of Oriental carpets, and to read and interpret the histories of forgotten emperors and the mysteries of long-forgotten gods from the colours and intricate flowery labyrinths tied in silk or wool to the warps of some dead sultan's lustrous tapestry.

Here in the long sky gallery hung my own rugs against the arabesque incrusted-ivory panels—Tabriz, Shiraz, Sehna, and

Saruk—a sombre blaze of colour shot with fire—all rare, some priceless; Turkish Kulah, softly silky as a golden lion's hide, Persian Sehna, shimmering with rose and violet lights, fiercely brilliant rugs from Samarkand, superbly flowered, secreting deep in every floral thicket traceries of the ancient Mongol conqueror; Feraghans glowing like jewel-sewn velvets set with the Herati and the lotus—symbols of Egypt or of China, as you please to interpret the oldest pattern in the world.

Far in the gallery's amber-tinted gloom the red of Ispahan dominated, subduing fiery vistas to smoldering harmony through which, like a vast sapphire set in opals, glimmered the superb lost Persian blue.

There was one other rug, an Eighur, the famous so-called "Babilu," or "Carpet of Belshazzar"; but it hung alone in imperial magnificence behind the locked doors of a marble room, which it seemed to fill with a soft lustre of its own, radiating from the mystic "Tree of Heaven" woven in its centre.

We were, as I say, in this gallery; Geraldine poring over an illuminated volume on cuneiform inscriptions, I, with pad and pencil, idly shifting and reshifting the Kufic key to the ancient cipher, which always left me stranded where I had begun with the stately repetition:

King of Kings—
King of Kings—
King of Kings—

As for Westover, my cousin, he was, as usual, in the laboratory fussing with his venomous extracts an occupation which, to my dismay, he had taken up within the year, working, as he explained, on the theory that every poison has its antidote. Yet it seemed to me that he was more anxious to in vent some new and subtle toxic than to devise the remedy.

From where I sat I could not see him, but the crystalline tinkle of his glass retorts and bottles distracted my attention from the pencilled calculations. Without moving my head, I glanced across the room at Geraldine. She looked up immediately, raising her level eyebrows in mute inquiry as though I had moved or spoken; then, realizing that I had not, she bent above the book once more, the warm colour stealing to her cheeks.

Within the year a wordless intimacy had grown up between us; we never understood it, never acknowledged it, and at times it disconcerted us.

I sat silent, tracing with my pencil series after series of futile Kufic combinations with the cuneiforms, but ever the first turn of the ancient key creaked in my ears,

King of Kings—
King of Kings—

until the triverbal reiteration wore on my nerves.

Geraldine leaned back abruptly, closing her book.

"I'm tired and nervous," she said. "You may wear out your eyes and temper if you choose—and you're doing the latter, for I'm as restless as an eel. Besides, I'm lonely, and I'm going back to the East—if you'll come, too."

I laughed, understanding what she meant by the "East."

"Will you come with me?" she insisted.

"Yes," I said, "whenever you are ready."

She sprang to her feet, scattering the illuminated pages over the floor, and stood an instant facing me, tall, dark-eyed, smiling, brushing back the lustrous hair from her cheeks.

"Where is Jim?" she asked—although we both knew.

"In the laboratory," I replied mechanically.

Still busy with her hair, she regarded me dreamily out of those dark, sweet eyes of hers.

"It would be wonderful," she mused, "if Jim should find an antidote to death; but I wish it were not necessary to kill so many little helpless creatures. Did you hear that pitiful sound in there yesterday? Was it something he was killing?"

"I don't know," I said. And after a silence: "What are you going to do?"

She shook her head vaguely and leaned against the window, looking out into the rain.

377

"Shall we go back to our inscriptions?" I suggested.

She shook her head again. After a while she turned away from the window, stifling a dainty yawn, and stretched out, languidly straightening up to the full height of her young body.

"I feel stupid," she said; "I'm tired of cryptograms and the pages of dusty books. I'm tired of the rain, too. The languor of April is in me. I'm homesick for lands I never knew. So come back to the East with me, Dick."

She held out her hand to me with a confident little smile; and knowing what she meant, I acquiesced in her caprice, and conducted her solemnly to the piano, leaving her before it.

She stood there for a space, musing, her lovely head bent; then, still standing, she struck a sequence of chords—chords pulsating with colour; and through them flashed strange little trills like threads of tinsel.

"This is an Eighur carpet I am dreaming of," she murmured, as the music swelled, glowing as tints and hues glow in the old dyes of the East.

Wave on wave of colour seemed to spread from the keys under her fingers; she looked back at me over her shoulder with a warning nod.

"I shall begin to weave very soon. Khiounnou horsemen may appear and frighten me for a moment—but I shall finish. Listen! I am at the loom."

Seating herself, she developed out of the flowing, sombre harmony a monotonous minor theme, suddenly checked by a distant rattle like the clatter of nomad lances on painted stirrups; then she picked up the thread of the melody again, dropped it, breathless for a moment's quivering silence, resumed it, twisting it into delicate arabesques, threading it across the dull, rich harmonies, at first slowly, then faster, faster, swift as the flying fingers of a nomad maid tying fretted silver in a Ghiordes knot. The whirring tempo was the cadence of the loom; soft feathery notes flew like carded wool; thicker, duller, softer grew the fabric, dense, silky, heavily lustrous.

Suddenly she broke the thread off short, the whole fabric

falling with a muffled shock.

"Why did you do that?" I demanded wrathfully.

"The rug is woven; the weaver is dead," she said.

"Oh, go on, Geraldine," I insisted; "don't stop half way in a thing like that. It's the East it's the real East, I tell you. How you do it—you who have never seen the East—Heaven only knows!"

"*U Allah Aalem*," she murmured; "it's in me." Then she looked back at me, laughing. "Centuries ago you and I heard that music along the Arax—or I sang it among the Tcherkess roses for you, perhaps—perhaps in the gardens of Trebizond."

"That might explain it," I said gravely. Lately she had found pleasure in a fancy that she and I had lived together in the East, centuries since, and that we were soon to return forever.

"You and I," she mused, touching the keys lightly—"and Jim, of course," she added.

"Of course," I said.

She dropped her head, striking chord on chord with nervous precision; and hanging in the wake of every ringing harmony a frail melody floated like the Chinese cloud band in a Kirman tapestry.

"What's that air?" I asked, fascinated.

"I don't know; it sounds pagan, doesn't it?—like the wicked beauty of Babylon. Do you hear how it beats on and on like the rhythm of naked feet—little, delicate, naked feet ablaze with gems—the feet of Herodiade perhaps—thud—thud—tching!— don't you hear them, Dick? And now listen to those silky, flowery trills! They re Asiatic; ancient Cathay is awaking—camel bells in the *hazar* of the Golden Emperor! Hark!—now you hear trumpets, don't you? Well, of course that must be the Mongols marching with the Prince of the Vanguard. Hark! How savagely the brutal Afghan theme breaks in with its fierce trampling and the *staccato* echo of Tekke drums! It's frightening me out of the East. I think we had better come home, Dick," she added, mischievously running into the latest popular street song.

"How on earth could you do that!" I exclaimed wrathfully.

"You're a futile mixture of feather brain and genius!"

But where was the genius hidden under that laughing and exquisite mask confronting me? Suddenly the delicate mask became grave.

"Let me laugh when I can, Dick," she said. "It is not often I laugh."

I was silent.

"Of course you may be horrid if you choose," she observed with a shrug, running a brilliantly inane series of trills from end to end of the key board. "But it's no use scolding, for I won't study, I won't compose, I won't try to do something, and I won't be serious. I'm shallow, I'm frivolous, I've the soul of a Trebizond dancing girl, and I like it. Now what are you going to do?"

"I'm going out," I said ungraciously.

Oh—alone?"

"Not if you'll come. It's stopped raining. Will you come? Oh, get your hat, Geraldine, and stop that torment of idiotic trills!"

"If Jim doesn't mind, I think I'll go and sit in the laboratory with him," she observed carelessly.

I looked at her without comment.

"I have a curious idea," she continued, "that he might like to have me around today while he is working."

I stared at her, but there was no bitterness in her tranquil smile as she leaned forward, resting her elbows on the polished rosewood case.

"So I won't go with you, Dick," she said slowly.

One of those intervals of restless silence, which within the year we had learned to dread, menaced us now. Mute, motionless, I watched the soft colour deepening in her face, then, impatient, roused myself and walked over to the laboratory. Westover looked up as I pushed aside the screen.

"Will you drive with us?" I asked. "The sun's out."

He declined, peering at me through his glass mask.

"Come on, Jim," I urged. "You've inhaled enough poison for one day. Take off your mask and wash your hands and drive us out to High Bridge. I'll telephone to the stable if you say the word, and they'll hook up the new four. Is it a go?"

"No," he said coldly, and turned on his heel, lifting a test tube to the light.

He was more taciturn and a trifle uglier than usual. I watched him for a moment warming the test tube over a burner, then without further parley replaced the screen, closed the double glass doors, and walked back to Geraldine.

"Doesn't Jim care to come?" she asked.

I said that her husband appeared to be absorbed in his work.

"Very well," she said, with airy composure; "trot along, Dicky—and if you see a bunch of jonquils growing on Fifth Avenue, you may pick them for me—or for that pretty girl you met at Lakewood—"

"I'll send you a bunch as big as a bushel."

"A bushel of flowers is as compromising as a declaration," she said. "Send them to her."

"There's only one way to settle it," I said; "I'll send them to the loveliest girl in the world—shall I?"

She assented, laughing uncertainly.

"I think I'll pay Jim a little call," she said, rising from the piano and walking slowly toward the laboratory.

A few moments later as I passed down the broad stairway I heard Westover's penetrating voice: "Let that glass tube alone, Geraldine! Why the devil can't you keep your hands off things when you come in here?"

I lingered for a while in the hallway, thinking that she might change her mind and come down, for she had left the laboratory to her husband, and I heard her moving about in her own apartment. She did not come, and after a little while I left the house, a sense of apprehension depressing me.

The asphalt of Fifth Avenue was still wet with the first warm rain of April, but the sun glittered on window and pavement and flashed along the polished panels of carriages crowding the avenue from curb to curb. A breath of spring had set the sparrows chattering and chirping; the movement of the throng, the bright gowns, the fresh faces of young girls, and the endless *façades* of glass reflecting it—all were pleasant to me, a man sensitive to impressions.

And so in the pale sunshine I sauntered on through the throng, now idling curiously by some shop window whither a display of jewels or curios attracted me, now strolling on again content with the soft colour in sky and sunlight.

I found a florist whose shop windows were filled with thickets of fragrant, fragile spring flowers; and every little scented blossom that I touched, choosing the freshest, nodded to the voiceless cadence of a name repeated—and: "Geraldine! Geraldine!" they nodded, so confidently, so sweetly, that what was I to do but send them to her?

And so I sauntered on again, threading the throng, half-minded to turn back, yet ever tempted on by idleness, until above me the twin spires of the cathedral glimmered, all silvered in the shimmering blue.

Halting, undecided, I presently became aware of an old man, his withered hands crossed before him, standing quite patiently under the cathedral terrace. Before him on the sidewalk rested a basket draped with a brilliant rug or two and heaped with tawdry rubbish—scarlet *fezzes*, slippers of spangled leather, tasselled charms of gilt, flimsy striped fabrics—all the worthless flummery known as "Oriental" to the good peoples of the West.

Few stopped to look; no one bought. As I passed him his dimmed gaze met mine; all the wistfulness of the very poor, all the mystery of the very, very old, was in his eyes. Moved by impulse, perhaps, I spoke to him in a low voice, using the Turkish language.

A dull animation came into his misty eyes.

"*Allahou Ekber*," he muttered, in a trembling voice; "it is sweet to hear your words, my son."

"Mussulman," I said, "who are you who recite the Tekbir here under the spires of a Roman church?"

"Is there harm in bearing witness to the glory of God here under the minarets of your cathedral?" he asked humbly.

"Spire and minaret are one to Him," I said. "Who are you,

Mussulman?"

"My name is Khassar," he said; "my nation Eighur; my Iort is the Issig-Kul; Baïon-Aoul my clan. I am an Eighur Turk, a Khodja; and I am able to write the Turkish language in Arabic and in Eighur-Mongol characters."

"Reverend father," I said, full of astonishment and pity, "how should a Khodja of the Baïon-Aoul come to this? Even the Tekrin horseman halts at the sea."

"It is written," he said feebly, "that we belong to God and we return to Him."

Troubled, I stood there on the sidewalk, oblivious of the knot of idlers around us, curious to hear two men so different conversing in a common tongue.

I wished to give him something, yet did not venture to humiliate him without pretence of buying.

"Here is my card," I said, "on which is written my name and where I live. Bring me these rugs tonight, *ata*. I wish to buy."

"You do not desire them," he said, shaking his head. "You know the East; you understand these rugs; you know they are worthless, acid-washed, singed, rubbed with pumice, smoked—every vile Armenian practice used! You know the dyes are aniline; that they are loosely tied, hastily and flimsily woven by Armenian dogs and sons of dogs. You mean kindness; you have done me enough by speaking to me."

He passed his trembling hand over his ragged beard.

"You who know carpets and love them," he quavered; "listen attentively. I have a strip to show—not here—but I could bring it."

"Bring it," I said gently.

He fumbled in the pocket of his tattered coat and presently brought to light a scrap of paper on which was scrawled some Persian characters.

"It is such a carpet as I have never seen," he said; "there is nothing in our history or our traditions to teach us the meaning of this carpet—nothing save that it is an Eighur rug inscribed in Persian and in an unknown script. I have traced the characters in a single *cartouche*. Read, my son."

And I read, translating freely:

Ten thousand thousand stars shine down on Babylon. The desert well reflects but one.

"I will bring the carpet," he said, after a silence. "I do not know its value; it has no beauty any longer; only the ghost of ancient splendour remains in the thin knots clinging to warp and weft. And it is old, my son, older than tradition. Upon it there is not one sign to teach us the mystery of its meaning."

He peered at me with his old, sad eyes, earnestly.

"I will bring it," he said. "Go with Ali, thou fair comrade of Hassan."

"May the Blessed Companions intervene for you," I said.

And so we parted, gravely and with circum stance, I to stroll homeward, touched, musing curiously upon this carpet of which a nomad Mussulman could make nothing. The Persian verse from the cartouche interested me, too, the refrain lingering persistently in my memory:

"Ten thousand thousand stars shine down on Babylon. The desert well reflects but one."

Never before, save on the imperial carpet known as Belshazzar's Rug, had I encountered any inscription mentioning Babylon. So, at the first glance, the nomad's rug should have some value. But speculation was futile—surely I ought to have learned that if unnumbered disappointments could teach me anything.

Thinking of these things, I passed along the noble avenue, retracing my steps to the big dusky house standing alone, with two old trees to guard—it relics, like the mansion, of the great city's infancy—the last old dwelling left marooned amid the arid wastes of commerce. Here my cousin and his wife lived with me in winter; I with them at their Lenox home in summer.

A brougham or two at the curb before the house warned me of clients waiting or of visitors for Geraldine—doubtless the latter, for it was now past five.

Under the circumstances I went in to second Geraldine—for

Westover never troubled himself to be civil to her friends.

There were people there, and tea—and a pretty, wordless welcome from Geraldine.

The violet-tinted April dusk brought candle light; people went away and others came; then, one by one, they left, and we were alone, Geraldine and I—and the new moon shining through the frail curtains. For a long time we talked together, aimlessly, of this and that which mattered nothing to anybody. A maid entered to draw the curtains. When she left, Geraldine laughed and picked up a cluster of yellow jonquils.

"Your courage failed you, after all," she said; "the loveliest woman in the world must go without my flowers tonight."

"She has them," I retorted.

"Do you mean me, Dick?" she said under her breath.

"Did you doubt it?"

She bowed her head. Silence, ever waiting to ensnare us, crept like a shadow in between us. And I would not have it.

"An old man is to bring a rug tonight," I said abruptly.

Geraldine stirred in her armchair, repeating in a low voice:

"*Ten thousand thousand stars shine down on Babylon. The desert well reflects but one. Abaddon none.*"

Bolt upright in my chair I listened, incredulous of my own ears.

"Where on earth did you hear that?" I demanded.

"I read it on Belshazzar's Rug in cuneiform with the Kufic key," she answered, watching me.

"You—all alone—interpreted that?" I asked, astounded.

"Yes. It is the cuneiform inscription in the gold *cartouche*."

Profound astonishment left me silent. She lay back in her chair with a little laugh of pure excitement.

"After you went out," she said, "I was horribly lonely, and I thought of you, and then I thought about the work you loved-the cuneiforms—and—as Jim did not seem to need me in the laboratory—I thought to myself: Suppose—suppose by luck I could unravel the inscription on the gold *cartouche*! Dick would be the happiest man in the world. And then you—your—flowers came, and I sat for a while alone with them. Then, on impulse, I jumped up and took the Kufic tables and all the combinations that you and I had tried together, and I slipped upstairs to the marble room and knelt down before Belshazzar's Rug. O Dick! the Tree of Heaven seemed to quiver in every jewelled branch and leaf!—it was only the draught from the closing door that moved the rug, but the mystic tree swayed there as the folds of the car pet moved, and I seemed to feel the mystery of the Prophet's Paradise stealing into me, penetrating me like the incense of forbidden wine—and I—I felt very Eastern and very pagan, kneeling there.

"It was strange, too; the intricate Kufic key seemed to be falling into place of its own impulse, symbol after symbol promising a linked symmetry of sense, until, almost before I was conscious of the miracle, it had been wrought there in the marble room; and my eyes were opened; and I, kneeling before the Tree of Heaven, read quite clearly what is written in the gold *cartouche* on the great carpet of Belshazzar. Dick! I prayed so hard that I might read it. And I have read it—for you!"

In the eloquence of her emotion she had risen, holding out both hands to me; I caught them, crushing them to my lips.

Ominous pulsating silence grew between us; her fingers relaxed and her hands fell from my lips. The stillness, intense, absolute, became a tension, a growing resistless force pressing us apart, slowly, inexorably driving me back step by step against the silk-hung wall, which I reached for, groping, steadying myself.

Never before had we been so swayed, so thrilled; never before had we been so reckless of the peril. Over us a magic snare had fallen, and we had evaded it—an unseen and delicate web, enmeshing us, drawing us together limb to limb, body to body, soul to soul, there on the kindling edges of destruction.

She sank back into the deep seat by the window, her white hands tightening on the gilded foliation of the chair's carved arms. And I saw how pale her face was and how her dark eyes were fixed steadily upon the floor as though destruction was a pit whose edge lay at her feet.

Presently I became aware that the world outside the curtained windows was moving still—had perhaps never halted on its way to wait upon our fate. And, crossing the room, I raised the shade and saw the new moon, low in the sky, kneeling amid the watching stars. Yellow rays from a street lamp illuminated the old trees foliage, edging with palest fire the tracery of newborn leaves, tufting each stem and twig, exquisite, delicately formal as the leafy labyrinths of the Tree of Heaven spreading above the flowery field of Belshazzar's Rug.

Khassar the nomad had come and gone, and his rug hung in the marble room, pale as the tinted shadow cast by the great carpet of Belshazzar.

The nomad's rug was clean but very ancient, and so worn, so time-eaten to the very warp, that the Kherdeh was all but obliterated in the *metnih*. But outside of that, between the outside band and the *ara*, or central line, there were traces of ancient glory and dimmed outlines of design; and I saw the twelve *cartouches* inscribed alternately in Persian and in cuneiform characters. There, too, were the worn remains of floral thickets haunted of beast and bird, intricate allegories, chronicles in colour and symbol, every leaf, every blossom, every creature fraught with mystic meaning; and there also, still faintly to be made out, the shadowy foliage of the Tree of Heaven.

"How much did you pay for that ghost of a rug?" demanded Westover, who had followed me upstairs after dressing for dinner.

When I told him he shrugged his shoulders, but made no comment. A moment later Geraldine entered, and his small eyes, no longer furtive, became fixed and dull.

"They say in the East," I remarked, "that when all colour is gone from an Eighur rug a lost soul takes it for its abode. Eighur women are supposed to have souls occasionally, and to lose them now and then."

"There are plenty of lost souls in town," observed Westover; "no doubt you'll have your choice of tenants for your carpet—or," he added, staring at space, "if you like I'll provide you."

I did not understand his remark, but it left a vaguely sinister impression. Geraldine, standing between us, her white fingers linked behind her, looked up at me very gravely.

"Do you know," she said, "that I am convinced that I wove that rug some centuries ago?"

"I have no doubt of it," I replied, smiling.

"Do you doubt it, Jim?" she asked gaily.

He did not reply.

"As a matter of fact," I said, "it was always believed that a young girl who dared to weave the Tree of Heaven into an Eighur carpet died when her task was ended—her entire physical and spiritual vitality entering into the sacred tree and in fusing it with mystic splendour."

"Oh, I died as you say," observed Geraldine gravely.

"I don't see that you infused much physical or spiritual splendour into that rug," observed Westover.

"I must die again, you know, Jim, and bring its vanished beauty back," she said gaily. "Shall I, Dick?—and leave you a priceless carpet as my bequest and monument?"

Westover turned on his heel, fidgeting with his collar. Recently his neck had grown fat behind the ears.

A few moments later dinner was announced.

We lingered late over dinner, I remember. Jim drank heavily—a habit which both Geraldine and I had long since left unnoticed, she shrinking from the sullen rebuff certain to follow even a playful protest, I understanding the utter hopelessness of interference. His mind, already shaken, would one day shatter, and the dreadful price be paid.

As he sat there sousing walnuts in port, in his altered features and swollen hands I seemed to divine something malicious and patient and powerful—that indescribable physical menace one feels in the inert brooding eye of the mentally and spiritually crippled.

When Geraldine rose he stood up unsteadily. After she had gone he lighted a cigar and turned his bloodshot eyes on me.

"Is that wine expensive?" he demanded, pointing to Geraldine's half-empty glass.

"Rather," I said.

He picked up the glass, examined it, sniffing at the contents.

"It's poor claret," he said. "Taste it. It's pure poison, I tell you."

"I'm sorry," I said indifferently.

Again he sniffed it. "Faugh!" he sneered, and threw it into the fireplace behind him. Then he got on his feet, heavily, muttering to himself, and stumbled off through the drawing-room.

For a while I sat there amid the shaded candles, staring at space. But I could not read the future pictured there amid the empty chairs and the flowers, already drooping in each crystal vase.

When at length I roused myself and went up stairs, passing her apartment I heard her singing to herself, and I wondered that she could.

I paused on the gallery stairway to listen; and she could not have heard my footsteps on the thick deep carpeting, yet she came to the door and opened it, looking up at me where I stood.

"You are going to the marble room. May I come and help you?" she asked sweetly. And as I was silent, she said again: "Let me be happy, won't you, Dick? Let me be where you are."

"Have I ever avoided you, Geraldine?"

I descended the steps, she laid her hand lightly on my arm, and together we mounted the stairway toward the gallery.

"I was singing a Hillah tent song when you passed," she said, "partly because I was lonely, and partly"—she hesitated, looking around at me "partly because I've come to the conclusion, Dick, that I was once at Belshazzar's feast in Cadimirra—for there's a great deal of wickedness in me—you'd never believe it, would you?"

She smiled at me so innocently, so adorably, that I laughed outright.

"I've heard that the maids of Babilu-Ki had a bowing acquaintance with the devil," I said. "Even an Eighur girl nodded pleasantly to Erlik now and then—according to the chronicles of the Tekrins."

"Oh, they surely did," she said. And, "Thank you, Dick," she added, as we reached the gallery; "when I am an old woman you must help me up the steep places."

"It is you who help me," I said lightly.

She stood, resting her arm on the table while I gathered up the mass of papers containing our cuneiform combinations and the Kufic key.

"All that is useless," she said suddenly. Her manner and smile had altered.

I looked up in surprise, and at the same instant she pushed the papers from beneath my hands.

"The memory of things forgotten centuries ago has returned to me," she said feverishly. "I am a pagan again. It was Istar who first taught my hands to weave and my fingers to tie the Sehna knot. I wove that carpet; what I have woven there I can read. Why do you laugh? Will you believe me if I translate the mystery of each inscription as easily as I read the gold *cartouche*? Come; we shall never need those papers again."

What new caprice was this? She was smiling, almost fixedly, and I thought that there was something in her overflushed face and in the starlike brilliancy of her eyes not quite normal. At the same moment the electric lights in the laboratory went out. Westover was evidently in there. I waited, expecting him to appear, but he did not. Again I reached for the papers, but Geraldine scattered them with a quick sweep of her hand.

"Won't you believe me? Won't you let me try?" she repeated almost impatiently.

With a quick movement she bent forward past me and shut off the lights in the gallery where we stood. Another second, and the lights in the marble room broke out fiercely; and there, full in the dazzling glory, I saw the great carpet of Belshazzar hanging, and beside it the Eighur rug—a pallid shadow on the wall.

Geraldine, hands clasped to her scarlet mouth, dark eyes fixed, moved forward slowly, opalescent tints flashing on her smooth bare arms and shoulders, her head a delicate silhouette against the glare.

I followed, pausing at her side, and we stood silently before the miracle, the great folds gently stirring in some unfelt current; and I saw the upper branches of the Tree of Heaven sway, and a thousand leaves, all glistening, quiver and subside.

"One can almost hear the rustling of the leaves," I whispered.

"I hear more than that," she murmured. "I hear my soul bidding me goodbye."

She smiled dreamily, turning to the faded Eighur carpet, and stepping back one pace, dropped her left arm, clasping my hand in hers.

"It was I who wove that carpet—I, maid of the Issig-Kul—and it was you, beloved of Hassan, who inspired it."

"What are you saying, Geraldine?" I began uneasily; "where did you ever hear my name linked with the name of Hassan?"

Her palm was burning hot, her eyes too bright. The fever of caprice possessed her, and her imagination was running riot.

There was a silence, through which a distant sound penetrated—the faint ring of glass somewhere in the laboratory. Westover was tying on his crystal mask.

She heard it, too, and she turned, looking me full in the eyes.

"Dick," she said, "he has slain my body. My soul is bidding me goodbye."

"It is my own that he is dragging to destruction, not yours," I muttered.

But she only clasped my hand tighter, the fixed smile stamped on her lips.

"Listen," she whispered, raising her arm. "This is what is written in the rose *cartouche* on the Eighur carpet that I made:

Roses of Babylon: Ashes of roses in Abaddon.

"Love and its awful penalty, Dick and the warning I wove, coffined in cryptogram! Listen again. The *cartouche* below was once topaz—for I wove it—I!

All Paradise the cost:
Warp and weft for souls so lost.

—Mine, Dick, mine!—lost in loving as I loved, centuries since. I have no soul; I have never had any since I lost it then. It is there, tenanting the phantom of an Eighur carpet. Do you not understand? There is my faded monument and refuge—that magic-woven sanctuary—that hiding place from hell!"

Her little feverish fingers tightened convulsively in mine; the colour flamed in her cheeks. Suddenly she crushed our clasped hands to her heart, and I felt it leaping madly.

"Geraldine," I stammered, "what is all this ghastly nonsense? Are you ill?"

"Listen! Listen!" she whispered; "the next *cartouche* was blue— the lost Persian blue! I know; why should I not know—I who wove it centuries ago? And thus it reads, O thou whom I loved to my destruction—thou whom I love!

Time and the Guest
Shall meet me twice—once East, once West.

"Ah, prophetess was I by Istar's favour—seeing I died for love. Do you not understand, Dick? Time and the Guest!—the Guest is Death—the Guest we all must entertain one day—and I twice—once in the East, once here in the West—here, now!"

"Geraldine, are you mad?" I whispered; "look at me!—turn and look at me, I say!"

But she shivered in my arms, whispering that she was ransoming her soul and mine. A distant sound broke from the laboratory, and we listened.

"Hush, beloved," she said breathlessly; "the last *cartouche* is black! And this is written there:

Soul, lotus-sealed,
Receive—thy—Paradise—

Her voice died out; a terrible pallor struck her face; she swayed where she stood, the smile frozen on her bloodless lips.

As I caught her to me, her head fell straight back and her body sank a dead weight in my arms. Then a dreadful thing occurred; the faded ancient tapestry glowed out like a live ember, kindling from end to end, brighter, fiercer, flaming into living fire; and the phantom Tree of Heaven, flashing, superbly jewelled, burst into magnificent florescence.

Blinded, almost stupefied, I staggered back, but the straining cry died in my throat as a voice is strangled in dreadful dreams. Again I strove to shout. The rug, glowing like a living ember, slowly faded before my eyes. Suddenly the last spark went out in a shower of whitening ashes.

Again I strove to cry out: "Jim! Jim!" but my lips stiffened with horror as I listened. For he was somewhere there in the darkness, laughing.

"It was in her wine," he chuckled—"and I saw her kiss the glass and look at you!—and you, there, staring at nothing! Stare at it now!"

And again: "Do you think I have never watched her?—and you? Now she's in hell, and we'll race for her on even terms once more."

Silence: a low, insane laugh, cut by a report and the crash of glass as he fell, shattering his masked face upon the floor.

After a long while I spoke, listening intently. Then I took up my burden.

And there was no sound save the soft stirring of her silken gown as I bore her through the darkness, my cold lips pressed to hers.

★ ★ ★ ★ ★ ★

He has never returned to America, but now that the time has come for me to fulfil my part, I do so, setting down what I know and what occult information I have received in letters from him, of the strange fate which overtook, separately, each and every man present at that farewell dinner at the Lenox Club.

My own fate is stranger still—to record these facts and take my position as his historian and his disciple.

The Sign of Venus

(A story from The Tree of heaven.)

In the card room the game, which had started from a chance suggestion, bid fair to develop into an all-night *séance*: the young foreign diplomat had shed his coat and lighted a fresh cigar; somebody threw a handkerchief over the face of the clock, and a sleepy club servant took reserve orders for two dozen siphons and other details.

"That lets me out," said Hetherford, rising from his chair with a nod at the dealer. He tossed his cards on the table, settled side obligations with the man on his left, yawned, and put on his hat.

Somebody remonstrated: "It's only two o clock, Hetherford; you have no white man's burden sitting up for you at home."

But Hetherford shook his head, smiling.

So a servant removed his chair, another man cut in, the dealer dealt cards all around. Presently from somewhere in the smoke haze came a voice, "Hearts." And a quiet voice retorted, "I double it."

Hetherford lingered a moment, then turned on his heel, sauntered out across the hallway and down the stairs into the court, refusing with a sign the offered cab.

Breathing deeply, yawning once or twice, he looked up at the stars. The night air refreshed him; he stood a moment, thoughtfully contemplating his half-smoked cigar, then tossed it away and stepped out into the street.

The street was quiet and deserted; darkened brownstone mansions stared at him through sombre windows as he passed; his footsteps echoed across the pavement like the sound of footsteps following.

His progress was leisurely; the dreary monotony of the house fronts soothed him. He whistled a few bars of a commonplace tune, crossed the deserted avenue under the electric lamps, and entered the dimly lighted street beyond.

Here all was silence; the doors of many houses were boarded up—sign that their tenants had migrated to the country. No shadowy cat fled along the iron railings at his approach; no night watchman prowled in deserted dooryards or peered at him from obscurity.

Strolling at ease, thoughts nowhere, he had traversed half the block, when an opening door and a glimmer of light across the sidewalk attracted his attention.

As he approached the house from whence the light came, a figure suddenly appeared on the stoop—a girl in a white ball gown—hastily descending the stone steps. Gaslight from the door way tinted her bared arms and shoulders. She bent her graceful head and gazed earnestly at Hetherford.

"I beg your pardon," she almost whispered; "might I ask you to help me?"

Hetherford stopped and wheeled short.

"I—I really beg your pardon," she said, "but I am in such distress. Could I ask you to find me a cab?"

"A cab!" he repeated uncertainly; "why, yes—I will with pleasure—" He turned and looked up and down the deserted street, slowly lifting his hand to his short moustache. "If you are in a hurry," he said, "I had better go to the nearest stables—"

"But there is something more," she said, in a tremulous voice; "could you get me a wrap—a cloak—anything to throw over my gown?"

He looked up at her, bewildered. "Why, I don't believe I—" he began, then fell silent before her troubled gaze. "I'll do anything I can for you," he said abruptly. "I have a raincoat at the club—if your need is urgent—"

"It is urgent; but there is something else—something more urgent, more difficult for me to ask you. I must go to Willow Brook—I must go now, tonight! And I—I have no money."

"Do you mean Willow Brook in Westchester?" he asked, astonished. "There is no train at this hour of the morning!"

"Then—then what am I to do?" she faltered. "I cannot stay another moment in that house."

After a silence he said: "Are you afraid of anybody in that house?"

"There is nobody in the house," she said with a shudder; "my mother is in Westchester; all the household are there. I—I came back—a few moments ago—unexpectedly—" She stammered and winced under his keen scrutiny; then the pallor of utter despair came into her cheeks, and she hid her white face in her hands.

Hetherford watched her for a moment.

"I don't exactly understand," he said gently, "but I'll do anything I can for you. I'll go to the club and get my raincoat; I'll go to the stables and get a cab; I haven't any money with me, but it would take only a few minutes for me to drive to the club and get some. . . . Please don't be distressed; I'll do anything you desire."

She dropped her arms with a hopeless gesture.

"But you say there is no train!"

"You could drive to the house of some of your friends—"

"No, no! Oh, my friends must never know of this!"

"I see," he said gravely.

"No, you don't see," she said unsteadily. "The truth is that I am almost frightened to death."

"Can you not tell me what has frightened you so?"

"If I tried to tell you, you would think me mad—you would indeed—"

"Try," he said soothingly.

"Why—why, it startled me to find myself in this house," she began. "You see, I didn't expect to come here; I didn't really want to come here," she added piteously. "Oh, it is simply dreadful to come—like this!" She glanced fearfully over her shoulder at the lighted doorway above, then turned to Hetherford as though dazed.

"Tell me," he said in a quiet voice.

Yes—I'll tell you. At first it was all dark—but I must have known I was in my own room, for I felt around on the dresser for the matches and lighted a candle. And when I saw that it was truly my own room, and when I caught sight of my own face in the mirror, it terrified me—" She pressed her fingers to her cheeks with a shudder. "Then I ran downstairs and lighted the gas in the hall and peered into the mirror; and I saw a face there—a face like my own—"

Pale, voiceless, she leaned on the bronze balustrade, fair head drooping, lids closed.

Presently, eyes still closed, she said: "You will not leave me alone here will you "Her voice died to a whisper.

"No of course not," he replied slowly.

There was an interval of silence; she passed her hand across her eyes and raised her head, looking up at the stars.

"You see," she murmured, "I dare not be alone; I *dare* not lose touch with the living. I suppose you think me mad, but I am not; I am only stunned. Please stay with me."

"Of course," he said in a soothing voice. "Everything will come out all right—"

"Are you sure?"

"Perfectly. I don't quite know what to say—how to reassure you and offer you any help—"

He fell silent, standing there on the sidewalk, worrying his short moustache. The situation was a new one to him.

"Suppose," he suggested, "that you try to take a little rest. I'll sit down on the steps—"

She looked at him in wide-eyed alarm. "Do you mean that I should go into that house—alone!"

"Well—you oughtn't to stand on the steps all night. It is nearly three o clock. You are frightened and nervous. Really you must go in and—"

"Then you must come, too," she said desperately. "This nightmare is more than I can endure alone. I'm not a coward; none of my race is. But I need a living being near me. Will you come?"

He bowed. She turned, hastily gathering her filmy gown, and mounted the shadowy steps without a sound; and he followed leisurely, even perhaps warily, every sense alert.

He was prepared to see the end of this encounter—see it through to an explanation if it took all summer. Of the situation, however, and of her, he had so far ventured no theory. The type of woman and the situation were perfectly new to him. He was aware that anything might happen in New York, and, closing the heavy front door, he was ready for it.

The hall gas jets were burning brightly, and in the darkened drawing-room he could distinguish the heavy outlines of furniture cased in dust coverings.

She asked him to strike a match and light the sconces in the drawing-room, and he did so, curiosity now thoroughly aroused.

As the gas flared up, shrouded pictures and furniture sprang into view surrounding him, and in the dusk of the room beyond he saw a ray of light glimmering on the foliated carving of a gilded harp.

Slowly he turned to the girl beside him. A warm shadow dimmed her delicate features, yet they were the loveliest he had ever looked upon.

Suddenly he understood the mute message of her eyes: "My imprudence places me at your mercy."

"Your helplessness places me at yours," he said aloud, scarcely conscious that he had spoken.

At that a bright flush transfigured her. "I trusted you the moment I saw you," she said impulsively. "Do you mind sitting there opposite me? I shall take this chair—rather near you—"

She sank into an armchair; and, touched and a trifle amused, he seated himself, at a little nod from her, awaiting her further pleasure.

She lay there for a minute or two without speaking, rounded arms resting on the gilt arms of the chair, eyes thoughtfully studying him.

"I've simply got to tell you everything," she said at length.

"It can do no harm, I think," he replied pleasantly.

"No; no harm. The harm has been done. Yet, with you sitting there so near me, I am not frightened now. It is curious," she mused, "that I should feel no apprehension now. And yet—and yet—"

She leaned toward him, dropping her linked fingers in her lap.

"Tell me, did you ever hear of the Sign of Venus?—the *Signum Veneris*?" she asked.

"I've heard of it—yes," he replied, surprised. And as she said nothing, he went on: "The distinguished gentleman who occupies the chair of Applied Psychics at the university lectures on the Sign of Venus, I believe."

"Did you attend the lectures?" she asked calmly.

He said he had not, smiling a trifle.

"I did."

"They were probably amusing," he ventured.

"Not very. Psychic phenomena bored me; I went during Lent. Psychic phenomena—" She hesitated, embarrassed at his amusement. "I suppose you laugh at that sort of thing."

"No, I don't laugh at it. Queer things occur, they say. All I know is that I myself have never seen anything happen that could not be explained by natural laws."

"I have," she said.

He bent his head in polite acquiescence.

"I went to the lectures," she said. "I am not very intellectual; nothing he said interested me very much—which was, of course, suitable for a Lenten amusement."

She leaned a little nearer, small hands tightly interlaced on her knee.

"His lecture on the Sign of Venus was the last." She lifted a white finger, drawing the imaginary *Signum Veneris* in the air.

Hetherford nodded gravely.

"The lecture," she continued, "ended with an explanation of the Sign of Venus—how, contemplating it by starlight, one might pass into that physical unconsciousness which leaves the mind free to control the soul."

She held out her left hand toward him. On a stretched finger a ring glistened, mounted with the Sign of Venus blazing in brilliants.

"I had this made specially," she said; "not that I had any particular desire to test it—no curiosity. It never occurred to me that here in New York one could—could—"

"What?" asked Hetherford dryly.

"—could leave one's own body at will."

"I don't believe it could be accomplished in New York," he said with great gravity. "And that's a pretty safe conclusion to come to, is it not?"

She dropped her eyes, silent for a moment, resting her delicate chin on the palm of her hand. Then she lifted her eyes to him calmly, and the direct beauty of her gaze disturbed him.

"No, it is not a safe conclusion to come to. Listen to me. Last night they gave a dance at the Willow Brook Hunt. It was nearly two o clock this morning when I left the club house and started home across the lawn with my mother and the maid——"

"But how on earth could—" he began, then begged her pardon and waited.

She continued serenely: "The night was warm and lovely, and it was clear starlight. When I entered my room I sent the maid away and sat down by the open window. The scent of the flowers and the beauty of the night made me restless; I went downstairs, unbolted the door, and slipped out through the garden to the *pergola*. My hammock hung there, and I lay down in it, looking out at the stars."

She drew the ring from her finger, holding it out for him to see.

"The starlight caught the gems on the Sign of Venus," she said under her breath; "that was the beginning. And then—I don't know why—as I lay there idly turning the ring on my finger, I found myself saying, 'I must go to New York: I must leave my body here asleep in the hammock and go to my own room in Fifty-eighth Street.'"

A curious little chill passed over Hetherford.

"I said it again and again—I don't know why. I remember the ring glittered; I remember it grew brighter and brighter. And then—and then! I found myself upstairs in the dark, groping over the dresser for the matches."

Again that faint chill touched Hetherford.

"I was stupefied for a moment," she said tremulously; "then I suspected what I had done, and it frightened me. And when I lighted the candle, and saw it was truly my own room—and when I caught sight of my own face in the mirror—terror seized me; it was like a glimpse of something taken unawares. For, do you know that although in the glass I saw my own face, the face was not looking back at me." She dropped her head, crushing the ring in both hands. "The reflected face was far lovelier than mine; and it was mine, I think, yet it was not looking at me, and it moved when I did not move. I wonder—I wonder"

The tension was too much. "If that be so," he said, steadying his voice—"if you saw a face in your mirror, the face was your own." He made an impatient gesture, rising to his feet at the same moment. "All that you have told me can be explained," he said.

"How can it? At this very moment I am asleep in my hammock."

"We will deal with that later," he said, smiling down at her. "Where is there a looking-glass?"

"There is one in the hallway." She rose, slipping the ring on her finger, and led the way to where an oval gilt mirror hung partly covered with dust cloths.

He cast aside the coverings. "Now look into the glass," he said gaily.

She raised her head and faced the mirror for an instant.

"Come here," she whispered; and he stepped behind her,

looking over her shoulder.

In the glass, as though reflected, he saw her face, *but the face was in profile!*

A shiver passed over him from head to foot.

"Did I not tell you?" she whispered. "Look! See, the other face is moving, while I am still!"

"There's something wrong about the glass, of course," he muttered; "it's defective."

"But who is that in the glass?"

"It is you—your profile. I don't exactly understand. Good Lord! It's turning away from us!"

She shrank against the wall, wide-eyed, breathing rapidly.

"There is no use in our being frightened," he said, scarcely knowing what he uttered. "This is Fifty-eighth Street, New York, 1903." He shook his shoulders, squaring them, and forced a smile. "Don't be frightened; there's an explanation for all this. You are not asleep in Westchester; you are here in your own house. You mustn't tremble so. Give me your hand a moment."

She laid her hand in his obediently; it shook like a leaf. He held it firmly, touching the fluttering pulse.

"You are certainly no spirit," he said, smiling; "your hand is warm and yielding. Ghosts don't have hands like that, you know."

Her fingers lay in his, quite passive now, but the pulse quickened.

"The explanation of it all is this," he said: "You have had a temporary suspension of consciousness, during which time you, without being aware of what you were doing, came to town from Willow Brook. You believe you went to the dance at the Hunt Club, but probably you did not. Instead, during a lapse of consciousness, you went to the station, took a train to town, came straight to your own house—" He hesitated.

"Yes," she said, "I have a key to the door. Here it is." She drew it from the bosom of her gown; he took it triumphantly.

"You simply awoke to consciousness while you were groping for the matches. That is all there is to it; and you need not be frightened at all!" he announced.

"No, not frightened," she said, shaking her head; "only—only I wonder how I can get back. I've tried to fix my mind on my ring—on the Sign of Venus—I cannot seem to—"

"But that's nonsense!" he protested cheerfully. "That ring has nothing to do with the matter."

"But it brought me here! Truly I am asleep in my hammock. Won't you believe it?"

"No; and you mustn't, either," he said impatiently. "Why, just now I explained to you—"

"I know," she said, looking down at the ring on her hand; "but you are wrong—truly you are."

"I am not wrong," he said, laughing. "It was only a dream—the dance, the return, the hammock—all these were parts of a dream so in tensely real that you cannot shake it off at once."

"Then—then *who* was that we saw in the mirror?"

"Let us try it again," he said confidently. She suffered him to lead her again to the mirror; again they peered into its glimmering depths, heads close together.

A second's breathless silence, then she caught his hand in both of hers with a low cry; for the strange profile was slowly turning toward them a face of amazing beauty—her own face transfigured, radiantly glorified.

"My soul!" she gasped, and would have fallen at his feet had he not held her and supported her to the stairs, where she sank down, hiding her face in her arms.

As for him, he was terribly shaken; he strove to speak, to reason with her, with himself, but a stupor chained body and mind, and he only leaned there on the newel post, vaguely aware of his own helplessness.

Far away in the night the bells of a church began striking the hour—one, two, three, four. Presently the distant rattle of a wagon sounded. The city stirred in its slumbers.

He found himself bending beside her, her passive hands in his once more, and he was saying: "As a matter of fact, all this is quite capable of an explanation. Don't be distressed—please don't be frightened or sad. We've both had some sort of hallucination, that's—all really that is all."

"I am not frightened now," she said dreamily. "I am quite sure that—that I am not dead. I am only asleep in my hammock. When I awake—"

Again, in spite of himself, he shivered.

"Will you do one more thing for me?" she asked.

"Yes—a million."

"Only one. It is unreasonable, it is perhaps silly—and I have no right to ask—"

"Ask it," he begged.

"Then—then, will you go to Willow Brook? Now?"

"Now?" he repeated blankly.

"Yes." She looked down at him with the shadow of a smile touching lips and eyes. "I am asleep in the hammock; I sleep very, very soundly—and very, very late into the morning. They may not find me there for a long while. So would you mind going to Willow Brook to awaken me?"

"I—I—but you do not expect me to leave you here and find you in Westchester!" he stammered.

"You need not go," she said quietly. "If you will telephone to the house and ask somebody to go out to the *pergola*—"

"No," he said, "I will go; I will go anywhere on earth for you."

He stood up, his senses in a whirl. She rose, too, leaning lightly on the balustrade.

"Thank you," she said sweetly. "When you awake me, give me this." She held out the *Signum Veneris*; and he took it, and bending his head slowly, raised it to his lips.

It was almost morning when he entered his own house. In a dull trance he dressed, turned again to the stairs, and crept out into the shadowy street.

People began to pass him; an early electric tram whizzed up Forty-second Street as he entered the railway station. Presently he found himself in a car, clutching his ticket in one hand, her ring in the other.

"It is I who am mad, not she," he muttered as the train glided from the station, through the long yard, dim in morning mist, where green and crimson lanterns still sparkled faintly.

Again he pressed the *Signum Veneris* to his lips. "It is I who am mad—love mad!" he whispered as the far treble warning of the whistle aroused him and sent him stumbling out into the soft fresh morning air.

The rising sun smote him full in the eyes as he came in sight of the club house among the still green trees, and the dew on the lawn flashed like the gems of the *Signum Veneris* on the ring he held so tightly.

Across the club house lawn stood another house, circled with gardens in full bloom; and to the left, among young trees, the white columns of a *pergola* glistened, tinted with rose from the early sun.

There was not a soul astir as he crossed the lawn and entered the garden, brushing the dew from overweighted blossoms as he passed.

Suddenly, at a turn in the path, he came upon the *pergola*, and saw a brilliant hammock hanging in the shadow.

Over the hammock's fringe something light and fluffy fell in folds like the billowy frills of a ball-gown. He stumbled forward, dazed, incredulous, and stood trembling for an instant.

Then, speechless, he sank down beside her, and dropped the ring into the palm of her half-closed and unconscious hand.

A ray of sunlight fell across her hair; slowly her blue eyes unclosed, smiling divinely.

And in her partly open palm the Sign of Venus glimmered like dew silvering a budding rose.

The Case of Mr. Helmer

(A story from The Tree of heaven.)

He had really been too ill to go; the penetrating dampness of the studio, the nervous strain, the tireless application, all had told on him heavily. But the feverish discomfort in his head and lungs gave him no rest; it was impossible to lie there in bed and do nothing; besides, he did not care to disappoint his hostess. So he managed to crawl into his clothes, summon a cab, and depart. The raw night air cooled his head and throat; he opened the cab window and let the snow blow in on him.

When he arrived he did not feel much better, although Catharine was glad to see him. Some body's wife was allotted to him to take in to dinner, and he executed the commission with that distinction of manner peculiar to men of his temperament.

When the women had withdrawn and the men had lighted cigars and cigarettes, and the conversation wavered between municipal reform and *contes drolatiques*, and the Boznovian *attaché* had begun an interminable story, and Count Fantozzi was emphasizing his opinion of women by joining the tips of his overmanicured thumb and forefinger and wafting spectral kisses at an annoyed Englishman opposite, Helmer laid down his unlighted cigar and, leaning over, touched his host on the sleeve.

"Hello! what's up, Philip?" said his host cordially; and Helmer, dropping his voice a tone below the sustained pitch of conversation, asked him the question that had been burning his feverish lips since dinner began.

To which his host replied, "What girl do you mean?" and

bent nearer to listen.

"I mean the girl in the fluffy black gown, with shoulders and arms of ivory, and the eyes of Aphrodite."

His host smiled. "Where did she sit, this human wonder?"

"Beside Colonel Farrar."

"Farrar? Let's see"—he knit his brows thoughtfully, then shook his head. "I can't recollect; we're going in now and you can find her and I'll—"

His words were lost in the laughter and hum around them; he nodded an abstracted assurance at Helmer; others claimed his attention, and by the time he rose to signal departure he had for gotten the girl in black.

As the men drifted toward the drawing-rooms, Helmer moved with the throng. There were a number of people there whom he knew and spoke to, although through the increasing feverishness he could scarce hear himself speak. He was too ill to stay; he would find his hostess and ask the name of that girl in black, and go.

The white drawing-rooms were hot and over-thronged. Attempting to find his hostess, he encountered Colonel Farrar, and together they threaded their way aimlessly forward.

"Who is the girl in black, Colonel?" he asked; "I mean the one that you took in to dinner."

"A girl in black? I don't think I saw her."

"She sat beside you!"

"Beside *me*?" The Colonel halted, and his inquiring gaze rested for a moment on the younger man, then swept the crowded rooms.

"Do you see her now?" he asked.

"No," said Helmer, after a moment.

They stood silent for a little while, then parted to allow the Chinese minister thoroughfare—a suave gentleman, all antique silks, and a smile "thousands of years old." The minister passed, leaning on the arm of the general commanding at Governor's Island, who signalled Colonel Farrar to join them; and Helmer drifted again, until a voice repeated his name insistently, and his hostess leaned forward from the brilliant group surrounding her, saying: "What in the world is the matter, Philip? You look wretchedly ill."

"It's a trifle close here—nothing's the matter."

He stepped nearer, dropping his voice: "Catharine, who was that girl in black?"

"What girl?"

"She sat beside Colonel Farrar at dinner—or I thought she did—"

"Do you mean Mrs. Van Siclen? She is in white, silly!"

"No—the girl in black."

His hostess bent her pretty head in perplexed silence, frowning a trifle with the effort to re member.

"There were so many," she murmured; "let me see—it is certainly strange that I cannot recollect. Wait a moment! Are you sure she wore black? Are you *sure* she sat next to Colonel Farrar?"

"A moment ago I was certain—" he said, hesitating. "Never mind, Catharine; I'll prowl about until I find her."

His hostess, already partly occupied with the animated stir around her, nodded brightly; Helmer turned his fevered eyes and then his steps toward the cool darkness of the conservatories. But he found there a dozen people who greeted him by name, demanding not only his company but his immediate and undivided attention.

"Mr. Helmer might be able to explain to us what his own work means," said a young girl, laughing.

They had evidently been discussing his sculptured group, just completed for the new *façade* of the National Museum. Press and public had commented very freely on the work since the un veiling a week since; critics quarrelled concerning the significance of the strange composition in marble. The group was at the same time repellent and singularly beautiful; but nobody denied its technical perfection. This was the sculptured group: A vaquero, evidently dying, lay in a loose heap among some desert rocks. Beside him, chin on palm, sat an exquisite winged figure, calm eyes fixed on the dying man. It was plain that death was near; it was stamped on the ravaged visage, on the collapsed frame. And yet, in the dying boy's eyes there was nothing of agony, no fear, only an intense curiosity as the lovely winged figure gazed straight into the glazing eyes.

"It may be," observed an attractive girl, "that Mr. Helmer will say with Mr. Gilbert,

'*It is really very clever,*
But I don't know what it means.'

Helmer laughed and started to move away. "I think I d better admit that at once," he said, passing his hand over his aching eyes; but the tumult of protest blocked his retreat, and he was forced to find a chair under the palms and tree ferns. "It was merely an idea of mine," he protested, good-humouredly, "an idea that has haunted me so persistently that, to save myself further annoyance, I locked it up in marble."

"Demoniac obsession?" suggested a very young man, with a taste for morbid literature.

"Not at all," protested Helmer, smiling; "the idea annoyed me until I gave it expression. It doesn't bother me anymore."

"You said," observed the attractive girl, "that you were going to tell us all about it."

"About the idea? Oh, no, I didn't promise that—"

"Please, Mr. Helmer!"

A number of people had joined the circle; he could see others standing here and there among the palms, evidently pausing to listen.

"There is no logic in the idea," he said, uneasily "nothing to attract your attention. I have only laid a ghost—"

He stopped short. The girl in black stood there among the others, intently watching him. When she caught his eye, she nodded with the friendliest little smile; and as he started to rise she shook her head and stepped back with a gesture for him to continue.

They looked steadily at one another for a moment.

"The idea that has always attracted me," he began slowly, "is

409

purely instinctive and emotional, not logical. It is this: As long as I can remember I have taken it for granted that a person who is doomed to die, never dies utterly alone. We who die in our beds—or expect to—die surrounded by the living. So fall soldiers on the firing line; so end the great majority—never absolutely alone. Even in a murder, the murderer at least must be present. If not, something else is there.

"But how is it with those solitary souls isolated in the world—the lone herder who is found lifeless in some vast, waterless desert, the pioneer whose bones are stumbled over by the tardy pickets of civilization—and even those nearer us—here in our city—who are found in silent houses, in deserted streets, in the solitude of salt meadows, in the miserable desolation of vacant lands beyond the suburbs?"

The girl in black stood motionless, watching him intently.

"I like to believe," he went on, "that no living creature dies absolutely and utterly alone. I have thought that, perhaps in the desert, for instance, when a man is doomed, and there is no chance that he could live to relate the miracle, some winged sentinel from the uttermost outpost of Eternity, putting off the armour of invisibility, drops through space to watch beside him so that he may not die alone."

There was absolute quiet in the circle around him. Looking always at the girl in black, he said:

"Perhaps those doomed on dark mountains or in solitary deserts, or the last survivor at sea, drifting to certain destruction after the wreck has foundered, finds death no terror, being guided to it by those invisible to all save the surely doomed. That is really all that suggested the marble—quite illogical, you see."

In the stillness, somebody drew a long, deep breath; the easy reaction followed; people moved, spoke together in low voices; a laugh rippled up out of the darkness. But Helmer had gone, making his way through the half light toward a figure that moved beyond through the deeper shadows of the foliage—moved slowly and more slowly. Once she looked back, and he followed, pushing forward and parting the heavy fronds of fern and palm and masses of moist blossoms. Suddenly he came upon her, standing there as though waiting for him.

"There is not a soul in this house charitable enough to present me," he began.

"Then," she answered laughingly, "charity should begin at home. Take pity on yourself—and on me. I have waited for you."

"Did you really care to know me?" he stammered.

"Why am I here alone with you?" she asked, bending above a scented mass of flowers. "Indiscretion may be a part of valour, but it is the best part of—something else."

That blue radiance which a starless sky sheds lighted her white shoulders; transparent shadow veiled the contour of neck and cheeks.

"At dinner," he said, "I did not mean to stare so—but I simply could not keep my eyes from yours—"

"A hint that mine were on yours, too?"

She laughed a little laugh so sweet that the sound seemed part of the twilight and the floating fragrance. She turned gracefully, holding out her hand.

"Let us be friends," she said, "after all these years."

Her hand lay in his for an instant; then she withdrew it and dropped it caressingly upon a cluster of massed flowers.

"Forced bloom," she said, looking down at them, where her fingers, white as the blossoms, lay half buried. Then, raising her head, "You do not know me, do you?"

"Know you?" he faltered; "how could I know you? Do you think for a moment that I could have forgotten you?"

"Ah, you have not forgotten me!" she said, still with her wide smiling eyes on his; "you have not forgotten. There is a trace of me in the winged figure you cut in marble—not the features, not the massed hair, nor the rounded neck and limbs—but in the eyes. Who living, save yourself, can read those eyes?"

"Are you laughing at me?"

"Answer me; who alone in all the world can read the message in those sculptured eyes?"

"Can you?" he asked, curiously troubled.

"Yes; I, and the dying man in marble."

"What do you read there?"

"Pardon for guilt. You have foreshadowed it unconsciously—the resurrection of the soul. That is what you have left in marble for the mercilessly just to ponder on; that alone is the meaning of your work."

Through the throbbing silence he stood thinking, searching his clouded mind.

"The eyes of the dying man are your own," she said. "Is it not true?"

And still he stood there, groping, probing through dim and forgotten corridors of thought toward a faint memory scarcely perceptible in the wavering mirage of the past.

"Let us talk of your career," she said, leaning back against the thick foliage—"your success, and all that it means to you," she added gaily.

He stood staring at the darkness. "You have set the phantoms of forgotten things stirring and whispering together somewhere within me. Now tell me more; tell me the truth."

"You are slowly reading it in my eyes," she said, laughing sweetly. "Read and remember."

The fever in him seared his sight as he stood there, his confused gaze on hers.

"Is it a threat of hell you read in the marble?" he asked.

"No, nothing of destruction, only resurrection and hope of Paradise. Look at me closely."

"Who are you?" he whispered, closing his eyes to steady his swimming senses. "When have we met?"

"You were very young," she said under her breath—"and I was younger—and the rains had swollen the Canadian river so that it boiled amber at the fords; and I could not cross—alas!"

A moment of stunning silence, then her voice again: "I said nothing, not a word even of thanks when you offered aid. . . I-was not too heavy in your arms, and the ford was soon passed—soon passed. That was very long ago." Watching him from shadowy sweet eyes, she said:

"For a day you knew the language of my mouth and my arms around you, there in the white sun glare of the river. For every kiss taken and retaken, given and forgiven, we must account—for everyone, even to the last.

"But you have set a monument for us both, preaching the resurrection of the soul. Love is such a little thing—and ours endured a whole day long! Do you remember? Yet He who created love, designed that it should last a lifetime. Only the lost outlive it."

She leaned nearer:

"Tell me, you who have proclaimed the resurrection of dead souls, are you afraid to die?"

Her low voice ceased; lights broke out like stars through the foliage around them; the great glass doors of the ballroom were opening; the illuminated fountain flashed, a falling shower of silver. Through the outrush of music and laughter swelling around them, a clear far voice called "Françoise!"

Again, close by, the voice rang faintly, "Françoise! Françoise!"

She slowly turned, staring into the brilliant glare beyond.

"Who called?" he asked hoarsely.

"My mother," she said, listening intently. "Will you wait for me?"

His ashen face glowed again like a dull ember. She bent nearer, and caught his fingers in hers.

"By the memory of our last kiss, wait for me!" she pleaded, her little hand tightening on his.

"Where?" he said, with dry lips. "We cannot talk here!—we cannot say here the things that must be said."

"In your studio," she whispered. "Wait for me."

"Do you know the way?"

"I tell you I will come; truly I will! Only a moment with my mother—then I will be there!"

Their hands clung together an instant, then she slipped away into the crowded rooms; and after a moment Helmer followed, head bent, blinded by the glare.

"You are ill, Philip," said his host, as he took his leave. "Your face is as ghastly as that dying *vaquero's*—by Heaven, man, you *look* like him!"

"Did you find your girl in black?" asked his hostess curiously.

"Yes," he said; "goodnight."

The air was bitter as he stepped out—bitter as death. Scores of carriage lamps twinkled as he descended the snowy steps, and a faint gust of music swept out of the darkness, silenced as the heavy doors closed behind him.

He turned west, shivering. A long smear of light bounded his horizon as he pressed toward it and entered the sordid avenue beneath the iron arcade which was even now trembling under the shock of an oncoming train. It passed overhead with a roar; he raised his hot eyes and saw, through the tangled girders above, the illuminated disk of the clock tower—all distorted—for the fever in him was disturbing everything—even the cramped and twisted street into which he turned, fighting for breath like a man stabbed through and through.

"What folly!" he said aloud, stopping short in the darkness. "This is fever—all this. She could not know where to come—"

Where two blind alleys cut the shabby block, worming their way inward from the avenue and from Tenth Street, he stopped again, his hands working at his coat.

"It is fever, fever!" he muttered. "She was not there."

There was no light in the street save for the red fire lamp burning on the corner, and a glimmer from the Old Grapevine Tavern across the way. Yet all around him the darkness was illuminated with pale unsteady flames, lighting him as he groped through the shadows of the street to the blind alley. Dark old silent houses peered across the paved lane at their aged counterparts, waiting for him.

And at last he found a door that yielded, and he stumbled into the black passageway, always lighted on by the unsteady pallid flames which seemed to burn in infinite depths of night.

414

"She was not there—she was never there," he gasped, bolting the door and sinking down upon the floor. And, as his mind wandered, he raised his eyes and saw the great bare room growing whiter and whiter under the uneasy flames.

"It will burn as I burn," he said aloud—for the phantom flames had crept into his body. Suddenly he laughed, and the vast studio rang again.

"Hark!" he whispered, listening intently. "Who knocked?"

There was someone at the door; he managed to raise himself and drag back the bolt.

"You!" he breathed, as she entered hastily, her hair disordered and her black skirts powdered with snow.

"Who but I?" she whispered, breathless. "Listen! do you hear my mother calling me? It is too late; but she was with me to the end."

Through the silence, from an infinite distance, came a desolate cry of grief—"Françoise!"

He had fallen back into his chair again, and the little busy flames enveloped him so that the room began to whiten again into a restless glare. Through it he watched her.

The hour struck, passed, struck and passed again. Other hours grew, lengthening into night. She sat beside him with never a word or sigh or whisper of breathing; and dream after dream swept him, like burning winds. Then sleep immersed him so that he lay senseless, sightless eyes still fixed on her. Hour after hour—and the white glare died out, fading to a glimmer. In densest darkness, he stirred, awoke, his mind quite clear, and spoke her name in a low voice.

"Yes, I am here," she answered gently.

"Is it death?" he asked, closing his eyes.

"Yes. Look at me, Philip."

His eyes unclosed; into his altered face there crept an intense curiosity. For he beheld a glimmering shape, wide-winged and deep-eyed, kneeling beside him, and looking him through and through.

The Story of Major Weir

It must have been a sad scandal to this peculiar community (the "Bowhead Saints") when Major Weir, one of their number, was found to have been so wretched an example of human infirmity. The house occupied by this man still exists, though in an altered shape, in a little court accessible by a narrow passage near the first angle of the street. His history is obscurely reported; but it appears that he was of a good family in Lanarkshire, and had been one of the ten thousand men sent by the Scottish Covenanting Estates in 1641 to assist in suppressing the Irish Papists. He became distinguished for a life of peculiar sanctity, even in an age when that was the prevailing tone of the public mind. According to a contemporary account:

"His garb was still a cloak, and somewhat dark, and he never went without his staff. He was a tall black man, and ordinarily looked down to the ground; a grim countenance, and a big nose. At length he became so notoriously regarded among the Presbyterian strict sect, that if four met together, be sure Major Weir was one. At private meetings he prayed to admiration, which made many of that stamp court his converse. He never married, but lived in a private lodging with his sister, Grizel Weir. Many resorted to his house, to join with him, and hear him pray; but it was observed that he could not officiate in any holy duty without the black staff, or rod, in his hand, and leaning upon it, which made those who heard him pray admire his flood in prayer, his ready extemporary expression, his heavenly gesture; so that he was thought more angel than man, and was termed by some of the holy sisters ordinarily 'Angelical Thomas.'"

Plebeian imaginations have since fructified regarding the staff, and crones will still seriously tell how it could run a message to a shop for any article which its proprietor wanted; how it could answer the door when anyone called upon its master; and that it used to be often seen running before him, in the capacity of a link-boy, as he walked down the Lawnmarket.

After a life characterised externally by all the graces of devotion, but polluted in secret by crimes of the most revolting nature, and which little needed the addition of wizardry to excite the horror of living man, Major Weir fell into a severe sickness, which affected his mind so much, that he made an open and voluntary confession of all his wickedness. The tale was at first so incredible, that the provost, Sir Andrew Ramsay, refused for some time to take him into custody. At length himself, his sister (partner of one of his crimes), and his staff, were secured by the magistrates, together with certain sums of money, which were found wrapped up in rags in different parts of the house.

One of these pieces of rag being thrown into the fire by a bailie who had taken the whole in charge, flew up the chimney, and made an explosion like a cannon. While the wretched man lay in prison, he made no scruple to disclose the particulars of his guilt, but refused to address himself to the Almighty for pardon. To every request that he would pray, he answered in screams:

"Torment me no more—I am tormented enough already!" Even the offer of a Presbyterian clergyman, instead of an established Episcopal minister of the city, had no effect upon him. He was tried April 9, 1670, and being found guilty, was sentenced to be strangled and burnt between Edinburgh and Leith. His sister, who was tried at the same time was sentenced to be hanged in the Grass-market. The execution of the profligate Major took place, April 14, at the place indicated by the judge.

When the rope was about his neck, to prepare him for the fire, he was bid to say: "Lord, be merciful to me!" but he answered, as before: "Let me alone—I will not—I have lived as a beast, and I must die as a beast!" After he had dropped lifeless

417

in the flames, his stick was also cast into the fire; and, "what-ever incantation was in it," says the contemporary writer already quoted,[1] "the persons present own that it gave rare turnings, and was long a-burning, as also himself."

The conclusion to which the humanity of the present age would come regarding Weir—that he was mad—is favoured by some circumstances; for instance, his answering one who asked if he had ever seen the devil, that "the only feeling he ever had of him was in the dark." What chiefly countenances the idea, is the unequivocal lunacy of the sister. This miserable woman confessed to witchcraft, and related, in a serious manner, many things which could not be true. Many years before, a fiery coach, she said, had come to her brother's door in broad day, and a stranger invited them to enter, and they proceeded to Dalkeith.

On the way, another person came and whispered in her brother's ear something which affected him; it proved to be supernatural intelligence of the defeat of the Scottish army at Worcester, which took place that day. Her brother's power, she said, lay in his staff. She also had a gift for spinning above other women, but the yarn broke to pieces in the loom. Her mother, she declared, had also been a witch. "The secretes thing that I, or any of the family could do, when once a mark appeared upon her brow, she could tell it them, though done at a great distance."

This mark could also appear on her own forehead when she pleased. At the request of the company present, "she put back her head-dress, and seeming to frown, there was an exact horseshoe shaped for nails in her wrinkles, terrible enough, I assure you, to the stoutest beholder."[2] At the place of execution she acted in a furious manner, and with difficulty could be prevented from throwing off her clothes, in order to die, as she said, "with all the shame she could."

The treatise just quoted makes it plain that the case of Weir

---

1. The Rev. Mr. Frazer, Minister of Wardlaw, in his *Divine Providences* (MS Adv. Lib.) dated 1670.
2. *Satan's Invisible world Discovered.*

and his sister had immediately become a fruitful theme for imaginations of the vulgar. We there receive the following story:—

> Some few days before he discovered himself, a gentlewoman coming from the Castle-hill, where her husband's niece was lying-in of a child, about midnight perceived about the Bowhead three women in windows, shouting, laughing, and clapping their hands. The gentlewoman went forward, 'till, at Major Weir's door, there arose, as from the street, a woman about the length of two ordinary females, and stepped forward. The gentlewoman, not as yet excessively feared, bid her maid step on, if by the lantern they could see what she was; but haste what they could, this long-legged spectre was still before them, moving her body with a vehement cachinnation and great unmeasurable laughter.
>
> At this rate the two strove for place, 'till the giantess came to a narrow lane in the Bow, commonly called the Stinking Close, into which she turning, and the gentlewoman looking after her, perceived the close full of flaming torches (she could give them no other name), and as if it had been a great number of people stentoriously laughing, and gaping with tahees of laughter. This sight, at so dead a time of night, no people being in the windows belonging to the close, made her and her servant haste home, declaring all that they saw to the rest of the family.

For upwards of a century after Major Weir's death, he continued to be the bugbear of the Bow, and his house remained uninhabited. His apparition was frequently seen at night, flitting, like a black and silent shadow, about the street. His house, though known to be deserted by everything human, was sometimes observed at midnight to be full of lights, and heard to emit strange sounds, as of dancing, howling, and, what is strangest of all, spinning. Some people occasionally saw the Major issue from the low close at midnight, mounted on a black horse without a head, and gallop off in a whirlwind of flame.

Nay, sometimes the whole of the inhabitants of the Bow would be roused from their sleep at an early hour of the morning by the sound as of a coach and six, first rattling up the Lawnmarket, and then thundering down the Bow, stopping at the head of the terrible close for a few minutes, and then rattling and thundering back again—being neither more or less than Satan come in one of his best equipages to take home the Major and his sister, after they had spent a night's leave of absence in their terrestrial dwelling.

About fifty years ago, when the shades of superstition began universally to give way in Scotland, Major Weir's house came to be regarded with less terror by the neighbours, and an attempt was made by the proprietor to find a person who should be bold enough to inhabit it. Such a person was procured in William Patullo, a poor man of dissipated habits, who, having been at one time a soldier and a traveller, had come to disregard in a great measure the superstitions of his native country, and was now glad to possess a house upon the low terms offered by the landlord, at whatever risk.

Upon its being known that Major Weir's house was about to be re-inhabited, a great deal of curiosity was felt by people of all ranks as to the result of the experiment; for there was scarcely a native of the city who had not felt, since his boyhood, an intense, interest in all that concerned that awful fabric, and yet remembered the numerous terrible stories which he had heard respecting it. Even before entering upon his hazardous undertaking, William Patullo was looked upon with a flattering sort of interest, similar to that which we feel respecting a regiment on the march to active conflict. It was the hope of many that he would be the means of retrieving a valuable possession from the dominion of darkness. But Satan soon let them know that he does not tamely relinquish any of the outposts of his kingdom.

On the very first night after Patullo and his spouse had taken up their abode in the house, as the worthy couple were lying awake in their bed, not unconscious of a certain degree of fear—a dim uncertain light proceeding from the gathered embers of their fire, and all being silent around them—they suddenly saw a form like that of a calf, which came forward to the bed, and, setting its forefeet upon the stock, looked steadfastly at the unfortunate pair. When it had contemplated them thus for a few minutes, to their great relief it at length took itself away, and, slowly retiring, gradually vanished from their sight. As might be expected, they deserted the house next morning; and for another half-century no other attempt was made to embank this part of the world of light from the aggressions of the world of darkness.

It may be here mentioned that, at no very remote time, there were several houses in the Old Town which had the credit of being haunted. It is said there is one at this day in the Lawnmarket (a fiat), which had been shut up from time immemorial. The story goes that one night, as preparations were making for a supper-party, something occurred which obliged the family, as well as all the assembled guests, to retire with precipitation, and lock up the house. From that night it has never once been opened, nor was any of the furniture withdrawn: the very goose which was undergoing the process of being roasted at the time of the occurrence, is still at the fire!

No one knows to whom the house belongs; no one inquires after it; no one living ever saw the inside of it; it is a condemned house! There is something peculiarly dreadful about a house under these circumstances. What sights of horror might present themselves if it were entered! Satan is the *ultimus hæres* of all such unclaimed property!

One Over

(A story from Police.)

1

Professor Farrago had remarked to me that morning:

"The city of New York always reminds me of a slovenly, fat woman with her dress unbuttoned behind."

I nodded.

"New York's architecture," said I, "—or what popularly passes for it—is all in front. The minute you get to the rear a pitiable condition is exposed."

He said: "Professor Jane Bottomly is all façade; the remainder of her is merely an occipital backyard full of theoretical tin cans and broken bottles. I think we all had better resign."

It was a fearsome description. I trembled as I lighted an inexpensive cigar.

The sentimental feminist movement in America was clearly at the bottom of the Bottomly affair.

Long ago, in a reactionary burst of hysteria, the North enfranchised the Ethiopian. In a similar sentimental explosion of dementia, some sixty years later, the United States wept violently over the immemorial wrongs perpetrated upon the restless sex, opened the front and back doors of opportunity, and sobbed out, "Go to it, ladies!"

They are still going.

Professor Jane Bottomly was wished on us out of a pleasant April sky. She fell like a meteoric mass of molten metal upon the Bronx Park Zoological Society splashing her excoriating personality over everybody until everybody writhed.

I had not yet seen the lady. I did not care to. Sooner or later I'd be obliged to meet her but I was not impatient.

Now the Field Expeditionary Force of the Bronx Park Zoological Society is, perhaps, the most important arm of the service. Professor Bottomly had just been appointed official head of all field work. Why? Nobody knew. It is true that she had written several combination nature and love romances. In these popular volumes trees, flowers, butterflies, birds, animals, dialect, sobs, and sun-bonnets were stirred up together into a saccharine mess eagerly gulped down by a provincial reading public, which immediately protruded its tongue for more.

The news of her impending arrival among us was an awful blow to everybody at the Bronx. Professor Farrago fainted in the arms of his pretty stenographer; Professor Cornelius Lezard of the Batrachian Department ran around his desk all day long in narrowing circles and was discovered on his stomach still feebly squirming like an expiring top; Dr. Hans Fooss, our beloved Professor of Pachydermatology sat for hours weeping into his noodle soup. As for me, I was both furious and frightened, for, within the hearing of several people, Professor Bottomly had remarked in a very clear voice to her new assistant, Dr. Daisy Delmour, that she intended to get rid of me for the good of the Bronx because of my reputation for indiscreet gallantry among the feminine employees of the Bronx Society.

Professor Lezard overhead that outrageous remark and he hastened to repeat it to me.

I was lunching at the time in my private office in the Administration Building with Dr. Hans Fooss—he and I being too busy dissecting an unusually fine specimen of Dingue to go to the Rolling Stone Inn for luncheon—when Professor Lezard rushed in with the scandalous libel still sizzling in his ears.

"Everybody heard her say it!" he went on, wringing his hands. "It was a most unfortunate thing for anybody to say about you before all those young ladies. Every stenographer and typewriter there turned pale and then red."

"What!" I exclaimed, conscious that my own ears were growing large and hot. "Did that outrageous woman have the bad taste to say such a thing before all those sensitive girls!"

"She did. She glared at them when she said it. Several blondes and one brunette began to cry."

"I hope," said I, a trifle tremulously, "that no typewriter so far forgot herself as to admit noticing playfulness on my part."

"They all were tearfully unanimous in declaring you to be a perfect gentleman!"

"I am," I said. "I am also a married man—irrevocably wedded to science. I desire no other spouse. I am ineligible; and everybody knows it. If at times a purely scientific curiosity leads me into a detached and impersonally psychological investigation of certain—ah—feminine idiosyncrasies—"

"Certainly," said Lezard. "To investigate the feminine is more than a science; it is a duty!"

"Of a surety!" nodded Dr. Fooss.

I looked proudly upon my two loyal friends and bit into my cheese sandwich. Only men know men. A jury of my peers had exonerated me. What did I care for Professor Bottomly!

"All the same," added Lezard, "you'd better be careful or Professor Bottomly will put one over on you yet."

"I am always careful," I said with dignity.

"All men should be. It is the only protection of a defenceless coast line," nodded Lezard.

"*Und* neffer, neffer commid nodding to paper," added Dr. Fooss. "Don'd neffer write it, 'I lofe you like I was going to blow up alretty!' *Ach, nein*! Don'd you write down somedings. Effery man he iss entitled to protection; *und* so iss it he iss protected."

Stein in hand he beamed upon us benevolently over his knifeful of sauerfisch, then he fed himself and rammed it down with a hearty draught of Pilsner. We gazed with reverence upon Kultur as embodied in this great Teuton.

"That woman," remarked Lezard to me, "certainly means to get rid of you. It seems to me that there are only two possible ways for you to hold down your job at the Bronx. You know it, don't you?"

I nodded. "Yes," I said; "either I must pay marked masculine attention to Professor Bottomly or I must manage to put one over on her."

"Of course," said Lezard, "the first method is the easier for *you*—"

"Not for a minute!" I said, hastily; "I simply couldn't become frolicsome with her. You say she's got a voice like a drill-sergeant and she goose-steps when she walks; and I don't mind admitting she has me badly scared already. No; she must be scientifically ruined. It is the only method which makes her elimination certain."

"But if her popular nature books didn't ruin her scientifically, how can we hope to lead her astray?" inquired Lezard.

"There is," I said, thoughtfully, "only one thing that can really ruin a scientist. Ridicule! I have braved it many a time, taking my scientific life in my hands in pursuit of unknown specimens which might have proved only imaginary. Public ridicule would have ended my scientific career in such an event. I know of no better way to end Professor Bottomly's scientific career and capability for mischief than to start her out after something which doesn't exist, inform the newspapers, and let her suffer the agonising consequences."

Dr. Fooss began to shout:

"The idea iss *schön!* colossal! *prachtvol! ausgezeichnet! wunderbar! wunderschön! gemütlich*—" A large, tough noodle checked him. While he laboured with Teutonic imperturbability to master it Lezard and I exchanged suggestions regarding the proposed annihilation of this fearsome woman who had come ravening among us amid the peaceful and soporific environment of Bronx Park.

It was a dreadful thing for us to have our balmy Lotus-eaters' paradise so startlingly invaded by a large, loquacious, loud-voiced lady who had already stirred us all out of our agreeable, traditional and leisurely inertia. Inertia begets cogitation, and cogitation begets ideas, and ideas beget reflexion, and profound reflexion is the fundamental cornerstone of that immortal temple in which the goddess Science sits asleep between her dozing sisters, Custom and Religion.

This thought seemed to me so unusually beautiful that I wrote it with a pencil upon my cuff.

While I was writing it, quietly happy in the deep pleasure that my intellectual allegory afforded me, Dr. Fooss swabbed the last morsel of nourishment from his plate with a wad of rye bread, then bolting the bread and wiping his beard with his fingers and his fingers on his waistcoat, he made several guttural observations too profoundly German to be immediately intelligible, and lighted his porcelain pipe.

"*Ach wass!*" he remarked in ruminative fashion. "*Dot Frauenzimmer* she iss to raise hell alretty determined. *Von* Pachydermatology she knows nodding. Maybe she leaves me alone, maybe it is to be *'raus mit* me. *I' weis' ni'*! It iss *aber besser* one over on dat lady to put, yess?"

"It certainly is advisable," replied Lezard.

"Let us try to think of something sufficiently disastrous to terminate her scientific career," said I. And I bowed my rather striking head and rested the point of my forefinger upon my forehead. Thought crystallises more quickly for me when I assume this attitude.

Out of the corner of my eye I saw Lezard fold his arms and sit frowning at infinity.

Dr. Fooss lay back in a big, deeply padded armchair and closed his prominent eyes. His pipe went out presently, and now and then he made long-drawn nasal remarks, in German, too complicated for either Lezard or for me to entirely comprehend.

"We must try to get her as far away from here as possible," mused Lezard. "Is Oyster Bay *too* far and too cruel?"

I pondered darkly upon the suggestion. But it seemed unpleasantly like murder.

"Lezard," said I, "come, let us reason together. Now *what* is woman's besetting emotion?"

"Curiosity?"

"Very well; assuming that to be true, what—ah—quality particularly characterizes woman when so beset."

"Ruthless determination."

"Then," said I, "we ought to begin my exciting the curiosity of Professor Bottomly; and her ruthless determination to satisfy that curiosity should logically follow."

"How," he asked, "are we to arouse her curiosity?"

"By pretending that we have knowledge of something hitherto undiscovered, the discovery of which would redound to our scientific glory."

"I see. She'd want the glory for herself. She'd swipe it."

"She would," said I.

"Tee—hee!" he giggled; "Wouldn't it be funny to plant something phony on her—"

I waved my arms rather gracefully in my excitement:

"That is the germ of an idea!" I said. "If we could plant something—something—far away from here—very far away—if we could bury something—like the Cardiff Giant—"

"Hundreds and hundreds of miles away!"

"Thousands!" I insisted, enthusiastically.

"Tee-hee! In Tasmania, for example! Maybe a Tasmanian Devil might acquire her!"

"There exists a gnat," said I, "in Borneo—*Gnatus soporificus*—and when this tiny gnat stings people they never entirely wake up. It's really rather a pleasurable catastrophe, I understand. Life becomes one endless cat-nap—one delightful *siesta*, with intervals for light nourishment.... She—ah—could sit very comfortably in some pleasant retreat and rock in a rocking-chair and doze quite happily through the years to come....And from your description of her I should say that the Soldiers' Home might receive her."

"It won't do," he said, gloomily.

"Why? Is it too much like crime?"

"Oh not at all. Only if she went to Borneo she'd be sure to take a mosquito-bar with her."

In the depressed silence which ensued Dr. Fooss suddenly

made several Futurist observations through his nose with monotonous but authoritative regularity. I tried to catch his meaning and his eye. The one remained cryptic, the other shut.

Lezard sat thinking very hard. And as I fidgetted in my chair, fiddling nervously with various objects lying on my desk I chanced to pick up a letter from the pile of still unopened mail at my elbow.

Still pondering on Professor Bottomly's proposed destruction, I turned the letter over idly and my preoccupied gaze rested on the postmark. After a moment I leaned forward and examined it more attentively. The letter directed to me was postmarked Fort Carcajou, Cook's Peninsula, Baffin Land; and now I recalled the handwriting, having already seen it three or four times within the last month or so.

"Lezard," I said, "that lunatic trapper from Baffin Land has written to me again. What do you suppose is the matter with him? Is he just plain crazy or does he think he can be funny with me?"

Lezard gazed at me absently. Then, all at once a gleam of savage interest lighted his somewhat solemn features.

"Read the letter to me," he said, with an evil smile which instantly animated my own latent imagination. And immediately it occurred to me that perhaps, in the humble letter from the wilds of Baffin Land, which I was now opening with eager and unsteady fingers, might lie concealed the professional undoing of Professor Jane Bottomly, and the only hope of my own ultimate and scientific salvation.

The room became hideously still as I unfolded the pencil-scrawled sheets of cheap, ruled letter paper.

Dr. Fooss opened his eyes, looked at me, made porcine sounds indicative of personal well-being, relighted his pipe, and disposed himself to listen. But just as I was about to begin, Lezard suddenly laid his forefinger across his lips conjuring us to densest silence.

For a moment or two I heard nothing except the buzzing of flies. Then I stole a startled glance at my door. It was opening slowly, almost imperceptibly.

But it did not open very far—just a crack remained. Then, listening with all our might, we heard the cautiously suppressed breathing of somebody in the hallway just outside of my door.

Lezard turned and cast at me a glance of horrified intelligence. In dumb pantomime he outlined in the air, with one hand, the large and feminine amplification of his own person, conveying to us the certainty of his suspicions concerning the unseen eavesdropper.

We nodded. We understood perfectly that *she* was out there prepared to listen to every word we uttered.

A flicker of ferocious joy disturbed Lezard's otherwise innocuous features; he winked horribly at Dr. Fooss and at me, and uttered a faint click with his teeth and tongue like the snap of a closing trap.

"Gentlemen," he said, in the guarded yet excited voice of a man who is confident of not being overheard, "the matter under discussion admits of only one interpretation: a discovery—perhaps the most vitally important discovery of all the centuries—is imminent.

"Secrecy is imperative; the scientific glory is to be shared by us alone, and there is enough of glory to go around.

"Mr. Chairman, I move that epoch-making letter be read aloud!"

"I second dot motion!" said Dr. Fooss, winking so violently at me that his glasses wabbled.

"Gentlemen," said I, "it has been moved and seconded that this epoch-making letter be read aloud. All those in favour will kindly say 'aye.'"

"Aye! Aye!" they exclaimed, fairly wriggling in their furtive joy.

"The contrary-minded will kindly emit the usual negation," I went on. . . . "It seems to be carried. . . . It *is* carried. The chairman will proceed to the reading of the epoch-making letter."

I quietly lighted a five-cent cigar, unfolded the letter and read aloud:

Joneses Shack,
Golden Glacier, Cook's Peninsula, Baffin Land,
March 15, 1915.

Professor, Dear Sir:

I already wrote you three times no answer having been rec'd perhaps you think I'm kiddin' you're a dam' liar I ain't.

Hoping to tempt you to come I will hereby tell you more'n I told you in my other letters, the terminal moraine of this here Golden Glacier finishes into a marsh, nothing to see for miles excep' frozen tussock and mud and all flat as hell for fifty miles which is where I am trappin' it for mink and otter and now ready to go back to Fort Carcajou. i told you what I seen stickin' in under this here marsh, where anything sticks out the wolves have eat it, but most of them there ellerphants is in under the ice and mud too far for the wolves to git 'em.

I ain't kiddin' you, there is a whole herd of furry ellerphants in the marsh like as they were stuck there and all lay down and was drownded like. Some has tusks and some hasn't. Two ellerphants stuck out of the ice, I eat onto one, the meat was good and sweet and joosy, the damn wolves eat it up that night, I had cut stakes and rost for three months though and am eating off it yet.

Thinking as how ellerphants and all like that is your graft, I being a keeper in the Mouse House once in the Bronx and seein' you nosin' around like you was full of scientific thinks, it comes to me to write you and put you next.

If you say so I'll wait here and help you with them ellerphants. Livin' wages is all I ask also eleven thousand dollars for tippin' you wise. I won't tell nobody till I hear from you. I'm hones' you can trus' me. Write me to Fort Carcajou if you mean bizness. So no more respectfully,
James Skaw.

When I finished reading I cautiously glanced at the door, and, finding it still on the crack, turned and smiled subtly upon

430

Lezard and Fooss.

In their slowly spreading grins I saw they agreed with me that somebody, signing himself James Skaw, was still trying to hoax the Great Zoological Society of Bronx Park.

"Gentlemen," I said aloud, injecting innocent enthusiasm into my voice, "this secret expedition to Baffin Land which we three are about to organise is destined to be without doubt the most scientifically prolific field expedition ever organised by man.

"Imagine an entire herd of mammoths preserved in mud and ice through all these thousands of years!

"Gentlemen, no discovery ever made has even remotely approached in importance the discovery made by this simple, illiterate trapper, James Skaw."

"I thought," protested Lezard, "that *we* are to be announced as the discoverers."

"We are," said I, "the discoverers of James Skaw, which makes us technically the finders of the ice-preserved herd of mammoths—*technically*, you understand. A few thousand dollars," I added, carelessly, "ought to satiate James Skaw."

"We could name dot glacier after him," suggested Dr. Fooss.

"Certainly—the Skaw Glacier. That ought to be enough glory for him. It ought to satisfy him and prevent any indiscreet remarks," nodded Lezard.

"Gentlemen," said I, "there is only one detail that really troubles me. Ought we to notify our honoured and respected Chief of Division concerning this discovery?"

"Do you mean, should we tell that accomplished and fascinating lady, Professor Bottomly, about this herd of mammoths?" I asked in a loud, clear voice. And immediately answered my own question: "No," I said, "no, dear friends. Professor Bottomly already has too much responsibility weighing upon her distinguished mind. No, dear brothers in science, we should steal away unobserved as though setting out upon an ordinary field expedition. And when we return with fresh and immortal laurels such as no man before has ever worn, no doubt that our generous-minded Chief of Division will weave for us further wreaths to crown our brows—the priceless garlands of professional approval!" And I made a horrible face at my co-conspirators.

Before I finished Lezard had taken his own face in his hands for the purpose of stifling raucous and untimely mirth. As for Dr. Fooss, his small, porcine eyes snapped and twinkled madly behind his spectacles, but he seemed rather inclined to approve my flowers of rhetoric.

"*Ja*," said he, "so iss it *besser* oursellufs dot *gefrozenss* herd *von elephanten* to discover, und, by and by, *die elephanten bei der Pronx Bark* home yet again once more to bring. We shall therefore much praise thereby *bekommen. Ach wass!*"

"Gentlemen," said I, distinctly, "it is decided, then, that we shall say nothing concerning the true object of this expedition to Professor Bottomly."

Lezard and Fooss nodded assent. Then, in the silence, we all strained our ears to listen. And presently we detected the scarcely heard sound of cautiously retreating footsteps down the corridor.

When it was safe to do so I arose and closed my door.

"I think," said I, with a sort of infernal cheerfulness in my tones, "that we are about to do something jocose to Jane Bottomly."

"A few," said Professor Lezard. He rose and silently executed a complicated ballet-step.

"I shall *laff*," said Dr. Fooss, earnestly, "*und* I shall *laff*, und I shall *laff—ach Gott* how I shall *laff* my pally head off!"

I folded my arms and turned romanesquely toward the direction in which Professor Bottomly had retreated.

"Viper!" I said. "The Bronx shall nourish you in its bosom no more! Fade away, Ophidian!"

The sentiment was applauded by all. There chanced to be in my desk a bottle marked: "That's all!" On the label somebody had written: "Do it now!" We did.

3

It was given out at the Bronx that our field expedition to

Baffin Land was to be undertaken solely for the purpose of bringing back living specimens of the five-spotted Arctic wood-cock—*Philohela quinquemaculata*—in order to add to our ono-matology and our glossary of onomatopoeia an ontogenesis of this important but hitherto unstudied sub-species.

I trust I make myself clear. Scientific statements should be as clear as the Spuyten Duyvil. *Sola in stagno salus!*

But two things immediately occurred which worried us; Professor Bottomly sent us official notification that she ap-proved our expedition to Baffin Land, designated the steamer we were to take, and enclosed tickets. That scared us. Then to add to our perplexity Professor Bottomly disappeared, leaving Dr. Daisy Delmour in charge of her department during what she announced might be "a somewhat prolonged absence on business."

And during the four feverish weeks of our pretended prepa-rations for Baffin Land not one word did we hear from Jane Bottomly, which caused us painful inquietude as the hour ap-proached for our departure.

Was this formidable woman actually intending to let us de-part alone for the Golden Glacier? Was she too lazy to rob us of the secretly contemplated glory which we had pretended awaited us?

We had been so absolutely convinced that she would forbid our expedition, pack us off elsewhere, and take charge herself of an exploring party to Baffin Land, that, as the time for our leav-ing drew near we became first uneasy, and then really alarmed.

It would be a dreadful jest on us if she made us swallow our own concoction; if she revealed to our colleagues our pretended knowledge of the Golden Glacier and James Skaw and the sup-posedly ice-imbedded herd of mammoths, and then publicly forced us to investigate this hoax.

More horrible still would it be if she informed the newspa-pers and gave them a hint to make merry over the three wise men of the Bronx who went to Baffin Land in a boat.

"*What* do you suppose that devious and secretive female is up to?" inquired Lezard who, within the last few days, had grown thin with worry. "Is it possible that she is sufficiently degraded to suspect us of trying to put one over on her? Is that what she is now doing to us?"

"*Terminus est*—it is the limit!" said I.

He turned a morbid eye upon me. "She is making a monkey of us. That's what!"

"*Suspendenda omnia naso*," I nodded; "*tarde sed tute*. When I think aloud in Latin it means that I am deeply troubled. *Suum quemque scelus agitat*. Do you get me, Professor? I'm sorry I attempted to be sportive with this terrible woman. The curse of my scientific career has been periodical excesses of frivolity. See where this frolicsome impulse has landed me!—*super abyssum ambulans. Trahit sua quemque voluptas; transeat in exemplum!* She means to let us go to our destruction on this mammoth *frappé* affair."

But Dr. Fooss was optimistic:

"I tink she iss alretty herselluf by dot Baffin Land ge-gone," he said. "I tink she has *der* bait ge-swallowed. Ve vait; ve see; *und* so iss it ve know."

"But why hasn't she stopped our preparations?" I demanded. "If she wants all the glory herself why does she permit us to incur this expense in getting ready?"

"No mans can to know *der* vorkings of *der* mental brocess by a *Frauenzimmer*," said Dr. Fooss, wagging his head.

The suspense became nerve-racking; we were obliged to pack our camping kits; and it began to look as though we would have either to sail the next morning or to resign from the Bronx Park Zoological Society, because all the evening papers had the story in big type—the details and objects of the expedition, the discovery of the herd of mammoths in cold storage, the prompt organization of an expedition to secure this unparalleled deposit of prehistoric *mammalia*—everything was there staring at us in violent print, excepting only the name of the discoverer and the names of those composing the field expedition.

"She means to betray us after we have sailed," said Lezard,

greatly depressed. "We might just as well resign now before this hoax explodes and bespatters us. We can take our chances in vaudeville or as lecturing professors with the movies."

I thought so, too, in point of fact we all had gathered in my study to write out our resignations, when there came a knock at the door and Dr. Daisy Delmour walked in.

Oddly enough I had not before met Dr. Delmour personally; only formal written communications had hitherto passed between us. My idea of her had doubtless been inspired by the physical and intellectual aberrations of her chief; I naturally supposed her to be either impossible and corporeally redundant, or intellectually and otherwise as weazened as last year's Li-che nut.

I was criminally mistaken. And why Lezard, who knew her, had never set me right I could not then understand. I comprehended later.

For the feminine assistant of Professor Jane Bottomly, who sauntered into my study and announced herself, had the features of Athene, the smile of Aphrodite, and the figure of Psyche. I believe I do not exaggerate these scientific details, although it has been said of me that any pretty girl distorts my vision and my intellectual balance to the detriment of my calmer reason and my differentiating ability.

"Gentlemen," said Dr. Delmour, while we stood in a respectful semi-circle before her, modestly conscious of our worth, our toes turned out, and each man's features wreathed with that politely unnatural smirk which masculine features assume when confronted by feminine beauty. "Gentlemen, on the eve of your proposed departure for Baffin Land in quest of living specimens of the five-spotted *Philohela quinquemaculata*, I have been instructed by Professor Bottomly to announce to you a great good fortune for her, for you, for the Bronx, for America, for the entire civilized world.

"It has come to Professor Bottomly's knowledge, recently I believe, that an entire herd of mammoths lie encased in the mud and ice of the vast flat marshes which lie south of the terminal moraine of the Golden Glacier in that part of Baffin Land known as Dr. Cook's Peninsula.

"The credit of this epoch-making discovery is Professor Bottomly's entirely. How it happened, she did not inform me. One month ago today she sailed in great haste for Baffin Land. At this very hour she is doubtless standing all alone upon the frozen surface of that wondrous marsh, contemplating with reverence and awe and similar holy emotions the fruits of her own unsurpassed discovery!"

Dr. Delmour's lovely features became delicately suffused and transfigured as she spoke; her exquisite voice thrilled with generous emotion; she clasped her snowy hands and gazed, enraptured, at the picture of Dr. Bottomly which her mind was so charmingly evoking.

"Perhaps," she whispered, "perhaps at this very instant, in the midst of that vast and flat and solemn desolation the only protuberance visible for miles and miles is Professor Bottomly. Perhaps the pallid Arctic sun is setting behind the majestic figure of Professor Bottomly, radiating a blinding glory to the zenith, illuminating the crowning act of her career with its unearthly aura!"

She gazed at us out of dimmed and violet eyes.

"Gentlemen," she said, "I am ordered to take command of this expedition of yours; I am ordered to sail with you tomorrow morning on the Labrador and Baffin Line steamer *Dr. Cook*.

"The object of your expedition, therefore, is not to be the quest of *Philohela quinquemaculata*; your duty now is to corroborate the almost miraculous discovery of Professor Bottomly, and to disinter for her the vast herd of frozen mammoths, pack and pickle them, and get them to the Bronx.

"Tomorrow's morning papers will have the entire story: the credit and responsibility for the discovery and the expedition belong to Professor Bottomly, and will be given to her by the press and the populace of our great republic.

"It is her wish that no other names be mentioned. Which is right. To the discoverer belongs the glory. Therefore, the marsh is to be named Bottomly's Marsh, and the Glacier, Bottomly's Glacier.

"Yours and mine is to be the glory of laboring incognito under the direction of the towering scientific intellect of the age, Professor Bottomly.

"And the most precious legacy you can leave your children—if you get married and have any—is that you once wielded the humble pick and shovel for Jane Bottomly on the bottomless marsh which bears her name!"

After a moment's silence we three men ventured to look sideways at each other. We had certainly killed Professor Bottomly, scientifically speaking. The lady was practically dead. The morning papers would consummate the murder. We didn't know whether we wanted to laugh or not.

She was now virtually done for; that seemed certain. So greedily had this egotistical female swallowed the silly bait we offered, so arrogantly had she planned to eliminate everybody excepting herself from the credit of the discovery, that there seemed now nothing left for us to do except to watch her hurdling deliriously toward destruction. *Should* we burst into hellish laughter?

We looked hard at Dr. Delmour and we decided not to—yet.

Said I: "To assist at the final apotheosis of Professor Bottomly makes us very, very happy. We are happy to remain *incognito*, mere ciphers blotted out by the fierce white light which is about to beat upon Professor Bottomly, fore and aft. We are happy that our participation in this astonishing affair shall never be known to science.

"But, happiest of all are we, dear Dr. Delmour, in the knowledge that *you* are to be with us and of us, *incognito* on this voyage now imminent; that you are to be our revered and beloved leader.

"And I, for one, promise you personally the undivided devotion of a man whose entire and austere career has been dedicated to science—in *all* its branches."

I stepped forward rather gracefully and raised her little hand to my lips to let her see that even the science of gallantry had not been neglected by me.

Dr. Daisy Delmour blushed.

"Therefore," said I, "considering the fact that our names are not to figure in this expedition; and, furthermore, in consideration of the fact that *you* are going, we shall be very, very happy to accompany you, Dr. Delmour." I again saluted her hand, and again Dr. Delmour blushed and looked sideways at Professor Lezard.

4

It was, to be accurate, exactly twenty-three days later that our voyage by sea and land ended one Monday morning upon the gigantic terminal moraine of the Golden Glacier, Cook's Peninsula, Baffin Land.

Four pack-mules carried our luggage, four more bore our persons; an arctic dicky-bird sat on a bowlder and said, "Pilly-willy-willy! Tweet! Tweet!"

As we rode out to the bowlder-strewn edge of the moraine the rising sun greeted us cordially, illuminating below us the flat surface of the marsh which stretched away to the east and south as far as the eye could see.

So flat was it that we immediately made out the silhouettes of two mules tethered below us a quarter of a mile away.

Something about the attitude of these mules arrested our attention, and, gazing upon them through our field-glasses we beheld Professor Bottomly.

That resourceful lady had mounted a pneumatic hammock upon the two mules, their saddles had sockets to fit the legs of the galvanized iron tripod.

No matter in which way the mules turned, sliding swivels on the hollow steel frames regulated the hammock slung between them. It was an infernal invention.

There lay Jane Bottomly asleep, her black hair drying over the hammock's edge, gilded to a peroxide lustre by the rays of the rising sun.

I gazed upon her with a sort of ferocious pity. Her professional days were numbered. *I* also had her number!

"How majestically she slumbers," whispered Dr. Delmour to me, "dreaming, doubtless, of her approaching triumph."

Dr. Fooss and Professor Lezard, driving the pack-mules ahead of them, were already riding out across the marsh.

"Daisy," I said, leaning from my saddle and taking one of her gloved hands into mine, "the time has come for me to disillusion you. There are no mammoths in that mud down there."

She looked at me in blue-eyed amazement.

"You are mistaken," she said; "Professor Bottomly is celebrated for the absolute and painstaking accuracy of her deductions and the boldness and the imagination of her scientific investigations. She is the most cautious scientist in America; she would never announce such a discovery to the newspapers unless she were perfectly certain of its truth."

I was sorry for this young girl. I pressed her hand because I was sorry for her. After a few moments of deepest thought I felt so sorry for her that I kissed her.

"You mustn't," said Dr. Delmour, blushing.

The things we mustn't do are so many that I can't always remember all of them.

"Daisy," I said, "shall we pledge ourselves to each other for eternity—here in the presence of this immemorial glacier which moves a thousand inches a year—I mean an inch every thousand years—here in these awful solitudes where incalculable calculations could not enlighten us concerning the number of cubic tons of mud in that marsh—here in the presence of these innocent mules—"

"Oh, look!" exclaimed Dr. Delmour, lifting her flushed cheek from my shoulder. "There is a man in the hammock with Professor Bottomly!"

I levelled my field-glasses incredulously. Good Heavens! There *was* a man there. He was sitting on the edge of the hammock in a dejected attitude, his booted legs dangling.

And, as I gazed, I saw the arm of Professor Bottomly raised as though groping instinctively for something in her slumber—saw her fingers close upon the blue-flannel shirt of her companion, saw his timid futile attempts to elude her, saw him inexorably hauled back and his head forcibly pillowed upon her ample chest.

"Daisy!" I faltered, "what does yonder scene of presumable domesticity mean?"

"I—I haven't the faintest idea!" she stammered.

"Is that lady married! Or is this revelry?" I asked, sternly.

"She wasn't married when she sailed from N-New-York," faltered Dr. Delmour.

We rode forward in pained silence, spurring on until we caught up with Lezard and Fooss and the pack-mules; then we all pressed ahead, a prey, now, to the deepest moral anxiety and agitation.

The splashing of our mule's feet on the partly melted surface of the mud aroused the man as we rode up and he scrambled madly to get out of the hammock as soon as he saw us.

A detaining feminine hand reached mechanically for his collar, groped aimlessly for a moment, and fell across the hammock's edge. Evidently its owner was too sleepy for effort.

Meanwhile the man who had floundered free from the hammock, leaped overboard and came hopping stiffly over the slush toward us like a badly-winged snipe.

"Who are you?" I demanded, drawing bridle so suddenly that I found myself astride of my mule's ears. Sliding back into the saddle, I repeated the challenge haughtily, inwardly cursing my horsemanship.

He stood balancing his lank six feet six of bony altitude for a few moments without replying. His large gentle eyes of baby blue were fixed on me.

"Speak!" I said. "The reputation of a lady is at stake! Who are you? We ask, before we shoot you, for purpose of future identification."

He gazed at me wildly. "I dunno who I be," he replied. "My

name *was* James Skaw before that there lady went an' changed it on me. She says she has changed my name to hers. I dunno. All I know is I'm married."

"*Married!*" echoed Dr. Delmour.

He looked dully at the girl, then fixed his large mild eyes on me.

"A mission priest done it for her a month ago when we was hikin' towards Fort Carcajou. Hoon-hel are you?" he added.

I informed him with dignity; he blinked at me, at the others, at the mules. Then he said with infinite bitterness:

"You're a fine guy, ain't you, a-wishin' this here lady onto a pore pelt-hunter what ain't never done nothin' to you!"

"Who did you say I wished on you?" I demanded, bewildered.

"That there lady a-sleepin' into the nuptool hammick! You wished her onto me—yaas you did! Whatnhel have I done to you, hey?"

We were dumb. He shoved his hand into his pocket, produced a slug of twist, slowly gnawed off a portion, and buried the remains in his vast jaw.

"All I done to you," he said, "was to write you them letters sayin's as how I found a lot of ellerphants into the mud.

"What you done to me was to send that there lady here. Was that gratitood? Man to man I ask you?"

A loud snore from the hammock startled us all. James Skaw twisted his neck turkey-like, and looked warily at the hammock, then turning toward me:

"Aw," he said, "she don't never wake up till I have breakfast ready."

"James Skaw," I said, "tell me what has happened. On my word of honor I don't know."

He regarded me with lack-lustre eyes.

"I was a-settin' onto a bowlder," said he, "a-fig-urin' out whether you was a-comin' or not, when that there lady rides up with her led-mule a trailin'.

"Sez she: 'Are you James Skaw?'

441

"Yes, marm,' sez I, kinder scared an' puzzled.

"'Where is them ellerphants?' sez she, reachin' down from her saddle an' takin' me by the shirt collar, an' beatin' me with her umbrella.

"Sez I, 'I have wrote to a certain gent that I would show him them ellerphants for a price. Bein' strictly hones' I can't show 'em to no one else until I hear from him.'

"With that she continood to argoo the case with her umbrella, never lettin' go of my shirt collar. Sir, she argood until dinner time, an' then she resoomed the debate until I fell asleep. The last I knowed she was still conversin'.

"An' so it went next day, all day long, an' the next day. I couldn't stand it no longer so I started for Fort Carcajau. But she bein' onto a mule, run me down easy, an' kep' beside me conversin' volooble.

"Sir, do you know what it is to listen to umbrella argooment every day, all day long, from sun-up to night-fall? An' then some more?

"I was loony, I tell you, when we met the mission priest. 'Marry me,' sez she, 'or I'll talk you to death!' I didn't realise what she was sayin' an' what I answered. But them words I uttered done the job, it seems.

"We camped there an' slep' for two days without wakin.' When I waked up I was convalescent.

"She was good to me. She made soup an' she wrapped blankets onto me an' she didn't talk no more until I was well enough to endoor it.

"An' by'm'by she brooke the nooze to me that we was married an' that she had went as far as to marry me in the sacred cause of science because man an' wife is one, an' what I knowed about them ellerphants she now had a right to know.

"Sir, she had put one over on me. So bein' strickly hones' I had to show her where them ellerphants lay froze up under the marsh."

Where the ambition of this infatuated woman had led her appalled us all. The personal sacrifice she had made in the name of science awed us.

Still when I remembered that detaining arm sleepily lifted from the nuptual hammock, I was not so certain concerning her continued martyrdom.

I cast an involuntary glance of critical appraisal upon James Skaw. He had the golden hair and beard of the early Christian martyr. His features were classically regular; he stood six feet six; he was lean because fit, sound as a hound's tooth, and really a superb specimen of masculine health.

Curry him and trim him and clothe him in evening dress and his physical appearance would make a sensation at the Court of St. James. Only his English required manicuring.

The longer I looked at him the better I comprehended that detaining hand from the hammock. *Fabas indulcet fames.*

Then, with a shock, it rushed over me that there evidently had been some ground for this man's letters to me concerning a herd of frozen mammoths.

Professor Bottomly had not only married him to obtain the information but here she was still camping on the marsh!

"James Skaw," I said, tremulously, "where are those mammoths?"

He looked at me, then made a vague gesture:

"Under the mud—everywhere—all around us."

"Has *she* seen them?"

"Yes, I showed her about a hundred. There's one under you. Look! you can see him through the slush."

"Ach Gott!" burst from Dr. Fooss, and he tottered in his saddle. Lezard, frightfully pale, passed a shaking hand over his brow. As for me my hair became dank with misery, for there directly under my feet, the vast hairy bulk of a mammoth lay dimly visible through the muddy ice.

What I had done to myself when I was planning to do Professor Bottomly suddenly burst upon me in all its hideous proportions. Fame, the plaudits of the world, the highest scientific honours—all these in my effort to annihilate her, I had deliberately thrust upon this woman to my own everlasting detriment and disgrace.

A sort of howl escaped from Dr. Fooss, who had dismounted and who had been scratching in the slush with his feet like a hen. For already this slight gallinaceous effort of his had laid bare a hairy section of frozen mammoth.

Lezard, weeping bitterly, squatted beside him clawing at the thin skin of ice with a pick-axe.

It seemed more than I could bear and I flung myself from my mule and seizing a spade, fell violently to work, the tears of rage and mortification coursing down my cheeks.

"Hurrah!" cried Dr. Delmour, excitedly, scrambling down from her mule and lifting a box of dynamite from her saddle-bags.

Transfigured with enthusiasm she seized a crowbar, traced in the slush the huge outlines of the buried beast, then, measuring with practiced eye the irregular zone of cleavage, she marked out a vast oval, dug holes along it with her bar, dropped into each hole a stick of dynamite, got out the batteries and wires, attached the fuses, covered each charge, and retired on a run toward the moraine, unreeling wire as she sped upward among the bowlders.

Half frantic with grief and half mad with the excitement of the moment we still had sense enough to shoulder our tools and drive our mules back across the moraine.

Only the mule-hammock in which reposed Professor Bottomly remained on the marsh. For one horrid instant temptation assailed me to press the button before James Skaw could lead the hammock-mules up to the moraine. It was my closest approach to crime.

With a shudder I viewed the approach of the mules. James Skaw led them by the head; the hammock on its bar and swivels swung gently between them; Professor Bottomly slept, lulled, no doubt, to deeper slumber by the gently swaying hammock.

When the hammock came up, one by one we gazed upon its unconscious occupant.

And, even amid dark and revengeful thoughts, amid a mental chaos of grief and fury and frantic self-reproach, I had to admit to myself that Jane Bottomly was a fine figure of a woman, and good-looking, too, and that her hair was all her own and almost magnificent at that.

With a modiste to advise her, a maid to dress her, I myself might have—but let that pass. Only as I gazed upon her fresh complexion and the softly parted red lips of Professor Bottomly, and as I noted the beautiful white throat and prettily shaped hands, a newer, bitterer, and more overwhelming despair seized me; and I realized now that perhaps I had thrown away more than fame, honours, applause; I had perhaps thrown away love!

At that moment Professor Bottomly awoke. For a moment her lilac-tinted eyes had a dazed expression, then they widened, and she lay very quietly looking from one to another of us, cradled in the golden glory of her hair, perfectly mistress of herself, and her mind as clear as a bell.

"Well," she said, "so you have arrived at last." And to Dr. Delmour she smilingly extended a cool, fresh hand.

"Have you met my husband?" she inquired.

We admitted that we had.

"James!" she called.

At the sound of her voice James Skaw hopped nimbly to do her bidding. A tender smile came into her face as she gazed upon her husband. She made no explanation concerning him, no apology for him. And, watching her, it slowly filtered into my mind that she liked him.

With one hand in her husband's and one on Dr. Delmour's arm she listened to Daisy's account of what we were about to do to the imbedded mammoth, and nodded approval.

James Skaw turned the mules so that she might watch the explosion. She twisted up her hair, then sat up in her hammock; Daisy Delmour pressed the electric button; there came a deep jarring sound, a vast upheaval, and up out of the mud rose *five or six dozen mammoths* and toppled gently over upon the surface of the ice.

Miserable as we were at such an astonishing spectacle we raised a tragic cheer as Professor Bottomly sprang out of her hammock and, telling Dr. Delmour to get a camera, seized her husband and sped down to where one of the great, hairy frozen beasts lay on the ice in full sunshine.

And then we tasted the last drop of gall which our over-slopping cup of bitterness held for us; Professor Bottomly climbed up the sides of the frozen mammoth, dragging her husband with her, and stood there waving a little American flag while Dr. Delmour used up every film in the camera to record the scientific triumph of the ages.

Almost idiotic with the shock of my great grief I reeled and tottered away among the bowlders. Fooss came to find me; and when he found me he kicked me violently for some time. "*Esel dumkopf!*" he said.

When he was tired Lezard came and fell upon me, showering me with kicks and anathema.

When he went away I beat my head with my fists for a while. Every little helped.

After a time I smelled cooking, and presently Dr. Delmour came to where I sat huddled up miserably in the sun behind the bowlder.

"Luncheon is ready," she said.

I groaned.

"Don't you feel well?"

I said that I did not.

She lingered apparently with the idea of cheering me up. "It's been such fun," she said. "Professor Lezard and I have already located over a hundred and fifty mammoths within a short distance of here, and apparently there are hundreds, if not thousands, more in the vicinity. The ivory alone is worth over a million dollars. Isn't it wonderful!"

She laughed excitedly and danced away to join the others. Then, out of the black depth of my misery a feeble gleam illuminated the Stygian obscurity. There was one way left to stay my approaching downfall—only one. Professor Bottomly meant to get rid of me, "for the good of the Bronx," but there remained a way to ward off impending disaster. And though I had lost the opportunity of my life by disbelieving the simple honesty of James Skaw,—and though the honours and emoluments and applause which ought to have been mine were destined for this determined woman, still, if I kept my head, I should be able to hold my job at the Bronx.

Dr. Delmour was immovable in the good graces of Professor Bottomly; and the only way for me to retain my position was to marry her.

The thought comforted me. After a while I felt well enough to arise and partake of some luncheon.

They were all seated around the campfire when I approached. I was welcomed politely, inquiries concerning my health were offered; but the coldly malevolent glare of Dr. Fooss and the calm contempt in Lezard's gaze chilled me; and I squatted down by Daisy Delmour and accepted a dish of soup from her in mortified silence.

Professor Bottomly and James Skaw were feasting connubially side by side, and she was selecting titbits for him which he dutifully swallowed, his large mild eyes gazing at vacancy in a gentle, surprised sort of way as he gulped down what she offered him.

Neither of them paid any attention to anybody else.

Fooss gobbled his lunch in a sort of raging silence; Lezard, on the other side of Dr. Delmour, conversed with her continually in undertones.

After a while his persistent murmuring began to make me uneasy, even suspicious, and I glared at him sideways.

Daisy Delmour, catching my eye, blushed, hesitated, then leaning over toward me with delightful confusion she whispered:

"I know that you will be glad to hear that I have just promised to marry your closest friend, Professor Lezard—"

447

"What!" I shouted with all my might, "have *you* put one over on me, too?"

Lezard and Fooss seized me, for I had risen and was jumping up and down and splashing them with soup.

"Everybody has put one over on me!" I shrieked. "Everybody! Now I'm going to put one over on myself!"

And I lifted my plate of soup and reversed it on my head.

They told me later that I screamed for half an hour before I swooned.

Afterward, my intellect being impaired, instead of being dismissed from my department, I was promoted to the position which I now hold as President Emeritus of the Consolidated Art Museums and Zoological Gardens of the City of New York.

I have easy hours, little to do, and twenty ornamental stenographers and typewriters engaged upon my memoirs which I dictate when I feel like it, steeped in the aroma of the most inexpensive cigar I can buy at the Rolling Stone Inn.

There is one typist in particular—but let that pass.

Vir sapit qui pauca loquitor.

The Bridal Pair

(A story from The Tree of Heaven.)

CHAPTER 1

"If I were you," said the elder man, "I should take three months' solid rest."

"A month is enough," said the younger man. "Ozone will do it; the first brace of grouse I bag will do it—" He broke off abruptly, staring at the line of dimly lighted cars, where negro porters stood by the vestibuled sleepers, directing passengers to staterooms and berths.

"Dog all right, doctor?" inquired the elder man pleasantly. 'All right, doctor," replied the younger; "I spoke to the baggage master, There was a silence; the elder man chewed an unlighted cigar reflectively, watching his companion with keen narrowing eyes.

The younger physician stood full in the white electric light, lean head lowered, apparently preoccupied with a study of his own shadow swimming and quivering on the asphalt at his feet.

"So you fear I may break down?" he observed, without raising his head.

"I think you're tired out," said the other.

"That's a more agreeable way of expressing it," said the young fellow. "I hear"—he hesitated, with a faint trace of irritation—I understand that Forbes Stanly thinks me mentally unsound."

"He probably suspects what you're up to," said the elder man soberly.

"Well, what will he do when I announce my germ theory? Put me in a strait-jacket?"

"He'll say you're mad, until you prove it; every physician will agree with him—until your radium test shows us the microbe of insanity."

"Doctor," said the young man abruptly, "I'm going to admit something—to you."

"All right; go ahead and admit it."

"Well, I am a bit worried about my own condition."

"It's time you were," observed the other.

"Yes—it's about time. Doctor, I am seriously affected."

The elder man looked up sharply.

"Yes, I'm—in love."

"Ah!" muttered the elder physician, amused and a trifle disgusted; "so that's your malady, is it?"

"A malady—yes; not explainable by our germ theory—not affected by radio-activity. Doctor, I'm speaking lightly enough, but there's no happiness in it."

"Never is," commented the other, striking a match and lighting his ragged cigar. After a puff or two the cigar went out. "All I have to say," he added, "is, don't do it just now. Show me a scale of pure radium and I'll give you leave to marry every spinster in New York. In the meantime go and shoot a few dozen harmless, happy grouse; they can't shoot back. But let love alone. . . . By the way, who is she?"

"I don't know."

"You know her name, I suppose?"

The young fellow shook his head. "I don't even know where she lives," he said finally.

After a pause the elder man took him gently by the arm: "Are you subject to this sort of thing? Are you susceptible?"

"No, not at all."

"Ever before in love?"

"Yes—once.".

"When?"

"When I was about ten years old. Her name was Rosamund—aged eight. I never had the courage to speak to her. She died recently, I believe."

The reply was so quietly serious, so destitute of any suspicion of humour, that the elder man's smile faded; and again he cast one of his swift, keen glances at his companion.

"Won't you stay away three months?" he asked patiently.

But the other only shook his head, tracing with the point of his walking stick the outline of his own shadow on the asphalt.

A moment later he glanced at his watch, closed it with a snap, silently shook hands with his equally silent friend, and stepped aboard the sleeping car.

Neither had noticed the name of the sleeping car.

It happened to be the Rosamund.

Chapter 2

Loungers and passengers on Wildwood station drew back from the platform's edge as the towering locomotive shot by them, stunning their ears with the clangour of its melancholy bell.

Slower, slower glided the dusty train, then stopped, jolting; eddying circles of humanity closed around the cars, through which descending passengers pushed.

"Wildwood! Wildwood!" cried the trainmen; trunks tumbling out of the forward car descended with a bang!—a yelping, wagging setter dog landed on the platform, hysterically grateful to be free; and at the same moment a young fellow in tweed shooting clothes, carrying gripsack and gun case, made his way forward toward the baggage master, who was being jerked all over the platform by the frantic dog.

"Much obliged; I'll take the dog," he said, slipping a bit of silver into the official's hand, and receiving the dog's chain in return.

"Hope you'll have good sport," replied the baggage master. "There's a lot o' birds in this country, they tell me. You've got a good dog there."

The young man smiled and nodded, released the chain from

his dog's collar, and started off up the dusty village street, followed by an urchin carrying his luggage.

The landlord of the Wildwood Inn stood on the veranda, prepared to receive guests. When a young man, a white setter dog, and a small boy loomed up, his speculative eyes became suffused with benevolence.

"How-de-so, sir?" he said cordially. "Guess you was with us three year since—stayed to supper. Ain't that so?"

"It certainly is," said his guest cheerfully. "I am surprised that you remember me."

"Be ye?" rejoined the landlord, gratified. "Say! I can tell the name of every man, woman, an child that has ever set down to eat with us. You was here with a pair o' red bird dawgs; shot a mess o' birds before dark, come back pegged out, an' took the ten-thirty to Noo York. Hey? Yaas, an' you was cussin' round because you couldn't stay an' shoot for a month."

"I had to work hard in those days," laughed the young man. "You are right; it was three years ago this month."

"Time's a flyer; it's fitted with triple screws these days," said the landlord. "Come right in an' make yourself to home. Ed! O Ed! Take this bag to 13! We're all full, sir. You ain't scared at No. 13, be ye? Say! if I ain't a liar you had 13 three years ago! Waal, now!—ain't that the dumbdest—But you can have what you want Monday. How long was you calkerlatin' to stay?".

"A month—if the shooting is good."

"It's all right. Orrin Plummet come in last night with a mess o pa'tridges. He says the woodcock is droppin' in to the birches south o' Sweetbrier Hill."

The young man nodded, and began to remove his gun from the service-worn case of sole leather.

"Ain't startin' right off, be ye?" inquired his host, laughing.

"I can't begin too quickly," said the young man, busy locking barrels to stock, while the dog looked on, thumping the veranda floor with his plumy tail.

The landlord admired the slim, polished weapon. "That's the instroment!" he observed. "That there's a slick bird dawg, too.

Guess I'd better fill my ice box. Your limit's thirty of each—cock an' parridge. After that there's ducks."

"It's a good, sane law," said the young man, dropping his gun under one arm.

The landlord scratched his ear reflectively. "Lemme see," he mused; "wasn't you a doctor? I heard tell that you made up pieces for the papers about the idjits an' loonyticks of Rome an' Roosia an' furrin climes."

"I have written a little on European and Asiatic insanity," replied the doctor good-humouredly.

"Was you over to them parts?"

"For three years." He whistled the dog in from the road, where several yellow curs were walking round and round him, every hair on end.

The landlord said: "You look a little peaked yourself. Take it easy the fust, is my advice."

His guest nodded abstractedly, lingering on the veranda, pre-occupied with the beauty of the village street, which stretched away westward under tall elms. Autumn-tinted hills closed the *vista*; beyond them spread the blue sky.

"The cemetery lies that way, does it not?" inquired the young man.

"Straight ahead," said the landlord. "Take the road to the Holler."

"Do you"—the doctor hesitated—"do you recall a funeral there three years ago?"

"Whose?" asked his host bluntly.

"I don't know."

"I'll ask my woman; she saves them funeral pieces an' makes a album."

"Friend o' yours buried there?"

"No."

The landlord sauntered toward the barroom, where two fellow taxpayers stood shuffling their feet impatiently.

"Waal, good luck, Doc," he said, without intentional offense; "supper's at six. We'll try an' make you comfortable."

"Thank you," replied the doctor, stepping out into the road, and motioning the white setter to heel.

"I remember now," he muttered, as he turned northward, where the road forked; "the cemetery lies to the westward; there should be a lane at the next turning—"

He hesitated and stopped, then resumed his course, mumbling to himself: "I can pass the cemetery later; she would not be there; I don't think I shall ever see her again. . . . I—I wonder whether I am—perfectly—well—"

The words were suddenly lost in a sharp indrawn breath; his heart ceased beating, fluttered, then throbbed on violently; and he shook from head to foot.

There was a glimmer of a summer gown under the trees; a figure passed from shadow to sunshine, and again into the cool dusk of a leafy lane.

The pallor of the young fellow's face changed; a heavy flush spread from forehead to neck; he strode forward, dazed, deafened by the tumult of his drumming pulses. The dog, alert, suspicious, led the way, wheeling into the bramble-bordered lane, only to halt, turn back, and fall in behind his master again.

In the lane ahead the light summer gown fluttered under the foliage, bright in the sunlight, almost lost in the shadows. Then he saw her on the hill's breezy crest, poised for a moment against the sky.

When at length he reached the hill, he found her seated in the shade of a pine. She looked up serenely, as though she had expected him, and they faced each other. A moment later his dog left him, sneaking away without a sound.

When he strove to speak, his voice had an unknown tone to him. Her upturned face was his only answer. The breeze in the pinetops, which had been stirring lazily and monotonously, ceased.

Chapter 3

Her delicate face was like a blossom lifted in the still air; her upward glance chained him to silence. The first breeze broke the spell: he spoke a word, then speech died on his lips; he stood twisting his shooting cap, confused, not daring to continue.

The girl leaned back, supporting her weight on one arm, fingers almost buried in the deep green moss.

"It is three years today," he said, in the dull voice of one who dreams; "three years today. May I not speak?"

In her lowered head and eyes he read acquiescence; in her silence, consent.

"Three years ago today," he repeated; "the anniversary has given me courage to speak to you. Surely you will not take offense; we have travelled so far together!—from the end of the world to the end of it, and back again, here—to this place of all places in the world! And now to find you here on this day of all days—here within a step of our first meeting place—three years ago today! And all the world we have travelled over since never speaking, yet ever passing on paths parallel—paths which for thousands of miles ran almost within arms distance—"

She raised her head slowly, looking out from the shadows of the pines into the sunshine. Her dreamy eyes rested on acres of golden-rod and hillside brambles quivering in the September heat; on fern-choked gullies edged with alder; on brown and purple grasses; on pine thickets where slim silver birches glimmered.

"Will you speak to me?" he asked. "I have never even heard the sound of your voice."

She turned and looked at him, touching with idle fingers the soft hair curling on her temples Then she bent her head once more, the faintest shadow of a smile in her eyes.

"Because," he said humbly, "these long years of silent recognition count for something! And then the strangeness of it!— the fate of it—the quiet destiny that ruled our lives—that rules them now—now as I am speaking, weighting every second with its tiny burden of fate."

She straightened up, lifting her half-buried hand from the moss; and he saw the imprint there where the palm and fingers had rested.

"Three years that end today—end with the new moon," he said. "Do you remember?"

"Yes," she said.

He quivered at the sound of her voice. "You were there, just beyond those oaks," he said eagerly; "we can see them from here. The road turns there—"

"Turns by the cemetery," she murmured.

"Yes, yes, by the cemetery! You had been there, I think."

"Do you remember that?" she asked.

"I have never forgotten—never!" he repeated, striving to hold her eyes to his own; "it was not twilight; there was a glimmer of day in the west, but the woods were darkening, and the new moon lay in the sky, and the evening was very clear and still."

Impulsively he dropped on one knee beside her to see her face; and as he spoke, curbing his emotion and impatience with that subtle deference which is inbred in men or never acquired, she stole a glance at him; and his worn visage brightened as though touched with sunlight.

"The second time I saw you was in New York," he said—"only a glimpse of your face in the crowd—but I knew you."

"I saw you," she mused.

"Did you?" he cried, enchanted. "I dared not believe that you recognized me."

"Yes, I knew you. . . . Tell me more."

The thrilling voice set him aflame; faint danger signals tinted her face and neck.

"In December," he went on unsteadily, "I saw you in Paris—I saw only you amid the thousand faces in the candlelight of Notre Dame."

"And I saw you. . . . And then?"

"And then two months of darkness. . . . And at last a light—moonlight—and you on the terrace at Amara."

"There was only a flower bed—a few spikes of white hyacinths between us," she said dreamily.

He strove to speak coolly. "Day and night have built many a wall between us; was that you who passed me in the starlight, so close that our shoulders, touched, in that narrow street in Samarkand? And the dark figure with you—"

"Yes, it was I and my attendant."

"And . . . you, there in the fog—"

"At Archangel? Yes, it was I."

"On the Goryn?"

"It was I. . . . And I am here at last—with you. It is our destiny."

CHAPTER 4

So, kneeling there beside her in the shadow of the pines, she absolved him in their dim confessional, holding him guiltless under the destiny that awaits us all.

Again that illumination touched his haggard face as though brightened by a sun ray stealing through the still foliage above. He grew younger under the level beauty of her gaze; care fell from him like a mask; the shadows that had haunted his eyes faded; youth awoke, transfiguring him and all his eyes beheld.

Made prisoner by love, adoring her, fearing her, he knelt beside her, knowing already that she had surrendered, though fearful yet by word or gesture or a glance to claim what destiny was holding for him holding securely, inexorably, for him alone.

He spoke of her kindness in understanding him, and of his gratitude; of her generosity, of his wonder that she had ever noticed him on his way through the world.

"I cannot believe that we have never before spoken to each other," he said; "that I do not even know your name. Surely there was once a corner in the land of childhood where we sat together when the world was younger."

She said, dreamily: "Have you forgotten?"

"Forgotten?"

"That sunny corner in the land of childhood."

"Had you been there, I should not have forgotten," he replied, troubled.

"Look at me," she said. Her lovely eyes met his; under the penetrating sweetness of her gaze his heart quickened and grew restless and his uneasy soul stirred, awaking memories.

"There was a child," she said, "years ago; a child at school. You sometimes looked at her, you never spoke. Do you remember?"

He rose to his feet, staring down at her.

"Do you remember?" she asked again.

"Rosamund! Do you mean Rosamund? How should you know that?" he faltered.

The struggle for memory focused all his groping senses; his eyes seemed to look her through and through.

"How can you know?" he repeated unsteadily. "You are not Rosamund. . . . Are you? . . . She is dead. I heard that she was dead. . . . Are you Rosamund?"

"Do you not know?"

"Yes; you are not Rosamund. . . . What do you know of her?"

"I think she loved you."

"Is she dead?"

The girl looked up at him, smiling, following with delicate perception the sequence of his thoughts; and already his thoughts were far from the child Rosamund, a sweetheart of a day long since immortal; already he had forgotten his question, though the question was of life or death.

Sadness and unrest and the passing of souls concerned not him; she knew that all his thoughts were centred on her; that he was already living over once more the last three years, with all their mystery and charm, savouring their fragrance anew in the exquisite enchantment of her presence.

Through the autumn silence the pines began to sway in a wind unfelt below. She raised her eyes and saw their green crests shimmering and swimming in a cool current; a thrilling sound stole out, and with it floated the pine perfume, exhaling in the sunshine. He heard the dreamy harmony above, looked up; then, troubled, somber, moved by he knew not what, he knelt once more in the shadow beside her—close beside her.

She did not stir. Their destiny was close upon them. It came in the guise of love.

He bent nearer. "I love you," he said. "I loved you from the first. And shall forever. You knew it long ago."

She did not move.

"You knew I loved you?"

"Yes, I knew it."

The emotion in her voice, in every delicate contour of her face, pleaded for mercy. He gave her none, and she bent her head in silence, clasped hands tightening.

And when at last he had had his say, the burning words still rang in her ears through the silence. A curious faintness stole upon her, coming stealthily like a hateful thing. She strove to put it from her, to listen, to remember and understand the words he had spoken, but the dull confusion grew with the sound of the pines.

"Will you love me? Will you try to love me?"

"I love you," she said; "I have loved you so many, many years; I—I am Rosamund—"

She bowed her head and covered her face with both hands.

"Rosamund! Rosamund!" he breathed, enraptured.

She dropped her hands with a little cry; the frightened sweetness of her eyes held back his outstretched arms. "Do not touch me," she whispered; "you will not touch me, will you?—not yet—not now. Wait till I understand!" She pressed her hands to her eyes, then again let them fall, staring straight at him. "I loved you so!" she whispered. "Why did you wait?"

"Rosamund! Rosamund!" he cried sorrowfully, "what are you saying? I do not understand; I can understand nothing save that I worship you. May I not touch you?—touch your hand, Rosamund? I love you so."

"And I love you. I beg you not to touch me—not yet. There is something—some reason why—"

"Tell me, sweetheart."

"Do you not know?"

"By Heaven, I do not!" he said, troubled and amazed.

She cast one desperate, unhappy glance at him, then rose to her full height, gazing out over the hazy valleys to where the mountains began, piled up like dim sun-tipped clouds in the north.

The hill wind stirred her hair and fluttered the white ribbons at waist and shoulder. The golden-rod swayed in the sunshine. Below, amid yellow treetops, the roofs and chimneys of the village glimmered.

"Dear, do you not understand?" she said. "How can I make you understand that I love you—too late?"

"Give yourself to me, Rosamund; let me touch you—let me take you—"

"Will you love me always?"

"In life, in death, which cannot part us. Will you marry me, Rosamund?"

She looked straight into his eyes. "Dear, do you not understand? Have you forgotten? I died three years ago today."

The unearthly sweetness of her white face startled him. A terrible light broke in on him; his heart stood still.

In his dull brain words were sounding—his own words, written years ago: "When God takes the mind and leaves the body alive, there grows in it, sometimes, a beauty almost supernatural."

He had seen it in his practice. A thrill of fright penetrated him, piercing every vein with its chill. He strove to speak; his lips seemed frozen; he stood there before her, a ghastly smile stamped on his face, and in his heart, terror.

"What do you mean, Rosamund?" he said at last.

"That I am dead, dear. Did you not understand that? I—I thought you knew it—when you first saw me at the cemetery, after all those years since childhood.... Did you not know it?" she asked wistfully. "I must wait for my bridal."

Misery whitened his face as he raised his head and looked out across the sunlit world.

Something had smeared and marred the fair earth; the sun grew gray as he stared.

Stupefied by the crash, the ruins of life around him, he stood mute, erect, facing the west.

She whispered, "Do you understand?"

'Yes," he said; "we will wed later. You have been ill, dear; but it is all right now—and will always be—God help us! Love is stronger than all— stronger than death."

"I know it is stronger than death," she said, looking out dreamily over the misty valley.

He followed her gaze, calmly, serenely reviewing all that he must renounce, the happiness of wedlock, children—all that a man desires.

Suddenly instinct stirred, awaking man's only friend—hope. A lifetime for the battle!—for a cure! Hopeless? He laughed in his excitement. Despair?—when the cure lay almost within his grasp! the work he had given his life to! A month more in the laboratory—two months—three— perhaps a year. What of it? It must surely come—how could he fail when the work of his life meant all in life for her?

The light of exaltation slowly faded from his face; ominous, foreboding thoughts crept in; fear laid a shaky hand on his head which fell heavily forward on his breast.

Science and man's cunning and the wisdom of the world!

"O God," he groaned, "for Him who cured by laying on His hands!"

Chapter 5

Now that he had learned her name, and that her father was alive, he stood mutely beside her, staring steadily at the chimneys and stately dormered roof almost hidden behind the crimson maple foliage across the valley—her home.

She had seated herself once more upon the moss, hands clasped upon one knee, looking out into the west with dreamy eyes.

"I shall not be long," he said gently. "Will you wait here for me? I will bring your father with me."

"I will wait for you. But you must come before the new moon. Will you? I must go when the new moon lies in the west."

"Go, dearest? Where?"

"I may not tell you," she sighed, "but you will know very soon—very soon now. And there will be no more sorrow, I think," she added timidly.

"There will be no more sorrow," he repeated quietly.

"For the former things are passing away," she said.

He broke a heavy spray of golden-rod and laid it across her knees; she held out a blossom to him—a blind gentain, blue as her eyes. He kissed it.

"Be with me when the new moon comes," she whispered. "It will be so sweet. I will teach you how divine is death, if you will come."

"You shall reach me the sweetness of life," he said tremulously.

"Yes—life. I did not know you called it by its truest name."

So he went away, trudging sturdily down the lane, gun glistening on his shoulder.

Where the lane joins the shadowy village street his dog skulked up to him, sniffing at his heels.

A mill whistle was sounding; through the red rays of the setting sun people were passing.

Along the row of village shops loungers followed him with vacant eyes. He saw nothing, heard nothing, though a kindly voice called after him, and a young girl smiled at him on her short journey through the world.

The landlord of the Wildwood Inn sat sunning himself in the red evening glow.

"Well, doctor," he said, "you look tired to death. Eh? What's that you say?"

The young man repeated his question in a low voice. The landlord shook his head.

"No, sir. The big house on the hill is empty—been empty these three years. No, sir, there ain't no family there now. The old gentleman moved away three years ago."

"You are mistaken," said the doctor; "his daughter tells me he lives there."

"His—his daughter?" repeated the landlord. "Why, doctor, she's dead." He turned to his wife, who sat sewing by the open window: "Ain't it three years, Marthy?"

"Three years today," said the woman, biting off her thread. "She's buried in the family vault over the hill. She was a right pretty little thing, too."

"Turned nineteen," mused the landlord, folding his newspaper reflectively.

CHAPTER 6

The great gray house on the hill was closed, windows and doors boarded over, lawn, shrubbery, and hedges tangled with weeds. A few scarlet poppies glimmered above the brown grass. Save for these, and clumps of tall wild phlox, there were no blossoms among the weeds.

His dog, which had sneaked after him, cowered as he turned northward across the fields.

Swifter and swifter he strode; and as he stumbled on, the long sunset clouds faded, the golden light in the west died out, leaving a calm, clear sky tinged with the faintest green.

Pines hid the west as he crept toward the hill where she awaited him. As he climbed through dusky purple grasses, higher, higher, he saw the new moon's crescent tipping above the hills; and he crushed back the deathly fright that clutched at him and staggered on.

"Rosamund!"

The pines answered him.

"Rosamund!"

The pines replied, answering together. Then the wind died away, and there was no answer when he called.

East and south the darkening thickets, swaying, grew still. He saw the slim silver birches glimmering like the ghosts of young trees dead; he saw on the moss at his feet a broken stalk of golden-rod.

The new moon had drawn a veil across her face; sky and earth were very still.

While the moon lasted he lay, eyes open, listening, his face pillowed on the moss. It was long after sunrise when his dog came to him; later still when men came.

And at first they thought he was asleep.

Un Peu D'amour

(A story from Police.)

When I returned to the plateau from my investigation of the crater, I realized that I had descended the grassy pit as far as any human being could descend. No living creature could pass that barrier of flame and vapour. Of that I was convinced.

Now, not only the crater but its steaming effluvia was utterly unlike anything I had ever before beheld. There was no trace of lava to be seen, or of pumice, ashes, or of volcanic *rejecta* in any form whatever. There were no sulphuric odours, no pungent fumes, nothing to teach the olfactory nerves what might be the nature of the silvery steam rising from the crater incessantly in a vast circle, ringing its circumference halfway down the slope.

Under this thin curtain of steam a ring of pale yellow flames played and sparkled, completely encircling the slope.

The crater was about half a mile deep; the sides sloped gently to the bottom.

But the odd feature of the entire phenomenon was this: the bottom of the crater seemed to be entirely free from fire and vapour. It was disk-shaped, sandy, and flat, about a quarter of a mile in diameter. Through my field-glasses I could see patches of grass and wild flowers growing in the sand here and there, and the sparkle of water, and a crow or two, feeding and walking about.

I looked at the girl who was standing beside me, then cast a glance around at the very unusual landscape.

We were standing on the summit of a mountain some two

thousand feet high, looking into a cup-shaped depression or crater, on the edges of which we stood.

This low, flat-topped mountain, as I say, was grassy and quite treeless, although it rose like a truncated sugar-cone out of a wilderness of trees which stretched for miles below us, north, south, east, and west, bordered on the horizon by towering blue mountains, their distant ranges enclosing the forests as in a vast amphitheatre.

From the centre of this enormous green floor of foliage rose our grassy hill, and it appeared to be the only irregularity which broke the level wilderness as far as the base of the dim blue ranges encircling the horizon.

Except for the log bungalow of Mr. Blythe on the eastern edge of this grassy plateau, there was not a human habitation in sight, nor a trace of man's devastating presence in the wilderness around us.

Again I looked questioningly at the girl beside me and she looked back at me rather seriously.

"Shall we seat ourselves here in the sun?" she asked.

I nodded.

Very gravely we settled down side by side on the thick green grass.

"Now," she said, "I shall tell you why I wrote you to come out here. Shall I?"

"By all means, Miss Blythe."

Sitting cross-legged, she gathered her ankles into her hands, settling herself as snugly on the grass as a bird settles on its nest.

"The phenomena of nature," she said, "have always interested me intensely, not only from the artistic angle but from the scientific point of view.

"It is different with father. He is a painter; he cares only for the artistic aspects of nature. Phenomena of a scientific nature bore him. Also, you may have noticed that he is of a—a slightly impatient disposition."

I had noticed it. He had been anything but civil to me when I arrived the night before, after a five-hundred mile trip on a mule, from the nearest railroad—a journey performed entirely alone and by compass, there being no trail after the first fifty miles.

To characterize Blythe as slightly impatient was letting him down easy. He was a selfish, bad-tempered old pig.

"Yes," I said, answering her, "I did notice a negligible trace of impatience about your father."

She flushed.

"You see I did not inform my father that I had written to you. He doesn't like strangers; he doesn't like scientists. I did not dare tell him that I had asked you to come out here. It was entirely my own idea. I felt that I *must* write you because I am positive that what is happening in this wilderness is of vital scientific importance."

"How did you get a letter out of this distant and desolate place?" I asked.

"Every two months the storekeeper at Windflower Station sends in a man and a string of mules with staples for us. The man takes our further orders and our letters back to civilization."

I nodded.

"He took my letter to you—among one or two others I sent——"

A charming colour came into her cheeks. She was really extremely pretty. I liked that girl. When a girl blushes when she speaks to a man he immediately accepts her heightened colour as a personal tribute. This is not vanity: it is merely a proper sense of personal worthiness.

She said thoughtfully:

"The mail bag which that man brought to us last week contained a letter which, had I received it earlier, would have made my invitation to you unnecessary. I'm sorry I disturbed you."

"*I* am not," said I, looking into her beautiful eyes.

I twisted my moustache into two attractive points, shot my cuffs, and glanced at her again, receptively.

She had a far-away expression in her eyes. I straightened my necktie. A man, without being vain, ought to be conscious of his own worth.

"And now," she continued, "I am going to tell you the various reasons why I asked so celebrated a scientist as yourself to come here."

I thanked her for her encomium.

"Ever since my father retired from Boston to purchase this hill and the wilderness surrounding it," she went on, "ever since he came here to live a hermit's life—a life devoted solely to painting landscapes—I also have lived here all alone with him.

"That is three years, now. And from the very beginning—from the very first day of our arrival, somehow or other I was conscious that there was something abnormal about this corner of the world."

She bent forward, lowering her voice a trifle:

"Have you noticed," she asked, "that so many things seem to be *circular* out here?"

"Circular?" I repeated, surprised.

"Yes. That crater is circular; so is the bottom of it; so is this plateau, and the hill; and the forests surrounding us; and the mountain ranges on the horizon."

"But all this is natural."

"Perhaps. But in those woods, down there, there are, here and there, great circles of crumbling soil—*perfect* circles a mile in diameter."

"Mounds built by prehistoric man, no doubt."

She shook her head:

"These are not prehistoric mounds."

"Why not?"

"Because they have been freshly made."

"How do you know?"

"The earth is freshly upheaved; great trees, partly uprooted, slant at every angle from the sides of the enormous piles of newly upturned earth; sand and stones are still sliding from the raw ridges."

She leaned nearer and dropped her voice still lower:

"More than that," she said, "my father and I both have seen

one of these huge circles *in the making!*"

"What!" I exclaimed, incredulously.

"It is true. We have seen several. And it enrages father."

"Enrages?"

"Yes, because it upsets the trees where he is painting land-scapes, and tilts them in every direction. Which, of course, ruins his picture; and he is obliged to start another, which vexes him dreadfully."

I think I must have gaped at her in sheer astonishment.

"But there is something more singular than that for you to investigate," she said calmly. "Look down at that circle of steam which makes a perfect ring around the bowl of the crater, half-way down. Do you see the flicker of fire under the vapour?"

"Yes."

She leaned so near and spoke in such a low voice that her fragrant breath fell upon my cheek:

"In the fire, under the vapours, there are little animals."

"What!!"

"Little beasts live in the fire—slim, furry creatures, smaller than a weasel. I've seen them peep out of the fire and scurry back into it. . . . *Now* are you sorry that I wrote you to come? And will you forgive me for bringing you out here?"

An indescribable excitement seized me, endowing me with a fluency and eloquence unusual:

"I thank you from the bottom of my heart!" I cried; "—from the depths of a heart the emotions of which are entirely and exclusively of scientific origin!"

In the impulse of the moment I held out my hand; she laid hers in it with charming diffidence.

"Yours is the discovery," I said. "Yours shall be the glory. Fame shall crown you; and perhaps if there remains any reflected light in the form of a by-product, some modest and negligible little ray may chance to illuminate me."

Surprised and deeply moved by my eloquence, I bent over her hand and saluted it with my lips.

She thanked me. Her pretty face was rosy.

It appeared that she had three cows to milk, new-laid eggs to gather, and the construction of some fresh butter to be accomplished.

At the bars of the grassy pasture slope she dropped me a curtsey, declining very shyly to let me carry her lacteal paraphernalia.

So I continued on to the bungalow garden, where Blythe sat on a camp stool under a green umbrella, painting a picture of something or other.

"Mr. Blythe!" I cried, striving to subdue my enthusiasm. "The eyes of the scientific world are now open upon this house! The searchlight of Fame is about to be turned upon you—"

"I prefer privacy," he interrupted. "That's why I came here. I'll be obliged if you'll turn off that searchlight."

"But, my dear Mr. Blythe—"

"I want to be let alone," he repeated irritably. "I came out here to paint and to enjoy privately my own paintings."

If what stood on his easel was a sample of his pictures, nobody was likely to share his enjoyment.

"Your work," said I, politely, "is—is———"

"Is what!" he snapped. "*What* is it—if you think you know?"

"It is entirely, so to speak, *per se*—by itself—"

"What the devil do you mean by that?"

I looked at his picture, appalled. The entire canvas was one monotonous vermillion conflagration. I examined it with my head on one side, then on the other side; I made a funnel with both hands and peered intently through it at the picture. A menacing murmuring sound came from him.

"Satisfying—exquisitely satisfying," I concluded. "I have often seen such sunsets—"

"What!"

"I mean such prairie fires—"

"Damnation!" he exclaimed. "I'm painting a bowl of nasturtiums!"

"I was speaking purely in metaphor," said I with a sickly smile.

"To me a nasturtium by the river brink is more than a simple flower. It is a broader, grander, more magnificent, more stupendous symbol. It may mean anything, everything—such as sunsets and conflagrations and *Götterdämmerungs*! Or—" and my voice was subtly modulated to an appealing and persuasive softness—"it may mean nothing at all—chaos, void, vacuum, negation, the exquisite annihilation of what has never even existed."

He glared at me over his shoulder. If he was infected by Cubist tendencies he evidently had not understood what I said.

"If you won't talk about my pictures I don't mind your investigating this district," he grunted, dabbing at his palette and plastering a wad of vermilion upon his canvas; "but I object to any public invasion of my artistic privacy until I am ready for it."

"When will that be?"

He pointed with one vermilion-soaked brush toward a long, low, log building.

"In that structure," he said, "are packed one thousand and ninety-five paintings—all signed by me. I have executed one or two every day since I came here. When I have painted exactly ten thousand pictures, no more, no less, I shall erect here a gallery large enough to contain them all.

"Only real lovers of art will ever come here to study them. It is five hundred miles from the railroad. Therefore, I shall never have to endure the praises of the *dilettante*, the patronage of the idler, the vapid rhapsodies of the vulgar. Only those who understand will care to make the pilgrimage."

He waved his brushes at me:

"The conservation of national resources is all well enough—the setting aside of timber reserves, game preserves, bird refuges, all these projects are very good in a way. But I have dedicated this wilderness as a last and only refuge in all the world for true Art! Because true Art, except for my pictures, is, I believe, now practically extinct!...You're in my way. Would you mind getting out?"

I had sidled around between him and his bowl of nasturtiums, and I hastily stepped aside. He squinted at the flowers, mixed up a flamboyant mess of colour on his palette, and daubed away with unfeigned satisfaction, no longer noticing me until I started to go. Then:

"What is it you're here for, anyway?" he demanded abruptly. I said with dignity:

"I am here to investigate those huge rings of earth thrown up in the forest as by a gigantic mole." He continued to paint for a few moments:

"Well, go and investigate 'em," he snapped. "I'm not infatuated with your society."

"What do you think they are?" I asked, mildly ignoring his wretched manners.

"I don't know and I don't care, except, that sometimes when I begin to paint several trees, the very trees I'm painting are suddenly heaved up and tilted in every direction, and all my work goes for nothing. *That* makes me mad! Otherwise, the matter has no interest for me."

"But what in the world could cause—"

"I don't know and I don't care!" he shouted, waving palette and brushes angrily. "Maybe it's an army of moles working all together under the ground; maybe it's some species of circular earthquake. I don't know! I don't care! But it annoys me. And if you can devise any scientific means to stop it, I'll be much obliged to you. Otherwise, to be perfectly frank, you bore me."

"The mission of Science," said I solemnly, "is to alleviate the inconveniences of mundane existence. Science, therefore, shall extend a helping hand to her frailer sister, Art—"

"Science can't patronize Art while I'm around!" he retorted. "I won't have it!"

"But, my dear Mr. Blythe—"

"I won't dispute with you, either! I don't like to dispute!" he shouted. "Don't try to make me. Don't attempt to inveigle me into discussion! I know all I want to know. I don't want to know anything you want me to know, either!"

I looked at the old pig in haughty silence, nauseated by his conceit.

After he had plastered a few more tubes of vermilion over his canvas he quieted down, and presently gave me an oblique glance over his shoulder.

"Well," he said, "what else are you intending to investigate?"

"Those little animals that live in the crater fires," I said bluntly.

"Yes," he nodded, indifferently, "there are creatures which live somewhere in the fires of that crater."

"Do you realize what an astounding statement you are making?" I asked.

"It doesn't astound *me*. What do I care whether it astounds you or anybody else? Nothing interests me except Art."

"But—"

"I tell you nothing interests me except Art!" he yelled. "Don't dispute it! Don't answer me! Don't irritate me! I don't care whether anything lives in the fire or not! Let it live there!"

"But have you actually seen live creatures in the flames?"

"Plenty! *Plenty!* What of it? What about it? Let 'em live there, for all I care. I've painted pictures of 'em, too. That's all that interests me."

"What do they look like, Mr. Blythe?"

"Look like? *I* don't know! They look like weasels or rats or bats or cats or—stop asking me questions! It irritates me! It depresses me! Don't ask any more! Why don't you go in to lunch? And—tell my daughter to bring me a bowl of salad out here. *I've* no time to stuff myself. Some people have. *I* haven't. You'd better go in to lunch.... And tell my daughter to bring me seven tubes of Chinese vermilion with my salad!"

"You don't mean to mix—" I began, then checked myself before his fury.

"I'd rather eat vermilion paint on my salad than sit here talking to *you*!" he shouted.

I cast a pitying glance at this impossible man, and went into the house. After all, he was *her* father. I *had* to endure him.

After Miss Blythe had carried to her father a large bucket of lettuce leaves, she returned to the veranda of the bungalow.

A delightful luncheon awaited us; I seated her, then took the chair opposite.

A delicious omelette, fresh biscuit, salad, and strawberry preserves, and a tall tumbler of iced tea imbued me with a sort of mild exhilaration.

Out of the corner of my eye I could see Blythe down in the garden, munching his lettuce leaves like an ill-tempered rabbit, and daubing away at his picture while he munched.

"Your father," said I politely, "is something of a genius."

"I am so glad you think so," she said gratefully. "But don't tell him so. He has been surfeited with praise in Boston. That is why we came out here."

"Art," said I, "is like science, or tobacco, or tooth-wash. Every man to his own brand. Personally, I don't care for his kind. But who can say which is the best kind of anything? Only the consumer. Your father is his own consumer. He is the best judge of what he likes. And that is the only true test of art, or anything else."

"How delightfully you reason!" she said. "How logically, how generously!"

"Reason is the handmaid of Science, Miss Blythe."

She seemed to understand me. Her quick intelligence surprised me, because I myself was not perfectly sure whether I had emitted piffle or an epigram.

As we ate our strawberry preserves we discussed ways and means of capturing a specimen of the little fire creatures which, as she explained, so frequently peeped out at her from the crater fires, and, at her slightest movement, scurried back again into the flames. Of course I believed that this was only her imagination. Yet, for years I had entertained a theory that fire supported certain unknown forms of life.

"I have long believed," said I, "that fire is inhabited by living organisms which require the elements and temperature of active combustion for their existence—micro-organisms, but not," I added smilingly, "any higher type of life."

"In the fireplace," she ventured diffidently, "I sometimes see curious things—dragons and snakes and creatures of grotesque and peculiar shapes."

I smiled indulgently, charmed by this innocently offered contribution to science. Then she rose, and I rose and took her hand in mine, and we wandered over the grass toward the crater, while I explained to her the difference between what we imagine we see in the glowing coals of a grate fire and my own theory that fire is the abode of living *animalculae*.

On the grassy edge of the crater we paused and looked down the slope, where the circle of steam rose, partly veiling the pale flash of fire underneath.

"How near can we go?" I inquired.

"Quite near. Come; I'll guide you."

Leading me by the hand, she stepped over the brink and we began to descend the easy grass slope together.

There was no difficulty about it at all. Down we went, nearer and nearer to the wall of steam, until at last, when but fifteen feet away from it, I felt the heat from the flames which sparkled below the wall of vapour.

Here we seated ourselves upon the grass, and I knitted my brows and fixed my eyes upon this curious phenomenon, striving to discover some reason for it.

Except for the vapour and the fires, there was nothing whatever volcanic about this spectacle, or in the surroundings.

From where I sat I could see that the bed of fire which encircled the crater; and the wall of vapour which crowned the flames, were about three hundred feet wide. Of course this barrier was absolutely impassable. There was no way of getting through it into the bottom of the crater.

A slight pressure from Miss Blythe's fingers engaged my attention; I turned toward her, and she said:

"There is one more thing about which I have not told you. I feel a little guilty, because *that* is the real reason I asked you to come here."

"What is it?"

"I think there are emeralds on the floor of that crater."

475

"Emeralds!"

"I *think* so." She felt in the ruffled pocket of her apron, drew out a fragment of mineral, and passed it to me.

I screwed a jeweller's glass into my eye and examined it in astonished silence. It was an emerald; a fine, large, immensely valuable stone, if my experience counted for anything. One side of it was thickly coated with vermilion paint.

"Where did this come from?" I asked in an agitated voice.

"From the floor of the crater. Is it *really* an emerald?"

I lifted my head and stared at the girl incredulously.

"It happened this way," she said excitedly. "Father was painting a picture up there by the edge of the crater. He left his palette on the grass to go to the bungalow for some more tubes of colour. While he was in the house, hunting for the colours which he wanted, I stepped out on the veranda, and I saw some crows alight near the palette and begin to stalk about in the grass. One bird walked right over his wet palette; I stepped out and waved my sun-bonnet to frighten him off, but he had both feet in a sticky mass of Chinese vermilion, and for a moment was unable to free himself.

"I almost caught him, but he flapped away over the edge of the crater, high above the wall of vapour, sailed down onto the crater floor, and alighted.

"But his feet bothered him; he kept hopping about on the bottom of the crater, half running, half flying; and finally he took wing and rose up over the hill.

"As he flew above me, and while I was looking up at his vermilion feet, something dropped from his claws and nearly struck me. It was that emerald."

When I had recovered sufficient composure to speak steadily, I took her beautiful little hand in mine.

"This," said I, "is the most exciting locality I have ever visited for purposes of scientific research. Within this crater may lie millions of value in emeralds. You are probably, today, the wealthiest heiress upon the face of the globe!"

I gave her a winning glance. She smiled, shyly, and blushingly withdrew her hand.

For several exquisite minutes I sat there beside her in a sort of heavenly trance. How beautiful she was! How engaging—how sweet—how modestly appreciative of the man beside her, who had little beside his scientific learning, his fame, and a kind heart to appeal to such youth and loveliness as hers!

There was something about her that delicately appealed to me. Sometimes I pondered what this might be; sometimes I wondered how many emeralds lay on that floor of sandy gravel below us.

Yes, I loved her. I realised it now. I could even endure her father for her sake. I should make a good husband. I was quite certain of that.

I turned and gazed upon her, meltingly. But I did not wish to startle her, so I remained silent, permitting the chaste language of my eyes to interpret for her what my lips had not yet murmured. It was a brief but beautiful moment in my life.

"The way to do," said I, "is to trap several dozen crows, smear their feet with glue, tie a ball of Indian twine to the ankle of every bird, then liberate them. Some are certain to fly into the crater and try to scrape the glue off in the sand. Then," I added, triumphantly, "all we have to do is to haul in our birds and detach the wealth of Midas from their sticky claws!"

"That is an excellent suggestion," she said gratefully, "but I can do that after you have gone. All I wanted you to tell me was whether the stone is a genuine emerald."

I gazed at her blankly.

"You are here for purposes of scientific investigation," she added, sweetly. "I should not think of taking your time for the mere sake of accumulating wealth for my father and me."

There didn't seem to be anything for me to say at that moment. Chilled, I gazed at the flashing ring of fire.

And, as I gazed, suddenly I became aware of a little, pointed muzzle, two pricked-up ears, and two ruby-red eyes gazing intently out at me from the mass of flames.

The girl beside me saw it, too.

"Don't move!" she whispered. "That is one of the flame crea-tures. It may venture out if you keep perfectly still."

Rigid with amazement, I sat like a stone image, staring at the most astonishing sight I had ever beheld.

For several minutes the ferret-like creature never stirred from where it crouched in the crater fire; the alert head remained pointed toward us; I could even see that its thick fur must have possessed the qualities of asbestos, because here and there a hair or two glimmered incandescent; and its eyes, nose, and whiskers glowed and glowed as the flames pulsated around it.

After a long while it began to move out of the fire, slowly, cautiously, cunning eyes fixed on us—a small, slim, wiry, weasel-like creature on which the sunlight fell with a vitreous glitter as it crept forward into the grass.

Then, from the fire behind, another creature of the same sort appeared, another, others, then dozens of eager, lithe, little ani-mals appeared everywhere from the flames and began to frisk and play and run about in the grass and nibble the fresh, green, succulent herbage with a snipping sound quite audible to us.

One came so near my feet that I could examine it minutely.

Its fur and whiskers seemed heavy and dense and like asbestos fibre, yet so fine as to appear silky. Its eyes, nose, and claws were scarlet, and seemed to possess a glassy surface.

I waited my opportunity, and when the little thing came nos-ing along within reach, I seized it.

Instantly it emitted a bewildering series of whistling shrieks, and twisted around to bite me. Its body was icy.

"Don't let it bite!" cried the girl. "Be careful, Mr. Smith!"

But its jaws were toothless; only soft, cold gums pinched me, and I held it twisting and writhing, while the icy temperature of its body began to benumb my fingers and creep up my wrist, paralyzing my arm; and its incessant and piercing shrieks deaf-ened me.

In vain I transferred it to the other hand, and then passed it from one hand to the other, as one shifts a lump of ice or a hot potato, in an attempt to endure the temperature: it shrieked and squirmed and doubled, and finally wriggled out of my stiffened and useless hands, and scuttled away into the fire.

It was an overwhelming disappointment. For a moment it seemed unendurable.

"Never mind," I said, huskily, "if I caught one in my hands, I can surely catch another in a trap."

"I am so sorry for your disappointment," she said, pitifully.

"Do *you* care, Miss Blythe?" I asked.

She blushed.

"Of course I care," she murmured.

My hands were too badly frost-nipped to become eloquent. I merely sighed and thrust them into my pockets. Even my arm was too stiff to encircle her shapeful waist. Devotion to Science had temporarily crippled me. Love must wait. But, as we ascended the grassy slope together, I promised myself that I would make her a good husband, and that I should spend at least part of every day of my life in trapping crows and smearing their claws with glue.

That evening I was seated on the veranda beside Wilna—Miss Blythe's name was Wilna—and what with gazing at her and fitting together some of the folding box-traps which I always carried with me—and what with trying to realise the pecuniary magnificence of our future existence together, I was exceedingly busy when Blythe came in to display, as I supposed, his most recent daub to me.

The canvas he carried presented a series of crimson speckles, out of which burst an eruption of green streaks—and it made me think of stepping on a caterpillar.

My instinct was to placate this impossible man. He was *her* father. I meant to honour him if I had to assault him to do it.

"Supremely satisfying!" I nodded, chary of naming the subject. "It is a stride beyond the art of the future: it is a flying leap out of the Not Yet into the Possibly Perhaps! I thank you for enlightening me, Mr. Blythe. I am your debtor."

He fairly snarled at me:

"What are *you* talking about!" he demanded.

I remained modestly mute.

To Wilna he said, pointing passionately at his canvas:

"The crows have been walking all over it again! I'm going to paint in the woods after this, earthquakes or no earthquakes. Have the trees been heaved up anywhere recently?"

"Not since last week," she said, soothingly. "It usually happens after a rain."

"I think I'll risk it then—although it did rain early this morning. I'll do a moonlight down there this evening." And, turning to me: "If you know as much about science as you do about art you won't have to remain here long—I trust."

"What?" said I, very red.

He laughed a highly disagreeable laugh, and marched into the house. Presently he bawled for dinner, and Wilna went away. For her sake I had remained calm and dignified, but presently I went out and kicked up the turf two or three times; and, having foozled my wrath, I went back to dinner, realising that I might as well begin to accustom myself to my future father-in-law.

It seemed that he had a mania for prunes, and that's all he permitted anybody to have for dinner.

Disgusted, I attempted to swallow the loathly stewed fruit, watching Blythe askance as he hurriedly stuffed himself, using a tablespoon, with every symptom of relish.

"Now," he cried, shoving back his chair, "I'm going to paint a moonlight by moonlight. Wilna, if Billy arrives, make him comfortable, and tell him I'll return by midnight." And without taking the trouble to notice me at all, he strode away toward the veranda, chewing vigorously upon his last prune.

"Your father," said I, "is eccentric. Genius usually is. But he is a most interesting and estimable man. I revere him."

"It is kind of you to say so," said the girl, in a low voice.

I thought deeply for a few moments, then:

"Who is 'Billy?'" I inquired, casually.

I couldn't tell whether it was a sudden gleam of sunset light on her face, or whether she blushed.

"Billy," she said softly, "is a friend of father's. His name is William Green."

"Oh."

"He is coming out here to visit—father—I believe."

"Oh. An artist; and doubtless of mature years."

"He is a mineralogist by profession," she said, "—and some-what young."

"Oh."

"Twenty-four years old," she added. Upon her pretty face was an absent expression, vaguely pleasant. Her blue eyes became dreamy and exquisitely remote.

I pondered deeply for a while:

"Wilna?" I said.

"Yes, Mr. Smith?" as though aroused from agreeable meditation.

But I didn't know exactly what to say, and I remained uneasily silent, thinking about that man Green and his twenty-four years, and his profession, and the bottom of the crater, and Wilna—and striving to satisfy myself that there was no logical connection between any of these.

"I think," said I, "that I'll take a bucket of salad to your father."

Why I should have so suddenly determined to ingratiate myself with the old grouch I scarcely understood: for the construction of a salad was my very best accomplishment.

Wilna looked at me in a peculiar manner, almost as though she were controlling a sudden and not unpleasant inward desire to laugh.

Evidently the finer and more delicate instincts of a woman were divining my motive and sympathizing with my mental and sentimental perplexity.

So when she said: "I don't think you had better go near my father," I was convinced of her gentle solicitude in my behalf.

"With a bucket of salad," I whispered softly, "much may be accomplished, Wilna." And I took her little hand and pressed it gently and respectfully. "Trust all to me," I murmured.

She stood with her head turned away from me, her slim hand

481

resting limply in mine. From the slight tremor of her shoulders I became aware how deeply her emotion was now swaying her. Evidently she was nearly ready to become mine.

But I remained calm and alert. The time was not yet. Her father had had his prunes, in which he delighted. And when pleasantly approached with a bucket of salad he could not listen otherwise than politely to what I had to say to him. Quick action was necessary—quick but diplomatic action—in view of the imminence of this young man Green, who evidently was *persona grata* at the bungalow of this irritable old dodo.

Tenderly pressing the pretty hand which I held, and saluting the finger-tips with a gesture which was, perhaps, not wholly ungraceful, I stepped into the kitchen, washed out several heads of lettuce, deftly chopped up some youthful onions, constructed a seductive French dressing, and, stirring together the crisp ingredients, set the savoury masterpiece away in the ice-box, after tasting it. It was delicious enough to draw sobs from any pig.

When I went out to the veranda, Wilna had disappeared. So I unfolded and set up some more box-traps, determined to lose no time.

Sunset still lingered beyond the chain of western mountains as I went out across the grassy plateau to the cornfield.

Here I set and baited several dozen aluminium crow-traps, padding the jaws so that no injury could be done to the birds when the springs snapped on their legs.

Then I went over to the crater and descended its gentle, grassy slope. And there, all along the borders of the vapoury wall, I set box-traps for the lithe little denizens of the fire, baiting every trap with a handful of fresh, sweet clover which I had pulled up from the pasture beyond the cornfield.

My task ended, I ascended the slope again, and for a while stood there immersed in pleasurable premonitions.

Everything had been accomplished swiftly and methodically within the few hours in which I had first set eyes upon this extraordinary place—everything!—love at first sight, the delightfully lightning-like wooing and winning of an incomparable maiden and heiress; the discovery of the fire creatures; the solving of the emerald problem.

And now everything was ready, crow-traps, fire-traps, a bucket of irresistible salad for Blythe, a modest and tremulous avowal for Wilna as soon as her father tasted the salad and I had pleasantly notified him of my intentions concerning his lovely offspring.

Daylight faded from rose to lilac; already the mountains were growing fairy-like under that vague, diffuse lustre which heralds the rise of the full moon. It rose, enormous, yellow, unreal, becoming imperceptibly silvery as it climbed the sky and hung aloft like a stupendous arc-light flooding the world with a radiance so white and clear that I could very easily have written verses by it, if I wrote verses.

Down on the edge of the forest I could see Blythe on his camp-stool, madly besmearing his moonlit canvas, but I could not see Wilna anywhere. Maybe she had shyly retired somewhere by herself to think of me.

So I went back to the house, filled a bucket with my salad, and started toward the edge of the woods, singing happily as I sped on feet so light and frolicsome that they seemed to skim the ground. How wonderful is the power of love!

When I approached Blythe he heard me coming and turned around.

"What the devil do *you* want?" he asked with characteristic civility.

"I have brought you," said I gaily, "a bucket of salad."

"I don't want any salad!"

"W-what?"

"I never eat it at night."

I said confidently:

"Mr. Blythe, if you will taste this salad I am sure you will not regret it." And with hideous cunning I set the bucket beside him on the grass and seated myself near it. The old dodo grunted and continued to daub the canvas; but presently, as though forgetfully, and from sheer instinct, he reached down into the bucket, pulled out a leaf of lettuce, and shoved it into his mouth.

My heart leaped exultantly. I had him!

"Mr. Blythe," I began in a winningly modulated voice, and, at the same instant, he sprang from his camp-chair, his face distorted.

"There are onions in this salad!" he yelled. "What the devil do you mean! Are you trying to poison me! What are you following me about for, anyway? Why are you running about under foot every minute!"

"My dear Mr. Blythe," I protested—but he barked at me, kicked over the bucket of salad, and began to dance with rage.

"What's the matter with you, anyway!" he bawled. "Why are you trying to feed me? What do you mean by trying to be attentive to me!"

"I—I admire and revere you—"

"No you don't!" he shouted. "I don't want you to admire me! I don't desire to be revered! I don't like attention and politeness! Do you hear! It's artificial—out of date—ridiculous! The only thing that recommends a man to me is his bad manners, bad temper, and violent habits. There's some meaning to such a man, none at all to men like you!"

He ran at the salad bucket and kicked it again.

"They all fawned on me in Boston!" he panted. "They ran about underfoot! They bought my pictures! And they made me sick! I came out here to be rid of 'em!"

I rose from the grass, pale and determined.

"You listen to me, you old grouch!" I hissed. "I'll go. But before I go I'll tell you why I've been civil to you. There's only one reason in the world: I want to marry your daughter! And I'm going to do it!"

I stepped nearer him, menacing him with outstretched hand:

"As for you, you pitiable old dodo, with your bad manners and your worse pictures, and your degraded mania for prunes, you are a necessary evil that's all, and I haven't the slightest respect for either you or your art!"

"Is that true?" he said in an altered voice.

"True?" I laughed bitterly. "Of course it's true, you miserable dauber!"

"D-dauber!" he stammered.

"Certainly! I *said* 'dauber,' and I mean it. Why, your work would shame the pictures on a child's slate!"

"Smith," he said unsteadily, "I believe I have utterly misjudged you. I believe you are a good deal of a man, after all—"

"I'm man enough," said I, fiercely, "to go back, saddle my mule, kidnap your daughter, and start for home. And I'm going to do it!"

"Wait!" he cried. "I don't want you to go. If you'll remain I'll be very glad. I'll do anything you like. I'll quarrel with you, and you can insult my pictures. It will agreeably stimulate us both. Don't go, Smith—"

"If I stay, may I marry Wilna?"

"If you ask me I won't let you!"

"Very well!" I retorted, angrily. "Then I'll marry her anyway!"

"That's the way to talk! Don't go, Smith. I'm really beginning to like you. And when Billy Green arrives you and he will have a delightfully violent scene—"

"What!"

He rubbed his hands gleefully.

"He's in love with Wilna. You and he won't get on. It is going to be very stimulating for me—I can see that! You and he are going to behave most disagreeably to each other. And I shall be exceedingly unpleasant to you both! Come, Smith, promise me that you'll stay!"

Profoundly worried, I stood staring at him in the moonlight, gnawing my moustache.

"Very well," I said, "I'll remain if—"

Something checked me, I did not quite know what for a moment. Blythe, too, was staring at me in an odd, apprehensive way. Suddenly I realised that under my feet the ground was stirring.

"Look out!" I cried; but speech froze on my lips as beneath

485

me the solid earth began to rock and crack and billow up into a high, crumbling ridge, moving continually, as the sod cracks, heaves up, and crumbles above the subterranean progress of a mole.

Up into the air we were slowly pushed on the ever-growing ridge; and with us were carried rocks and bushes and sod, and even forest trees.

I could hear their tap-roots part with pistol-like reports; see great pines and hemlocks and oaks moving, slanting, settling, tilting crazily in every direction as they were heaved upward in this gigantic disturbance.

Blythe caught me by the arm; we clutched each other, balancing on the crest of the steadily rising mound.

"W-what is it?" he stammered. "Look! It's circular. The woods are rising in a huge circle. What's happening? Do you know?"

Over me crept a horrible certainty that *something living* was moving under us through the depths of the earth—something that, as it progressed, was heaping up the surface of the world above its unseen and burrowing course—something dreadful, enormous, sinister, and *alive*!

"Look out!" screamed Blythe; and at the same instant the crumbling summit of the ridge opened under our feet and a fissure hundreds of yards long yawned ahead of us.

And along it, shining slimily in the moonlight, a vast, viscous, ringed surface was moving, retracting, undulating, elongating, writhing, squirming, shuddering.

"It's a worm!" shrieked Blythe. "Oh, God! It's a mile long!"

As in a nightmare we clutched each other, struggling frantically to avoid the fissure; but the soft earth slid and gave way under us, and we fell heavily upon that ghastly, living surface.

Instantly a violent convulsion hurled us upward; we fell on it again, rebounding from the rubbery thing, strove to regain our feet and scramble up the edges of the fissure, strove madly while the mammoth worm slid more rapidly through the rocking forests, carrying us forward with a speed increasing.

Through the forest we tore, reeling about on the slippery

back of the thing, as though riding on a ploughshare, while trees clashed and tilted and fell from the enormous furrow on every side; then, suddenly out of the woods into the moonlight, far ahead of us we could see the grassy upland heave up, cake, break, and crumble above the burrowing course of the monster.

"It's making for the crater!" gasped Blythe; and horror spurred us on, and we scrambled and slipped and clawed the billowing sides of the furrow until we gained the heaving top of it.

As one runs in a bad dream, heavily, half-paralyzed, so ran Blythe and I, toiling over the undulating, tumbling upheaval until, half-fainting, we fell and rolled down the shifting slope onto solid and unvexed sod on the very edges of the crater.

Below us we saw, with sickened eyes, the entire circumference of the crater agitated, saw it rise and fall as avalanches of rock and earth slid into it, tons and thousands of tons rushing down the slope, blotting from our sight the flickering ring of flame, and extinguishing the last filmy jet of vapour.

Suddenly the entire crater caved in and filled up under my anguished eyes, quenching for all eternity the vapour wall, the fire, and burying the little denizens of the flames, and perhaps a billion dollars' worth of emeralds under as many billion tons of earth.

Quieter and quieter grew the earth as the gigantic worm bored straight down into depths immeasurable. And at last the moon shone upon a world that lay without a tremor in its milky lustre.

"I shall name it *Verma gigantica*," said I, with a hysterical sob; "but nobody will ever believe me when I tell this story!"

Still terribly shaken, we turned toward the house. And, as we approached the lamplit veranda, I saw a horse standing there and a young man hastily dismounting.

And then a terrible thing occurred; for, before I could even shriek, Wilna had put both arms around that young man's neck, and both of his arms were clasping her waist.

Blythe was kind to me. He took me around the back way and put me to bed.

And there I lay through the most awful night I ever experienced, listening to the piano below, where Wilna and William Green were singing, "Un Peu d'Amour."

LEONAUR

ALSO FROM LEONAUR
AVAILABLE IN SOFTCOVER OR HARDCOVER WITH DUST JACKET

THE COMPLETE FOUR JUST MEN: VOLUME 2 *by Edgar Wallace*—*The Law of the Four Just Men & The Three Just Men*—disillusioned with a world where the wicked and the abusers of power perpetually go unpunished, the Just Men set about to rectify matters according to their own standards, and retribution is dispensed on swift and deadly wings.

THE COMPLETE RAFFLES: 1 *by E. W. Hornung*—*The Amateur Cracksman & The Black Mask*—By turns urbane gentleman about town and accomplished cricketer, life is just too ordinary for Raffles and that sets him on a series of adventures that have long been treasured as a real antidote to the 'white knights' who are the usual heroes of the crime fiction of this period.

THE COMPLETE RAFFLES: 2 *by E. W. Hornung*—*A Thief in the Night & Mr Justice Raffles*—By turns urbane gentleman about town and accomplished cricketer, life is just too ordinary for Raffles and that sets him on a series of adventures that have long been treasured as a real antidote to the 'white knights' who are the usual heroes of the crime fiction of this period.

THE COLLECTED SUPERNATURAL AND WEIRD FICTION OF WILKIE COLLINS: VOLUME 1 *by Wilkie Collins*—Contains one novel 'The Haunted Hotel', one novella 'Mad Monkton', three novelettes 'Mr Percy and the Prophet', 'The Biter Bit' and 'The Dead Alive' and eight short stories to chill the blood.

THE COLLECTED SUPERNATURAL AND WEIRD FICTION OF WILKIE COLLINS: VOLUME 2 *by Wilkie Collins*—Contains one novel 'The Two Destinies', three novellas 'The Frozen deep', 'Sister Rose' and 'The Yellow Mask' and two short stories to chill the blood.

THE COLLECTED SUPERNATURAL AND WEIRD FICTION OF WILKIE COLLINS: VOLUME 3 *by Wilkie Collins*—Contains one novel 'Dead Secret,' two novelettes 'Mrs Zant and the Ghost' and 'The Nun's Story of Gabriel's Marriage' and five short stories to chill the blood.

FUNNY BONES *selected by Dorothy Scarborough*—An Anthology of Humorous Ghost Stories.

MONTEZUMA'S CASTLE AND OTHER WEIRD TALES *by Charles B. Cory*—Cory has written a superb collection of eighteen ghostly and weird stories to chill and thrill the avid enthusiast of supernatural fiction.

SUPERNATURAL BUCHAN *by John Buchan*—Stories of Ancient Spirits, Uncanny Places & Strange Creatures.

LEONAUR

ALSO FROM LEONAUR
AVAILABLE IN SOFTCOVER OR HARDCOVER WITH DUST JACKET

MR MUKERJI'S GHOSTS *by S. Mukerji*—Supernatural tales from the British Raj period by India's Ghost story collector.

KIPLINGS GHOSTS *by Rudyard Kipling*—Twelve stories of Ghosts, Hauntings, Curses, Werewolves & Magic.

www.ingramcontent.com/pod-product-compliance
Lightning Source LLC
Chambersburg PA
CBHW030747030726
47497CB00001B/169